Collected Stories

Books by Harry Mark Petrakis

Novels

Lion at my Heart
The Odyssey of Kostas Volakis
A Dream of Kings
In the Land of Morning
The Hour of the Bell
Nick the Greek
Days of Vengeance

Short Stories

Pericles on 31st Street
The Waves of Night
A Petrakis Reader
Collected Stories

Autobiography

Stelmark
Reflections: A Writer's Life, A Writer's Work

Collected Stories

HARRY MARK PETRAKIS

LAKE VIEW Press

Lake View Press
p o box 578279
Chicago, IL 60657

Library of Congress Cataloging-in-Publication Data

Petrakis, Harry Mark.
The collected stories of Harry Mark Petrakis.

I. Title.
PS3566.E78S5 1986 813'.54 86-20859
ISBN 0-941702-14-6

For my great-nieces and great-nephews,
to read on winter nights.

CONTENTS

Foreword — xi
Dark Eye — 3
The Wooing of Ariadne — 10
The Miracle — 21
The Journal of a Wife Beater — 28
The Castle — 37
A Day's Journey — 52
Courtship of the Blue Widow — 63
The Bastards of Thanos — 75
The Song of Rhodanthe — 83
The Passing of the Ice — 92
Pericles on 31st St. — 103
Homecoming — 114
The Legacy of Leontis — 126
The Prison — 134
The Siege of Minerva — 141
Between Sleep and Death — 151
Pa and the Sad Turkeys — 159
Chrisoula — 169
Matsoukas — 179
End of Winter — 185
The Waves of Night — 193
The Eyes of Love — 220
The Return of Katerina — 231
The Last Escapade — 237
Rosemary — 247
The Ballad of Daphne and Apollo — 259
The Judgment — 271

The Shearing of Samson — 281
Zena Dawn — 292
The Victim — 300
A Hand for Tomorrow — 306
The Witness — 316
The Sweet Life — 326
Song of Songs — 337

FOREWORD

I considered writing a foreword to these stories explaining what I wished them to achieve. I decided that was superfluous. One's stories, like one's children, must make their own way in the world. Each reader must determine whether they are entertaining and moving and, perhaps, revealing in what they portray of human beings.

In the last couple of decades, the novels I've written have been gratifying and the main source of our support. But my attachment to the short story remains. From time to time the longing to write one is reawakened and I grope for a few opening lines. It's like pushing a small frail vessel out to sea. Will it stay afloat? Will the journey itself produce some magic of discovery? Nothing should be totally clear because the earth is a realm of infinite complexity, and unrequited love as well as unjustified suffering must be accepted as part of the mystery.

Beyond the writing, I've also had the fulfillment of reading my stories hundreds of times before high school, college, library and club audiences. In these readings I am witness to the universal appeal and joy of stories as an audience laughs with me or shares melancholy or a feeling of renewal.

There have been storytellers from the time men dwelt in caves and huddled around fires, and there will be stories as long as humans survive. Reading and telling stories will continue in libraries, on the grass in the sunshine of summer parks, at twilight when friends gather, during those hours when one grows weary of the tumult of TV.

I'm sure that stories will endure even if the horror occurs and we are driven to find refuge in concrete catacombs beneath the earth and air our hatreds and weapons have destroyed. In that darkest of hours, the human voice will remain, obeying the enjoinment of King Lear, ". . . so we'll pray and sing and tell old tales."

Harry Mark Petrakis
Dune Acres, Indiana
June, 1986

Collected Stories

We lived for about two years in Los Angeles while I worked on a couple of screenplays, including one for my novel *A Dream of Kings.* We made friends then with some Greek actors, who eagerly joined us to share my wife's tasty Greek meals. These dinners were always climaxed by some hours of vigorous dancing and singing, led by the character actors Nick Dennis and Chris Marks, with the versatile Jim Harakas playing a spirit-stirring guitar.

Late one night they performed a Karaghiozis play, the old Turkish-Greek puppet theater I had not seen since childhood. Something of their voices and gestures caught me, and several days later I began writing the story.

Since one cannot dedicate a story when it is published in a magazine, I have the chance now to acknowledge my debt to Nick, Chris, and Jim for "Dark Eye." They were wonderful friends, and I miss our buoyant and salubrious parties.

DARK EYE

My father was a drunkard. Every two weeks when he received his wages from the owner of the grocery where he worked, he'd begin making the rounds of the taverns on the street. In the normal course of his journey, we would not see him for the weekend and even the following Monday. But by ten o'clock on those Friday nights he did not come home, my mother had a neighbor look after me and then went out to find my father. This wasn't a difficult search because there were only a certain number of taverns he frequented. When she located him he would be furious at her before his companion sots. She endured his tirade silently, until, momentarily purged by his outburst and after purchasing several bottles as hostages for the weekend, he allowed her to lead him home.

He drank steadily through Saturday and Sunday. I kept fearfully out of his way but he ignored me, hoarding his revilement for my mother.

"Tell me, woman!" he cried. "Tell me what devil's blindness made me choose a wife like you, a dried fig, a bloodless stone, a deaf and dumb bitch!"

It seemed incredible to me, even as a child, that anyone might wish to abuse my mother. She was a slender and lovely woman with a complexion so pale and fine that tiny violet veins were visible just beneath the surface of her skin. She spoke softly and moved with a lucent grace. Sometimes, playing alone, I felt a longing to look at her and I'd go to find her in another room, sit close beside her for a while, warm and nested in her presence. The moments I treasured most were those we shared when she sat before her mirror at night, brushing her long glistening hair that was dark as a blackbird's wing. I watched her then with a curious tension in my body.

My father was a tall, burly man who might once have been regarded by some as handsome, until indulgence and self-pity had scarred his face with weak, ugly circles. Whether drunk or sober, he moved in a shuffling and uncertain walk, defeat and failure rising like a fetid mist from his pores.

Although he worked at many different jobs, never able to hold even the menial ones for very long, he regarded himself as a Karaghiozis, the profession he had practiced in the old country, a puppetmaster of the shadow puppets once so popular throughout Greece. The art of the Karaghiozis was handed down from father to son and my father had learned his craft from his father. As a young man in Greece, he performed frequently at festivals and fairs, but the popularity of the plays declined. Just a few years after he married my mother, the plays were being requested only on a few special holidays. A new generation of children turned to other pursuits and only the old and infirm lamented the passing of the Karaghiozis.

My father must have come to America thinking that in the new country of myriad opportunities, he would be able to practice his craft. But the children who had never seen a Karaghiozis had other allegiances to Laurel and Hardy, Buster Keaton and baseball. And their parents were too involved with the artifacts of home and the rigors of business to bother with an old-country art.

Once, when I was eight or nine, and this was the only time, I remember my father performing the Karaghiozis. It was in the week before Christmas and I sat in the assembly hall of the church with perhaps a hundred other children on long low benches around me. A scattering of adults sat in chairs along the walls. On a small platform in front of us was a rectangular screen of thin, translucent muslin.

When the lights in the hall were turned off, the room was darkened except for the radiant screen casting eerie flickering lights across the faces of the children. From behind the screen came a rattling sound, as if pieces of wood were being shaken in a sack. A few men clapped, and then on the glowing screen a palace appeared, a courtyard and gardens, and in the foreground, a fountain. The brightly attired figure of a soldier appeared. He pranced a few steps and then cried, "Karaghiozis! Wake up, Karaghiozis! The sultan is coming!"

From behind the fountain snapped a great bald head, the face in profile containing a single huge dark eye. The head drew back down for a moment and then the silhouette of Karaghiozis leaped swiftly into view. A powerful body with one arm shrunk to no more than a hand emerging from his chest, the other arm long and apelike.

The sight of the weird figure caused the children to cry out, and with a wrenching of my flesh in fear, I joined my shriek to their cries.

A frantic sequence of scenes followed, characters appearing who shouted, danced, sang, quarreled, laughed and beat one another. There were dancers and beggars, soldiers and wrestlers, fishermen and sultans, gods and devils, a rabid throng inhabiting the screen with a violent and teeming world that my father created and controlled. His nimble hands directed their leaps and jumps and somersaults; his voice delivered their cries, harsh, shrill, tearful, deceiving, demonic. Above all the players loomed the figure of Karaghiozis, his dark eye piercing the screen. It seemed to look directly at me and I screamed in terror even while the children around me shouted and shrieked in glee.

When the lights went on at the end of the performance, I sat mute and exhausted. A vigorous clapping brought my father from behind the screen, his face flushed with power and triumph as he bowed, acknowledging the cheers and the applause. He stood afterward in the center of a group of admiring men, who slapped his shoulders and shook his hands. My mother hung smiling to his arm. I went to her to be consoled for my distress, but even while she held me against her body, I felt her love directed only toward my exultant father.

He never performed the Karaghiozis in public again. In the years that followed, he kept the cardboard figures of the players, perhaps twenty-five or thirty of them, in a footlocker at the rear of his closet. Sometimes, when he was drunk, he would pull out the footlocker, open it and sit down on the floor beside it. He would bring out the mad Karaghiozis and all his companions. He'd spread them around on the floor, pick them up, move their heads and arms. They often spoke only in his head, but when he could not contain himself, he cried voices between them. In the end, exhausted and unfulfilled, he would store them carefully away and go lamenting to his bed.

My father lost his job in the grocery, worked for a while in a laundry and then lost that job as well. During this period, my mother took work as a waitress to pay our rent and food. When he could not find money on which to drink, my father spent his time brooding.

I remember a night when my mother was still at work. My father had been locked alone in his bedroom for hours until he called me in. I found him on the floor beside the open footlocker with the Karaghiozis players spread around him. He wasn't drunk then, but his face was flushed and a frenzy glittered in his eyes. He motioned for me to sit beside him and, frightened, I obeyed.

"In the old country," he said, "a father teaches the Karaghiozis to his son. In this way, it is passed from generation to generation. My father taught me and I will teach you."

I trembled and nodded slowly.

"They don't want the Karaghiozis now," my father said with bitterness, "but someday it will be revived. The crowds will gather again and cheer and laugh and cry out for Karaghiozis." He looked at me with burning eyes. "You must be ready for that time."

He motioned to one of the cardboard players. "This one is Hachivat, Karaghiozis' friend; and this is Celebit, the dandy; and Tusuz Deli Bekir, the bellowing bully; Tiryaki, the opium smoker; Zenne, the dancer . . . and this one, this one is Karaghiozis."

He picked up the cardboard Karaghiozis and held him tenderly in his hands. I had never seen him look at any living creature with the warmth and love his face held as he looked at Karaghiozis. He moved slowly to hand the figure to me. "Hold him now and I'll show you how to control his head and arms."

The huge dark eye in the profiled face terrified me and I shrank away.

"What's the matter?" my father cried. "What are you afraid of? He won't hurt you! This is Karaghiozis!"

His anger fled and he tried to speak softly to reassure me.

"It will take time to teach you all the plays," he said. "You must learn them slowly and learn them well. Then you will be able to improvise plays of your own." He stared at me with naked and earnest eyes. "Do you know that once I could continue a dialog between Karaghiozis and his friend, Hachivat, for more than fifteen hours? Do you know that once the mayor of our village, watching me perform, hearing Karaghiozis talk of politics, the mayor offered me a position in his office? Do you know . . . ?"

His voice trailed off as he looked sadly at my locked and frightened face.

"Get out, little bastard," he said wearily. "Get out of my sight. Go to bed."

I hurried from the room to undress and climb shaking under the covers. I called to my mother when she came home and she came and sat beside me, consoling me by her presence until I had fallen asleep.

That night marked a change in my father, and he seemed more furiously bent on his own destruction. His credit was dried up at the taverns on our street and he made futile pilgrimages to other neighborhoods.

When he could not bully or steal money from my mother or my cousin Frosos, he begged and borrowed from friends and strangers along the street. Abandoning all efforts to find any kind of work, he whirled in a wind of drunken despair.

Any redeeming memory I had of him, any bond of blood remaining between us was demolished in the blustering, whining, raging moments when he cursed fate, the misfortune of his marriage, the madness that made him leave the old country. And in his frenzy his voice altered, becoming shrill and hoarse, taunting and pleading, demanding and denouncing, as if all the myriad tongues of the Karaghiozis players were crying through his lips.

My mother suffered as he suffered, prayed for him constantly and accepted all his curses and imprecations in silence. On those evenings when his helpless rage seemed to be tearing him apart, my mother said my prayers with me and put me to bed. She closed the doors between my room, the hall and their bedroom. I still heard faintly my father shouting and cursing for a while. Then a silence fell over the rooms, an ominous and terrible silence, although I did not understand until years later the way in which my mother took my father's rage and frenzy into her own frail body.

Once, only once, did I condemn my father to my mother. I was about twelve and it was after one of the worst of his rampages, when he had broken several dishes he knew my mother treasured, and finally, like a great beast, had collapsed in a heap on the floor. He lay sprawled on his back, his mouth open, harsh drunken snores erupting from his limp face. I whispered a wish to my mother that he might die.

She had never struck me before, but she beat me then. She beat me savagely with a belt while I screamed in shock and pain.

"Listen to me," she said, her face white and her eyes like knives. "Say such a thing again and I'll have the flesh hot from your back! In the old country your father was an artist, a great Karaghiozis. They came from villages a hundred miles away to see him perform. Now nobody cares for his skill and he rages and drinks to forget his grief and loss. Do you think a man whose soul is being torn apart can help himself? We can only love him and have faith in him. He has nothing else."

But I could not understand, and for turning my mother against me, for the beating she gave me, I hated him more.

My father died when I was fourteen. During one of his drunken sprees in the coldest part of winter, he had stumbled and fallen in an alley. The snow began and the thick flakes covered him. He lay concealed for hours until he was discovered. They took him to the hospital and called my mother. For three days and three nights, while he struggled to die, she fought to hold him to life. On the morning of the fourth day, cousin Frosos took me to the hospital. We walked the long ward filled with beds and strangers, and at the end, behind a screen, my father was dying.

He was curled on his side, one half of his face hidden, one arm extended in a twisting grasp for something that seemed just beyond his reach. His cheek was unshaven, his huge dark eye open, staring straight ahead. My mother, her face worn like a river stone by tears, led me to the bed and put my hand upon my father's hand. I felt the quiver of his flesh expiring under my fingers.

He could not turn his face to look at me, but the eye stirred restlessly. He looked no different than I remembered him many times before. He was helpless, the way I most favored him, because at those times he was unable to curse or to strike my mother.

Cousin Frosos led me away from the bed, and at the screen, I stopped and looked back one last time. A fly buzzed over my father's head and the dark eye in the dying face burned in a frantic effort to escape and follow the wings' swift flight.

I awoke that night to hear my mother scream. She was still at the hospital with my father, but I clearly heard the howl of desolation and loss that came torn from her soul. I knew my father was dead.

Through the following months, my mother grieved. Only forty, she seemed to age a year with each month. Still she worked and took care of me. I took a job after school and on weekends, and when payday came, I gave my mother every dollar that I made. In addition, there was a lodge insurance policy on my father's death that provided us with a small regular monthly sum. Strangely, as survivors, we lived better than we had lived when my father was alive. We might almost have been happy then, for the first time in my memory, except for the way my mother grew swiftly older, quietly, irrevocably mourning my father's death.

Sometimes late at night, when she thought I was asleep, I would see the light burning under her bedroom door. I would quietly open the door a narrow crack. She would be sitting on the floor, the open foot-locker beside her, the cardboard figures spread across her lap, her hands holding, her fingers fondling the wild, dark-eyed Karaghiozis.

When I finished high school, I received a tuition scholarship to a college several hundred miles away. My mother and I accepted the separation. I wrote her at regular intervals, telling her about my classes, the news of school, and avoided letting her know about my loneliness, the ways in which the past locked me in a shell I could not break. Her letters were brief, filled with admonitions for me to study and pray and live true in the eyes of God. Each time I saw her after the separation of a few months, I marked again the ravages of premature age, her hair grown dove gray, a web of wrinkles gathering around her eyes, a gaunt-ness at her throat.

When I graduated from college and walked to receive my diploma in a black cap and gown, my mother sat in the third row on the aisle, an old woman watching her son in his moment of fulfillment. I went to hug her afterward, holding her slim, frail body in my arms, wanting her to share the achievement she had helped make possible. Yet, in that moment, I held only a fragment of her in my arms, and with a cold chill sweeping my heart, I realized how faint a hold she retained upon the earth.

It was only a few months after my graduation that my mother died. She was less than fifty and should have had many more years to live. But she had no relish for life, and after I finished my schooling, her last bond to the earth was gone. She fell ill in the spring, lingered only a day and died as quietly as she had lived for the past eight years. It was as if the shadow she became after my father's death was suddenly brushed away by a light gust of wind.

I buried her, as she had wished, in the cemetery beside my father, one of two graves beside the stone fence. They would lie together forever, with no one to shield or console her against his abuse.

And on the same day she was buried, I carried the footlocker to the basement of the building in which we lived, and in the furnace, one by one, I burned the cardboard figures of the Karaghiozis' puppets. Hachivat, Celebit, Tusuz Deli Bekir, Tiryaki, Zenne, the beggars, soldiers, sultans, wrestlers and devils, all consigned to the flames. Karaghiozis himself I saved for last, and when the final fragments of the others had gone up in ashes and smoke, I put him into the flames. I knelt before the furnace door and watched trembling as his arms and legs curled and writhed and darkened in the fierce fire, his limbs shriveling in a final anguished spasm, his glowing dark eye suspended for an instant of torment after the rest of the figure was gone.

My father was a drunkard, a bastard who beat and abused my mother. Yet she loved him more than she loved anyone else on earth, remained true to him for the death in life, and in the end, joined him for the life in eternity.

How strong the bonds of faith, how deep the abyss of devotion. And how terrible and unfathomable the love that welds a man and woman together forever.

During my son John's senior year in Chesterton High School, I adapted three of my stories into one-act plays for his class to perform. One of those stories was "The Wooing of Ariadne," and I helped in the direction. Watching German and Irish and Swedish farm-belt youngsters coming slowly to encompass the emotional ebullience of a group of Greeks was a memorable experience. The young man who played Marko Palamas did a fine job and has never really recovered from that role. From time to time now, in his speech patterns and in the expansiveness of his gestures, I catch glimpses of the Spartan wrestler and sailor who wooed Ariadne.

THE WOOING OF ARIADNE

I knew from the beginning she must accept my love—put aside foolish female protestations. It is the distinction of the male to be the aggressor and the cloak of the female to lend grace to the pursuit. Aha! I am wise to these wiles.

I first saw Ariadne at a dance given by the Spartan brotherhood in the Legion Hall on Laramie Street. The usual assemblage of prune-faced and banana-bodied women smelling of virtuous anemia. They were an outrage to a man such as myself.

Then I saw her! A tall stately woman, perhaps in her early thirties. She had firm and slender arms bare to the shoulders and a graceful neck. Her hair was black and thick and piled in a great bun at the back of her head. That grand abundance of hair attracted me at once. This modern aberration women have of chopping their hair close to the scalp and leaving it in fantastic disarray I find revolting.

I went at once to my friend Vasili, the baker, and asked him who she was.

"Ariadne Langos," he said. "Her father is Janco Langos, the grocer."

"Is she engaged or married?"

"No," he said slyly. "They say she frightens off the young men. They say she is very spirited."

"Excellent," I said and marveled at my good fortune in finding her unpledged. "Introduce me at once."

"Marko," Vasili said with some apprehension. "Do not commit anything rash."

I pushed the little man forward. "Do not worry, little friend," I said. "I am a man suddenly possessed by a vision. I must meet her at once."

We walked together across the dance floor to where my beloved stood. The closer we came the more impressive was the majestic swell of her breasts and the fine great sweep of her thighs. She towered over the insignificant apple-core women around her. Her eyes, dark and thoughtful, seemed to be restlessly searching the room.

Be patient, my dove! Marko is coming!

"Miss Ariadne," Vasili said. "This is Mr. Marko Palamas. He desires to have the honor of your acquaintance."

She looked at me for a long and piercing moment. I imagined her gauging my mighty strength by the width of my shoulders and the circumference of my arms. I felt the tips of my mustache bristle with pleasure. Finally she nodded with the barest minimum of courtesy. I was not discouraged.

"Miss Ariadne," I said, "may I have the pleasure of this dance?"

She stared at me again with her fiery eyes. I could imagine more timid men shriveling before her fierce gaze. My heart flamed at the passion her rigid exterior concealed.

"I think not," she said.

"Don't you dance?"

Vasili gasped beside me. An old prune-face standing nearby clucked her toothless gums.

"Yes, I dance," Ariadne said coolly. "I do not wish to dance with you."

"Why?" I asked courteously.

"I do not think you heard me," she said. "I do not wish to dance with you."

Oh, the sly and lovely darling. Her subterfuge so apparent. Trying to conceal her pleasure at my interest.

"Why?" I asked again.

"I am not sure," she said. "It could be your appearance, which bears considerable resemblance to a gorilla, or your manner, which would suggest closer alliance to a pig."

"Now that you have met my family," I said engagingly, "let us dance."

"Not now," she said, and her voice rose. "Not this dance or the one after. Not tonight or tomorrow night or next month or next year. Is that clear?"

Sweet, sweet Ariadne. Ancient and eternal game of retreat and pursuit. My pulse beat more quickly.

Vasili pulled at my sleeve. He was my friend, but without the courage of a goat. I shook him off and spoke to Ariadne.

"There is a joy like fire that consumes a man's heart when he first sets eyes on his beloved," I said. "This I felt when I first saw you." My voice trembled under a mighty passion. "I swear before God from this moment that I love you."

She stared shocked out of her deep dark eyes and, beside her, old prune-face staggered as if she had been kicked. Then my beloved did something which proved indisputably that her passion was as intense as mine.

She doubled up her fist and struck me in the eye! A stout blow for a woman that brought a haze to my vision, but I shook my head and moved a step closer.

"I would not care," I said, "if you struck out both my eyes. I would cherish the memory of your beauty forever."

By this time the music had stopped, and the dancers formed a circle of idiot faces about us. I paid them no attention and ignored Vasili, who kept whining and pulling at my sleeve.

"You are crazy!" she said. "You must be mad! Remove yourself from my presence or I will tear out both your eyes and your tongue besides!"

You see! Another woman would have cried, or been frightened into silence. But my Ariadne, worthy and venerable, hurled her spirit into my teeth.

"I would like to call on your father tomorrow," I said. From the assembled dancers who watched there rose a few vagrant whispers and some rude laughter. I stared at them carefully and they hushed at once. My temper and strength of arm were well known.

Ariadne did not speak again, but in a magnificent spirit stamped from the floor. The music began, and men and women began again to dance. I permitted Vasili to pull me to a corner.

"You are insane!" he said. He wrung his withered fingers in anguish. "You assaulted her like a Turk! Her relatives will cut out your heart!"

"My intentions were honorable," I said. "I saw her and loved her and told her so." At this point I struck my fist against my chest. Poor Vasili jumped.

"But you do not court a woman that way," he said.

"*You* don't, my anemic friend," I said. "Nor do the rest of these sheep. But I court a woman that way!"

He looked to heaven and helplessly shook his head. I waved good-by and started for my hat and coat.

"Where are you going?" he asked.

"To prepare for tomorrow," I said. "In the morning I will speak to her father."

I left the hall and in the street felt the night wind cold on my flushed cheeks. My blood was inflamed. The memory of her loveliness fed fuel to the fire. For the first time I understood with a terrible clarity the driven heroes of the past performing mighty deeds in love. Paris stealing Helen in passion, and Menelaus pursuing with a great fleet. In that moment if I knew the whole world would be plunged into conflict I would have followed Ariadne to Hades.

I went to my rooms above the tavern. I could not sleep. All night I tossed in restless frenzy. I touched my eye that she had struck with her spirited hand.

Ariadne! Ariadne! my soul cried out.

In the morning I bathed and dressed carefully. I confirmed the address of Langos, the grocer, and started to his store. It was a bright cold November morning, but I walked with a spring in my step.

When I opened the door of the Langos grocery, a tiny bell rang shrilly. I stepped into the store piled with fruits and vegetables and smelling of cabbages and greens.

A stooped little old man with white bushy hair and owlish eyes came toward me. He looked as if his veins contained vegetable juice instead of blood, and if he were, in truth, the father of my beloved, I marveled at how he could have produced such a paragon of women.

"Are you Mr. Langos?"

"I am," he said and he came closer. "I am."

"I met your daughter last night," I said. "Did she mention I was going to call?"

He shook his head somberly.

"My daughter mentioned you," he said. "In thirty years I have never seen her in such a state of agitation. She was possessed."

"The effect on me was the same," I said. "We met for the first time last night, and I fell passionately in love."

"Incredible," the old man said.

"You wish to know something about me," I said. "My name is Marko Palamas. I am a Spartan emigrated to this country eleven years ago. I am forty-one years old. I have been a wrestler and a sailor and fought with the resistance movement in Greece in the war. For this service I was decorated by the king. I own a small but profitable tavern on Dart Street. I attend church regularly. I love your daughter."

As I finished he stepped back and bumped a rack of fruit. An orange rolled off to the floor. I bent and retrieved it to hand it to him, and he cringed as if he thought I might bounce it off his old head.

"She is a bad-tempered girl," he said. "Stubborn, impatient and spoiled. She has been the cause of considerable concern to me. All the eligible young men have been driven away by her temper and disposition."

"Poor girl," I said. "Subjected to the courting of calves and goats."

The old man blinked his owlish eyes. The front door opened and a battleship of a woman sailed in.

"Three pounds of tomatoes, Mr. Langos," she said. "I am in a hurry. Please to give me good ones. Last week two spoiled before I had a chance to put them into Demetri's salad."

"I am very sorry," Mr. Langos said. He turned to me. "Excuse me, Mr. Poulmas."

"Palamas," I said. "Marko Palamas."

He nodded nervously. He went to wait on the battleship, and I spent a moment examining the store. Neat and small. I would not imagine he did more than hold his own. In the rear of the store there were stairs leading to what appeared to be an apartment above. My heart beat faster.

When he had bagged the tomatoes and given change, he returned to me and said, "She is also a terrible cook. She cannot fry an egg without burning it." His voice shook with woe. "She cannot make pilaf or lamb with squash." He paused. "You like pilaf and lamb with squash?"

"Certainly."

"You see?" he said in triumph. "She is useless in the kitchen. She is thirty years old, and I am resigned she will remain an old maid. In a way I am glad because I know she would drive some poor man to drink."

"Do not deride her to discourage me," I said. "You need have no fear that I will mistreat her or cause her unhappiness. When she is married to me she will cease being a problem to you." I paused. "It is true that I am not pretty by the foppish standards that prevail today. But I am a man. I wrestled Zahundos and pinned him two straight falls in Baltimore. A giant of a man. Afterward he conceded he had met his master. This from Zahundos was a mighty compliment."

"I am sure," the old man said without enthusiasm. "I am sure."

He looked toward the front door as if hoping for another customer.

"Is your daughter upstairs?"

He looked startled and tugged at his apron. "Yes," he said. "I don't know. Maybe she has gone out."

"May I speak to her? Would you kindly tell her I wish to speak with her."

"You are making a mistake," the old man said. "A terrible mistake."

"No mistake," I said firmly.

The old man shuffled toward the stairs. He climbed them slowly. At the top he paused and turned the knob of the door. He rattled it again.

"It is locked," he called down. "It has never been locked before. She has locked the door."

"Knock," I said. "Knock to let her know I am here."

"I think she knows," the old man said. "I think she knows."

He knocked gently.

"Knock harder," I suggested. "Perhaps she does not hear."

"I think she hears," the old man said. "I think she hears."

"Knock again," I said. "Shall I come up and knock for you?"

"No, no," the old man said quickly. He gave the door a sound kick. Then he groaned as if he might have hurt his foot.

"She does not answer," he said in a quavering voice. "I am very sorry she does not answer."

"The coy darling," I said and laughed. "If that is her game." I started for the front door of the store.

I went out and stood on the sidewalk before the store. Above the grocery were the front windows of their apartment. I cupped my hands about my mouth.

"Ariadne!" I shouted. "Ariadne!"

The old man came out the door running disjointedly. He looked frantically down the street.

"Are you mad?" he asked shrilly. "You will cause a riot. The police will come. You must be mad!"

"Ariadne!" I shouted. "Beloved!"

A window slammed open, and the face of Ariadne appeared above me. Her dark hair tumbled about her ears.

"Go away!" she shrieked. "Will you go away!"

"Ariadne," I said loudly. "I have come as I promised. I have spoken to your father. I wish to call on you."

"Go away!" she shrieked. "Madman! Imbecile! Go away!"

By this time a small group of people had assembled around the store and were watching curiously. The old man stood wringing his hands and uttering what sounded like small groans.

"Ariadne," I said. "I wish to call on you. Stop this nonsense and let me in."

She pushed farther out the window and showed me her teeth.

"Be careful, beloved," I said. "You might fall."

She drew her head in quickly, and I turned then to the assembled crowd.

"A misunderstanding," I said. "Please move on."

Suddenly old Mr. Langos shrieked. A moment later something broke on the sidewalk a foot from where I stood. A vase or a plate. I looked up, and Ariadne was preparing to hurl what appeared to be a water pitcher.

"Ariadne!" I shouted. "Stop that!"

The water pitcher landed closer than the vase, and fragments of glass struck my shoes. The crowd scattered, and the old man raised his hands and wailed to heaven.

Ariadne slammed down the window.

The crowd moved in again a little closer, and somewhere among them I heard laughter. I fixed them with a cold stare and waited for some one of them to say something offensive. I would have tossed him around like a sardine, but they slowly dispersed and moved on. In another moment the old man and I were alone.

I followed him into the store. He walked an awkward dance of agitation. He shut the door and peered out through the glass.

"A disgrace," he wailed. "A disgrace. The whole street will know by nightfall. A disgrace."

"A girl of heroic spirit," I said. "Will you speak to her for me? Assure her of the sincerity of my feelings. Tell her I pledge eternal love and devotion."

The old man sat down on an orange crate and weakly made his cross.

"I had hoped to see her myself," I said. "But if you promise to speak to her, I will return this evening."

"That soon?" the old man said.

"If I stayed now," I said, "it would be sooner."

"This evening," the old man said and shook his head in resignation. "This evening."

I went to my tavern for a while and set up the glasses for the evening trade. I made arrangements for Pavlakis to tend bar in my place. Afterward I sat alone in my apartment and read a little of majestic Pindar to ease the agitation of my heart.

Once in the mountains of Greece when I fought with the guerrillas in the last year of the great war, I suffered a wound from which it seemed I would die. For days high fever raged in my body. My friends brought a priest at night secretly from one of the captive villages to read the last rites. I accepted the coming of death and was grateful for many things. For the gentleness and wisdom of my old grandfather, the loyalty of my companions in war, the years I sailed between the ports of the seven seas, and the strength that flowed to me from the Spartan earth. For one thing only did I weep when it seemed I would leave life, that I had never set ablaze the world with a burning song of passion for one woman. Women I had known, pockets of pleasure that I tumbled for quick joy, but I had been denied mighty love for one woman. For that I wept.

In Ariadne I swore before God I had found my woman. I knew by the storm-lashed hurricane that swept within my body. A woman whose majesty was in harmony with the earth, who would be faithful and beloved to me as Penelope had been to Ulysses.

That evening near seven I returned to the grocery. Deep twilight had fallen across the street, and the lights in the window of the store had been dimmed. The apples and oranges and pears had been covered with brown paper for the night.

I tried the door and found it locked. I knocked on the glass, and a moment later the old man came shuffling out of the shadows and let me in.

"Good evening, Mr. Langos."

He muttered some answer. "Ariadne is not here," he said. "She is at the church. Father Marlas wishes to speak with you."

"A fine young priest," I said. "Let us go at once."

I waited on the sidewalk while the old man locked the store. We started the short walk to the church.

"A clear and ringing night," I said. "Does it not make you feel the wonder and glory of being alive?"

The old man uttered what sounded like a groan, but a truck passed on the street at that moment and I could not be sure.

At the church we entered by a side door leading to the office of Father Marlas. I knocked on the door, and when he called to us to enter we walked in.

Young Father Marlas was sitting at his desk in his black cassock and with his black goatee trim and imposing beneath his clean-shaven cheeks. Beside the desk, in a dark blue dress sat Ariadne, looking somber and beautiful. A bald-headed, big-nosed old man with flint and fire in his eyes sat in a chair beside her.

"Good evening, Marko," Father Marlas said and smiled.

"Good evening, Father," I said.

"Mr. Langos and his daughter you have met," he said and he cleared his throat. "This is Uncle Paul Langos."

"Good evening, Uncle Paul," I said. He glared at me and did not answer. I smiled warmly at Ariadne in greeting, but she was watching the priest.

"Sit down," Father Marlas said.

I sat down across from Ariadne, and old Mr. Langos took a chair beside Uncle Paul. In this way we were arrayed in battle order as if we were opposing armies.

A long silence prevailed during which Father Marlas cleared his throat several times. I observed Ariadne closely. There were grace and poise even in the way her slim-fingered hands rested in her lap. She was a dark and lovely flower, and my pulse beat more quickly at her nearness.

"Marko," Father Marlas said finally. "Marko, I have known you well for the three years since I assumed duties in this parish. You are most regular in your devotions and very generous at the time of the Christmas and Easter offerings. Therefore, I find it hard to believe this complaint against you."

"My family are not liars!" Uncle Paul said, and he had a voice like hunks of dry hard cheese being grated.

"Of course not," Father Marlas said quickly. He smiled benevolently at Ariadne. "I only mean to say—"

"Tell him to stay away from my niece!" Uncle Paul burst out.

"Excuse me, Uncle Paul," I said very politely. "Will you kindly keep out of what is not your business."

Uncle Paul looked shocked. "Not my business?" He looked from Ariadne to Father Marlas and then to his brother. "Not my business?"

"This matter concerns Ariadne and me," I said. "With outside interference it becomes more difficult."

"Not my business!" Uncle Paul said. He couldn't seem to get that through his head.

"Marko," Father Marlas said, and his composure was slightly shaken. "The family feels you are forcing your attention upon this girl. They are concerned."

"I understand, Father," I said. "It is natural for them to be concerned. I respect their concern. It is also natural for me to speak of love to a woman I have chosen for my wife."

"Not my business!" Uncle Paul said again, and shook his head violently.

"My daughter does not wish to become your wife," Mr. Langos said in a squeaky voice.

"That is for your daughter to say," I said courteously.

Ariadne made a sound in her throat, and we all looked at her. Her eyes were deep and cold, and she spoke slowly and carefully as if weighing each word on a scale in her father's grocery.

"I would not marry this madman if he were one of the Twelve Apostles," she said.

"See!" Mr. Langos said in triumph.

"Not my business!" Uncle Paul snarled.

"Marko," Father Marlas said. "Try to understand."

"We will call the police!" Uncle Paul raised his voice. "Put this hoodlum under a bond!"

"Please!" Father Marlas said. "Please!"

"Today he stood on the street outside the store," Mr. Langos said excitedly. "He made me a laughingstock."

"If I were a younger man," Uncle Paul growled, "I would settle this without the police. Zi-ip!" He drew a callused finger violently across his throat.

"Please," Father Marlas said.
"A disgrace!" Mr. Langos said.
"An outrage!" Uncle Paul said.
"He must leave Ariadne alone!" Mr. Langos said.
"We will call the police!" Uncle Paul said.
"Silence!" Father Marlas said loudly.
With everything suddenly quiet he turned to me. His tone softened.
"Marko," he said and he seemed to be pleading a little. "Marko, you must understand."

Suddenly a great bitterness assailed me, and anger at myself, and a terrible sadness that flowed like night through my body because I could not make them understand.

"Father," I said quietly, "I am not a fool. I am Marko Palamas and once I pinned the mighty Zahundos in Baltimore. But this battle, more important to me by far, I have lost. That which has not the grace of God is better far in silence."

I turned to leave and it would have ended there.

"Hoodlum!" Uncle Paul said. "It is time you were silent!"

I swear in that moment if he had been a younger man I would have flung him to the dome of the church. Instead I turned and spoke to them all in fire and fury.

"Listen," I said. "I feel no shame for the violence of my feelings. I am a man bred of the Spartan earth and my emotions are violent. Let those who squeak of life feel shame. Nor do I feel shame because I saw this flower and loved her. Or because I spoke at once of my love."

No one moved or made a sound.

"We live in a dark age," I said. "An age where men say one thing and mean another. A time of dwarfs afraid of life. The days are gone when mighty Pindar sang his radiant blossoms of song. When the noble passions of men set ablaze cities, and the heroic deeds of men rang like thunder to every corner of the earth."

I spoke my final words to Ariadne. "I saw you and loved you," I said gently. "I told you of my love. This is my way—the only way I know. If this way has proved offensive to you I apologize to you alone. But understand clearly that for none of this do I feel shame."

I turned then and started for the door. I felt my heart weeping as if waves were breaking within my body.

"Marko Palamas," Ariadne said. I turned slowly. I looked at her. For the first time the warmth I was sure dwelt in her body radiated within the circles of her face. For the first time she did not look at me with her eyes like glaciers.

"Marko Palamas," she said and there was a strange moving softness in the way she spoke my name. "You may call on me tomorrow."

Uncle Paul shot out of his chair. "She is mad too!" he shouted. "He has bewitched her!"

"A disgrace!" Mr. Langos said.

"Call the police!" Uncle Paul shouted. "I'll show him if it's my business!"

"My poor daughter!" Mr. Langos wailed.

"Turk!" Uncle Paul shouted. "Robber!"

"Please!" Father Marlas said. "Please!"

I ignored them all. In that winged and zestful moment I had eyes only for my beloved, for Ariadne, blossom of my heart and black-eyed flower of my soul!

The old priest in this story is another of the Greek Orthodox clergymen I often use in my stories. I think my father's having been a priest has much to do with my fondness for them as principals. None of the fictional priests are totally my father, but fragments of him appear in them all. From time to time I have used his gentleness, patience, humor, and, from a period near the end of his life when he was battered by illness and the ingratitude of those he had served, the weariness and resignation that saturated his spirit.

The rake, Barbaroulis, offers a good contrast to the priest. In accordance with prehistoric Homeric practice, they fire insults and satirical couplets at one another, a smoking fusillade that conceals their mutual affection and respect.

This story also satisfies my boyhood expectations, when I wavered between dreams of becoming a saint and the exciting prospect of turning out to be a venerable sinner.

THE MIRACLE

He was weary of tears and laughter. He felt perhaps he had been a priest too long. His despair had grown until it seemed, suddenly, bewilderingly, he was an entity, separate and alone. His days had become a burden.

The weddings and baptisms which once provided him with pleasure had become a diversion, one of the myriad knots upon the rope of his faith. A rope he was unable to unravel because for too long he had told himself that in God rested the final and reconciling truth of the mystery that was human life.

In the middle of the night the ring of the doorbell roused him from restless sleep. His housekeeper, old Mrs. Calchas, answered. Word was carried by a son or a daughter or a friend that an old man or an old woman was dying and the priest was needed for the last communion. He dressed wearily and took his bag and his book, a conductor on the train of death who no longer esteemed himself as a puncher of tickets.

He spent much time pondering what might have gone wrong. He thought it must be that he had been a priest too long. Words of solace and consolation spoken too often became tea bags returned to the pot too many times. Yet he still believed that love, all forms of love, represented the only real union with other human beings. Only in this way, in loving and being loved, could the enigmas be transcended and suffering be made bearable.

When he entered the priesthood forty years before, he drew upon the springs of love he had known. The warmth of his mother who embodied for him the home from which he came, bountiful nature and the earth. The stature of his father as the one who taught him, who showed him the road to the world. Even the fragmented recollection of the sensual love of a girl he had known as a boy helped to strengthen the bonds of his resolve. He would never have accepted his ordination if he did not feel that loving God and God's love for all mankind could not be separated. If he could not explain all the manifestations of this love, he could at least render its testaments in compassionate clarity.

But with increasing anguish his image seemed to have become disembodied from the source. He felt himself suddenly of little value to those who suffered. Because he knew this meant he was failing God in some improvident way, a wounding shame was added to his weariness.

Sometimes in the evening he stopped by the coffeehouse of Little Macedonia. There the shadows were cool and restful and the sharp aroma of brandies and virulent cigars exorcised melancholy for a little while. He sat with his old friend of many years, Barbaroulis, and they talked of life and death.

Barbaroulis was a grizzled and growling veteran of three wars and a thousand tumbled women. An unrepentant rake who counted his years of war and lechery well spent. An old man in the twilight of his life with all the fabled serenity of a saint.

"Hurry, old noose-collar," Barbaroulis said. "I am half a bottle of mastiha ahead."

"I long ago gave up hope of matching you in that category," the priest said.

Barbaroulis filled both their glasses with a flourish. "Tell me of birth and marriage and death," he said.

"I have baptized one, married two, and buried three this last week," the priest said.

Barbaroulis laughed mockingly. "What a delightful profession," he said. "A bookkeeper in the employ of God."

"And whose employ are you in?" the priest asked.

"I thought you knew," the old man said. "Can you not smell sulfur and brimstone in my presence?"

"An excuse for not bathing more often," the priest said.

"You are insolent," the old man growled. He called out in his harsh loud voice and a waiter exploded out of the shadows with another bottle of mastiha. Barbaroulis drew the cork and smelled the fragrance with a moan of pleasure. "The smell of mastiha and the smell of a lovely woman have much in common," he said. "And a full bottle is like a lovely woman before love."

"Your head and a sponge have much in common, too," the priest said. "Wine and women are ornaments and not pillars of life."

"Drink up, noose-collar," Barbaroulis said. "Save your sermons for Sunday."

The priest raised the glass to his lips and slowly sipped the strong tart liquid. It soothed his tongue and for a brief illusive moment eased his spirit. "The doctor has warned you about drinking," he said to Barbaroulis. "Yet you seem to be swilling more than ever before."

"When life must be reduced to an apothecary's measure," Barbaroulis snorted, "it is time to get out. I am not interested in remaining alive with somber kidneys and a placid liver. Let the graduate undertakers who get me marvel at my liver scarred like the surface of a withered peach and at my heart seared by a thousand loves like a hunk of meat in incredible heat."

"You are mad, old roué," the priest said. "But sometimes I see strange order in your madness."

"Even a madman would renounce this world," Barbaroulis said with contempt. "Why should anyone hesitate giving up the culture of the bomb and the electric chair? We are a boil on the rump of the universe and all our vaunted songs are mute farts in the darkness of eternity."

"You assemble the boil and the fart," the priest said, "from the condition of your liver and your heart."

"When will you admit, noose-collar," Barbaroulis laughed, "that the limousine of faith has a broken axle?"

"When you admit," the priest said, "that the hungry may eat fish without understanding the dark meaning in its eye." He finished his drink and rose regretfully to go.

"Leaving already?" Barbaroulis said. "You come and go like a robin after crumbs."

"There is a world outside these shadows," the priest said.

"Renounce it!" Barbaroulis said. "Forsake it! Join me here and we will both float to death on exultant kidneys."

"You are a saint," the priest said. "Saint Barbaroulis of the Holy Order of Mastiha. Your penance is to drink alone."

"What is your penance?"

The priest stood for a moment in the shadows and yearned to stay awhile longer. The taste of the mastiha was warm on his tongue and his weariness was eased in the fragrant dark. "Birth and marriage and death," he said and waved the old man goodby.

On Sunday mornings he rose before dawn and washed and dressed. He sat for a little while in his room and reviewed his sermon for the day. Then he walked the deserted streets to the church.

There was a serenity about the city at daybreak on Sunday, a quiet and restful calm before the turmoil of the new week. Only a prowling tomcat, fierce as Barbaroulis, paused to mark the sound of his steps in the silence. At the edge of the dark sky the first light glittered and suspended the earth between darkness and day.

The church was damp from the night and thick with shadows. In a few moments old Janco shuffled about lighting the big candles. The flames flickered light across the icons of the white bearded saints.

He prepared for the service. He broke the bread and poured the wine for the communion. Afterward he dressed slowly in his vestments and bound the layers and cords of cloth together. He passed behind the iconostasis and through a gap in the partition saw that the first parishioners were already in church awaiting the beginning of the service. First, the very old and infirm regarding the ornaments of God somberly and without joy. They would follow every word and gesture of the liturgy grimly. Their restless and uneasy fingers reflected the questions burning in their minds. Would the balance sheet of their lives permit them entry into the city of God? Was it ever too late to take solace in piety and assurance in sobriety?

After them the middle-aged entered. Men and women who had lived more than half their lives and whose grown children had little need for them anymore. Strange aches and pains assailed them and they were unable to dispel the dark awareness of time as enemy instead of friend.

Then the young married couples with babies squirming in their arms, babies whose shrill voices cried out like flutes on scattered islands. In the intervals when they were not soothing the infants, the young parents would proffer their devotions a little impatiently while making plans for the things to be done after church.

Finally the very young girls and boys, distraught and inattentive, secured to the benches by the eyelocks of stern parents. They had the arrogance of youth, the courage of innocence, and the security of good health.

When the service was over they all mingled together for a moment and then formed into lines to pass before him for bread. Old Janco began snuffing out the candles in the warm and drowsy church. The shadows returned garnished by incense. The church emptied slowly and the last voices echoed a mumble like the swell of a receding wave. In the end only he remained and with him the men and women standing in the rear of the darkened church waiting to see him alone.

"Father, my daughter is unmarried and pregnant. A boy in our neighborhood is guilty. I swear I will kill him if he does not marry her."

"Father, my husband drinks. For ten years he has promised to give it up. Sometimes there isn't money enough to buy food for the children's supper."

"Father, all day I look after my mother in her wheelchair. I cannot sleep at night because I dream of wishing her dead."

"Father, my child is losing his sight. The doctors say there is nothing that can be done."

"Father, ask God to have mercy on me. I have sinned with my brother's wife."

"Father, pray for me."

Until the last poor tormented soul was gone, and he stood alone in the dark and empty church. In the sky outside a bird passed trailing its winged and throaty cry. He knelt and prayed. He asked to be forgiven his sins of weariness and despair and to be strengthened against faltering and withdrawal. For a terrible instant he yearned for the restful sleep of death.

There was a night that summer when the doorbell rang long after midnight. He woke from a strange and disordered sleep to the somber voice of Mrs. Calchas. Barbaroulis was dying.

He dressed with trembling hands and went into the night. His friend lived in a rooming house a few blocks away and the landlady, a grim-faced Medusa, let the priest in. She told him the doctor had come and gone. There was nothing more to be done.

Barbaroulis lay in an old iron-postered bed, a decayed giant on a quilt-and-cotton throne. When he turned his head at the sound of the door, the priest saw that dying had refashioned the flesh of his face, making the cheeks dark and tight and the eyes webbed and burning.

"I was expecting Death, the carrion crow," Barbaroulis said. "You enter much too softly."

"Did you wake me for nothing?" the priest said. "Is your ticket perhaps for some later train?"

Barbaroulis grinned, a twisting of flesh around his mouth, and the husks of his teeth glittered in the dim light. "I sent for you to get it," he said.

"Get what?"

"The bottle of mastiha," Barbaroulis said. "My mouth is parched for some mastiha."

"The custom is for communion," the priest said.

"Save it," Barbaroulis said. "There is a flask of mastiha in the corner behind the books. I have hidden it from that dragon who waits like a banshee for my wake."

The priest brought him the flask. The great nostrils of Barbaroulis twitched as he smelled the sharp aroma. He made a mighty effort to raise his head and the priest helped him. The touch of the old man's expiring flesh swept the priest with a mutilating grief. A little liquid dribbled down the old man's chin. Breathing harshly, he rested his head back against the pillow. "A shame to waste any," he said.

"Tomorrow I will bring a full bottle," the priest said, "and serve it to you out of the communion chalice. We might get away with it."

"Drink it yourself in my memory," Barbaroulis said. "I will not be here."

"Where is your courage?" the priest asked gruffly to cover emotion. "I have seen men sicker by far rise to dance in a week."

"No more dancing for Barbaroulis," the old man said slowly and the mocking rise and fall of his voice echoed from the hidden corners of the room. "The ball is over, the bottle empty, the strumpets asleep. Pack me a small bag for a short trip. Only the lightest of apparel."

"A suit of asbestos," the priest said.

"I have no regrets," Barbaroulis twisted his mouth in a weird grin. "I have burned the earth as I found it. And if word could be carried far and fast enough a thousand women would mourn for me and rip their petticoats in despair."

"Are you confessing?" the priest asked.

"Just remembering," Barbaroulis said and managed a sly wink. "When I see your God," he said, "shall I give him a message from you?"

"You won't have time," the priest said. "The layover between trains will be brief."

The old man's dark parched lips stirred against each other in silent laughter. "Old noose-collar," he said, "a comfort to the end."

"Saint Barbaroulis," the priest said. "The Holy Order of Mastiha."

"What a time we could have had," Barbaroulis said. "The two of us wenching and fighting and drinking. What a roisterer I could have made of you."

"What about you in church?" the priest said. "You might have become a trustee and passed the collection plate on Sunday. Who would have dared drop a slug before your fierce and vigilant eyes? Gregory of Nazianzus would have been a minor saint beside you."

Barbaroulis laughed again with a grating sound as if bone were being rubbed against bone. Then the laughter faltered and a long shudder swept his body. His fingers, stiff as claws, curled in frenzy upon the sheet.

The priest watched the terrible struggle and there was nothing he could do but grip the old man's hand tightly in his own.

Barbaroulis made a sign with his raging eyes and the priest moved closer quickly. A single moment had transformed the old man's face into a dark and teeming battleground of death. His lips stirred for a moment without sound and then he spoke in a low hoarse whisper and each word came bitten slowly from between his teeth.

"I have known a thousand men and women well," he drew a long fierce rasp of breath. "I have loved only one." His voice trailed away and the priest moved closer to his lips that trembled to finish. "A priest who reflects the face of his God."

Then his mouth opened wider and his teeth gleamed. For a moment he seemed to be screaming in silence and then a short violent rush of air burst from his body.

The priest sat there for a long time. In death the old man seemed to have suddenly become half man, half statue, something between flesh and stone. Finally the priest rose and closed the dead man's eyes and bent and kissed his cheek.

He left the room. The street was black but the roofs of houses were white in the glow of the waning moon. A wind stirred the leaves of a solitary tree and then subsided.

His friend had been a man of strife and a man of contention. But into the darkness the old man had borne the priest's grief and his sorrow. In his final moment Barbaroulis had fed his loneliness and appeased his despair. And as he walked, he cried, and the great bursting tears of Lazarus ran like wild rivers down his cheeks.

I have read this story before several hundred college and club audiences across the United States. The girls in the audience will clap for Nitsa and hiss Vasili, and the boys will cheer Vasili and boo Nitsa. The result is like an old movie, where one cheers or hisses, depending upon one's sympathies. No other story I have written has provided me as much fun.

In the question periods that follow the reading, someone invariably asks if the story is autobiographical. I explain solemnly that my wife and I have a nonaggression pact. If I do not beat her, she will not beat me.

THE JOURNAL OF A WIFE BEATER

October 2: Today I beat my wife, Nitsa, for the first time! I preserve this momentous event for future generations by beginning this Journal and recording this first entry with some pride.

I did not beat her hard, really not hard at all. I gave her several clouts across her head with my open palm, enough to make her stagger and daze her a little. Then I led her courteously to a chair to show her I was not punishing her in anger.

"Why?" she asked, and there were small tears glistening in the corners of her eyes.

"Nothing of great significance," I said amiably. "The coffee you served me was not hot enough this morning and after the last few washings my shirts have not had enough starch. Yesterday and the day before you were late in arriving at the restaurant. All of these are small imprudences that display a growing laxity on your part. I felt it was time to suggest improvement."

She watched me with her lips trembling. How artfully women suffer!

"You have never struck me before," she said thoughtfully. "In the year since we married, Vasili, you have never struck me before."

"One does not wish to begin correction too soon," I said. "It would be unjust to expect a new bride to attain perfection overnight. A period of flexibility is required."

Her big black eyes brooded, but she said nothing.

"You understand," I said consolingly. "This does not mean I do not love you." I shook my head firmly to emphasize my words. "It is exactly because I do care for you that I desire to improve you. On a number of occasions in my father's house I can remember him beating my mother. Not hard you understand. A clout across the head, and a box upon the ear. Once when she left the barn door open and the cows strayed out, he kicked her, but that was an exception. My mother was a happy and contented woman all her life."

The conversation ended there, but Nitsa was silent and meditative as we prepared for bed. She did not speak again until we were under the covers in the darkness.

"Vasili," she asked quietly, "will you strike me again?"

"Only when I feel you need it," I said. "It should not be required too often. You are a sensible girl and I am sure are most anxious to please me by being a good wife and a competent homemaker."

She turned away on her pillow and did not say another word.

October 3: I slept splendidly last night!

October 5: Since I have a few moments of leisure this evening, I will fill in certain background information about Nitsa and myself so that future generations may better understand this record of an ideal marriage relationship.

First I must record my immense satisfaction in the results of the beating. Nitsa has improved tremendously the past two days. She has taken the whole affair as sensibly as any man could have wished.

Her good sense was what first impressed me about Nitsa. I met her about a year ago at a dance in the church hall, sponsored by the Daughters of Athens. I drank a little beer and danced once with each of a number of young ladies whose zealous mothers beamed at me from chairs along the wall. I might add here that before my marriage a year ago I was a very desirable catch for some fortunate girl. I was just a year past forty, an inch above average height, with all of my own hair and most of my own teeth, a number of which have been capped with gold. I had, and of course still have, a prosperous restaurant on Dart Street and a substantial sum in United States Savings Bonds. Finally, I myself was interested in marriage to a well-bred young lady. My first inclination was to return to Greece and select some daughter born to respect the traditions of the family; but as our parish priest, Father Antoniou, pointed out with his usual keen discernment, this would have been grossly unfair to the countless girls in our community who hoped for me as a bridegroom. Although marriage to any one of them would dismay the others, it would be better than if I scorned them all for a wife from overseas.

Nitsa impressed me because she was not as young as most of the other girls, perhaps in her late twenties, a tall athletic-looking girl who appeared capable of bearing my sturdy sons. She was not as beautiful a girl as I felt I deserved, but she made a neat and pleasant appearance. Most attractive young girls are too flighty and arrogant. They are not sensible enough to be grateful when a successful man pays them attention. Bringing one of them into a man's home is much the same as bringing in a puppy that has not yet been housebroken. Too much time is spent on fundamentals!

Imagine my delight when, in inquiry regarding Nitsa's family that night, I learned that she was the niece of our revered priest, Father Antoniou, visiting him from Cleveland.

I danced several American dances with her to demonstrate that I was not old-fashioned and spoke to her at some length of my assets and my prospects. She listened with unconcealed interest. We sat and drank coffee afterward until a group of my friends called to me to lead one of the old country dances. Conscious of her watching me, I danced with even more than my usual grace and flourish, and leaped higher off the floor than I had in some time.

A day or two later I spoke seriously to Father Antoniou. He was frankly delighted. He phoned his sister, Nitsa's mother in Cleveland, and in no time at all the arrangements were made. As I had accurately surmised, the whole family, including Nitsa, were more than willing.

Several weeks later we were married. It was a festive affair and the reception cost a little over a thousand dollars which I insisted her father pay. He was a housepainter who worked irregularly, but in view of the fact that Nitsa brought me no dowry I felt he should demonstrate the good faith of the family by paying for the reception.

Nitsa and I spent a honeymoon weekend at the Mortimer Hotel so I could return to count the cash when the restaurant closed each evening. As it was, God only knows what the waitresses stole from me those two days. During our absence I had the bedroom of my apartment painted, and after considerable deliberation bought a new stove. I write this as proof of my thoughtfulness. The stove I had was only twelve years old, but I am worldly enough to understand how all women love new stoves. If permitted by weak and easily swayed husbands they would trade them in on newer models every year.

In recalling our first year together, while it was not quite what I expected, I was not completely disillusioned. There was a certain boldness and immodesty about Nitsa which I found displeasing, but one must bear with this in a healthy young woman.

As time went on she spent a good part of the day with me in the restaurant taking cash. She became familiar enough with my business so that when the wholesale produce and meat salesman called she could be trusted to order some of the staple items. But I noticed a certain laxity developing, a carelessness in her approach to her responsibilities, and remembering my father's success with my mother, it was then I beat her for the first time.

I am so pleased that it seems to have prompted unreserved improvement. Bravo, Vasili!

October 7: It is after midnight and I am alone in the restaurant which is closed until morning. I am sitting at the small table in the kitchen and can hardly bear to write the shameful and disgraceful episode which follows.

Last night after returning from the restaurant I went to bed because I was tired. Nitsa came into the room as I was slipping under the covers. I had noticed a rather somber quietness about her all that day, but I attributed it to that time of the female month. When she had donned her night clothes and gotten into bed beside me, I raised my cheek for her to kiss me goodnight. She turned her back on me and for a moment I was peeved, but remembering her indisposition, I turned off the lamp and said nothing.

I fell asleep shortly and had a stirring dream. I fought beside Achilles on the plains before Troy. I carried a mighty shield and a long sword. Suddenly a massive Trojan appeared before me and we engaged each other in combat. After I brilliantly parried a number of his blows he seemed to recognize he was doomed. He retreated and I pressed him hard. While we slashed back and forth, another Trojan rose beside me as if he had sprung from the earth, and swung his weapon at my head. I raised my shield swiftly but not quite in time and the flat of his sword landed across my head. The pain was so terrible I shrieked out loud, and suddenly the plains of Troy and the helmeted warriors were all swept away and my eyes exploded open to the sight of Nitsa bent over me, calmly preparing to strike again!

I bellowed and clawed to sit up, and tried desperately to flee from the bed. The stick she swung bounced again across my head and the pain was ferocious. I fell off the bed in a tangle of sheets at her feet; then I jumped up frantically and ran to the other side of the bed, looking back in desperation to see if she followed. She stood dreadfully calm with the stick still in her hand.

"Are you mad!" I shouted. My nose seemed to be swelling and my head stung and I tasted blood from my cut lip. "You must be mad or in the employ of the devil! You have split me open!"

"I owed you one," she said quietly.

I looked at her in astonishment and rubbed my aching head. I could not comprehend the desecration of a wife striking her husband. "Your senses have come apart," I bellowed. "You might have broken my head!"

"I don't think so," she said. "You have an unusually dense head."

I was horrified. On top of my injuries her insolence could not be tolerated. I ran around the bed and pulled the stick from her hands. I swung it up and down. When it landed across her shoulders she winced and gave a shrill squeal. Then I went to bathe my swollen head. A harrowing and terrible experience indeed!

October 11: Plague and damnation! Blood and unspeakable horror! She has done it again.

That wench of evil design waited just long enough for the swelling of my nose to recede and my lip to heal. All week she had been quiet and reserved. She came to work promptly and performed her duties efficiently. While I could never forget that night in bed when she struck me, I was willing to forgive. Women are by nature as emotionally unstable as dogs under the mad light of a full moon. But I am a generous man and in this foul manner was my generosity rewarded.

It happened shortly after the rush at lunch was over. The restaurant was deserted except for Nitsa at the register and the waitresses chattering beside the urns of coffee. I was sitting at the small table in the kitchen, smoking a cigar, and pondering whether to order short ribs or pork loins for lunch on Thursday. Suddenly I was conscious of an uneasy chill in the center of my back. A strange quick dread possessed me and I turned swiftly around and Nitsa was there. Almost at the same instant the pot she was swinging landed with a horrible clatter on my head. I let out a roar of outrage and pain, and jumped up holding my thundering head. I found it impossible to focus my eyes, and for a frenzied moment I imagined I was surrounded by a dozen Nitsas. I roared again in fear and anger, and ran to seek sanctuary behind the big stove. She made no move to follow me but stood quietly by the table with the pot in her hand.

"You must be mad!" I shrieked. "I will call the doctor and have him exchange your bloody head!"

The dishwasher, who had come from the back room where he had been eating, watched us with his great idiot eyes, and the waitresses, cousins of imbeciles, peered through the porthole of the swinging door.

"I owed you one," Nitsa said quietly. She put down the pot and walked from the kitchen past the awed and silent waitresses.

As I write this now, words are inadequate to describe my distress. Fiercer by far than the abominable lump on my head is the vision of chaos and disorder. In the name of all that is sacred, where is the moral and ordered world of my father?

October 15: Disturbed and agitated as I have been for the past few days, tonight I decided something had to be done. I went to speak to Father Antoniou.

Nitsa, that shrew, has been at the restaurant for several days now acting as if nothing had happened. She joked with the customers and took cash calmly. Heartless wench without the decency to show some shred of remorse!

Last night I slept locked in the bathroom. Even then I was apprehensive and kept one eye open on the door. While it was true that by her immoral standards we were even, she could not be trusted. I feared she would take it into her stony soul to surge into a shameful lead. Finally tonight, because I knew the situation had become intolerable, I visited the priest.

He greeted me courteously and took me into his study. He brought out a bottle of good sherry. We sat silent for a moment, sipping the fine vintage.

"You may speak now, my dear friend," he said gently. "You are troubled."

"How can you tell, Father?" I asked.

He smiled sagely. He was indeed a fountain of wisdom.

"Well, Father," I struggled for the mortifying words. "It is Nitsa. To put it plainly, she has struck me not once, but twice, with a stout stick and a heavy pot."

He sat upright in his chair.

"May God watch over us!" he said. "Surely, Vasili, you are jesting!"

I made my cross and bent my head to show him the hard lump that still dwelt there. He rose from his chair and came to examine it. When he touched the lump, I jumped.

He paced the floor in agitation, his black cassock swirling about his ankles.

"She must be demented," he said slowly. "The poor girl must be losing her mind."

"That is what I thought at first," I said seriously. "But she seems so calm. Each time she strikes me she merely says, 'I owed you one.'"

"Aaaaah!" the priest said eagerly. "Now we approach the core of truth." His voice lowered. "What did you do to her for which she seeks revenge?" He winked slyly. "I know you hot-blooded Spartans. Perhaps a little too passionate for a shy young girl?"

"Nothing, Father!" I said in indignation, although I could not help being pleased at his suggestion. "Absolutely nothing."

"Nothing?" he repeated.

"I have clouted her several times across her head," I said. "My prerogative as a husband to discipline my wife. Certainly nothing to warrant the violence of her blows."

"Incredible," the priest said. He sat silent and thoughtful, then shook his head. "A woman raising her hand to her husband in my parish, and that woman my niece. Incredible!" He wrung his hands fretfully. "A stain upon the sacred vows of marriage." He paused as if struck by a sudden thought. "Tell me, Vasili, has she been watching much television? Sometimes it tends to confuse a woman."

"Our picture tube is burned out now several months, Father," I said.

"Incredible," the priest said.

"Perhaps if you talk to her, Father," I said. "Explain what it is to be a dutiful wife. Define the rights of a husband."

The priest shook his head sadly. "When I first entered the priesthood," he said somberly, "I learned never to attempt to reason with a woman. The two words should never be used in the same sentence. The emancipation of these crafty scheming descendants of Eve has hurled man into a second Dark Ages."

I was impressed by the gravity of his words and had to agree I had spoken hastily.

"My son," the priest said finally, a thin edge of desperation in his voice. "I confess I am helpless to know what to advise. If you came to seek counsel because she drank to excess or because she had succumbed to the wiles of another man . . . but for this! I will have to contact the Bishop."

I sipped my sherry and felt anger coming to a head on my flesh as if it were a festered boil pressing to break. I, Vasili Makris, subjected to these indignities! Humiliated before my own dishwasher! Driving my parish priest to consult with the Bishop!

"There is only one answer, Father," I said, and my voice rang out boldly, a Homeric call to battle. "I have clouted her too lightly. There is nothing further to be done but for me to give her a beating she will not forget!" I waved my hand. "Rest assured I will remember my own strength. I will not break any bones, but I will teach her respect." I became more pleased with that solution by the moment. "That is the answer, Father," I said. "A beating that will once and for all end this insufferable mutiny!"

We watched each other for a long wordless moment. I could sense that good man struggling between a moral objection to violence and an awareness there was no other way.

"They who live by the sword," he said dolefully, and he paused to permit me to finish the quotation in my mind. "This cancer must be cut out," he said, "before it spreads infection through the parish."

He raised his glass of wine and toasted me gravely.

"Consider yourself embarked on a holy crusade," he said in a voice trembling with emotion. "Recapture the sanctity of your manhood. Go, Vasili Makris, with God."

I kissed his revered hand and left.

October 17: The promised retribution has been delayed because a waitress has been sick and I cannot afford to incapacitate Nitsa at the same time. But I vow her reprieve will be brief!

October 19: Tonight is the night! The restaurant is closed and we are alone. I am sitting in the kitchen making this entry while she finishes cleaning out the urns of coffee. When the work is all done I will call her into the kitchen for judgment.

Nitsa! Misguided and arrogant woman, your hour of punishment is here!

October 23: In the life of every noble man there are moments of decisive discovery and events of inspired revelation. I hasten with fire and zeal to record such an experience in this Journal!

That epic night when Nitsa came to the kitchen of the restaurant after finishing her work, without a word of warning I struck her. Quick as a flash she struck me back. I was prepared for that and hit her harder. She replied with a thump on my head that staggered me. I threw all hesitation to the winds and landed a fierce blow upon her. Instead of submitting, she became a flame of baleful fury. She twisted violently in search of some weapon to implement her rage, and scooped up a meat cleaver off the block! I let out a hoarse shout of panic and turned desperately and fled! I heard her pounding like a maddened mare after me, and I made the door leading to the alley and bounded out with a wild cry! I forgot completely the accursed stairs and spun like a top in the air and landed on my head. I woke in the hospital where I am at present and X-rays have indicated no damage beyond a possible concussion that still causes me some dizziness.

At the first opportunity I examined myself secretly for additional reassurance that some vital part of me had not been dismembered by that frightful cleaver. Then I sat and recollected each detail of that experience with somber horror. A blow now and then, delivered in good faith, is one of the prerogatives of marriage. Malevolent assault and savage butchery are quite another matter!

However, as my first sense of appalled outrage and angry resentment passed, I found the entire situation developing conclusive compensations. I had fancied myself married to a mortal woman and instead I was united to a Goddess, a fierce Diana, a cyclonic Juno! I realized with a shock of recognition that one eagle had found another, perched on Olympian peaks, high above the obscure valley of pigeons and sheep.

O fortunate woman! You have gained my mercy and forbearance and have proven to my satisfaction that you deserve my virile love and are worthy of my intrepid manhood!

Nitsa, rejoice! You need no longer tremble or fear that I will ever strike you again!

This story, like "Dark Eye," resulted from the time we spent in California. The good actors and actresses we met were always eager for work which was unfailingly scarce because of the number of performers available.

In some ways I think an aspiring writer is more fortunate than an aspiring actor and actress. A writer can improve and develop his craft by writing even if he isn't able to sell what he writes. But to grow and mature as a performer, an actor requires a script, a director, a theatre or a film, and an audience.

As a youth I had a desire to act myself, and we still have an old framed photograph of me as an unkempt-bearded and baggy-costumed Creon the King, in an early performance of *Antigone*. I deflected my energies into writing but the genes were only temporarily submerged. Diana and I have sons who are fine actors and who write and aspire to make films.

Having chosen a writer's life, I have scant authority as I warn them of the hazards and uncertainties of their chosen professions.

THE CASTLE

Lou opened his eyes to streamers of sunlight slipping through the blinds. He stretched under the covers and breathed the aromas of the morning, coffee, bacon, and bougainvillea from the courtyard. He heard the hungry cry of a baby in an adjoining apartment, the cry silenced abruptly as if it had been given a bottle or its mother's breast.

He threw off his covers and moved swiftly out of bed, standing naked in the center of the bedroom, pacing his strong, muscled body through a series of pushups and deep-knee bends. He finished with a flurry of slaps across his firm belly and remembered suddenly that it was his birthday.

Fifty, he thought with a surge of panic, his forties ended forever. He started to the bathroom, pausing to examine himself carefully before the full-length mirror on the closet door. He was in better condition than most thirty year olds and he defied anyone who did not know the truth to guess that he looked any older than forty.

"I'm in my prime now, goddamit," he spoke to his reflection.

"Hunger and disappointment have kept me lean as an old wolf. And I can still outrun the dogs and outwit the hunters!" He scowled fiercely at his image, daring it to disagree. He laughed and continued into the bathroom.

He emerged from the shower, toweling himself briskly and dressed with even more than his usual care. He put on a yellow shirt with faint brown stripes and his best herringbone sportcoat. Before leaving his apartment he dialed his agent. The voice of the switchboard operator grated in his ear.

"Gutwillig, Gruenbaum and Alter."

"Good morning, honey," Lou said. "Is that scourge of the studios, Sam Vigil, there?"

"No, he isn't, Mr. Phillips," the woman said. "Shall I have him call you?"

"I'd appreciate that," Lou said. "I'd really appreciate that very much since I been calling him for three days without getting any answer. Tell him today is my birthday and to call and offer me his best wishes. Better yet, tell him to call me with some heartening news about a splendid role in some major film."

After he hung up, he dialed his answering service.

"I'm leaving home now," he said. "I'll be at Paramount for lunch, maybe Universal later in the afternoon. I'll check with you later."

He left his apartment feeling his spirits buoyant. He was a year older, that was true, but that also meant an additional year of experience as an actor. Thirty years in the business, parts in almost a hundred television series and films. He was respected as a craftsman and he was liked as a decent human being in a profession where pricks grew like weeds.

He walked along the balcony, smelling the hibiscus, watching the sunlight glittering across the clear blue water of the pool. On the diving board the wife of an assistant art director lay sunbathing on her stomach, one slender, tanned leg swinging idly in the air. The tiny fold of her silk bikini barely covered her shapely buttocks.

"Good morning, Mrs. Renrow," he said cheerfully. She raised her head off her towel, her blond hair awry, her face, arms and shoulders shimmering with oil.

"Good morning, Mr. Phillips," she said. She had a coquettish way of tilting her head and curling her lips in a pout copied from an old Brigitte Bardot movie. She was bored and restless, needing only the snap of a man's fingers to set her loose. But Lou avoided playing the marriage circuit. In addition he had heard her fighting shrilly with her husband and her voice repelled him.

"Are you shooting today?" she asked.

"Some publicity stills at Paramount," he said casually. "An interview for a Boston paper in the afternoon. Nothing too important, really."

He smiled at her, waving goodby, and walked around the board along the flagstones leading to the street. He felt her eyes appraisingly on his back. Wondering about my stroke, he thought with amusement, how deep I dive and how often I come up for air.

He parked his four year old Honda in the Melrose parking lot and twisted from behind the wheel. He didn't enjoy the small, cramped car but drove it because the model changes were slight and concealed its age. He walked between parked cars to the main entrance of Paramount. At a little past eleven the canteen truck stood outside the gate, the side panel open to reveal trays of sandwiches and a silver urn of coffee. Gathered around the canteen were shabby cowboys and spacemen and some GI's from a new series modeled on MASH. He paused to exchange greetings with a few players he knew and swiftly noted a strange young guard checking visitors at the gate. Even when he had no appointment, the old guards who knew him allowed him entrance without question. The younger guards he handled with the proper blend of civility and impatience.

As he neared the gate, preparing to respond to the young guard's query, he recognized one of the old guards sitting inside the guardhouse.

"How you doing, Al?" Lou called. The young guard paused with the question unasked.

"Hi ya, Lou," Albert smiled. "How's it going?"

"Fine! Fine!" Lou said heartily. "It's my birthday today. Forty-eight."

"Congratulations, Lou," Albert said. "Hope you make it to a hundred."

"I'm counting on it," Lou said. "I want to see what's coming after Women's Liberation."

Albert and the young guard laughed. Lou waved them a salute and sauntered past the guardhouse into the lot.

Inside the commissary he slipped around the crowd waiting in line for tables and nodded at the hostess.

"My friends are holding a chair for me, honey," he said. She stepped aside and for a moment he stood poised on the threshold of the noisy, turbulent room, breathing in the fervid spirit of laughter, gossip and excitement. He saw the white-haired figure of Paul Sher waving to him from a corner. He waved back, moving between the tables, asking and answering questions in almost the same breath.

"How are you, Tony?" he said. "Saw you in Festival. You were tremendous! Stole the scene from Gere... Larry, when did you get back? How was Spain?... Esther, what did I tell you about that director? Gift Package makes three bombs in a row... What part is that? You know I won't do less than three weeks. If it's a cameo, I'll talk to him. Where they shooting? Warners? O.K."

He talked loudly so that people at adjoining tables paused eating and looked up at him. When they didn't recognize him they looked back down, but that was still better than if they had not looked at all. Someone, someday, might suddenly see in him the perfect casting for a lead in a film.

By the time he reached the corner where Paul and Jim Retsas were sitting, Lou was in the full heat and rhythm of the commissary.

Jim Retsas, a bit actor in his early forties with a gaunt, harried face, shook his head in disgust.

"You come across the goddam room like you're Johnny Carson," he said.

"Let them know I'm here," Lou winked. He swung a leg lithely over the back of his chair and motioned at Paul's plate.

"I'm eating chicken croquettes," Paul said. He was a distinguished looking actor in his late sixties. Casting offices called him for mute parts as generals and admirals. Paul had spent so many hours before the camera in uniform, he claimed he deserved veteran's benefits.

The waitress, a slender, pretty blonde girl, appeared with her pencil and pad.

"Grilled ham and cheese, honey," Lou said. "Fries and coffee." He studied her ungirdled bottom as she walked away, not because he was interested at that moment but because a man was expected to stare after a pretty girl. If he didn't evidence interest in girls, people hinted at other attractions. Not that he minded working with Gays, but he wanted his own gender made clear.

"Happy birthday, Lou," Paul smiled. "Many happy returns."

"You remembered," Lou said gratefully. "Thank you, Paul."

"What else has he got to remember?" Jim sneered. "Appointments with directors? Readings for new parts? Publicity photographs? Personal appearances? What the hell else does he have to remember except birthdays?"

"Will you stop crying!" Paul said reprovingly. "You've become cynical. That's why nobody will give you work anymore. You've lost faith in our great industry."

"What does faith have to do with this goddam sausage factory?" Jim said. "To get ahead here you need to be a broad with an amiable slit, have a father who is a banker, or be a Jew."

"You're a bigot and you're nuts!" Lou said impatiently. "This town is jammed with talent before and behind the cameras and they worked like hell to get there! When you've been around as long as Paul and I have been, you'll see things from outside your asshole!"

"I hope to hell they shoot me before that happens!" Jim said violently.

"Before I spend the next twenty years batting out my brains like you guys, I hope someone will give me a small part in a western where they're using real bullets instead of blanks!"

"Will you shut up!" Paul cried. "It's Lou's birthday and for his sake, quit your endless carping for an hour at least." He paused. "Before I forget, Lou, I'm throwing a little party for you this evening. Just a few friends. We'll have a few drinks and eat some spaghetti."

"You're a hell of a friend, Paul," Lou said earnestly. He sighed and stared toward the alcove off the commissary where the stars, producers, directors and studio executives lunched. He recognized Kirk Douglas at one table, Walter Matthau at another. Then, with a shock of excitement, he saw Sid Lanzman, the director of the picture ten years earlier in which Lou had been nominated for an Oscar as best supporting actor. Lanzman had been making films in Europe and Lou had not seen him in years.

Lou rose jubilantly from the table and walked swiftly toward the alcove, bracing himself as he had done a hundred times to meet a rebuff. When he entered the alcove he saw that Lanzman was sitting with Jack Lemmon. He walked up to their table and clapped the director on the shoulder. Lanzman looked up and hesitated.

"How are you, Sidney?" Lou said. "Lou Phillips. *The Guns of Montana*."

A flash of recognition swept the director's face. He rose quickly from his chair.

"For cri' sakes, Lou!" he said warmly. "I haven't seen you since we did *Montana*! Where the hell you been keeping yourself?"

"I've been doing some films and television in New York," Lou said. He looked down at Jack Lemmon and nodded pleasantly, without any awe or deference, one actor to another. "I'm sorry to interrupt your lunch."

"Lou Phillips here is a hell of an actor," Lanzman said to Jack Lemmon. "Does both comedy and drama marvelously. We worked together in three pictures. He was nominated for a supporting Oscar in the last one. He should have won!"

"A nomination is honor enough," Lou said.

"That's right, Lou," Lanzman agreed fervently.

"We might be able to use him in our picture," Jack Lemmon smiled at Lou.

"It would be an honor to work with you, Mr. Lemmon," Lou said. "Sit down now, Sid, and finish your lunch. Casting here has my number so give me a call in a few days. We can have a beer together."

"I will for sure, Lou," Lanzman said earnestly. "You helped make Montana a picture they compared to Stagecoach. I'd love to have us working together again. I'll call you for sure."

Lou waved and started away from the table. He sensed the director talking about him. He straightened his shoulders and felt an added buoyance in his step. He was fifty but the day augured well.

"See you goddam punk cynic," Lou said in a low, exulting voice to jim when he got back to their table. "People in this industry respect talent. Some are bastards but there are honest, loyal people too. That was Sid Lanzman. He directed *The Guns of Montana* when I was nominated for best supporting actor."

"I know," Jim said wearily. "I've heard."

"Is he directing Jack Lemmon in a film?" Paul asked excitedly. "Did he say there might be a part in it for you?"

"Lemmon said it!" Lou said. "Lemmon looked right at me and said to Sid, 'Let's use this man.' "

"No!" Paul exclaimed.

"They'll use you," Jim said morosely and stared at the legs of a short-skirted girl walking by. "Don't worry. They'll use you."

Lou, secure in the euphoria of the meeting, laughed.

"Jesus, you're sure a miserable bastard," he said. "They should cast you as a gravedigger in a picture about Forest Lawn."

On their way out of the commissary, they stopped in the washroom. Paul went into one of the stalls while Lou washed his hands and combed his hair. Jim stood before a urinal.

"The best part of my day," he said gravely. "I imagine I'm pissing on my agent. He gets the first strong blast. Then I give it to all the casting directors followed by the assistant casting directors. As I dribble down to the end I manage a few drops for my ex-wife and, with a final shake, I include the goddam cook at the only lunchroom will allow me credit when I'm broke." He moved away from the urinal, zipping his pants with satisfaction.

Lou grinned, shaking his head. "I'm going down to casting," he said.

"Don't forget, Lou," Paul's voice came from the stall. "My place about eight o'clock."

When Lou entered the casting director's office he saw the middle-aged secretary look up nervously. Like a poor bitch guarding the hen-house, Lou thought, never certain where the next assault will fall. He gave her a warm, reassuring smile.

"Mr. Flanders isn't back from lunch yet," she said.

Lou frowned at his watch, a busy man pursued by numerous appointments. "Are you expecting him soon?"

She looked at him warily, afraid any mention of time might encourage his return.

"Have we called you on a part?" she asked.

"I'm Lou Phillips. Sam Vigil is my agent," Lou said. "I saw Mr. Flanders last week about a role in the *Tide City* series. He asked me to check back." He maintained the same confident tone knowing that any faltering on his part would stiffen her rejection.

"I remember you now, Mr. Phillips." She looked at the appointment calendar on her desk. "Mr. Flanders is busy all afternoon," she said. "If you were going to be on the lot tomorrow around two to two-thirty, you might stop in. I can't promise he'll see you but he has some free time then."

"I'll be at Universal tomorrow and may be tied up all day," Lou said. "I'll try to make it back here but tell Mr. Flanders he will be hearing from Sid Lanzman about me. We worked together in a film that brought me an Oscar nomination. He'd like us to work together again."

"I'll tell him, Mr. Phillips," she said. For the first time a fragment of respect entered her voice.

Outside the casting office Lou entered a phone booth and dialed his answering service. The phone rang four times before the operator answered.

"Four rings, honey," he said sharply. "I've told you to catch calls by the second ring. This is a busy town. Some people hang up after the second ring."

"I'm sorry, Mr. Phillips," the woman's tone suggested he could screw himself. "No messages," she said and he sensed a perverse satisfaction in her voice.

He lingered for a moment in the street outside the booth. A big, well-dressed man chewing a cigar and a smaller, harried man flying at his heels passed by. The big man spoke to the smaller one without bothering to turn his head.

"For this part I need a young Paul Newman," he said.

The smaller man clutched at his sleeve, trying desperately to slow him down.

"I got him, Lionel!" he cried fervently. "I tell you, I got him."

Lou walked slowly toward the facade of a western set beyond Stage 5. He passed a saloon, general store, bank and livery stable, silent and deserted under the midday sun. At any moment a group of horsemen might come thundering around the corner, guns blazing, sparks flying from their horses' hooves.

He stood before the saloon trying to remember when he had last worked in a film. He tried not to dwell upon the time but in this naked, solitary moment he could not conceal the truth. Two years, he thought, Jesus Christ, I haven't worked in a film for two years.

He stared at the set around him. It resembled the set where he had played the great final scene in *The Guns of Montana*. Durango, the gunman he portrayed, was the last of the outlaw gang to die. Wounded and cornered he waited as the young killer raised his gun to finish him off.

"Go to hell, Webb," he said slowly, his lips releasing the remembered lines. "And after I'm dead every punk in the territory will be gunning for you. You'll sleep with your gun in your hand, never turning your back on a man, never trusting a woman. Someday they'll kill you. Remember me then."

The young killer fired, his gun blazing flame. Lou felt the searing pain as the bullets struck his flesh. He felt himself falling, twisting his body, striking the ground, the sun bursting for the last time across his eyes.

There had been a moment of silence until the director's jubilant voice cried, "Cut!" He sat up slowly, hearing the grips and other players begin to applaud. Lanzman ran over, pulled him to his feet and hugged him.

The poignant beauty of the memory made Lou bite his lip. It had been a great scene, beautifully played. He wasn't Laurence Olivier or Robert DeNiro but he was as good as most of the actors in the town. What was the trouble then? Why couldn't he find work?

Perhaps overseas production was to blame, television taking over with the endless situation comedies. Maybe a time came for an actor when he was too old for most roles, not yet old enough to be retired. He had saved some money when he worked, collected some residuals each month. He wasn't starving but he was like a good watch that wasn't being used, a good watch whose parts were growing rusty.

"Goddam it," he said softly, and he spoke to the silent street, the deserted set, the rain rigging and the arc light cables. "Goddam it, Goddam it . . ."

He drove slowly down Hollywood Boulevard, past the marquees of theatres, restaurants, book and souvenir shops. The street teemed with youths in jeans and ragged jackets. Passing Grauman's Chinese Theatre, he parked in a nearby lot. He bought a bouquet of roses from a florist. On the way back to his car he entered the forecourt of Grauman's, walking among the slabs marked with the prints and signatures of stars. A family of tourists, a husband, wife and several children examined the slabs, uttering exclamations of delight when they discovered a familiar name.

"You want to see Jimmy Durante's nose?" he asked. "Right over there." The children followed his hand. "And the great John Barrymore's profile. Of course," he smiled, "you kids are too young to remember Jimmy Durante and John Barrymore but they were giants."

He waved goodby to the family, feeling a warmth at having shared their pleasure. He returned to his car and after driving a few blocks turned off Hollywood Boulevard. He ascended winding streets, passing stucco houses, the gardens ornamented with bird of paradise and hibiscus. Between the houses he caught glimpses of the landscape of Hollywood, its rooftops and terraces partially obscured by a layer of smog. He turned off the street under the arched entrance to a long, white-stoned building surrounded by a wide expanse of gardens. He parked beside a row of cars and carried the roses through the front door into a reception room.

"What lovely roses, Mr. Phillips," Mrs. Lawson, the receptionist greeted him. "Just as lovely as the chrysanthemums you brought Miss Carby on Tuesday."

"How is Jenny today?"

"She seems better, Mr. Phillips," Mrs. Lawson said. "She's on the terrace."

He walked from the hall onto the terrace that ran the length of the building, into an eerie and silent world burnished under the rays of the sun. A half dozen patients reclined in chairs. A few nurses sat nearby. He saw Jenny and walked toward her. She sat in a wicker armchair, a light spread wrapped about her legs, her hands together in her lap. Her face looked toward the Universal studio sound stages gleaming like toy blocks in the distance far below.

He bent and gently kissed her temple. She raised her face to him, a tremulous movement that left the tautness of her cheeks unchanged.

Her features were delicate and lovely, brown, soft hair framing the pale oval of her face. Even now, cowled with a faded fragility, she reflected the stunning beauty she had been before the breakdown from the drugs. She might still have been beautiful but for her eyes. Their surfaces seemed almost without pupils as if these had been driven down into her body in a frantic retreat. The world entered that sanctuary only through soft voices and a gentle touch. In that way whatever had been unendurable before was muted and dissolved for her now.

"How are you, Jenny?" he sat down beside her. He placed the flowers across her knees and raised her slim fingers to his lips.

"We're shooting my new picture at Paramount," he said softly. "There's a very talented young actress working with me named Sally Field. She's very good," he stroked her fingers, "but she's not the actress you are."

A slight wind carried the scent of bougainvillea about their heads. She lowered her head to watch the rose petals fluttering.

"There's a part in this picture for you, Jenny," he said, "as soon as you're feeling better. John Huston told me he needed an actress with your ability, a part like you played in *Love Song*. Remember?"

A network of flesh wrinkled about her eyes. She seemed to be holding her breath, suspended at the edge of understanding.

"A marvelous part for you, Jenny!" he tried to keep his voice from trembling. "It will win you an Oscar nomination for sure!"

Her lips parted suddenly as if she were about to speak. He struggled for these moments, seeking desperately to prevent her from slipping irrevocably away.

As quickly as her excitement came, it passed. He felt her fingers limp once more. As the sun moved slightly in the sky, the shadows tracking behind it, they sat in silence. He was grateful when the aseptic, soft-footed nurse appeared.

"Time for your nap now, dear," she said. For an instant Lou felt the pressure of Jenny's fingers, as if she were unwillling to relinquish the comfort of his touch.

Lou released her hand gently. The nurse folded the spread from Jenny's lap and helped her rise. Slowly, suspended like a marionette between them, they walked her inside.

"I'll take her from here," the nurse said, "and we'll put her lovely flowers in water." Jenny turned slightly and looked at Lou. She seemed to be staring at some reflection from within herself and not at him. He kissed her cheek and watched the nurse walking her slowly down the corridor to her room.

Paul Sher's party began about eight o'clock in his small apartment in the Hollywood Belden Apartments. People who had been invited were joined by others who had not been asked but who brought a bottle to assure their welcome. The party grew and spilled through the hallways and into adjoining apartments. By ten o'clock a hundred people thronged the lobby and the area around the swimming pool. There were supporting actors and a few featured players maintaining a careful separation from the cluster of extras. There were sound and film editors, unit publicists, an assistant director who hadn't worked in five years, an ex-cowboy singing star trying for a comeback in westerns where no one sang. There were also a number of attractive young girls aspiring to starlet status.

Lou felt his somberness at visiting Jenny overcome as he drank and talked. In a growing euphoria he felt himself staunchly allied to this amorphous, festive gathering. When he was pointed out as the original reason for the party, someone offered him congratulations. He sought to retain the faces that swirled around him and absorb the snatches of conversation.

"I tell you, Harold, Len is a major American writer, right up there with Hemingway, Faulkner and Irving Wallace."

"I wouldn't do a series on television if they begged me. It ruins your timing."

"So I says to the counterman, 'Hey, there's lipstick on my cup,' and he says, 'Lucky you, maybe she's nice.' "

"What does an actor learn after thirty years in this profession, Mr. Phillips?" A dark-haired, good-looking young man asked Lou respectfully.

"He learns to play a scene as simply as he can," Lou said, "and not burden it with all kinds of methods and motivations. He respects his fellow actors and clearly speaks the words in his script."

"But Stanislavski says . . . " the young man began.

Jim Retsas, moving drunkenly from group to group, paused near them. "Screw Stanislavski!" he shouted and then he stumbled away.

"I just can't be that casual about it," the young man said.

"About screwing Stanislavski?" A woman asked smirking.

The young man glared at her and spoke to Lou.

"I mean if I'm playing a fighter, I have to live the part both on and off the camera. On the street I walk like a fighter, talk like a fighter, think like a fighter."

"The only trouble is you might begin to believe you really are a fighter," Lou said, "and get into a fight that get's your ass knocked off."

A studio publicist named Weldman came up and caught Lou by the arm. He pulled him away from the group. His face was wreathed in excitement and sweat.

"I just heard the goddam marvelous news!" he said in a low, trembling voice. "Congratulations, Lou, I think it's marvelous! You deserve this break! Simply marvelous!"

"What the hell are you raving about?"

The publicist winked, including himself in the grand conspiracy.

"All right! All right!" he whispered hoarsely. "Keep it quiet if you like, but I got the word from someone at the top. Your old director, Lanzman, has tabbed you for a co-starring role with Jack Lemmon in his new film!"

With a surge of jubilation, Lou wondered if there had been a swift development from the meeting at lunch. Lanzman had been delighted to see him and perhaps he had spoken to Lemmon about him. He tried to believe that might have happened and then reluctantly accepted it wasn't true.

Rumbles and rumors, whispers and tattlings, diffused across the town like smog. Everything magnified, from the number of lovers a leading actress indulged at one time, to a half-dozen stars assured selection for the same starring role. Everything had to be enlarged because ordinary events and commonplace decisions were inadequate to feed the voracious hunger. Everybody knew that ninety percent of what circulated as true was unfounded gossip, but they all played the game of believing with the fervor of zealots.

"There's nothing certain yet," Lou said. "Lemmon and Sid are still discussing it." He marveled how easily he helped perpetuate the rumor. Yet the other man was so eager to believe that even if Lou had emphatically denied the story, the publicist would have become even more convinced it was true.

There was a sudden commotion at the other end of the pool. A girl and her boyfriend had jumped into the water fully clothed. A crowd gathered quickly along the edge, shouting encouragement as the couple splashed around gaily. Someone else jumped or was pushed in. Weldman moved away to join the watchers.

Lou was weary suddenly of shrill laughter and brittle voices. He walked away from the revelers toward the darker opposite end of the long pool. In the shadows he noticed someone sitting on the edge. When he got closer he made out the figure of a girl dangling her bare feet in the water. She had long blonde hair and was wearing a gold blouse, a dark velvet vest, and bell-bottomed trousers that she had pulled up above her knees. When she looked up at him he saw she was young, in her early twenties, with a pretty face he felt he had seen before.

"Happy birthday, Lou Phillips," she said.

"How did you know?" he asked in surprise. "In this mob I thought the reason for the party had been forgotten."

"Paul invited me," she said. "Besides I recognized you. I've seen all the films made the past ten years at least twice." She patted the stone ledge beside her.

He sat crosslegged on the edge of the pool beside her. She began swinging her bare legs and feet, just below the surface of the water, raising a slight spray of foam. Through the ripples her feet gleamed slim and pale.

"I'm sure I've seen you before," he said. "You're an actress, aren't you?"

She nodded gravely.

"My name is Deborah Lacey," she said. "Not really, but that's the name I use. My real name is Betty Schroeder. The Schroeders are an old theatre family. My grandfather was in movies fifty years ago."

"Was he an actor?"

"He played piano for the patrons at the old silent films," she said. "Tunes to suit the action on the screen." A mischievous smile played about her mouth. "He was an industry pioneer."

"He sure was," Lou said.

"You're a real actor, though," she said. "Paul says you're one of the best."

"I don't know about that," Lou said, but he was pleased. "Sometimes I feel I've been around since DeMille did *The Squaw Man* in 1913."

A burst of laughter erupted from the other end of the pool. The couple had been pulled dripping from the water, shrieking for towels and martinis. They moved toward the entrance of the building, a portion of the crowd following them inside. In the diminishment of voices, the humming of cicadas trailed across the night.

"Where are you from?" Lou asked.

"Milwaukee."

"Where have you studied?"

"Goodman Theatre in Chicago for three years," she said. "Two years of summer stock. I did *The Little Foxes* and *Oklahoma* before coming out here two years ago."

"Had any luck?"

"A few walk-ons," she said. "I got a few lines of dialogue once in a movie with Elizabeth Taylor. I got those lines by sleeping with an associate producer who promised me a co-starring role."

She spoke quietly, without apparent rancor or bitterness, as if it were a lesson she had learned, a mistake she would not repeat.

"Are you a good actress?"

She bent slightly to slip her hand beneath the water. She drew out her hand, her wet fingers glistening and trickling a few drops of water down her leg.

"Yes," she said, pronouncing the solitary word as if it were an invocation. There was a certainty in her voice, a conviction that reminded him of Jenny as she had been years before she'd begun taking drugs. For a moment he felt a desolate beating of his heart.

"Being a good actress isn't always enough," he said, and he couldn't keep a harshness from his voice.

"I'm not just waiting for the breaks," she said. "I'm going to acting school here too, studying dancing and singing. I want to be ready when my chance comes."

"There's more than getting ready," he said. "Don't be foolish and don't be impatient. Work hard and stay away from booze and coke. Don't abuse your body or your soul." A sliver of moon glittered in the sky and he thought of it shining over the silent, deserted terrace of the hospital in the hills above Hollywood. "If you can't find the strength to endure, this place breaks you and breaks your dreams."

"I know what you're saying," she said quietly. "Yet I never regret coming here or my decision to be an actress. Even when I'm disappointed, I'm never really unhappy. Because you see I am an actress and I live in the Castle." She looked at him, her face warm and lucent with her devotion. "Some only stay inside a little while and some stay forever. A few become kings and queens but all of us live in the Castle."

She stared down at the water and between the strands of her hair, her ear gleamed small and delicate as the ear of a child. He was caught by her wistful and graceful beauty.

"There you are, goddamit!" A strident voice burst behind them. Lou looked up sharply and saw a tall young man holding a drink in each hand. He was about the girl's age, with a handsome, callow face and a surly mouth. "You ask for a drink and then make me chase to hell and gone to find you!"

Feeling them pitted like intimate antagonists against one another, Lou started to rise and leave.

"Don't go," the girl said to him. She reached up brusquely for the drink. When the young man handed it to her, she raised it to her mouth. She took a sip and then extended her arm and the glass out over the water.

"There's too much tonic," she said. She tipped the glass and poured the drink into the water.

The young man stared at her in rage. "Bitch!" he spit hoarsely and turned to walk quickly away.

Lou and the girl sat in silence for a while. From the small group still left at the other end of the pool, a guitarist began to play, a soft and plaintive song drifting across the night.

"Young lovers are like bulls," she said finally, ruefully. "You can give them your body but not your thoughts or your dreams." Her face seemed suddenly pale and weary in the faint light. He felt an urge to hold and console her. As if she understood, she shifted closer to him. "I'm sad now and don't want to be alone," she said.

He felt his longing like an ache in his body.

"Come home with me," he said.

A silence drew out thin between them. Then he felt her hand, her fingers still wet and cold from the water, moving against his hand in a tentative bond. He took her fingers into his palm.

"You're not mean though, are you?" she asked. "That scares me." She pointed in the direction the young man had gone. "One night he broke my nose." She raised her head, pushing aside her hair, and showed him her profile. "See?" she said. "There's a little ridge where it didn't mend properly. I'm saving my money to have it reset."

"I'm not mean," he said, and he felt a sudden tenderness toward her.

"And will you tell me about this town?" she said. "About the stars you've known and worked with? The directors and the scenes and all the things you've seen and learned?"

"I'll tell you everything I know," he said earnestly.

She smiled then, her fine lips drawing back about her even white teeth. He helped her as she raised her feet dripping from the water. She bent and picked up her sandals and swung them by the straps across her shoulder.

He was suddenly conscious of the beauty of the night extending over the canyons and hills. Around them whirled the fragrance of countless flowers. He took her hand and they started around the pool, the strains of the guitar growing fainter as they walked through the passage that led to the street.

Sometime before dawn he woke with a start. He opened his eyes to a slashed pattern of shadow and light across the ceiling of his room. Almost at once he felt the girl in bed beside him, her body still and relaxed in sleep. He moved carefully to avoid waking her, sliding his body to the edge of the mattress. He sat there a moment and looked down at her.

She slept on her side, her mouth misshapen against the crease of the pillow. A matted strand of her blonde hair severed her cheek from eye to throat. One bare arm lay outside the covers, the angular bone of her shoulder sloping to her breast and a small, forlorn nipple, like a withered olive, all that remained from the table of love.

He had thought her vibrant and lovely, but now, empty of desire, he saw that she only reflected a surface radiance of youth and dreams that resembled so many other girls. An aura of adornment hung over them for a little while until bitterness and humiliation stripped the facade away. 'Whoever lives here lives in the Castle,' she had said. But it wasn't really a castle, he thought grimly, it was a snare into which the romantic young were drawn like rabbits to be maimed or killed.

He rose restlessly from the bed and walked into the next room. From the window he looked down upon the silent courtyard, the pool speckled by an eerie red and yellow glow from the lights burning within the clumps of shrubs and flowers. The setting glittered like the backdrop and cutouts for an exterior scene in a movie. He sensed the presence of the cameras hidden from sight, the director waiting for him to appear. He stifled a senseless impulse to run downstairs.

But I'm not a rabbit, he thought savagely. I'm an old wolf, hardened by hunger, made cunning by numerous lures. I've beaten despair down many times and I'll batter it away again.

He returned to the bedroom and slipped quietly into bed. The girl stirred in her sleep and nestled against him. He clasped her thigh gently in reassurance and then turned away.

Watching the window for the first light, he was impatient for morning so he could call Sam Vigil and tell him about the film he might make with Jack Lemmon.

In the writing workshops that I've been teaching for almost three decades, I suggest to my students that there isn't any such thing as ordinary experience. The major events and even the apparently minor occurences in our daily lives are all extraordinary because they're happening to us, and because each human being is genetically unique. In that way it doesn't matter how many others have lived and loved before us. When we breathe and love, we experience anew what Margaret Mead called the "world of the first rose and the first lark-song."

What is also unique to each of us are those moments when we glimpse our lives with a curious detachment. In those sometimes melancholy and yet consoling perceptions, we sense our individual fate somehow linked to an infinitely larger and more providential destiny that encompasses our planet, Earth, and the universe of stars.

That is where we begin and where we end.

A DAY'S JOURNEY

As he opened the door to the kitchen, Peter saw their deaf white cat perched on the ledge of the window. She stared through the glass at the yard, a landscape she prowled on her forays to freedom. The whiteness of her fur caught the morning glint of dew from the brown and red October leaves on the trees.

At the reflection of his body in the glass, she stretched indolently and leaped gracefully from the ledge to the floor. She crossed the kitchen to her empty bowl, her bushy tail waving like a regal plume. Before feeding her, he usually made coffee and drank his orange juice while she waited patiently. He altered his ritual and gave her some vittles at once, imagining surprise in her usually inscrutable eyes.

After plugging in the coffee, he returned to the bedroom. Sophie lay curled beneath the blankets of their bed, only a portion of her dark hair visible. He walked quietly into the bathroom to shave, recalling with remorse their argument the night before. What perversity was it, he wondered, that made them choose the last few moments before going to sleep to carp at one another?

At the end of October they would have been married 24 years. They had met in high school, remained sweethearts through college, and had married when Sophie was 22 and he was 24. They had endured the disappointments and frustrations of his early years of writing and finally shared the modest success and pleasure of his first published books. They had two children, grown now into a daughter of 18 and a son of 21. Sue had entered college as a freshman that fall. Jeff had gotten his degree from Circle Campus and lived in an apartment in the city, working and studyng acting.

Peter shaved slowly, gazing at his reflection with amiable resignation. If he could benignly accept the physical changes the years had brought him, he was less hopeful about his emotional alterations. He seemed to be passing a cycle of longer depressions, the most recent one deepening thorugh the summer into a pervasive weariness. Summer activities, cycling and tennis, had rendered it bearable, but he felt a stirring of fear when he thought of winter.

He emerged from the shower, relishing the freshness of his body after the soaping and rinsing. He returned to the bedroom and started to dress as Sophie stirred and pushed aside the covers, swinging her legs from the bed. She frowned with the effort to break the crust of sleep. She walked barefoot to the bathroom and left the door open. In a moment he heard the sound of her voiding with irritation. When love is strained, he thought, even a small familiarity can be aggravating.

She came from the bathroom with her hair brushed and a robe over her nightgown. She had been a pretty girl when they married and she remained a lovely woman, dark-haired and dark-eyed with a winsome smile that recalled a much younger girl. Generally cheerful, the departure of their youngest child from home had left her peevish and morose. For the first time in 20 years, she and Peter were left alone, their small frictions sharpened, while he couldn't provide her the reassurance she needed.

She sat on the edge of the bed, watching him moodily.

"I didn't sleep a wink last night," she said.

"I'm sorry."

"Arguments don't seem to bother you," she said. "You slept fine. I heard you snoring."

He looped his tie and watched her stiff, unforgiving image in the mirror.

"You hurt me last night," she said.

"I didn't mean to."

"You never mean to hurt," she said, "but you do. I could never say the things to you that you say to me."

"I try to tell you the things I feel."

"You seem to want to hurt me. Is that what you feel?"

"Listen, Sophie," he said earnestly, "let's not start arguing again now. I'll be gone all day and you'll sit here brooding."

For a moment, they were both silent.

"What are we going to do?" she asked, a tremor softening her voice. "What will happen to us if we can't get along anymore?"

She remained sitting on the bed and he walked to her and bent to kiss her cheek. He started to embrace her, but she kept her hands clasped stiffly in her lap.

"Will you be home for dinner?"

"I better go see mom at the home," he said. "So don't expect me before ten." The prospect of that visit to the nursing home where his mother had been confined for three years further dampened his mood.

"See if you can take Jeff to dinner before you go to see mom," she said. "I worry that he isn't eating enough."

"I'll try to take him out," he said.

He pulled the car from the garage and backed out the driveway. He drove down the street, passing the tennis courts, and saw Parry and Elder playing. He honked and they waved. He wished he could have been playing with them.

Driving several blocks under the overhanging branches of trees, he watched the leaves fluttering to the hood of his car and then being swept to the road. At the stop sign before the entrance to the expressway, he stared away from the city in the direction of the country. Then he turned onto the ramp that led downtown.

He spent the morning in the library making notes for an article. About 12:00, he picked up Merrill from the magazine editorial office and they strolled to a nearby restaurant. In addition to being a good editor, Merrill was an old, trusted friend.

"This is the second lunch you're buying me in three weeks," Peter said as they slipped into a booth. "I'm always delighted to accept when you phone, but aren't you afraid you'll spoil me?"

"I'm generous as well as a splendid editor," Merrill said, "especially with the magazine's money." He was a slimly built man in his fifties with a gentle voice that seemed out of place in the abrasive surroundings of a magazine office.

They drank Scotch and then ordered a second round. They were at ease with one another and ate leisurely, talking of writing and books. Afterward, waiting for the waiter to bring them coffee, Merrill pulled a letter from his pocket. Peter felt his heart leap when he saw it was from Rachel.

"I didn't want to give it to you before we ate," Merrill said. "You would have tried to be casual and not open it and that would have distracted your appetite and diminished the quality of conversation.

This way, you enjoyed your lunch, I enjoyed the talk, and now you have your letter."

"You're a remarkable man." Peter nodded thanks and slipped the envelope in his pocket. "The last letter you delivered from her was almost a year ago," he said. "She wrote then that she was planning to get married. Maybe this letter is to tell me she's getting divorced."

"You have a fertile imagination," Merrill said. "That's why I admire your writing. More likely, she wants to borrow money from you to help her husband open a tavern."

"If that's true, she'll find that getting money from a free-lance writer is harder than walking on water."

For a moment they sat silent, drinking their coffee.

"What if she wants the two of you back together again?" Merrill asked.

"We made that decision years ago," Peter said. "I had Sophie and the children, and three to one are heavy odds. Besides, Rachel was young and attractive and I knew she'd find someone else to love again."

Merrill reached for the check.

"Have another cup of coffee and read your letter," he said. "Give your sweet Sophie my love."

Peter delayed opening the letter, a nostalgia for those love-possessed days sweeping over him. He had met Rachel at a writer's conference shortly after she had been divorced. Her wretchedness touched his loneliness and they spent an awkward, faltering night together. When he returned home, he expected that would end the encounter. But he wrote her and she wrote him back, addressing her letter to a post office box he had rented.

They made arrangements to meet in a town between the cities where they lived. They spent the weekend at a Holiday Inn, and the first night they were together, he became ill, crouched for an hour over the stool in the bathroom. She had been gentle and reassuring. They had gone to bed later and slept fitfully. He felt better but, ashamed of his weakness, he yearned for morning so they could dress and leave. In the dark, wakeful hours of the night, they began to talk. Rachel told him of growing up in New Orleans, sailing in summer with her father, and her marriage at 18 to a man who concealed his alcoholism from her. When he began bouts of drinking and started to beat her, she left him.

Peter told her about Sophie, his daughter and his son, and his years of struggle to write. They crammed a year of conversation and intimacy into that hour when the earth hung silent and suspended between darkness and light. They fell asleep in each other's arms, and when they woke later in the morning, they made love.

That began one of the happiest years of his life. He loved Sophie, but his love for Rachel was untroubled by all the distresses of marriage and family. Rachel moved to the city where he lived. She found work and they spent weekends together, Peter telling Sophie he was researching assignments. In all their years of marriage he had never been unfaithful to her before. That reserve of trust covered his sometimes clumsy tracks.

But their own sexual unions had grown less frequent, and Sophie finally understood something was wrong. One night, she teased Peter into believing she knew and would forgive his escapade. Because the lies and deception had become harder for him to bear, he told her everything. She cried bitterly for hours and didn't speak to him for days.

He could not bear to lose Sophie and his children, so he and Rachel separated, crying as they parted.

Sophie had never forgiven him for the betrayal. Even as they talked and pledged renewed effort to mend the elements that had driven them apart, he would come home in the evenings and know by her reddened eyes that she had been crying. Although he asked her bitterly if she wanted them both to suffer for the rest of their lives, he knew the war between memory and forgetting had already been lost.

The waiter poured him another cup of hot coffee. He noticed the restaurant was almost empty. He held the letter in his hands a moment longer and then slit open the envelope slowly, pulling out the pages written in Rachel's small, neat hand.

She had been married and was well and content. Her days were filled with work, her evenings with friends, her weekends riding at a nearby stable. She and her husband were planning to buy a house with an attic converted to a studio where she could paint.

She had wondered about Peter, and had written to find out how he was and whether Sophie and his children were well. She sent him love and asked him to write her a friendly note soon.

As he folded the letter back into the envelope, he wasn't sure how much of what he felt was disappointment and how much relief. He rose and left the restaurant.

His son Jeff worked in a Baskin-Robbins ice-cream shop a few blocks from his apartment. He got off work about 4:30, and when Peter rang his bell at five, Jeff opened the door and greeted his father with a hug. Peter tugged gently at the young man's neatly trimmed beard.

"You still resemble a Hasidic scholar," he said. He entered the cramped studio room that had a mattress on the floor with crumpled bedclothes, a bookcase of books, a small black-and-white TV, and a stereo. The walls were decorated with theater posters. "How's work going?" Peter asked.

"Fine," Jeff said. "From scooping ice cream, I'm developing the biceps of a boxer and a taste for exotic flavors. You want a beer, Pa?"

"Sure," Peter said. "I started a diet this morning but fell off at lunch."

Jeff opened cans of beer for them and they sat down in the alcove of a kitchen.

"What's happening in school?" Peter asked.

"We're rehearsing Beckett's *Waiting for Godot,*" Jeff said excitedly. "We all took turns playing Vladimir and Estragon. Our teacher Schroeder—I've told you before what a fine director he is—said I was one of the best in capturing the nuances of character."

"That's great!"

"Later, in the winter, we'll perform a play by O'Neill. I have a good chance for one of the leading roles. That will be a great opportunity for me."

"I'll buy out the whole dress circle on opening night," Peter said, "and invite numerous dignitaries to witness my son's triumph."

"Maybe I'll even get a plug in Kup's column," Jeff said. "Can't you see it? 'Writer's Son Wows Critics in Theatrical Debut.' " He winked at his father. "Anyway, it shows I'm taking the right attitude, eh, Pa?"

Peter's harping about artists who demonstrated the right attitude of total effort was a family joke, and he laughed.

"Been playing any tennis?" he asked.

"Not since you and I had that last tough match."

"If I hadn't gotten that cramp, I would have beaten you," Peter said.

"Sure, sure!"

"Come out to the house soon and I'll show you!"

"I'll do that," Jeff said. "Maybe next weekend. By the way, I got a postcard from Sue."

He rose and walked to the bookcase. Peter looked unhappily about the dark, shabby room so unlike the light-splashed bedroom his son occupied in their house. But he knew that home was the place where children lived and home was the place they had to leave. This small dwelling belonged to Jeff, to enter and depart as he wished, to share with his friends.

Jeff brought back the card from Sue, a scrawled message within a ring of doodles that read "Sharing a bathroom with 12 girls. You would enjoy my misery. Love, Sue."

"I can just imagine!" Peter laughed. He thought of how silent the mornings at home were without his daughter, how much he missed the wild rushing in and out of the bathroom; the buzzing of the hair dryer; the young, fresh scent of her sparking the house.

"She'll be all right," Jeff said. "Sue is spunky and she's got the right attitude, too." He smiled at his father. "You driving back home now?"

"I'm going to the nursing home later to see grandmother," Peter said. "I planned to have dinner in Greek Town first. How about some thick, juicy lamb chops?"

"I'd like to join you, Pa, but I can't," Jeff said. "I'm meeting some friends for pizza and then we're going to see the new Altman film at the Biograph."

"Another time then," Peter said.

He hadn't really been hungry after lunch with Merrill and he didn't go to Greek Town. He had a hamburger at MacDonald's and lingered over his coffee. Finally, he drove west to the nursing home. When he parked in the adjoining lot, he stared unhappily at the red-bricked one-story building he had been visiting once or twice a week for years.

His mother was 88 years old and had survived his father by almost 25 years. For 20 of those years, she lived in her own house by herself, except for some students as lodgers. When she could no longer live alone, she moved in with Sophie and Peter. But she had been a strong, resolute woman, accustomed to taking command, and the three years she lived with them were marked with frictions. She tried to regulate the children's hours, influence their choice of friends, compel their attendance at church.

At the end of her third year with them, she developed pneumonia and was confined in the hospital, seriously ill. When she grew better, the doctor recommended a convalescent facility before she returned home. Peter located a good, clean home and moved her there. Her improvement was slow, one week passing into another until the temporary convalescence became a permanent confinement. That seemed justified to doctor, family, and friends because she also exhibited signs of forgetfulness and confusion.

Peter felt guilty about her confinement. Hard as she had been to live with, she deserved the dignity of dying with her family instead of among strangers. He never visited her without feeling the burden of that remorse.

He entered the reception area, greeting the pleasant aide at the desk. His passage down the corridor into the wing where his mother stayed was marked by greetings to patients he had come to know. Mrs. Murphy, small, frail, her swollen feet clad in oversized booties. Cornelia, who had once been a dancer, still animated in her eighties, her white hair twined into girlish braids. Esther, the tall German lady stumping up and down the corridor in her walker, who could say in a lucid moment, "Old age is not a time for vanity."

There were fewer men than women in the home, and they seemed less able to accept their helplessness. There was Vincent, whose legs were amputated, snarling at anyone who came near him. Satterly, who wheeled his wheelchair around, wearing red slippers, flirting loudly with the young aides. Soft-voiced and grave Mr. Kern, who always asked Peter for a bus schedule as if there were an urgent journey he had to make. And so many others, faces and voices he had come to know in the three years, patients in the home one week and dead the following week, nothing remaining of their presence after the nurses peeled the name tags from the closets and doors.

He paused outside the room his mother shared with one other patient and peered inside. She lay on her bed, her body curled almost into a ball, the tips of her felt slippers visible beneath the hem of her gown. He thought she was sleeping until he stood over the bed and saw her watching him. He bent and kissed her, inhaling the sour, wasted odors that rose from her body.

"How did you know I was here?" she asked, the question with which she often greeted Peter.

"They told me at the church," he spoke loudly because of her slight deafness. He helped her sit up, feeling the seat of her gown, grateful she was not soiled. She sat on the edge of the bed, her white hair disordered, her fingers trembling. One of her slippers fell off, and he knelt and replaced it and pulled up her white cotton socks.

Holding her around the waist and by the arm, he walked her slowly to the bathroom. He drew the curtain across the doorway and tugged up her gown, guiding her onto the commode that fitted over the stool. He asked her to call him when she had finished, repeating the statement several times.

He brushed the sheets of her bed and pulled up the covers. He folded a towel across the seat of her wheelchair and plucked the tangled strands of hair from her brush so he could fix her hair. By the time he finished the familiar sequence, she called his name from the bathroom. The cry whirled him into a distant past when he had been a child and she summoned him for dinner or an errand. Now, in the cycle that saw their roles reversed, he went to clean her and help her from the stool.

They sat together in the dining room, his chair beside her wheelchair, before the large window that looked out on the grounds and the street. Dinner was over and only a few patients remained at the tables. One old woman slept with her head cradled in her arms on a table while another played with a tattered fragment of bright ribbon on her gown. An old man tugged and strained in frustration against the restraints that bound him to his chair. In the corner, a television set droned a program that no one watched.

His mother stared through the glass at the lights of passing cars. When a gust of wind hurled some dry leaves against the window, the motion caught her eye and she looked up.

He tried to draw her into conversation, telling her of a wedding he and Sophie had attended. She listened and seemed to understand but did not respond. When he slipped into a reverie of his own, she startled him, speaking in a loud, shrill voice.

"How are the children?"

"Fine!" he said. "Fine!" He repeated the word vigorously.

"Where are they now?"

"Sue is in school . . . in college," he said. "Jeff is working and going to school. They both send you love."

She nodded slowly and fell silent again. From the nearby kitchen, he heard the clatter of dishes and pots being washed by the crew of high-school boys and girls, laughing and teasing one another. Their buoyant voices carried in strangely cheerful echoes across the somber silence.

When he wheeled his mother back to her room, the lights in the corridor had been lowered, most of the patients put to bed. From the dark rooms they passed, he heard whispers and pleas. Several voices called to him for help, but he had learned when he had gone to aid them in the past that they only wanted the closeness of another human being.

His mother's roommate, Mrs. Kravitz, was bedridden and never spoke except to call out her own name in a hoarse voice. When they entered, she called out, "Angelina! Angelina!" He had heard it many times, thinking of Poe's croaking raven.

He helped his mother into the bathroom again. While she sat on the commode, he washed her face and hands and massaged her feet with lotion. He tugged off her gown and slipped a clean one over her head. He walked her back to the bed and had her lean forward so he could pin on a diaper. He helped her into bed, took off her slippers, and placed them carefully beside her chair. Before raising the guardrail, he bent and kissed her dry, scarred cheek. She kissed him back.

He sat beside her bed for a while, waiting for her to fall asleep. She breathed in shallow spasms, from time to time opening her eyes to see if he was still there. After an hour, grown weary, he rose to leave.

"Are you going now?"

"Yes," he said.

"I'll be alone then," she said.

"You have Mrs. Kravitz here in the next bed," he said consolingly.

His mother twisted her head and stared through the guardrail at the woman who never spoke except to cry out her own name.

"Yes, I have her," his mother said gravely. "And that's like having no one."

Startled by the accuracy of her observation, he began to laugh and then restrained an urge to cry.

He undressed in the bathroom of his house and then slipped wearily into bed beside Sophie's warm body. He pulled the cover gently to his chest and held his breath for a moment to check her breathing. He felt her stir beside him.

"Sophie?"

She didn't answer, but he knew she was awake.

"Haven't you slept yet?" he asked.

"No," she said quietly.

"How was your day?"

"I wrote some letters and mailed the things to Sue that she wanted," Sophie said. "Florence came over about six and we had some supper. How was your day?"

"I had lunch with Merrill and then had a beer with Jeff in his flat,' he said. "We couldn't eat together because he had plans. But he's fine."

"Has he cut off his beard yet?"

"No."

"He should cut it off," she said. "He looks better when he's clean-shaven."

She moved under the covers and he felt her bare toes graze his ankle.

"How was mom?"

"About the same," he said. "Leonard is still in the hospital, and Mrs. Webb—she was the nurse in the wing tonight—told me he wasn't expected to live."

"Poor man," Sophie said. "He fights to live when he would be better off dead."

"The home is full of the fighters of life, the survivors," he said.

"Did you see Mrs. Murphy?"

"She was sitting in the corridor by the desk where she always is," he said. "She asked about you and sent you her love."

"She's a sweet lady," Sophie said.

She moved again, sliding her body closer to him, her thigh hesitantly pressing his thigh. He thought how strange that after 24 years of marriage she should still be so shy. Perhaps traits from youth remained features of character one carried into old age. The sweetness of Mrs. Murphy, the coquettishness of Cornelia with her snow-white hair twined into a young girl's braids.

He reached beneath the covers and gently clasped Sophie's breast. She let out her breath with a sigh. He was surprised that he had touched her. Drained by the long day and the oppressing aura of the nursing home, he hadn't any desire to make love. Yet he continued to fondle her breast, and she reached up and touched his cheek, her fingers stroking his lips.

They kissed and made love then, as they had made love so many times before, their bodies sparking under caresses and gropings. He pushed aside the covers and tugged her nightgown above her thighs, tickling her so that she giggled. The flash of her naked legs in the shadowed room excited him and, in the sweep of desire, his apathy vanished.

She nestled quietly in his arms while a thin film of sweat dried on his body. Warm in the afterglow of passion, he recalled the events of the day. The letter from Rachel, the beer and banter with his son, his mother's face when he raised the guardrail on her frail body. He remembered her saying she had no one and he was grateful because he had Sophie.

"I love you, Sophie," he said.

"I love you, too, Peter," she said, her voice sleepy and low. They nestled closer and he tried not to move so that she could fall asleep.

The wind rose and rattled the sash of their windows. He had a fleeting image of the autumn trees about the house, the wind severing the leaves so they drifted down, silently seeking the haven of the earth. They sheltered on the ground beside all other things, passing away, finally, like youth and love and dreams. In a strangely tranquil awareness of that truth, he felt Sophie and himself linked to the past, the present, and the future; to the living, the dying, and the unborn.

He closed his eyes, thankful in that moment for the sleep that embraced him like a sister of death.

When this story was published, in 1958 in *The Atlantic,* the magazine received a batch of outraged letters from indignant readers who felt the esteemed periodical had abandoned a tradition of respectability by publishing such indecent trash.

How times have changed! Through a bloody war, three assassinations, the immorality of Watergate, boundaries of taste have been expanded to include the powerful books of Henry Miller and the films of the flexuous Linda Lovelace. Against this climate of almost total freedom as to what can be read and seen, the assault of Mike Larakis on the formidable ramparts of the Widow Angela creaks with the shuffle of a Victorian romance.

Yet I think the humor in the story saves it from being dated. Laughter, since the plays of Aristophanes, has a timeless and durable quality.

COURTSHIP OF THE BLUE WIDOW

Something happened to me the first time I saw the Widow Angela in the grocery of old Mantaris. More than just the restless stirring of flesh a man feels in the presence of a lovely woman. I was bothered as I am often bothered when I see a woman I like I cannot at once touch. After she walked out with the bread and cheese she had bought, I asked old Mantaris about her.

He rubbed his big knuckled fingers across the leathery skin of his cheeks. He shook his head sadly. He drew a long breath and sighed.

"She is a woman, that one," he said. "She was born and reared in the mountains of the old country. A grown woman at fourteen. She came to this country and married a giant of a man who worked in produce. Then her man died."

"How long has her man been dead?" I asked.

He shook his head slowly, trying to remember.

"Two years ago," he said. "Maybe a little longer. He was a Spartan. A big man with the arms of a wrestler. She has been in mourning ever since."

Two years and maybe longer. Too long for a woman built as the Widow Angela was built to set a seal upon her heart.

Then I understood what had bothered me about her. She was tall and dark with dark hair pinned back into a prim bun. Her face was pale and clean of powder or rouge. Her lips were full but untouched by lipstick. The black dress she wore was a plain dark folding of cloth high across her breasts and full across her thighs. She was without any of the artifices women use to point up their womanliness. In some strange way this made her more beautiful than any woman I had ever seen.

"She sleeps in a widow's bed," Mantaris said, and his voice shook with woe. "Her good husband sleeps in the cold earth." He paused and licked his thin dried lips. "I saw her once at a picnic with him some years ago. She danced in a line of women, taller than any other. That day she was not pale-cheeked as she is now but hot with life. Not one of your withered city women but a mountain woman wild with the flow of heroic blood."

"You are a patriarch now," I said. "A recorder of history and a recounter of legends. Stop bagging your bread and slicing your cheese long enough to advise me where she lives."

Suddenly one of his big long fingers pointed straight at my head like a gun. His leathery cheeks quivered and his eyes burned. "I know who you are," he said. "You are a Turk bent upon pillage and rape!" He clenched his fist and beat his chest. "You do not see the tragic nobleness of her grief. To see her now and remember her as she was hurts me here." He touched the region of his heart. His voice sharpened with contempt. "You are touched much further down."

"My friend," I said gently. "You do me an injustice. I too believe in the nobility of grief. Remember, I too am a Greek."

He shrugged and rippled noise through his lips. "It is true you are Greek," he said. "But there are Greeks and Greeks. Some are the descendants of lions, and others . . ."

I put my finger expectantly to my nose.

"Others come from goats," he said.

"She is a lovely woman," I said.

The hard lines of his face softened. "Yes . . ." he said. "Yes."

"A face like Helen to launch a thousand ships," I said.

He shook his head approvingly. "Yes," he said.

"She has breasts like great cabbages," I said.

He almost leaped to the ceiling. When he came down with his face flaming he slammed his open palm upon the counter. "Your head is a cabbage!" he yelled. "You have no respect!"

"You are right," I said. "My old dried-up friend, you are right."

He looked at me scornfully.

"What can you know," he said. "What can a young goat know of dignity and beauty?"

"A woman is going to waste while you call me names," I said. "I leave you to your cabbages."

"Then leave your head!" he shouted. "I'll weigh it with the rest."

I waved back from the door.

The next day was Sunday. All the night before I had tossed restlessly with dreams. I dreamed of the pale-faced Widow Angela whose body looked long asleep. There were fine cabbages in my dreams and an old toothless lion who guarded the gate to the patch.

In the early morning I shaved carefully and dressed and left my rooms. I crossed the square past the closed stores. I went to the church beside the Legion hall. I waited outside. From within I could hear the full deep tones of the organ and the chanting of the priest.

I waited there until the services ended. Until the doors were opened and the first men and women came out. When I saw Mantaris I called to him. He looked about and blinked in the sunlight and then saw me and came closer.

"Watch for her," I said. "Watch for the widow."

He looked at me in shock and surprise. "You are a crazy man!" he said. "Is your head on straight or do I call for help?"

"If you don't introduce me," I said, "I will accost her myself, here in front of the church."

"You would not dare!" he said, and then breathing hard he shook his head slowly. "You would. You are part Turk."

Then I saw her and my fingers tightened again around his arm. She came out into the sunlight and the black dress she wore saddened my heart. She wore a small dark hat over her dark hair and her cheeks were still pale and she walked stiffly without notice of those who walked around her.

The old man trembled at my side.

"God help me," he said, and he crossed himself quickly and I gave him a little push and we started through the crowd. A short way down the stone steps we caught up to her and he called out her name and she stopped and turned. He looked around once more desperately as if thinking of escape and then spoke quickly. "Good morning, Mrs. Angela," he said. I stood close behind him, a somber look upon my cheeks. "It is a bright morning," he said.

"Good morning, Mr. Mantaris," she said. "Yes, it is a bright morning."

I punched the old man in the back and he jumped. "Mrs. Angela," he said, and he seemed to have trouble getting the rest out. "May I present Mr. Larakis."

"How do you do, Mrs. Angela," I said, and I was very careful not to smile. One does not laugh before the watch fires of grief.

She looked from the old man to me and her face darkened slightly. The old man shifted in some sort of agony from one foot to the other. Then she nodded an acknowledgment slowly and turned to walk on.

I punched the old man in the ribs again to follow her. He turned on me snarling like he was going to take a chance and clout me. He would not budge. He stood like one of the pillars of the Parthenon. I left him spitting at me under his breath.

I had to run several steps to catch up to her. "Excuse me, Mrs. Angela," I said. "May I walk with you to the next corner? We are going the same way."

She turned again and looked at me darkly. I think what saved me was the cool and impersonal expression on my face. A shadow of a smile would have whipped me right there. She nodded without speaking and I fell into step beside her.

We walked silently for a little way and the cars passed in the street and the spring sun shone brightly in the sky.

"Forgive me, Mrs. Angela," I said. "I knew your husband. I was grieved when I heard of his death. I have been out of the city a long time."

She looked at me with those deep dark eyes and there was nothing I could understand on her face. Then her cheeks loosened just a little. "Thank you," she said quietly. "It was a terrible loss."

I spoke softly and sympathetically. "A fine man," I said. "Did he ever wrestle? I do not remember ever seeing a man with stronger-looking arms."

She shook her head slowly. I was sorry for the remembered pain returned to her cheeks. I am not a sadist. But this initial surgery was necessary. "He was not a wrestler," she said. "But he was very strong."

"I believe he once mentioned to me he came from Sparta?" I said.

"Yes," she said. "Kostas was a Spartan."

"Of course," I said. "Where else? Sparta stands for strength and courage."

We had reached the corner and she stopped and looked at me again. "He would have been pleased to hear you say that," she said. "Thank you, Mr. . . ."

"Larakis," I said. "Mike Larakis."

"Thank you, Mr. Larakis," she said. "Now I turn here."

I took a deep breath. I had to proceed carefully. Whoso diggeth a pit might fall therein. "Mrs. Angela," I said. "Please do not think I am disrespectful. It is only I have not been back in the city very long. My old friends are moved and gone. Can you understand what it is to be lonely?"

That one was a beauty. I could see the shaft of the arrow sticking out of her wonderful chest.

"I know what loneliness is," she said. She spoke those words with real feeling.

I pushed my advantage. "Would it be too forward of me to think you might permit me to have dinner with you?" I asked. "Some quiet restaurant where we might sit and talk?"

She looked at me closely and I felt unrest under the intensity of her gaze. Those big dark eyes were more than ornaments on the Widow Angela. Her soul poured through them. "I do not go out socially," she said. "Not since my Kostas died."

"Forgive me," I said. "I was too forward. I have offended you. I am sorry."

I apologize very well. Frankly, it is not an easily acquired skill.

She shook her head. "Please," she said. "I was not offended. Just that it has been so long."

"A little food," I said. "A little quiet talk with a friend. Surely to allow yourself that is not to show disloyalty to a sacred memory."

I could see her making up her mind. Her skin without make-up gleamed cleanly. I felt a smarting in my fingers. Sweet is a grief well ended.

"All right," she said.

"Thank you," I said humbly. "You are kind to a lonely man." I paused and looked thoughtfully into space. This needed a clincher so she would not change her mind. "I regret I cannot make it tonight," I said. "There is a meeting of one of the church organizations I have just joined." I paused again. "I would rather sit and talk with you," I said.

"You must attend your meeting," she said firmly. "We will make it another night."

"Tomorrow night," I said. "If you are free."

"Tomorrow night," she said.

"I will call for you," I said. "Do you live close by?"

"The brownstone house," she said. "That one across the street. I have the first-floor apartment."

"At six?" I said.

"At six," she said.

"Thank you," I said.

She turned and walked away and I watched with intense interest the fine great sway of her marvelous thighs and savored my small pleasure like a general who had won the first skirmish but needed yet to win the war.

On the following afternoon I stopped for a moment in the grocery. Mantaris was bagging warm bread from the oven in back of the store. As

I walked in he raised his head and sniffed as if an animal had entered.

"Good evening, old man," I said.

He stood glaring at me.

"I merely stopped by to let you know," I said. "Tonight I dine with the Widow Angela."

"You lie!"

"This is a serious matter," I said. "I never lie where love is involved."

"Love!" The old man looked as if he might strangle on the word. "You would not know love if it had teeth and bit you in the ass."

"I will let that pass," I said. "Tonight I dine with a Queen and feel kindly toward the peasants."

"Get out, boofo!" he cried. "Go and drop dead!"

I left the store smiling and went home to dress.

At six that evening I rang the bell of the Widow Angela. She opened the door and she was ready and we said good evening to one another and commented on the fine spring weather. She went to put on her hat and came back and we walked down the stairs. I led her toward the car. She shook her head.

"Such a lovely evening," she said. "Let us walk. There is a little restaurant a few blocks from here that I often pass and have never entered. May we go there tonight?"

"Certainly," I said.

The restaurant she had spoken of was a small one off Dart Street. A little bell rang over the door as we entered and we walked down a few stairs into a small room with a row of booths and candles on the tables. I could not have picked a better atmosphere myself.

A small dark man with a heavy mustache greeted us and ushered us to a booth. We sat down. I ordered a glass of wine. She hesitated, and finally nodded. We ordered another glass. I sat back and looked at her. Her face in the candled light of the booth was a page from an Old Testament psalm. David to Bathsheba. And Solomon's song.

"You are very kind," I said, "to take pity on a lonely man."

She shook her lovely head. "You must not say that," she said. "I have been lonely too. It was generous of you to ask."

I am fearfully and wonderfully made. I caused the Widow's heart to sing with joy.

"You are shy," she said. "I understood that yesterday when we walked from church. You must try to make friends."

I was trying to make friends. Angela, Angela, you have no idea how hard I was trying.

"I cannot help myself," I said. "As a child I was shy. I have never fully gotten over it."

The waiter brought the bottle of wine. He poured from it into our glasses. The wind gleamed dark red. "In wine there is truth," I said.

She raised the glass to her mouth. When she lowered it the stain of wine glittered wetly on her lips. "What is the truth?" she said.

"That you are lonely," I said. "That you mourn golden days that can never be again."

A sob seemed to catch in her throat. "Never again?" she said.

"Not in the same way," I hastened to add. "The past has its place. Memories remain sacred, but one must somehow live."

I filled her glass with wine. For a girl out of circulation for over two years she knocked off that wine like a champion.

"There are nights I cannot sleep," she said. "Nights when I lie awake and hear strange noises in the dark."

"Loneliness," I said. "There is nothing more terrible than loneliness." As an alternative, Larakis offered himself as chosen comforter. Lucky Angela.

We ordered a little food. I poured another glass of wine. In a little while bright patches of red adorned her cheeks and her teeth gleamed even and white when she smiled.

"It seems so long ago," she said, "since I have sat like this and tasted wine and talked a little."

"You are still young," I said. "You have your life ahead of you."

"And you?" she said. "You are young and have known loneliness. Is your life still ahead of you?"

"For both of us," I said.

She paused and took another sip of wine and held her head a little to the side watching me intently. "I am glad," she said.

There was a bright spring moon high over the city as we walked home together past the houses and the stores and I did not even try to hold her hand.

After she had opened the door to her apartment she stood in the doorway weaving just a little. The scent of midnight tables was about her body. Aroma of walnuts, wine, and fruit. "Will you come in for coffee?" she asked. Her face was hidden in the shadows and I could not see her eyes.

I was tempted. But as an expert in such matters I knew it was too soon. Timing in these things is the principal thing. Therefore if thou would emulate the master, get timing. And with all thy timing, get understanding.

"It is too late for you," I said. "You have been kind and I will not impose further upon your kindness."

"You are a good and gentle man," she said.

She was right. Only fools make a mock at sin.

"Tomorrow night?" I said.

"Tomorrow night," she said. She closed the door.

A week passed. A week in which I saw the Widow Angela every night. Twice we ate in the little restaurant with the candles. Once we drove to an inn outside the city and ate beside a tree-shaded lake. Once we went to a movie and it was a sad love story and she cried. Several times after taking her home I stopped in for a little midnight coffee. She showed me an album of family photographs. She had been a remarkably well-developed child. In later photographs I could not help being a little glad that I was not conducting this raid for plunder while her husband was alive. He looked a real brute of a man. I had no doubts, however, of my ability to equal or surpass his capacities in the main event.

All that week I never once tried to touch the Widow Angela. Several times in the past few nights I had the feeling she would not have objected too strongly if I had kissed her good night. I refused to match for pennies when a chance for a gold piece is involved.

Late Saturday afternoon it began to rain. I stopped in the grocery with two bottles of dark wine that were wrapped as gifts. Mantaris stared at the bottles.

"Won't be long now," I said.

He glared at me and pulled fiercely at his nose. "Why don't you leave her alone?" he said. "Why not a woman of the street or some other wench? Why the Widow Angela?"

"She is the Rose of Sharon," I said, "and the Lily of the Valley."

"You are a goat," he said. "You hold nothing sacred."

"You are a poor loser," I said.

"In the end you will give up," he said. "You will get nowhere with her."

"I will not give up," I said. "I am getting somewhere very fast."

"Get out!" he said. "You are a Turk! I spit back to your father's father!"

I looked around. "You have no fresh cabbages today?" I said.

He got red in the face and started to sputter.

"It does not matter," I said. "Tonight I think I pluck my own. Tonight, old man."

I heaped the coals of fire upon his head. He stood there and did not say another word.

On my way to the Widow it began to rain again. I ran from the car to the stairs making sure not to drop the wine. She stood smiling, waiting in the doorway. "Let me take your wet things," she said.

I gave her my raincoat and my hat. I carried the wine in myself. "A bad night," I said.

"It is very bad," she said.

"A good night to sit inside," I said. "The rain has chilled me."

She stood for a moment without answering and the light of the lamp shone across her face. Her lips were red with a touch of lipstick and there were marks of rouge upon her cheeks.

"I don't mind," she said.

She brought a corkscrew and little decorative glasses for the wine. I opened one of the bottles. We sat together on the couch. We heard the whipping sound of wind and rain against the window.

"It has been a nice week," she said.

"I have enjoyed it very much," I said.

I refilled our glasses of wine. We sat without speaking for a little while with only our hands moving our glasses to our lips. The room seemed guarded like a valley between great mountains.

There was a record player in the corner. I got off the couch and walked to it and snapped the switch. The turntable revolved and the needle lowered upon a record. An old country mountain dance. Angela sat watching me from the couch.

"Come and dance," I said. "I have seen you dance before."

"Where?" she asked.

"At a picnic," I said. "You were taller than any woman in the line. You were beautiful and full of fire."

She stood up. The music rang the quick shrill of melody. She came slowly to the machine. "I do not dance any more," she said.

"Why not?" I said.

"It is not right," she said.

I reached out and very gently touched the hair of the Widow Angela. I might have waited until she had more wine but I was not made of stone. Besides, there was something about that moment, something in the way she stood. I knew this was it.

She turned her head slightly and my hand fell away. For a moment I saw her face with the sad dark eyes and the full lips like moist fruit before a hungry man. "You must not touch me," she said.

I touched the nape of her neck, feeling the slight teasing softness of her hair across my fingers. "I want to touch you," I said, and I really meant that line. "Angela, Angela, all my body wants to touch you."

I saw the first press of uncertain breathing stir her breasts. She knew I had seen and the moment tightened under her disorder. "It is not right," she said. Her hand moved uneasily to her cheek. "It is not right that he should lie in the cold ground and that I should be warm and flushed."

"You are not dead," I said. "Angela, you are not dead. You are a living breathing woman. When you are dead you will be cold forever. Till then you must live."

She turned from me as I spoke. She stood with her back to me, her face to the wall, and her hair glistened darkly.

I snapped off the phonograph. The dance died sharply and a quick silence took its place. There was wild anticipation in my belly. I knew I had her then. I knew by the way she stood and would not look at me. Weeping may endure for a day, but Larakis cometh in the evening.

I reached for her and when she felt my hands she wantonly turned to meet me. I heard her breathing as if breathing were a punishment. Her eyes were closed and hollowed above her rouged cheeks and as I pulled her to me she opened them and they were frenzied and uncaring.

I kissed her full lips. My mouth hard upon her caught breath and the brazen scent of wine between us. The kiss broke and we shakenly drew breath and she stepped away for only a moment and then came back into my arms fiercely. I felt her fingers upon my face and on my throat and across my eyes. I quit goofing around. I started to pull her to the couch.

The buzzer rang a sharp shrill sound.

I felt her stiffen and I tried to catch my breath.

"We won't answer," I whispered. I caught her again. I reached for the great flowing hills of her breasts and felt them like fire beneath my hands.

Somebody pounded on the door.

We looked at each other. Her face, pale and shaken, reflecting my own.

"We must answer," she said huskily. She stepped away pulling weakly at her dress.

If I had had a gun in my hand at that moment I would have emptied it through the door without caring who it was. Instead I stumbled to it, cursing under my breath.

I flung it open and caught old Mantaris with his hand raised to pound again.

He looked startled and his mouth dropped open. The fierceness of my face must have scared blood out of him.

"What the hell do you want!" I roared.

He raised his hands in trembling defense. He stepped back and then looked around me quickly to where the Widow Angela stood. He spoke pleadingly to her watching me from the corner of his eye.

"Good evening, Mrs. Angela," he said and he reached down beside the door and brought up a large bag. "I am delivering your groceries."

I looked at him speechlessly. The Widow came closer to the door.

"Mr. Mantaris," she said, and her voice was still shaken. "I did not order any groceries."

The old man tried to look surprised and in his excitement and fear bounced up and down in the doorway.

"I was sure this was your order," he said. "Mrs. Angela, maybe you forgot about this order."

"Are you nuts," I said, and a strange unrest bit at my belly. "She said she didn't order any groceries. Now get the hell away from here."

"Mike," the Widow Angela said reprovingly. She had regained her composure.

"I am very sorry, Mr. Mantaris," she said quietly. "There has been a mistake. I did not order any groceries."

The old man stopped bouncing and the sweat crouched in little beads across his brown cheeks and forehead. "I am sorry. I am getting old," he said. "I became mixed up. Forgive me."

For the first time I looked at the bag of groceries. I almost choked. Right on the top as bold as you goddam please was a cabbage! That did it. I gave him a shove and slammed the door in his face.

I turned back to the Widow. I was confused but not discouraged. I had come so close I refused to believe I could not make up the lost ground. I went for her again.

She greeted me with her elbows and a tight face.

"Angela," I said. "My darling, don't turn me away."

She shook her head. She stood like a stranger in the room. "It was wrong," she said. "If that old man had not accidentally come at the moment he did, it would have been wrong."

I watched her moist lips move as she talked and remembered them soft under my own.

"You can't go to bed alone forever," I said harshly.

She shook her head and her eyes were deep and clear. "Not forever," she said. "When I find a man to love and marry who will love me, we will go to bed."

I heard her with the hearing of my ear and saw her with the seeing of my eye. There was a roaring beginning in my head and a sense of outrage in my loins. "You are crazy," I said.

"I was for a little while," she said. "I am all right now."

"I won't give you up," I said.

"I will not see you," she said.

"I will make you see me," I said.

"We can be friends," she said.

That word nearly strangled me.

Her face was set into hard firm lines. She wore her virtue like a coat of armor.

I had enough. A man's heart deviseth his way but the Lord directeth his steps. While I was missing from the couch, the fire burned out.

"Goodby," she said.

I stood there a moment. Nimrod, the mighty hunter, returning with an empty pouch.

"My hat and coat," I said haughtily.

She turned to get them and I took one last mournful look at her strong fine thighs and the slender turn of her trim ankles. She brought me back my things. She walked to the door and opened it. I walked past her and turned in the doorway standing in the same place that sneaky old bastard had stood a few moments before.

"Angela," I said. "You are doing us both wrong."

She turned and walked out of the room and left me in the doorway with the door still open. If she had at least closed the door or pushed me out, but she left me standing there with the door still open.

With what dignity I could muster I reached in and closed the door in my own face. I turned and walked down the stairs.

In the car I debated between throwing a rock through the window of the Mantaris grocery or going to Crotty's bar. I decided on the bar. If I hurried I knew a cigarette girl there that I might talk into taking the night off. She had a squeaky giggle and an unfortunate tendency to cold feet, but any port in a storm.

An ass is beautiful to an ass and a pig to a pig.

To hell with the Widow Angela.

I had been working several days on a review of a book of poems by the Greek poet from Alexandria, Constantine Cavafy. When I finished the review I was steeped in the aura of sadness surrounding the gentle, sybaritic old poet who revealed so precisely how age and death are always in the shadow of the delight of love. I began writing this story, but the poet who emerged, Thanos, was a totally different person, sharing with Cavafy only his love of the poem.

THE BASTARDS OF THANOS

The island hospital stood on a small hill overlooking the city, a battered stuccoed two-story building that had endured rain and wind and storm. At the foot of the hill the narrow winding streets teemed with the trade of bazaars, stalls and shops vending spices and silks, cheeses and wines, shrimp and squid. Greek and Jewish and Egyptian merchants haggled and bartered in a babble of harsh and reedy dialects and tongues.

From where Thanos lay in the corner bed of the second floor pauper's ward, he could see the harbor beyond the city, the piers and docks with a few freighters at anchor. He watched the ships make port and sail with the tide and on sharp clear days he marked the flight of gulls that skimmed and soared above the water. At other times he stared at the ceiling above his bed, the surface upon which particles of sun and cloud and the reflections of water shimmered like the billows of the sea itself. During these hours he fashioned his verses, appending each word slowly and arduously, composing another fragment of the long unfinished poem he had begun ten years before. In this way the day would pass until twilight curtained his window. He waited for the lights of the city and the harbor to flicker on proclaiming the beginning of another roisterous night of drinking, gambling and love.

Though there were twenty other occupied beds in his ward, a screen beside his bed and another at the foot shielded him from the remainder of the patients. He heard the clatter of utensils, the skirmishing murmur of voices, the curses and the groans. He inhaled the fetid stench of pus and decay mingled with the antiseptic scents of alcohol, iodine and carbolic acid. But the smells and the sounds of the ward came to him as if from a distance, while in his bed he breathed and endured the cesspool of his own body.

He knew he was dying. The scent of death rose like swamp mist from his pores, his flesh withering on his bones. Even his once strong hands now skewered between fatal illness and age, his fingers brittle twigs needing only a slight jerk to snap them from the frail stem of his wrists.

When he had first been brought to the hospital several months before, the diagnosis had been unanimous and clear. Accepting the coming of his death he fought all efforts to soften his abrasive will, to medicate and console him. He rejected the banal ministrations of the nurses and doctors, scorned their aseptic routine visits that merely served to chart his decline. He vehemently refused the drugs they sought to give him for his pain, unwilling to narcotize the wellsprings from which his poem flowed. He would suffer the pain until he could bear it no longer rather than dull his senses. And even if pain made him howl like a dog to the end he would seek to contour and define even the assembling spectres of darkness and death.

For a little while each morning he had his only visitor, the island Greek priest who came dutifully to attend him on his rounds of the sick. He was a meek and resigned man with a pale, sepulchral face. Fasts and prayer, celibacy and ingratitude, these had drained his spirit and he lived and moved like a shadow drawing what small warmth he could from the candles of his faith.

"How are you today, Thanos?" the priest asked in a frail voice that he tried to make sound vigorous. Thanos knew he regarded the few moments of his visit as a penance.

"Absurdity is still king," Thanos said. "And the poem is the only canon still worthy of faith."

The priest sat down awkwardly in the chair at the screen. He drew his bony legs cloaked in shabby black trousers together and stared at the worn tips of his scuffed shoes. He forced himself to look back at Thanos and managed a wan smile.

"You are looking better today," he said.

"You are a dreadful liar," Thanos said. "Each day all my selfish desires and my absurd vanities decline further into impotence and ugliness. In a short while I will be hollowed out, old as the ages, bare bone and dry brush. And you look about the same."

The priest fumbled his fingers together.

"How is the poem going?" he asked.

"It resembles the old man of the sea," Thanos said. "The Proteus who constantly eludes the grasp, forever changes his shape. But here and there in a word, in a line, it captures pleasure and folly, misfortune and love, vice and elegance, perfidy, betrayal, ineptitude, cunning."

"Is there a place in all of this for God?" the priest said.

"He is there too," Thanos said, "holding aloft the lance and the cup and the Holy Grail. Where He is the water does not flow, love is sterile, crops fail, and animals do not reproduce."

"You build a statue without a pedestal," the priest said patiently. "We are saved by hope and not by memory."

"Spare me your vesicular oblations," Thanos said. "I would not trade a single folly or vice of my life for an eternity of redemption. Your paradise is duller than the landscape of your dismal and surrendered face."

"I have had no reason to laugh in twenty years," the priest sighed. "Even a smile threatens to crack my jaw. Yet although I cannot help my sad face, God may still help you. Believe in Him and you may find your burdens lightened."

"I have always believed in the essentials," Thanos said. "Dancing and laughter, yeast and flour, grapes and wine, desire and love, noon and night, words and poems. Why should I forsake them now?"

"There are mysteries we can enter only through faith," the priest said.

"The mystery lies not in the end but in the beginning," Thanos said.

For a moment longer the priest wavered and then he slowly rose. He bent and raised his small black communion bag.

"I will see you again in the morning," he said. He hesitated and for an instant closed his eyes. When he opened them the lids were heavy with despair. "I pray for a sign," he said slowly. "A sign to prove the power and glory of God. A small miracle to enable you to accept communion."

Thanos uttered a low growl of laughter. "I have swallowed wine by the barrel," he said, "and savored bread by the ovenful. Your chalice of crumbs and droplets is an abomination."

The priest turned forlornly to leave.

Thanos called after him. The priest turned back.

"Show me a sign of His power and glory," Thanos said, "and I pledge to take your communion." He grinned a crooked tearing back of flesh from about his hardened and discolored gums. "But if you cannot provide me a sign then you must admit your life has been useless deprivation and waste. We may still be able to provide you a few meager vices with which to adorn your last years."

The priest coughed a final futile sigh and left.

Thanos did not mind the visits of the priest. He looked forward to them, secretly yearned for them to last longer. They offered him a momentary release from the sputtering and spasms of his organs as they expired.

After the priest had gone, he returned to his poem, forming the words deep in his throat, feeling them hiss and sing through the crumbling canyons of his body. He cherished the words born of sight, smell, touch, taste, hearing and spirit. The fertile element was life, the sterile element was death, and the purifying element was the poem. In the throes of his creation he could still feel the wild strong cries of his soul.

When he needed a respite from the words and lines, he assaulted his memories. He used the myriad events of his life as herbs and potions, sharpening the treasured reveries for battle against the great savage pain he knew would come just before the end. He carefully reviewed the succulent meals he had eaten, the juicy rare meats, the redolent oil and garlic salads, the candled midnight tables of walnuts, cheese and fruit. Upon the parched desert of his palate he trickled once more in fantasy the wines of Bordeaux and Burgundy, Porto and Marsala, still wines and sparkling wines, pale amber champagne and glowing ruby clarets.

He retraced his multifarious journeys across the world. An orphan at six, a seaman at fifteen, fifty years as a poet. He remembered the hundreds of women he had possessed, the countless courtships and consummations. The cycles of desire, the sadness after love, but also, reborn like the phoenix from the ashes, the love after sadness. He tried to extricate the hundreds of shimmering bodies, the lovely faces, knowing that many of them were dead now or grown cold and old with skin like ship's canvas and bodies gnarled and twisted like the trunks and branches of old island trees. But in the fertile valleys of his assignations they would always be young. Brown handsome Polynesians who walked with the pride of Queens. Black wenches in Africa with gleaming flanks and armored breasts. Coal-eyed Jewesses, descended of Bathsheba, like smoke in a man's arms. Moslem girl children with breasts like plums. Delicate yellow women with the shyness of virgins in their eyes and a whore's skill in the arts of love. He heard them whimpering and teasing in the rocking beds of a hundred ports. He fought to hold the vicarious heat of the visions, until finally, shaking and exhausted, he watched them fading into the twilight that engulfed his bed. He cried out then, a bitter lament deep in his body, for the joys he had once savored and would garner no more.

Early one morning in that week he had another visitor. During the night his pains had goaded him almost to the threshold of screams and he had found himself thinking with frenzy of the numbing drugs. The dawn came bleak and pale, the sky a gray shroud against his window. He was staring at the window when a young man entered between the screens around his bed, pausing for a moment as if he were expecting to find someone else.

Thanos turned his head on the pillow and for a time they stared at one another in silence. The youth was tall, with dark eyes and dark hair, dressed in a seaman's jacket, a seaman's knit cap in his hands. Against the sunweathered skin of his cheek the slit of a scar gleamed white.

"Are you Thanos, the poet?" he asked finally. He spoke in a low and earnest voice.

The pain had made Thanos angry and uneasy. "What do you want?" he asked harshly.

"My name is Petros," the young man said. "Petros Potamis. My mother was Magdalina."

"My mother was the Blessed Virgin," Thanos said. "What do you want?"

"Magdalina Potamis of Athens," Petros said tensely. "You were in Athens for a while years ago, weren't you?"

"I have been in fifty countries and in five hundred cities," Thanos said impatiently.

Petros raised his hand, fumbling with his fingers at the scar on his cheek.

"I am your son," he said.

For a startled moment Thanos was silent. Then he began to laugh, a mirthless sniggering from between his lips. Petros stood stolidly until his fit had subsided, until he could hoarsely regain his breath.

"I have no sons or daughters," Thanos said and snorted again. "I have never been chained in marriage and my unions have been unsanctified. You have made a mistake."

"I am your bastard son," the young man said quietly. "My mother was Magdalina Potamis and you knew her in Athens more than twenty years ago. She has married twice, has other children by those husbands, but you are my father. She told me when I was fifteen."

"We all dream of the father," Thanos said. "The comedy begins when we think we have found him."

"My mother told me you had been a sailor," Petros said. "When I was sixteen I went to sea. I asked about you in a score of ports. A few men remembered your drinking and your fighting. Some remembered you shouting out your poems." He gestured with his hands in awkward apology. "I even talked to a few of the women who remembered you."

"You heard about me in some brothel," Thanos cried, "and have come to mock me or to discover if I have an inheritance of treasure to leave. I have nothing but a thousand lines of an unfinished poem that will die soon with me."

Petros fumbled in the pocket of his jacket and brought out a small, worn and faded, paper-covered booklet.

"These are your poems," he said. "I have read them many times. On nights in the Islands of the Indies and on watch in the Galapagos. I have heard them echo in the cries of birds on the shores of Greenland."

"Where did you get the scar?" Thanos asked.

Petros shrugged a slight drawing together of his shoulder, his lips parting in a spare wry admission.

"A fight over a girl in Vera Cruz," he said.

"That could be evidence of my paternity," Thanos said with a snigger.

"My mother gave me the poems," Petros said. "There is one of them, a poem she told me you had written of her. Do you remember?"

"Read it to me," Thanos said.

The young man opened the booklet and began to read in a clear and strong voice.

> A single candle was not needed
> To light our hours close together.
>
> In the distance, the sea,
> The harbor white under the moon.
>
> On the flanks of the mountains,
> Wildflowers and the evening star.
>
> Secret places of our heart's love,
> Wind and night our bower.
>
> Old and ill I will still remember,
> In darkness savor once more the light.

From a yard below the hospital window, a rooster screamed raucously. A dog answered with a short harsh bark. Thanos struggled vainly to separate flowers sundered in the wind of years, petals scattered in the wake of endless tides. With the poem in his hands Petros waited in a silence like the drifting of a ship in a dead still sea, heart and soul ardent for the first quiver of wind.

"I remember," Thanos said. "I remember your mother now." He felt a shiver of pain moving in his blood.

A flame leaped into the youth's dark eyes.

"I have searched for you for six years," he said and his voice trembled. "Searching six years to find a father I had never seen. In Alexandria, two months ago, an old salt you had sailed with told me he had heard you were here. When we anchored yesterday I swept the city for you, wandered all night through the bars that had not seen you in months. Now I have found you and my ship sails in an hour on the tide."

"You found me in time," Thanos said. "A few more days might have been too late."

"I can stay if you want me to stay," Petros said. "I can jump ship and hide until after she sails. I can stay with you until you are well."

"There is no need of that," Thanos said. "I cannot escape the shipwreck of my body and the end of my voyage is very near."

"I knew I would find you," Petros said. "I swore to my mother I would find you."

"When you see her again, give her a message for me," Thanos said. "Tell her I loved her most of all."

"I will tell her," Petros cried softly. "As God is my judge, I will tell her in just those words."

"I have no possessions to leave you," Thanos said. "Remember these words, my only legacy to you. I was what you are. You will become what I am. Think of those words and you will unravel the way to live."

"I will," Petros said. "I will."

"Hurry now to your ship," Thanos said.

Petros came closer to the bed and knelt quickly. Before Thanos could draw his hand away the son had clasped his palm and gently kissed his stiff dry fingers. The touch of the youth's mouth upon his cold wasted flesh filled him with a strange quivering warmth.

Petros rose and moved toward the opening between the screens. He paused as if to make another plea or effort to remain.

"Don't miss your ship and your mates!" Thanos cried. "A hundred gilded ports are waiting for you, a hundred scented lovely girls. Hurry!"

The young man turned and fled.

Later that morning the priest came on his daily rounds. He stood for a moment uncertainly at the foot of the bed.

"How are you today, Thanos?" he asked.

"Rejoicing," Thanos said, and the words came with a slurring burden to his lips. "Because I am purified by every devilment, sanctified by every depravity, beyond sentiment and fatigue, nearing the realm of pure spirit."

The priest sat wearily down drawing the small black bag close to his feet.

"You are looking better today, Thanos," he said with a frail smile.

Thanos groaned. "Day by day you parrot your miasmic clichęs," he said. "A worthy spiritual leader for this parish of drunks, thieves, and syphilitics."

The priest looked submissively at his pale-fingered hands in his lap.

"I had a visitor this morning," Thanos said. "I have been waiting to tell you about him. A bastard son from a far-off port that I did not know I had whelped. He has been searching for me for six years and finds me on the eve of my death. What does St. John say to that?"

The priest rose trembling to his feet and made his cross. "God has heard my prayers," he said in a shaken voice. "To send you a son so close to the end. It is a sign of His power and His glory."

"It was a sign," Thanos said. "A moment of deliverance, an event of revelation."

"God be praised!" the priest cried softly and closed his eyes.

"If there is one son," Thanos said, "how many others might there be, bastard spawn of my wild beds, born of virgins and whores . . ."

"No!" the priest gasped. "That is not the sign I meant!"

"Think of it!" Thanos cried hoarsely. "Perhaps as many as fifty or more androgynous mongrels of my rampaging journeys, devoted to life and drink and love as I have been, a virile host to carry on after I am gone, hurling my unrepentant seed into myriad races and through endless generations!"

The priest shook his head, a moan of despair falling from his lips. "No," he pleaded. "That is not the meaning."

"That is my meaning," Thanos said.

The priest stood in silence for another moment. His breathing grew calmer slowly, his agitation quieted. The weariness and the resignation settled once more in his pale cheeks. He bent heavily for his small bag and turned slowly to leave.

"I will see you in the morning, Thanos," he said.

"Before you go," Thanos said, "I would like communion."

The priest stared at him numbly.

"Communion, you know, the last rites," Thanos said. "A sign is a sign and I honor my pledges."

For a labored moment the priest stared benumbed at Thanos. Then he placed his small bag on the chair. He opened the worn clasp and drew out the golden chalice, the tiny bottle of wine, the container of meager bread. He worked with slow stiff fumblings, praying under his breath as he blended the wine and the bread.

He brought the chalice to the bed. He dipped the small golden spoon into the wine and bent toward Thanos.

"My God, my God," he whispered, and there were tears in his eyes. "Thy mysterious ways are beyond thy servant's understanding."

Thanos parted his lips and received the tiny spoon of sweet wine and the sodden pellet of bread.

After the priest had gone, he lay staring at the ceiling. The arc of day gave way to the shades of dusk. In the twilight the wild rooster screamed again and he heard a savage burst of pain answer in his body.

He fought his fear and panic and slowly, carefully, he cast and forged the words and lines of his poem.

I have read this story to audiences almost as many times as I have read "The Journal of a Wife Beater," but the response is quite different. The origins of the story must go back to my youth, when I admired the lovely, black-haired and dark-eyed Greek girls in church, who were encircled by zealous brothers and grim fathers. Sometimes, staring at one of those girls, I would catch a brother bristling and quickly avert my glance. I remember thinking then how only the most reckless and foolhardy of suitors would dare to pass the inspection of that fierce and prickly Greek garrison.

THE SONG OF RHODANTHE

I was twenty-seven years old that spring. Papa had still not given up hope that a man would be found to marry me. My brothers, Kostas and Marko and Niko, were married and had numerous children of their own. They were all concerned about me.

It was true that I wanted to be married. Papa had presented a number of men to me for my approval. I was not beautiful but neither was I so homely that I had to accept one of them. They were either too old or too loud or red-faced from drinking too much beer and wine. I think Papa grieved most about me when wine made him tearful. His only daughter, twenty-seven, and still unmarried. Friends who were bachelors drank and grieved with him. In the end they offered themselves as suitors to ease Papa's despair.

After an evening with one of them Papa waited for my decision. I told him I refused to accept such a man.

"You are twenty-seven years old!" he cried. "A daughter still unmarried at twenty-seven is a plague on a man's spirit. I cannot sleep for worrying about you. My health is breaking down. At the market everyone asks me, Panfelio, is your daughter married yet? Is she even engaged? I cannot bear much more."

"Yes, Papa."

"What was the matter with Gerontis?" he asked.

"He is too old," I said, "and his false teeth whistle when he speaks."

"You are too choosy!" Papa shouted. "Remember you are twenty-seven years old."

"Yes, Papa."

"What was the matter with Makris?" he asked. "He is a younger man than Gerontis."

"He is younger," I said. "But he greases his hair until it drips oil down his cheeks and he spent all evening telling me how he can crack open a crate with his bare hands."

"I can still crack open a crate with my bare hands," Papa shouted. "Your poor Mama was never the worse for it. You forget, my girl, you are twenty-seven years old."

"Yes, Papa."

One evening a week, my brothers brought their wives and children to our house to eat supper. The wives were red-cheeked with great bosoms and ate like contented mares. The house became a bedlam with children hanging from the lamps and chairs collapsing with a sound of thunder. We assembled at the table and bowed our heads and Papa said grace.

"We are grateful, O Lord, that we are well and together and for the food upon this table. Bring us together again next week and let there be a man for Rhodanthe among us. Amen."

When dinner was over and it was time to leave, each of the wives of my brothers kissed me benevolently on the cheek. One after the other my big brothers embraced me sadly and kissed me somberly. Every parting was a festival of grief. Poor Rhodanthe.

I told Papa goodnight and kissed him tenderly because I loved him very much. He was foolish sometimes and shouted a great deal but I knew how much he loved me too.

I went to my room and prepared for bed. I sat before the mirror and brushed my long hair. In those moments I fiercely felt a wish to be married and raise children of my own. Sometimes I thought I wanted that as much for Papa and Kostas and Marko and Niko as for myself.

The last cold months of winter passed. The winds grew gentle. The rain fell during the night and in the daylight the earth smelled fresh as if it were awakened from a long sleep. One morning I saw a robin sitting on a branch of the cherry tree in our yard and I knew the spring had really come.

Each morning Kostas and Marko and Niko drove up in their trucks to have a cup of coffee while Papa ate breakfast. I knew they did that for me so that I would not feel too lonely during the day.

They sat around the kitchen table, big strong men that made the kitchen seem smaller than it really was. The cups looked tiny and fragile in their massive hands. They smoked cigars and spoke in loud gruff voices to each other. But they were soft and gentle when they spoke to me.

When they had left with Papa for the market, I washed the dishes and cleaned the house. I worked quickly and felt a glow in my cheeks.

Because that day was so beautiful I decided to take the bedding out to air. I carried the sheets and blankets to the back yard and draped them across a line. When I finished hanging them up I was a little out of breath.

There was the sound of whistling in the alley in back of the yard and a young man appeared. He was striding along with his hands in his pockets and his head flung back and a wild jubilant whistling ringing from his lips. I had heard whistling before, even the strong bass whistling of my brothers, but never a sound like he made. It was as if the spring had burst into song. As if the first slim green buds and the blades of new grass and the soft fresh wind had suddenly found a voice.

When he saw me standing there he paused. For a quick tight moment the whistling ceased. His hair was thick and dark and an untamed and errant curl glittered across his forehead. He smiled then and his smile was as reckless and daring as his whistle. Then he walked on quickly and the wild whistling rang out again. As the sound faded a terrible loneliness overcame me. I went quickly into the house.

That night at supper I broke a cup and spilled soup from the pot while pouring it into a bowl.

"What is the matter with you?" Papa said. "You are nervous as a cat tonight."

"Nothing is the matter, Papa," I said and felt a quick flame in my cheeks.

He cleared his throat and sighed heavily.

"It is not normal," he said somberly. "Twenty-seven years old and still unmarried. You will become sick."

"I will not become sick, Papa," I said. "Do not worry about me."

"How can I help worrying?" he said. "What kind of father would I be if I did not worry about my daughter, still unmarried at twenty-seven?" His lips quivered and he wiped a stray tear from his eye.

"Yes, Papa."

"You are too choosy!" he shouted. "You have not that right at your age. Gastis passed the market today. He asked how you were. He was taken with you. What in God's name was the matter with Gastis?"

"I have told you before, Papa," I said.

"Tell me again!"

"His face is like one of his grapefruit," I said. "He never smiles. Whatever time of day you are with him always appears to be night."

Papa threw up his hands in despair.

"One is too young," he said. "And one is too old. One laughs like an idiot and one does not laugh enough. One is a banana and one is a grapefruit. I am telling you, my girl, I am losing patience!"

"Yes, Papa."

"What kind of man do you want?" he shouted again. "Tell me what kind of man do you want?"

I paused for a moment in the doorway of the kitchen. A reckless excitement swept my tongue.

"I want a young man with dark hair," I said boldly. "And a wild dark curl across his forehead. A man who whistles and makes the earth burst into song."

Papa made his cross.

"What I have feared has come to pass," he said sadly. "You have become unbalanced."

"Yes, Papa," I said, and I ran back to him and kissed him gently. "Good night, Papa."

In the morning I could not wait for all of them to leave. They sat over their coffee for what seemed to be an eternity. Yet each time I looked at the clock I saw they were no later than they usually were.

When they had gone I ran to my room and carefully brushed my hair and tied it with my brightest ribbon. I touched my lips with a light red stain and pinched my cheeks. I went quickly downstairs and out the back door. A moment of panic seized me when I realized I could not just stand there waiting. I hurried back into the house and pulled the blankets from my bed and ran with them down the stairs. I had just finished hanging them when I heard the sound of the whistling again.

He came down the alley just as he had the morning before. His head flung back and his legs walking with great strong strides and that wonderful wild whistle singing on his lips.

When he saw me he stopped. He smiled again, a perfect and riotous smile. I could not help myself and smiled back. He walked slowly to the fence and carelessly and with a supple grace leaned his elbows upon it and put his face in his hands.

"You live here?" he asked. And he had a deep man's voice but not nearly as harsh a voice as Papa had, and with revelry in it, unlike the voices of Marko and Kostas and Niko.

"Yes," I said.

"With your husband?" he asked slyly.

"With my father," I said quickly. "I am not married."

"Good," he said, and he smiled again and threw back his head and laughed a festival of tuneful laughter from his throat. "Good," he said again and then he waved goodby and started striding down the alley.

There were a dozen questions I wanted to call after him, a dozen things I wanted to say. I was ashamed because I had answered and yet I felt strange and alive for the first time in my life. I looked at the budding leaves and at the first blades of grass and at the early tulips and felt a fervent kinship with them.

The next morning it rained and I was in despair. I could not stand in the rain waiting for him to pass, or hang blankets on a line in the downpour. After a while I gave up hoping it would stop in time and consoled myself that the following morning the sun might shine again.

I finished the kitchen and wiped the last breakfast cups without spirit. I hung the dish towel upon the rack, and heard a light tapping at the window.

My heart leaped because he was there. He waved to me through the rain-smeared glass. I ran to the door and flung it open. He came in dripping from the rain and the dark curly hair matted upon his head.

"You are soaked!" I said. "You'll catch cold! I'll get a towel."

He took the clean towel from my hands and began briskly to dry his hair. He rubbed his cheeks with vigor and smiled and shook his head.

"You weren't in the yard," he said.

I looked at him helplessly.

"It was raining so hard," I said. "I wasn't sure you would come."

When I realized what I had said I put my hand quickly to my mouth. But he only laughed softly.

"The rain is nothing," he said. "I missed you."

We looked at each other and there was taunting merriment in his dark eyes. I tried to think of something to say but all my senses seemed to have fled.

"I've got to go in a minute," he said. "I'll be late for work."

"A cup of coffee," I said. "It's still hot. It will warm you."

He came to the table and he was not as tall as any of my brothers and not as broad in the shoulders as my father, but there was grace and strength in the way he moved.

I brought the pot of coffee to the table and filled his cup. I could sense him watching me and I spilled some into the saucer.

"Weren't you afraid to let me in?" he said.

I turned away and shook my head.

"What's your name?" he said.

"Rhodanthe," I said. I put the pot back on the stove and then turned to face him.

"A pretty name," he said. "A name for a flower."

I looked down at the floor because I was sure the frantic beating of my heart would show in my cheeks.

"I know a great deal about you," he said and when I looked up he winked slyly. "I know more about you than you realize."

"You do?" I said.

"I know you are sometimes sad," he said, "because you do not smile. I know you are sometimes lonely because you do not laugh."

We were both silent for a moment and I marveled at how well he understood. And how natural it seemed that he should be sitting at my table drinking coffee.

He pushed back his cup and rose from the table and walked to the door. I followed him there and he turned and paused with his hand on the knob. He bent a little and kissed me. A quick impulsive kiss that brushed my lips with the grace of a spring wind.

I stepped back shocked.

"You had no right!" I said. "You should not have done that."

"I wanted to kiss you," he said and smiled wickedly. "I do what I want."

Then he was walking swiftly with long strong strides through the rain.

That night the family gathered again. All the rosy-cheeked wives and the multitude of children. I worked with a jubilation I found hard to conceal. I even sang a little to myself and several times noticed one of my brothers watching me strangely.

At the end of the meal the children scrambled from the table to resume playing in another room. The wives picked up the plates and carried them to the kitchen. Niko, the youngest of my brothers, caught my arm.

"What makes you sparkle tonight?" he said. "I have never seen you like this before." He gestured at Papa. "What has happened to this girl?"

I tried to shake off his hand but he laughed and held me tight. All of them watched me and I felt my cheeks flaming.

"She is blushing," Marko said. "Blushing like a schoolgirl."

"Let me go," I said to Niko, "or I will bring this plate of bones across your head."

"She is in love!" Kostas roared. "The girl's in love!"

A reverent quiet descended upon the room. The wives came from the kitchen to stand in the doorway with their eyes open to great bursting cups. Niko let me go slowly. All of them watched me in some kind of awe.

"Rhodanthe," Papa said and there was a great joy stirring in his voice. "Is this true?"

My heart went out to him. He was growing old and loved me so much. I looked at each of my brothers and felt a great wave of affection for them. I could even forgive their smug wives, secure in marriage to good men, who listened in the doorway.

"Yes," I said. "Yes."

"Thunder and lightning!" Kostas roared. He beat with his big fist upon the table. The dishes rattled and jumped.

"Hurrah!" Niko cried.

"I'll be damned!" Marko shouted.

Everybody looked at Papa. He silently made his cross and looked as if he were about to cry.

"God be praised," he said and his voice trembled. "I knew you must come to your senses. I have brought you some good men. Which one of them have you reconsidered?"

"Five bucks to a buck it's Makris!" Niko shouted.

"That grease pot?" Kostas cried. "She wouldn't touch him with a yardstick."

"It must be Gastis!" Marko said. "It has to be Gastis!"

"Silence!" Papa roared. "Silence!"

The room went quiet. No sound except for the shrieking children in the parlor.

"Silence those little monsters!" Papa roared again. One of the wives went quickly to the parlor and a moment later silence fell in every part of the house. She came back and softly closed the door.

"Which one is it?" Papa spoke to me gently.

I stood at the foot of the table and folded my hands. I took a deep breath and for one brief moment closed my eyes and then opened them again.

"It is none of the men you have brought home," I said.

They all looked shocked. A rumbling began around the table. Papa waved his hand fiercely for silence.

"I do not understand," he said slowly. "It is not Gastis or Makris or Sarantis or Gerontis or any of those other good men?"

"No, Papa," I said.

"Who the devil is it then?" Marko said angrily.

A flare of panic seized me but I had gone too far to turn back.

"A young man who passes on his way to work in the morning," I said. "He has dark and curly hair and he whistles in a way I have never heard anyone whistle before."

For a long startled moment no one spoke.

"She has gone nuts!" Kostas cried. He looked around for confirmation.

"Who is this guy?" Marko shouted. "I'll teach him to whistle at my sister!"

"Dirty hoodlum!" Niko spit between his teeth.

Papa beat with his fist upon the table. Everyone became quiet again.

"You are joking?" Papa said and he made an effort to laugh and one of the wives began to laugh with him. Papa stopped laughing and glared at her and she almost choked closing her mouth.

"I am not joking," I said. "He is a young man that I have spoken to a number of times. This morning we had coffee together."

"He had coffee with you this morning?" Marko shouted angrily. "In this house alone with you?"

"We'll have his teeth hot from his mouth!" Kostas cried.

"Dirty hoodlum!" Niko shouted. "Sneaking behind our backs!"

"Who is he?" Papa cried. "Who is he?"

"I don't know his name," I said. I knew how that sounded but I was becoming angry too.

Papa exploded for all of them. Shock and anger ripping his face. The wives cowered in the doorway.

"You don't know his name!" Papa thundered. "You don't know his name!"

They all began roaring at once. I bit my lips hard trying to stop the tears that burned to break from my eyes.

"I don't know his name!" I cried angrily. "I don't know his name! I know I love him! I heard him whistling and saw him and everything changed. This morning it rained and I could have cried because I would not see him and then he knocked on the window." They all sat staring at me and I struggled furiously to find words to overwhelm them. "There were other men I might have loved years ago," I said. "Men who were frightened off by your shouts and your fists. But you will not take this man from me. He told me he knew I was sad because I did not smile and that I was lonely because I did not laugh and then he kissed me!" I felt a tremor shake my body and my voice rose fiercely. "I don't know his name! I only know I love him!"

They were sorry afterwards. Papa came to my room and kissed me and cried a little. Then Marko and Niko and Kostas came and touched my hair gently with their big hands and tried to speak with their eyes. I forgave them because I knew how much they cared for me. And I consented to let Niko wait with me in the morning to see the young man.

But he did not come the next morning. I thought perhaps he knew about Niko and the following day I waited alone. I waited in the yard with the spring wild and tangled about my head and the blossoms breaking on the branches of the trees and the earth flowing and alive.

He did not come. And the spring passed into summer and the leaves grew long and green on the trees and the sunflowers bloomed among the stones and the birds were everywhere. The speckled robins and the gray starlings and the brownish redwings.

After a while I knew Papa and the others thought I had made it all up. That I had grown weary of the procession of sad suitors and made the story up to keep others away.

They do not understand that someday he will come back. On a morning when the green hearts of the lilac bushes tremble awake in the wind. When the first slim green buds break upon the branches of the maples and the catalpas.

He will come striding along with his hands in his pockets and his reckless head flung back and the wild jubilant whistle ringing on his lips. And I will feel once again that the early green buds and the first fragile flowers and the soft new winds have suddenly burst into song.

This story is one of my favorites and stems from a year when I worked as a night dispatcher in an ice depot. The theme encompasses decline and age as well as those resonances of the past I often draw upon in my stories. If these men are not Homeric Greeks but Polish icemen, I saw them as heroic figures suffering the same fate.

The fine film director Sam Peckinpah and I hoped to make this story into a film. We had worked together when he directed my story "Pericles on 31st Street," and I'd enjoyed the experience. He died last year, a loss to his friends and to those who admired his great films.

THE PASSING OF THE ICE

That morning, standing before Toby's desk in the dispatch office, Mike felt the moment of his discharge had come. The straw boss sat overflowing his chair with the great rolls of fat around his waist and loins, his heavy fingers leafing through the papers on the desk.

"How you feel today, Mike?" Toby asked.

"I feel fine," Mike said. "I feel like an iceman. How do you feel?"

"You look tired, Mike," Toby said. "A man should not look as tired as you so early in the morning."

"We are all tired," Mike said. "But a heavy man covers his weariness and a skinny man shows it to the bone."

The straw boss sat stiffly at the desk staring intently at the papers, as if he had forgotten anyone was there. His way was to loosen his grip just enough to allow a man to think he might escape, and then clamp his big hand on him tighter. Mike had seen others squirm and sweat before the desk. He showed no fear, because his dread was not of the fat man but of being forced to accept the measure of his days.

"Somebody left ice out." Toby spit the words between his thin lips. "An old hand like you should watch there is no goddam ice left on the trucks overnight."

"I'll watch," Mike said.

Outside the office the loaded trucks stood idling with the blocks wedged beneath the wheels. The voices of the drivers and helpers carried in a chorus of curses and laughter. J. C. would have his truck gassed and loaded with the cakes of four-hundred-pounders stacked to the tailgate.

"Why don't you give up?" Toby said, and his voice was a harsh and ugly whisper. "You can't move around on the cars like you used to. It won't be long anyway."

Mike felt a violence deep in his belly, the fury of a temper that had plagued his younger days. He waited until the hard knot eased, and tried to speak quietly.

"I get around," he said. "I work twice as hard because I know you don't want to lose me."

"Get out." Toby's eyes were bright in anger. "Get out, old man, and do your work."

Mike left the office. Outside he stood for a moment in the spring morning with the smell of the earth fresh and cool, and found himself trembling. He walked across the roadway to where J. C. waited in the cab of the truck, feeling that Toby had risen from his desk and was watching at the window.

"Roll your truck, Mike," Sargent cried from behind the wheel. "We late now."

On the running board of the next truck, tall and lean-flanked Noodles swung an arm toward the sky.

"O sun," Noodles sang. "You have displayed your backside long enough. Winter has been fierce and the icemen are weary. O sun, grow strong and warm poor old Noodles."

From the tailgate of Noodles' truck, his helper Gomez waved a greeting to Mike.

"This is the season," Gomez said, turning his face to the sky, "the time I would like to own a small farm and work in the fields."

"You, a farmer?" Noodles said. "Gomez, you couldn't grow foam on a glass of beer."

"You making noise with your mouth," Gomez said. "My father was a farmer. I would have been a good farmer."

"Sure you would have," Mike said. "Lay off quail hunting every night with Noodles, and save your money. Get back to the farm."

When Mike reached the truck, J. C. kicked out the blocks that wedged the wheels and swung into the cab beside him.

"Let 'em roll!" Mike shouted savagely. "C'mon, you dead-rumped coal hikers that call yourselves icemen. Roll them loads!"

Noodles waved and hollered something that was lost in the roar of the motors.

A few moments later, driving with the windows open and the air cool against his cheeks, Mike's trembling had eased. J. C. rode in silent fury beside him.

"The bastard was on you again," J. C. said. "The bastard was riding your back again." His black cheeks corded, and a curse came bitten from his mouth.

"What you talking about?" Mike said. "He poured me a cup of coffee and shared his chocolate doughnut with me. You got that big and friendly man all wrong."

They looked at each other and smiled. J. C. laughed. Mike felt the old pleasure returning, the rocking feel of the wheel in his hands, the pull of the loaded trailer, and a good friend beside him.

"You can smell the spring," Mike said. "In a few more weeks the summer, and then another year almost gone."

"To hell with the season," J. C. said. "Icemen freeze in winter and roast in summer. You know the ice don't care what time of year."

"Amen," Mike said.

Mike knew the ice. He had worked with the pick and tongs for almost forty years. Sometimes in the summer, with the dry railroad cars waiting to be iced, and in his rushing back to the hill to reload, he forgot for a little while that the icing was not the way it had been. Bungo was dead, and the great Orchowski no longer roared his wild songs from the top of the cars. Each year brought more icing machines, and the old icemen were gone. Now in the beginning of summer the young wandering Blacks and the Irish gandy dancers came to work on the trucks. They were strong without skill and lifted to show off their strength. Foolish young men who tried to lift the three- and four-hundred-pound blocks with their backs or with their arms. Mike tried to teach them how to lift by using their legs and how to hook the tongs just the right distance from the score marks. But he worked beside them uneasily, aware of how a man could be maimed or crushed by the carelessness of others.

There were a few good men among them. J. C., the young Black on the truck, had some of the strength and spirit of the old icemen. Noodles knew how to handle his Hilift. The dark and bitter Sargent could cut and throw the way Chino once had. But they were just a few among the sportive young men who came for the summer pay and took no pride in their work and left wearily in the autumn.

Mike had been the smallest of the giants, and now he was alone. But time and the ice had not left him untouched. Each year the burden of his back and legs began earlier in the day, until by the middle of the afternoon his muscles were knotted and each movement of icing was scored with pain. More and more often he was seized with a strange despair.

He could not do much of anything else. He could eat and drink and sleep and in season go to see a ball game. He could lie in the darkness next to Zeba and sometimes still feel the wild and sudden tenderness that briefly let his weariness drop aside. Afterward he could not help but laugh, remembering himself as a bantam rooster and the women as the hens. Of all the women he had known and loved, only Zeba remained. She had never been very pretty, and she was no longer young. Little pouches of flesh had gathered beneath her chin, and in the morning he noticed how the strap of her slip was held by a pin, or how the seam of her stocking might run all around her leg. But in the evening there was hot food on the table. When he brought J. C. home, she baked them spareribs and went down to the corner and brought them back cold beer. She was kind to his friend, and for this he was grateful. When it was time to go to bed, Zeba rubbed Mike's back and legs with ointment, her big warm hands bringing a temporary comfort to his body. Afterward they lay side by side, and she spoke of the years they had spent together. She talked low and soft in the dark room, and knowing his weariness, she did not ask a question or expect him to say a word. Sometimes she laughed at something she remembered, secretively, yet always including him. He would feel himself easing into the darkness and her voice fading and the last low stirrings of her laughter.

"How come I let you be my driver?" J. C. bared his teeth in a broad grin. "You too skinny to be a good driver for a big boy like me."

"Fat ass don't make a good iceman," Mike said.

J. C. laughed and stuck his big fist against his chest.

"Never been an ice crew like us," he said. "Someday we going to ice together in hell. Damn devil going to say, 'J. C., where that skinny driver you come down with? Oh, there he is hiding in the cab. All right, now you both here, let the number-one ice crew start to work and cool off hell.' "

"You crazy." Mike smiled. "I taught you all I know, and now you wear your pants too high. Between tall pockets and big feet you got a head like a sponge."

"I'm an iceman," J. C. said. "All icemen got a sponge for a head. It goes with the job."

"Amen," Mike said.

When they reached their first stop, at the Harley Depot, the yardmaster located their cars on the spur. Mike pulled the truck alongside the first car to be iced, and carrying picks and tongs, he and J. C. swung up on the back of the truck.

The elevator rose slowly to the height of the car. They began to work, cutting the blocks into chunks to fit the bunkers. Swiftly they fell into the rhythm, and the ice flew. To save their wind they did not speak, but J. C. hummed a broken snatch of melody. Their picks rose and fell, and the ice split into chunks for the tongs to grab and throw. They moved quickly and surely on the narrow runway. They closed the lids and lifted the plugs with a steady pull. As fast as they finished a car they moved on to the next.

A little past noon they stopped for lunch at Chino's small bar on Laramie Street. They ordered beef sandwiches garnished with pickle and onion, and steins of lager beer. Sitting in a rear booth of the darkened room, Mike was grateful for the chance to rest among the warm shadows.

Chino, bent with arthritis but still taller than most men, came to sit in the booth with them. He had been one of the icemen with Mike in the days of Bungo and Orchowski. When his joints became inflamed and his body twisted, he bought an interest in the small bar. He kept it shadowed, as if ashamed to be seen by the men who still worked the trucks.

"How's business, Chino?" Mike asked.

"Ain't doing nothing," the old iceman said gloomily. "We get a little movement at lunch, and the rest of the day is like a graveyard. See." He motioned with his stiff and swollen fingers around the room.

"Sure," J. C. said. "You stop watering your beer and stop making sandwiches so skinny, you get some more business."

"You just a punk," Chino said. "You don't know like Mike and me know. The ice is passing. There ain't no more trade from the locations. In a few more years the machines will do all the icing and the last icemen will be working in the goddam coalyards."

Mike shut his eyes, and for a moment the years fell away and he worked with Bungo and Orchowski, and Chino was a tall young giant, wilder than all the rest.

"You remember?" Chino said. "Mike, you remember how it used to be?"

"I remember," Mike said.

Chino twisted his head around like a frightened bird suddenly trying to take flight. He raised his hand from the table and held it for a moment poised in the air and then slowly lowered it again to the scarred surface of the wood.

"It ain't no use thinking about how it used to be," Chino said. "I think and think but it ain't no use. Things are just the way they are and nothing can change them. The old ice days are gone, and they ain't never going to come back."

J. C. finished the last of the beer in the stein and wiped his mouth with the back of his hand. "You make it sound like we all dead now," he said.

"You just a punk," Chino said. "You don't remember the ice trucks lined up for blocks. Tarpans and Shaws and the crews from Proviso. A few years back, even after I was off the Hilifts, they would fill this place for lunch. But not one of them a damn iceman like we was in the old days. Ain't that right, Mike?"

Mike stood up to leave, suddenly not wanting to listen to Chino any longer.

"You still talk just as much," Mike said. "By God, Chino, you talk as much now as before."

"I got a right," Chino said. "Business is bad and my back hurts and all I got to do is sit and remember."

"Stuff it," J. C. said. "Trouble with you is you see the whole world hung up. You ain't the only man pushing to see daylight."

"Listen, Chino," Mike said. "Tomorrow make the beef a little leaner. Today was too much fat." He put his hand briefly on the old man's shoulder and felt the block of strength between the swollen joints.

Outside, the sunlight hurt their eyes, and for a moment they stood squinting while the shavings of ice melting on the truck dripped into puddles in the gutter.

"He's right about one thing," J. C. said. "You the only iceman left. Rest of us don't count for crap."

"Chino and me make noise with our mouths"—Mike shook his head and spoke gruffly—"because we can't shake our rumps the way we used to."

He climbed into the cab of the truck. J. C. walked to the other side and swung in beside him.

"He's right anyway," J. C. said. "I know the old man is right because you the only hump at the hill don't scare when Toby talks. Rest of us call him bastard but inside we sweat. Maybe it's how you think about the ice. Not like the rest of us, just a job. I see you close and I know."

Mike turned the key, and the motor kicked over with a roar. Then he reached over and brought his bunched fist down hard on J. C.'s leg above the knee. The helper bellowed with a cry of pain that almost drowned the noise of the motor.

"You're right," Mike said. "No one any damn good but me."

J. C. rubbed his leg and began to laugh.

"Daddy," he said. "When I grow up, daddy, can I be an iceman like you?"

They laughed together, and Mike pulled the truck from the curb and started back to the hill to reload.

By the time they got to the big ice storage house at the top of the hill, the rest at lunch had worn off and Mike was aware again of the burden of his body. He backed the truck to the edge of the platform. He waited with his tongs at the ramp while J. C. opened the heavy door and entered the icehouse. In a moment the helper backed out swiftly dragging the first four-hundred-pound block, his powerful back and big-muscled arms handling the ice easily.

Mike watched him and marveled at his strength and realized that even in his prime years he had perhaps not been as strong as J. C. Yet he still could have beaten him at work, because cutting and throwing the ice were like something he had been born to do, the main reason he had been put on earth. Now, like Chino said, it was too late. No good to hide in a dark bar and remember the way it used to be in sunlight. No good to hang with the ice and fall under weariness and age.

"Sometimes," Mike said, and there was a fierce edge to his voice, "I want to drag out that ice and cut it down and throw it as far as I can, throw it to hell and gone. I want to empty the big house once of every last block and scatter every last damn chunk over the hill. Make the fat man sit up. Make everyone understand that after forty years an iceman doesn't just lay down his pick and tongs with a goddam whimper."

J. C. paused and watched him silently for a long moment and then finally flashed his big white teeth.

"You too little to empty the big house," he said. "A little chewed-up runt like you can't do it alone. You need J. C. help to cut down the big house."

"Shove it," Mike hooted. "The only edge you got is a fat head and feet six sizes bigger than you need."

Together they put on the last blocks to make a full load. They climbed back into the cab, and Mike started the truck down the hill. Another truck passed them going up the hill to reload, and Noodles and Gomez waved from the cab.

In front of the dispatch office, Toby stood by the gas pumps waiting for them.

"Hot dog," J. C. said. "Run over the bastard!"

Mike stopped and braked beside the pumps and kept the motor idling. Toby looked up at him unsmiling, and as he stood there without the partial cover of his desk, the great rolls of fat hung upon his frame and made him appear rooted, like some shapeless and heavy-footed animal, to the earth. In that moment Mike was aware how unlike the icemen the fat man was. Where they were lean and quick, he was leaden and slow. Where they tried to sing in their work, he was angry with envy and reminded them it was a burden.

"You took a long time loading," Toby said.

J. C. shifted restlessly beside him, and Mike did not say a word but marveled suddenly how clearly he saw the place of the fat man in the passing of the ice.

"When you come back in," Toby said, "put any ice left into the big house. Don't let any ice sit overnight on the damn truck."

"OK," Mike said, and for a moment he pitied the fat man and his load.

That night in the darkness of their rooms Zeba moved closer to him in the bed, and her body soothed the pain that rioted through his bones. He felt the pressure of her full breasts against his arm, and he twisted in the bed, curling closer to her warmth.

"Sleep," she said, and her voice was soft and husky in the darkness. "Sleep, my old rooster, sleep."

He touched her, but there was no desire in his hands and no wish for her to respond. He wanted only to rest, to banish weariness and pain.

When he fell asleep, in a restless dream the first days of the ice returned. He saw again the great heaving horses pulling the dray, hauling the ice with block and tackle. He worked swiftly beside the wild young men and cut and threw, and then he stood alone. There was only the mournful face of Chino and in a mist the lost faces of the giants and over them all the cloud of Toby, soft and angry, waiting for him to fall and for the mountains of ice to crumble.

He moaned in his sleep and felt Zeba's fingers and dimly heard her comforting voice. He moved gratefully against her body and slipped again into fitful sleep.

In the beginning of September, the pain which had cramped his body through the summer eased up. He was not sure whether he felt less weary because of the shorter hours on the truck or the first clear, cool days. In the early twilight, driving back from icing at one of the depots, he sang loudly, and J. C. joined in, and the two of them bellowed over the roaring of the old motor. Later, as they unloaded the few remaining blocks into the big house, a great round and orange moon hung in the sky above the hill.

September was the time of year the drivers and helpers lingered in the locker room after punching out. A few more weeks would see most of them gone, so they talked of the journeys they would make, following the sun. They would recall the rumble of the freights and the small dark towns that swept by in the night and, finally, the great sweet orchards with the ripe fruit like little pieces of sunlight. They talked confidently of returning in the spring, and at those times Mike tried to convince himself that perhaps he and Chino were wrong. The winter would be quiet as it had always been, but in the spring the Hilifts would rock down the hill again. The dry cars with empty bunkers would stand in long trains. The young Blacks would come up from the South, and the husky gandy dancers would tumble in off the freights, and among them would be another Bungo or another Chino, and they would bring the mighty ice days back. Even as he told himself that story, he did not really believe it might be true.

There was a day near the end of September. His pain returned fiercely late in the afternoon as they iced dry potato cars at Dart Street. He stood for a moment uneasy and surprised. It had been weeks since he had felt it quite so sharply.

A little later, uncomfortable in his chest and stomach, he had to catch his breath, and on a car runway he let go his tongs and straightened up quickly, feeling a cramp knotting in his chest. The ice seemed to have become heavier through the afternoon, and by the time they finished their last car and were on their way in, empty, his arms and back felt stiff and raw. When he pulled up the hill and parked, Noodles and Gomez had just unloaded the few blocks of ice left on their truck into the big house, and the four of them walked together down the hill.

The locker room was thick with smoke and laughter and the jubilation of men leaving to eat and meet their women. Mike sat on a bench in the corner beside a paned window and rested his head against the wall. He wanted to wash and change to the clean shirt hanging in his locker, but suddenly he was far too tired for the effort that required. J. C. came over and shook his shoulder gently.

"C'mon, daddy," J. C. said. "Your lady is baking spareribs and I'm invited. You feel better after some of them ribs."

Noodles turned from his locker and laughed.

"Couple of pigeons picking for ribs," he said. "Old Noodles going picking for something else with more meat on it than them ribs." He winked broadly and flexed his muscles. "I seen a gal today," he said. "She come out of no place while we was icing and just stand and watch. Pretty gal with big eyes and hair like golden corn."

"Sheik," Gomez said. "Oh, sheik."

"I told her, honey," Noodles said, "honey, you need an iceman?"

"She was shaken with your hot charm," J. C. said. "I bet she took one look at you and fell right down under the wheels of your truck." He laughed down at Mike, who tried to smile against the stiffness in his cheeks and around his mouth.

"She told me—" Noodles said slowly. "She told me she got an electric icebox."

"Sheik," Gomez said, "tell them what you told her then."

"I told her"—Noodles grinned and slapped his leg—"I told that gal wasn't nothing better than hand icing by an iceman who knew his stuff."

"That's what he told her." Gomez shook his head and chuckled.

The room seemed unreal to Mike, the stiffness spreading to his arms and a slow pounding beginning in his head. Through the grimy glass of the window he could see the shadowed rows of frame houses further down the hill with their kitchens lit for supper. And far over the edge of the city the sun had left a strange red glint in the twilight.

"I could tell that gal was crazy about me," Noodles said. "She probably still there waiting for me."

"I had a gal crazy about me once," Sargent said. "Waited for me every night when I got off work. I borrowed two dollars, and we chased down a preacher. Now we got six kids waiting for me every night when I get off work."

Mike wanted to sleep. He felt suddenly that it would be comforting to be able to lay his head down on the bench and close his eyes and have J. C. and the young icemen close by.

"You all right?" J. C. said. "Daddy, you with me?"

The faces of the men around the room blurred, and in quick panic Mike struggled and recalled them and then lost them again. In sweeping darkness and without moving he seemed to be stretching for something just out of reach. A terrible heat suddenly blazed in his chest, and he wanted to cry out, but the wonder of what was happening kept him silent. He was torn by fear and a strange joy. In the moment of deciding which was stronger, the heat burst within him.

The voices of the men fell away and there was silence in the room. J. C. stood beside the bench, and Noodles came to his side.

"He's sleeping," Noodles said. "He just fell down asleep."

The others moved and gathered uncertainly around the bench.

"He's dead," Sargent said quietly. "I seen them in the army. I know the look. He's a dead man."

"You talk crazy!" Noodles snapped at him. "Old Mike just sleeping!"

"Goddam!" Sargent said savagely. "I know a dead man when I see one. Was you in the army and seen the dead piled up like me, you know too."

"Someone call a doctor," Gomez said in a shocked voice. "Someone better go for a doctor."

"He's dead." Sargent shook his head. "Doctor don't do no good for a dead man."

"Jesus Christ," Noodles said, and made a quick sign of the cross. "Jesus Christ."

For the first time J. C. moved and bent slightly to peer closely at Mike and straightened up and looked around at the circle of men with a stunned and terrible grief on his face.

"He was tired and just died," J. C. said. "He been an iceman a long time, and he got tired and he died."

The silence spread again, and no one moved. One of the men cleared his throat, and another shifted restlessly from one foot to the other.

"Phone the fat man," Sargent said. "Tell him to turn off that TV. Tell him an iceman died."

J. C. reached down and put his arms under Mike's back and legs and lifted his body. He held him easily against his chest. He left the locker room, and no one made a move to follow.

He carried the body to the top of the hill. Once or twice he stopped and for a moment stood unmoving beneath the dark sky pinned with a crescent moon. He started walking again toward the row of parked trucks, and bracing the body against his knees, he opened the cab of Mike's truck and slid him in upon the seat. He fumbled on the floor and found Mike's pick and tongs.

He crossed the hill and climbed the ladder to the big house's platform. He opened the heavy door and in the pale light of the moon saw the blocks of ice in glistening rows waiting to be loaded on the trucks in the morning.

He hooked his tongs on a block in the nearest row and dragged it swiftly through the door to the edge of the platform. He swung his pick and split the scored block. The chunks fell apart, and he switched back to tongs and caught up the chunks one after the other, and swinging them between his legs, flung the ice out into the darkness. When he had finished one block he went in and dragged out another and cut it down and again scattered the ice across the earth. He worked faster and faster, and shattered shavings of ice stung his cheeks. He kept dragging out the blocks and cutting them down and heaving the ice into the darkness. His breathing became hoarse and tight in his chest, and he cut desperately and threw more savagely. He dragged out block after block, throwing farther and farther, the chunks cracking against other chunks that littered the ground.

When the big house was empty, he stood for a moment on the platform, his lungs heaving for air, and then with a great and final fling he hurled the pick and tongs far out into the night.

He climbed down the ladder and walked through the field of broken ice back to the truck. In the cab he moved Mike's head gently to rest against his shoulder. He turned the key, and the motor roared like an animal coming awake. He wheeled the truck out of line and started down the hill to take Mike home.

This was my first published story, accepted by *The Atlantic* in December 1956 and published in their April 1957 issue. I had been writing and submitting stories unsuccessfully for ten years. That December, I was working in real estate sales and the prospects were bleak for my family's Christmas. I wired the great *Atlantic* editor Edward Weeks, who had been encouraging and supportive of my efforts for years, that they had been holding the story more than three months. They could take as much time as they needed, but if there was any good news, I would be grateful to hear from them before Christmas. Since it is not good practice to wire editors about one's stories, I never really expected an answer. But, a day later, Ted Weeks wired me back that they were taking the story as an *Atlantic* First. He added his congratulations and best wishes for a Merry Christmas.

The ten years I had been writing without publishing, from the age of twenty-two until thirty-two, were in some way redeemed for me in that moment when I received the wire. I felt like Lazarus. . . .

PERICLES ON 31ST STREET

Louie Debella's bar was located on the corner of 31st Street and Dart Avenue, the last store in a group of five stores owned by Leonard Barsevick, who besides being a landlord operated the Lark Wholesale Clothing Company across the street.

My name is George. My last name is not important. I'm Louie Debella's night bartender and I count myself a good bartender. I might mention a few of the quality places I have tended bar, but that has nothing to do with this story.

If I have learned anything from fifteen years of tending bar it is that a bartender cannot take sides with anything that goes on across the bar. He has got to be strictly nonpartisan. A cousin of mine in South Bend, also in the business, once tried to mediate an argument about Calvin Coolidge. Somebody hit him in the back of the head with a bottle of beer that was not yet empty, and besides needing stitches he got wet. Now when I am on the job I never take sides. That is, I never did until the episode of Pericles.

As I understand it this fellow Pericles was a Greek general and statesman who lived back in those Greek golden years you read about in the school history books. From all reports he was a pretty complete sort of guy who laid down a set of rules and was tough on everybody who did not read them right.

If you are wondering what a Greek who lived a couple of thousand years ago has got to do with this story, I guess it all started because the storekeepers in our row of stores gathered in the bar in the evening after they locked their doors for a glass of beer.

The first man in was usually Dan Ryan, who had the butcher shop. Ryan was a heavy beer man and needed the head start on the others. A little later Olaf Johnson, who ran the Sunlight lunchroom, came in with Sol Reidman the tailor. Olaf had a huge belly that was impossible to keep under a coat. Sol liked nothing better than to tease Olaf about when the triplets were expected.

The last man in was Bernard Klioris, who had a little grocery next to Sol's tailor shop. Bernard usually got lost in the arguments, and swung back and forth like a kitchen door in a restaurant. He had a sad thin face and was not so bright, but among our patrons you could hardly tell.

Last Tuesday night after I had served Ryan his fourth beer, Olaf and Sol and Bernard came in together, with Olaf and Sol arguing as usual.

"She told me she was a Republican," Olaf said. "They want some lunk for Congress. I told her to come by you and get her petition signed."

Sol waggled his bald head indignantly. "Who gave you leave to advertise my business?" he said. "A man's politics is a sacred trust that belongs to him alone."

"She only had a petition, not a gun," Olaf said. "I knew you was a Republican so I sent her."

"How can anyone," Ryan said from the bar, "be in his right mind and still be a Republican?"

Sol waved a warning finger. "Be careful," he said. "You are stepping on the Constitution when you ridicule a man's politics."

"I read about the Constitution," Bernard said.

They lined up at the bar. I poured them beer. All they ever drank was beer.

The door opened and Nick Simonakis came in. He was the vendor who took his stand at night on the corner of 31st and Dart. He had a glassed-in wagon that he pushed into place under the street lamp, and from the wagon he sold hot dogs and tamales and peanuts. Several times during the evening he locked up the wagon and came into the bar for a glass of wine. He would sit alone at a table to the side of the room, his dark eyes in his hollow-cheeked face glaring at the room from above the white handlebar mustache. Every now and then he would sip his wine and shake his head, making his thick white hair hang more disordered over his forehead.

Other men might have thought he was a little crazy because sometimes he sat there alone talking to himself, but like I said, I do not take sides. At other times he gave up muttering and loudly berated the drinkers of beer. "Only Turks would drink beer," he said, "when they could drink wine. One for the belly and the other for wisdom." He would sip his wine slowly, mocking their guzzling of beer, and the storekeepers would try to ignore him.

"The sun-ripened grapes," Simonakis said, "hanging until they become sweet. Then the trampling by the young maidens to extract the lovely juices. A ceremony of the earth."

"Beer don't just grow in barrels," Olaf said. "Good beer takes a lot of making."

The old man laughed softly as if he was amused. "You are a Turk," he said. "I excuse you because you think and talk like a Turk."

"Say, old man," Sol said. "Someone wants a bag of peanuts. You are losing business."

Simonakis looked at Sol with bright piercing eyes. "I will lose business," he said. "I am drinking my wine."

"He must be rich," Ryan said, "and pushing business away. I wish I had gone into peddling peanuts myself."

"It is not a case of wealth," Simonakis said. "There is a time for labor and a time for leisure. A man must have time to sit and think. This made Greece great."

"Made who what?" Olaf asked with sarcasm.

The old man swept him with contempt. "In ancient Greece," he said coldly, "an elephant like you would have been packed on a mountaintop as bait for buzzards."

"Watch the language," Olaf said. "I don't have to take that stuff from an old goat like you."

"A land of ruined temples," Sol said, and he moved from the bar and carried his beer to a nearby table. "A land of philosophers without shoes."

"A land of men!" Simonakis spit out. "We gave the world learning and courage. We taught men how to live and how to die."

Ryan and Bernard and Olaf had followed Sol to the table, drawing their chairs.

"Would you mind, old man," Ryan said as he sat down, "leaving a little bit of credit to the Irish?"

"I give them credit," Simonakis said, "for inventing the wheelbarrow, and giving the world men to push it."

"Did you hear that!" Ryan said indignantly and looked fiercely at the old man.

The old man went on as if he had not heard. "A model of courage for the world," he said. "Leonidas with three hundred men holding the pass at Thermopylae against the Persian hordes. Themistocles destroying the great fleet of Xerxes at Salamis."

"That's history," Olaf said. "What have they done lately?"

Simonakis ignored him. He motioned to me and I took him the bottle of port. He raised the full glass and held it up and spoke in Greek to the wine as if performing some kind of ceremony. The men watched him and somebody laughed. Simonakis glared at them. "Laugh, barbarians," he said. "Laugh and forget your debt to Greece. Forget the golden age and the men like lions. Hide in your smoking cities and drown in your stinking beer."

"What a goat," Olaf said.

Sol shook his head sadly. "It is a pity to see a man ruined by drink," he said. "That wine he waves has soaked his head."

"Wheelbarrow indeed," Ryan said, and he glared back at the old man.

2

At that moment the front door opened and Leonard Barsevick, the landlord, walked in. He carried an air of elegance into the bar. Maybe because of his Homburg and the black chesterfield coat he wore.

The storekeepers greeted him in a respectful chorus. He waved his hand around like a politician at a beer rally and smiled broadly. "Evening, boys," he said. "Only got a few minutes but I couldn't pass by without stopping to buy a few of my tenants a beer. George, set up the drinks and mark it on my tab."

"Thank you, Mr. Barsevick," Olaf said. "You sure look like a million bucks tonight."

Barsevick laughed and looked pleased. "Got to keep up a front, Olaf," he said. "If a man in my position gets a spot on his suit he might as well give up."

"That's right, Mr. Barsevick," Ryan said. "A man in your position has got to keep up with the best and you sure do."

"Say, Mr. Barsevick," Bernard said. "You know the leak in the roof at my store I spoke to you about last month. It hasn't been fixed yet and that rain the other night . . ."

"Wait a minute, Bernie," Barsevick laughed. "Not tonight. If I promised to fix it, I'm going to have it fixed. Leonard Barsevick is a man of his word. Ain't that right, boys?"

They all nodded and Olaf said, "Yes, sir," emphatically.

"But not tonight," Barsevick said. "Tonight I'm out for a little relaxation with a baby doll that looks like Jayne Mansfield." He made a suggestive noise with his mouth.

"You're sure a lucky man, Mr. Barsevick," Olaf said admiringly.

"Not luck at all, Olaf," Barsevick said, and his voice took on a tone of serious confidence. "It's perseverance and the ability to get along with people. I always say if I didn't know how to get along with people I wouldn't be where I am today."

"That's sure right, Mr. Barsevick," Ryan said. The others nodded agreement.

"Fine," Barsevick beamed. "All right, boys, drink up, and pass your best wishes to Leonard Barsevick for a successful evening." He winked broadly.

The storekeepers laughed and raised their glasses. Everybody toasted Barsevick but Simonakis. He sat scowling at the landlord from beneath his shaggy brows. Barsevick noticed him.

"You didn't give this gentleman a drink, George," he said. "What are you drinking, sir?"

"He ain't no gentleman," Olaf said. "He is a peanut peddler."

"An authority on wheelbarrows," Ryan said.

Simonakis cocked a thumb at Barsevick. "Hurry, landlord," he said, "your Mansfield is waiting."

Barsevick gave him a cool glance, but the old man just looked bored. Finally the landlord gave up and turned away, pulling on his suede gloves. He strode to the door cutting a fancy figure and waved grandly. "Good night, boys," he said.

The boys wished him good night. Simonakis belched.

3

On the following Thursday the notices came from Barsevick's bookkeeper announcing a fifteen per cent rent increase all along the block. All the storekeepers got a notice of the raise becoming effective with the expiration of their leases about a month away. Louie was so disturbed he called me down in the middle of the afternoon and took off early.

That night the storekeepers were a sad bunch. They sat around the table over their beer, looking like their visas had expired.

"I don't understand it," Ryan said. "Mr. Barsevick knows that business has not been good. Fifteen per cent at this time makes for an awful load."

"With license fees and the rest," Olaf said, "a lunchroom ain't hardly worth while. I was not making nothing before. With this increase it ain't going to get no better."

"Two hands to sew pants will not be enough," Sol said. "I must sew with four hands, all my own."

Bernard looked distressed. "Mr. Barsevick must have a good reason," he said.

"He's got expenses," Olaf said.

"He should have mine," Ryan said. "Beef is up six cents a pound again."

Simonakis came into the bar pulling off his gloves. He ignored the men as he walked by them to his table against the wall and signaled to me for his bottle of wine.

"I am going to buy a wagon," Olaf said loudly, "and sell peanuts and hot dogs on the street."

"You must first," Simonakis said, "have the wisdom to tell them apart."

Olaf flushed and started to get up. Sol shook him down. "No time for games with crazy men tonight," Sol said. "This matter is serious. We must organize a delegation to speak to Mr. Barsevick. It must be explained that this increase imposes a terrible burden on us at this time. Perhaps a little later."

"Shoot him," Simonakis said. He waved the glass I had just filled with dark wine.

"You mind your own business, peddler," Ryan said. "Nobody is talking to you."

"A Greek would shoot him," Simonakis said. "But you are toads."

"I get my rent raised," Olaf said, "and now I got to sit here and be insulted by a peanut peddler."

The front door opened and the room went quiet.

Barsevick closed the door softly behind him and walked over to the storekeepers' table. He pulled up a chair and sat down like a sympathetic friend coming to share their grief.

I guess they were all surprised as I was and for a long moment no one spoke and Barsevick looked solemnly from one to the other. "I hope you do not mind my butting in, boys," he said and he motioned to me. "George, bring the boys a round on me."

"Mr. Barsevick," Ryan said, "the boys and me were just discussing. . ."

Barsevick raised his hand gravely. "I know, Danny," he said. "I know what you are going to say. I want to go on record first as saying there is nobody any sorrier than Leonard Barsevick about this. That is why I am here. My bookkeeper said I did not have to come over tonight and talk to you. I told him I would not stand for that, that you boys were not just tenants, you were friends of mine."

"It is a lot of money, Mr. Barsevick," Olaf said. "I mean if we were making more, things might be different."

"I know that, Olaf," Barsevick said. "Believe me, if there was any other way I would jump at the chance. I said to Jack, my bookkeeper, 'Isn't there any other way?' I swear to you boys he said, 'Mr. Barsevick, if that rent is not increased it will be charity.'"I brought the tray of fresh beer and set the glasses around the table. "Not that I mind a little help to my friends," Barsevick said, "but it is not good business. I would be ashamed before my competitors. 'There's Barsevick,' they would laugh, 'too soft to raise his tenants' rent.' They would put the screws on me and in no time at all I might be out of business."

Everybody was silent for a moment, probably examining the prospect of Leonard Barsevick put out of business because of his soft heart.

"We know you got expenses," Ryan said.

Barsevick shook his head mournfully. "You got no idea," he said. "I mean you boys got no idea. I am afraid sometimes for the whole economy. Costs cannot keep rising and still keep the country sound. Everything is going up. Believe me, boys, being a landlord and a businessman is hell."

"Shoot him," Simonakis said loudly.

Barsevick stopped talking and looked across the tables at the old man.

"He is a crazy man," Sol said. "That wine he drinks makes him talk to himself."

Barsevick turned back to the men but he was disturbed. He looked over at the old man once more like he was trying to understand and then started to get up. "I got to go now, boys," he said. "I'm working late tonight with my bookkeeper. If we see any other way to cut costs I will be glad to reconsider the matter of the increase. That is my promise to you boys as friends."

"We sure appreciate you stopping by, Mr. Barsevick," Ryan said. "We know there is many a landlord would not have bothered."

Barsevick shook his head vigorously. "Not Leonard Barsevick," he said. "Not even his worst enemy will say that Barsevick does not cut a straight corner when it comes to friends."

"We know that, Mr. Barsevick," Olaf said.

"We sure do," Bernard said.

"Shoot him," Simonakis said. "Shoot him before he gets away."

4

Barsevick whirled around and stared in some kind of shock at the old man. I guess he was trying very fast to figure out if the old man was serious.

"Don't pay him no mind, Mr. Barsevick," Olaf said. "He has been out in the rain too long."

"You are a demagogue." Simonakis spoke loudly to the landlord. "You wave your greedy fingers and tell them you are a friend. Aaaaaaaaa!" The old man smiled craftily. "I know your kind. In Athens they would tie you under a bull."

Barsevick stood there like rocks were being bounced off his head, his face turning a bright shade of red.

Sol motioned angrily at the old man. "Somebody wants a hot dog," he said. "You are losing business."

Simonakis looked at Sol for a moment with his mustache bristling, then looked at the others. "I have lost business," he said slowly. "You have lost courage."

A sound of hissing came from Barsevick, his red cheeks shaking off heat like a capped kettle trying to let off steam. "You goddam pig," he said huskily. "You unwashed old bum. You damn peddler of peanuts."

The old man would not give an inch. "You are a hypocrite," he said. "A hypocrite and a libertine. You live on the sweat of better men."

Barsevick's jaw was working furiously like he was trying to chew up the right words.

"Let me tell you," Simonakis said, and his voice took on a more moderate tone as if he were pleased to be able to pass information on to the landlord, "let me tell you how the hypocrite goes in the end. One day the people wake up. They know he is a liar and a thief. They pick up stones. They aim for his head." He pointed a big long finger at Barsevick and made a rattling sound rise from his throat. "What a mess a big head like yours would make."

Barsevick gasped and whirled to the men at the table. "He's threatening me," he shouted. "Did you hear him? Throw the old bastard out."

No one moved. I kept wiping glasses. A good bartender learns to keep working.

"Did you hear me!" Barsevick yelled. "Somebody throw him out."

"He is a crazy old man," Sol said. "He talks without meaning."

"Shut up!" Barsevick said. "You stick with him because you are no damn good either."

"I do not stick with him," Sol said, and he drew himself up hurt. "I am trying to be fair."

Barsevick turned to me. "George, throw him out!"

I kept wiping the glasses. "I am underpaid, Mr. Barsevick," I said. "My salary barely covers my work. Any extra service would be charity."

The old man took after him again. "Who likes you, landlord?" he said. "Be honest and speak truth before your tenants. Who likes you?"

"You shut up!" Barsevick shouted.

"I mean really likes you," Simonakis said. "I do not mean the poor girls you buy with your tainted money."

"I'll shut the old bastard up!" Barsevick hollered and started for the table against the wall.

Simonakis stood up and Barsevick stopped. The old man looked tall and menacing with his big hands and bright eyes and his white mustache standing out like a joyous challenge to battle. "You cannot shut up truth," Simonakis said. "And the truth is that you are a leech feeding on the labor of better men. You wish to become rich by making them poorer."

Barsevick stood a couple of tables away from the old man with his back bent a little waiting for a word to be raised in his defense. No one spoke and the old man stared at him with eyes like knives.

"You old bastard . . ." Barsevick said weakly.

Ryan made a sound clearing his throat. He wore a stern and studied look on his face. "Fifteen per cent is a steep raise," he said. "Right at this time when it is tough to make ends meet."

Barsevick whirled on him. "You keep out of this," he said. "You just mind your own business."

"I would say," Ryan said slowly, "fifteen per cent more rent to pay each month is my business."

"I'll make it twenty-five per cent," Barsevick shouted. "If you don't like it you can get out!"

"I have a lease," Ryan said quietly. He was looking at the landlord like he was seeing him for the first time.

"I will break it," Barsevick said. He looked angrily around at the other storekeepers. "I will break all your leases."

"I did not say nothing!" Bernard protested.

"The way of tyrants and thieves," Simonakis said. "All who oppose them suffer." He raised his head and fixed his eyes upon the ceiling. "O Pericles, lend us a stick so we may drive the tyrant from the market place."

"Stop calling me a tyrant," Barsevick fumed.

Simonakis kept his head raised praying to that guy Pericles.

"I'm going to put every one of you into the street," Barsevick said. "I'm going to teach you all not to be so damn smart."

Sol shook his head with measured contempt for the landlord on his face. "You will not put us out," he said. "First, you are too greedy for the rent. Second, you would not rent those leaking barns again without major repairs, and third . . ." He paused. "Third, I do not admire your personality."

"Amen," Bernard said. "My roof keeps leaking."

"O Pericles!" Simonakis suddenly cried out and everybody looked at him. "They are barbarians and not of Athens but they are honest men and need your help. Give them strength to destroy the common enemy. Lend them your courage to sweep out the tyrant."

"You are all crazy," Barsevick said and he looked driven and disordered. His tie was outside his coat and the Homburg perched lopsided over one ear.

"You are a tiger," Sol said. "Tell me what circus you live in and I will rent a cage to take you home."

"Do not be insulting," Ryan said to Sol. "You will hurt the landlord's feelings. He cannot help he has got a head like a loin of pork."

"You ignorant bastards!" Barsevick shouted.

Ryan got up and came over to the bar. He stepped behind and pulled out the little sawed-off bat Louie kept under the counter. He winked at me. "I am just borrowing it," he said. "I want to put a new crease in the landlord's hat."

Simonakis came back from calling on Pericles. "Do not strike him," he said. "Stone him. Stone him as they stoned tyrants in Athens." He looked at the floor and around the room excitedly searching for stones.

Barsevick in full retreat began to edge toward the door. He opened his mouth to try and speak some final word of defiance but one look at the bat in Ryan's hands must have choked off his wind.

"Tyrant!" Simonakis shouted.

"Vulture!" Olaf said. "Stop and eat on me, and I'll grind some glass for your salad!"

"Greedy pig!" Ryan said, and he waved the bat. "You try and collect that rent and we all move out!"

"Judas!" Sol said. "Come to me only to sew your shroud!"

"Fix my leaking roof!" Bernard said.

With one last helpless wail, Barsevick stumbled out through the door.

For a long moment after the door closed nobody moved. Then Ryan handed me back the bat. I put it under the counter. Olaf started to the bar with his glass. Bernard came after him. Soon all were lined up at the bar. All except Simonakis, who had gone back to sit down at his table staring moodily into his glass of wine.

Ryan turned his back to the bar and looked across the tables at Simonakis. He looked at him for a long time and no one spoke. The old man kept staring at his wine. Ryan looked back helplessly at Olaf and Sol and they watched him struggling. Bernard looked dazed. I held a wet towel in my hands and forgot to wipe the bar. When Ryan finally turned back to Simonakis, you could see he had made up his mind. He spoke slowly and carefully.

"Mr. Simonakis," he said.

The old man raised his head scowling.

"Mr. Simonakis," Ryan said. "Will you be kind enough to join my friends and me in a drink?"

The old man stopped scowling. He nodded gravely and stood up tall and straight, his mustache curved in dignity, and came to the bar. Ryan moved aside to make a place for him.

I began to pour the beer.

"No, George," Ryan said. "We will have wine this trip."

"Yes, sir," I said.

I took down the port and filled a row of small glasses.

Ryan raised his glass and looked belligerently at the others. "To the glory of Greece," he said.

The rest of them raised their glasses.

"To Athens," Sol said.

"To Mr. Simonakis," Olaf said.

"Ditto," Bernard said.

I took down another wineglass. I poured myself some wine. They all looked at me. I did not care I was abandoning a professional tradition of neutrality.

"To Pericles," I said.

Simonakis stroked his mustache and sipped his wine. The rest of us sipped right with him.

This was a painful story for me to reread, reminding me of a period in my life when everything seemed unfocused and unbalanced, when love aborted and helplessness wielded power.

Yet even in such bleak intervals a writer has a recourse denied most other human beings. By refashioning the memories of suffering into fiction, he lyricizes and softens them and, in this way, renders the pain a shade more bearable.

HOMECOMING

On the way into the city, Alex picked up a hitchhiker, a seedy youth about nineteen or twenty with long, thick hair and shaggy sideburns. He wore a faded leather jacket and carried a worn duffel bag.

They rode in silence for a while, Alex thinking about seeing Miriam again after almost three years. The youth stared out of the window. They entered the perimeter of the city, the highway burgeoning through a landscape of small shacks and stunted houses, wrecked and partially dismantled cars littering the weed-tangled yards.

"You live in Chicago?" Alex asked.

The youth shook his head.

"I'm catching a bus for San Francisco," he said.

"Got a job there?"

The youth was silent for a moment and then he turned and looked at Alex.

"I'm 1 A," he said. "I'm going to refuse induction. I heard the judges in Frisco give lighter jail sentences."

The words were spoken with such finality there seemed nothing to add. Alex nodded and didn't speak. The houses began to cluster more thickly on the land, old frame dwellings with decrepit, unpainted porches. Here and there a few solitary trees with tinted leaves formed a bright fresco of autumn.

"I was in Korea," Alex said. "No war makes sense. But I wouldn't have had the guts then to do what you're doing now."

"If you had," the youth spoke quietly without turning his head, "maybe we wouldn't have to go through this now."

"Maybe you're right," Alex shrugged wryly. "Seems so long ago I can't remember what I felt like then."

They rode in silence again along one of the expressways tracking into the heart of the city. The roofs of buildings gleamed below, their windows masked and blurred, concealing the men and women who lived inside. Only when they descended a ramp to the street did the inhabitants suddenly become visible. Alex dropped the youth a block from the bus depot.

"Good luck," Alex said.

"Thanks," the youth said. "Thanks for the lift too."

The light changed and Alex drove off. In the rearview mirror he saw the youth crossing the street against the light, the duffel bag bouncing against his leg as he walked with a certain and defiant stride.

The midday sun, waning with the glitter of October, shone across the expanse of Grant Park as he turned onto the outer drive and followed the curve of the lake. A boy and girl sat close together on one of the slopes of grass. He recalled the spring morning three years before when he and Miriam had lain against one of the same slopes, feeling the scales of winter peeling from their flesh. In the jubilation of the season and the sun they had danced a wild abandoned little dance together, an old man on a bench a hundred feet away staring at them as if they were mad.

Afterwards Alex kissed her and tasted on her lips the sweetness of the orange juice they had drunk a while before. Then, wordlessly, possessed by desire, they had hurried to the car and driven to her apartment a few miles away to make love.

The white caps of breakers rode the waves toward the shore. He felt a curious surge of hope, unlike the resignation he had endured driving across the country. He knew even before he had started, the probable futility of any effort to recover the love he and Miriam once had. But he had come doggedly anyway, driving instead of flying, preparing his words and at the same time perhaps delaying the foundering of the dream. Now, suddenly, between the surf and the sky he was no longer convinced he would fail.

Miriam had moved from her apartment to another place but she still worked for the same agency. He had phoned her from California on the day he left but when the operator rang her department he panicked and hung up, afraid she'd tell him not to come.

He pulled over to a wayside telephone and got out and dialed the number. A woman in her department told him Miriam was still out to lunch. He left no message and hung up.

He thought of waiting downtown on the chance she might leave work to see him before the end of the day. He knew that was unlikely and then, despondently, he decided to go and see his mother.

He followed the drive south and turned off at 67th Street. A few blocks later he pulled up before his sister and brother-in-law's house, a narrow, high stucco dwelling, a few sparse evergreens before the porch, the grass in need of cutting. As he emerged from the car a cluster of small black children on the porch next door fell silent and stared somberly at him. He waved to them, smiling, and one boy of about four started to wave back. An older girl snapped him as immobile as a tiny ebony statue.

He crossed the walk and ascended the stairs, bracing himself for the meeting with his mother whom he had not seen in the three years since his departure. In one of the few letters exchanged with his sister, she had told him the old lady was failing, senility, illness and old age combining to push her closer to death. In the last letter his mother had written him herself he could barely decipher her illegible scrawl.

He stood for a moment before the front door, seeing through the sheer curtains into the hallway and the small kitchen beyond. He recognized his mother's short, stocky body sitting at the kitchen table, bent over tea or a bowl of soup. He felt a strange cracking of the shell of the past, remembering all the times he had stood before this door and in the instant before inserting his key in the lock, seeing her at the table in the kitchen.

He rang the bell. He watched her head turn slightly, and then, slowly, heavily, she rose. She came shuffling toward the door, one shoulder lowered slightly because of the arthritis in her arm. He saw her fingers fumbling to pull aside the curtain and he bent toward the rim of the glass. She could not discern him clearly, continuing to peer fearfully through the window.

"Mama," he said loudly. "It's Alex. Alex."

He saw the tremor sweep her cheeks and she flung both hands toward the knob of the door. She struggled and tugged, unable to coordinate her fingers. He heard her crying out his name and, finally, she jerked the door open. For one spectral and horrible moment he saw how she had changed. Then he bent and embraced her, and that peculiar, indefinable odor he remembered from childhood, an odor of spice locked in a container a long time and when finally opened, mingling pungence with a thin asthenic staleness.

They sat in the small parlor, side by side on the old worn sofa, the afternoon sun raising a wraithlike mist in the corners of the room. She clutched one of his hands between her thin-fleshed fingers. Whenever he looked at the ravages of illness and age marking her face he felt compelled to turn away.

"Your sister and Chester are both gone in the morning before I wake up," she said in a soft plaintive voice. "Before I open my eyes I hear the emptiness of the house and know I got to be alone all the day till they come home at night. I pray to God, then, for him to let me die."

"Don't you have coffee with the neighbors anymore? What about Mrs. Garfakis?"

"She moved with her son to Glencoe," his mother said. "A lot of people are moving now. The Felton house next door was sold to colored about six months ago. Pretty soon the whole neighborhood will be black."

"They got to live someplace."

"They don't bother me," his mother said. "They wouldn't bother with an old lady. I stay in the house and keep the doors locked. But Chester worries about your sister." She paused and stared at him with her eyes frightened and pleading for reassurance. "Do I look very bad?" she asked slowly and raised her hand in a feeble, mournful gesture to her cheek.

For a moment they sat in silence. He was forced to look without flinching at the dark, withered lips, the webbed, ashen cheeks, the pulp of flesh at her throat. He searched her eyes for a vestige of the vigor he remembered but saw only the querulous lids, the pupils peering in terror from the prison of her body.

"Your hair is whiter," he said, "but you look fine."

She shook her head.

"I'm not well," she said drearily. "I can't eat anymore and can't hardly walk."

"Chester still at the mills?" he asked to divert her attention from herself.

"He's doing what he'll always be doing," his mother said. "Working in the mills and with your sister entering contests to win new cars and washing machines and t.v. sets. When they come home they eat and watch some t.v. and go to bed. They don't have a dozen words to say to each other or to me."

He recalled the lean and weary frame of his sister and the stolid, gentle man she had married. In the years he had lived with them he marveled at the unchanging pattern of their days, work, food, sleep, television, and occasionally, love. From his attic room early in the morning he could hear the creaking of the springs of their bed in the room below, his sister's muted moanings and sometimes a single hoarse cry from Chester. Only in their moment of union did he hear either of them utter a cry to indicate they were alive.

He felt an urgency suddenly to leave, get out into the air, abandon the tight, dismal house as he had fled from it three years before. He rose and his mother reached up to him with a spasm of anguish.

"Not yet!" she pleaded. "Don't leave yet, Alex!"

"Listen, Mama," he said gently. "I've got some important business, one of the reasons I came to town. But I'll be back first thing in the morning."

"I've got some bologna and cheese," she said. "Have a sandwich first and Chester has beer in the icebox."

"I can't now, really, Mama," he said. "I've got to go."

She looked up at him with her naked, glistening eyes. "There are vesper services at church tonight, son," she said. "I don't get to church much anymore. Marika and Chester sleep late Sunday mornings and I can't stand on my feet too long anyway. Can you take me to church tonight?"

He started to refuse, thinking of Miriam, and then his mother's wretched face muted his rejection.

"If the meetings finish early," he said, "and I can get away, I'll take you to church."

"Services start at eight o'clock," she said. "But if we're a little late, it's all right."

"Okay, Mama," he started restlessly for the door. When his hand touched the knob he heard her voice, thin and in the grip of some nameless fear.

"Alex?"

"Yes, Mama?"

"You try, my boy. You try to come and take me to church."

"I'll try, Mama."

He drove back downtown, anxious suddenly and impatient. He parked the car and walked to the small bar a block from Miriam's office where the two of them used to meet. He had a couple of drinks and about four o'clock he phoned her office. He waited in turbulence while someone called her.

"Yes?" Her tone was pleasant and unsuspecting.

"Miriam, it's Alex."

There was a moment of startled silence.

"How are you, Alex?" He sensed her wariness.

"I'm fine," he said. "I'm just passing through town on business and thought I'd call. How are you?"

"Oh, I'm fine," she said.

He heard a voice close to her raised in inquiry and she muffled the phone for a moment and answered. He heard the receiver moved back to her ear.

"Miriam," he spoke her name with a sudden urgency. "I'm at the Zebra down on Michigan. Remember? I wanted to see you, talk to you for a few moments. Can you come over after work?"

"Oh, I'm sorry," she said. "I can't, Alex. Some of us are going out to dinner tonight. I've got to hurry home and dress."

"Listen, Miriam," he said, and felt his throat harsh and dry. "If you could come down for just a few moments . . ."

"No, I . . ." he heard an irritation and hardness enter her voice.

"I've got to leave late tonight," he said. "Just one drink, please."

Someone in the office spoke to her again and she left the phone. He waited in a growing unrest until she returned.

"All right," she said. "I'll be down a few minutes after five. Just one drink."

"One drink," he said, and felt a leaping in his blood because he was going to see her again. He held the phone tightly in his fingers long after she had hung up.

He went back to the shadowed booth and drank a third scotch, feeling his spirit reinforced. He fashioned an eloquent structure of words to tell her why he wanted and needed her.

At five o'clock the door opened, letting in a burst of light, and he tensed. Two secretaries entered, laughing and excited, their miniskirted legs visible for an instant before the door closed. He signaled to the waitress to bring him another drink.

He tried to sort out the memories, the months that he recalled now with nostalgia. Those nights when he'd knock on her apartment door and she opened the door on the chain and peeked out at him, her short taffy-colored hair framing her adorable face.

It's your lover, he would say.

I have no lover, she would say. My husband and five children are asleep. Go away.

I promise not to wake them, he would say. Let me in and I'll give you a present.

What present, she would say.

My hands and my lips, he would say, my body and my heart.

My darling, she would say, and she'd open the door and he'd walk in and they'd embrace, their bodies pressed tightly against one another.

They would eat dinner together, the juicy steaks and the sparkling wine, the two of them seated across from one another at her small table, laughing, touching each other with their eyes, the wine glistening wetly on her lips.

She'd laugh and in a great torrent of words would tell him the events of her day, with the magic to make something special of each ordinary occurence. She'd use her hands and body and eyes to pantomime the scenes. And he had to laugh with her laughter that came deep from her slender body. Afterwards she'd come and sit on his lap and rest her cheek against his cheek and whisper her words of love.

"Alex?"

He looked up with a start and Miriam stood beside the booth. He started to rise and nearly upset his glass.

"I'm sorry," he said. "I was daydreaming. Sit down, Miriam. I'll get the waitress."

"I don't really want a drink," she said and she sat down in the booth across from him. "Let's just talk a few moments."

He stared at her face, seeing the remembered brightness of her eyes even in the shadows, the fine sensual curve of her lips.

"You're still lovely, Miriam," he said.

She stirred restlessly and looked down at the table for an instant. Then she looked back at him.

"How are you, Alex?" she said."

"I'm okay," he said. "I'm just in, like I told you, for a little while. I stopped by and saw my mother and thought I'd give you a ring."

"That's fine," she said.

The front door opened and several men and girls entered, filling the bar with their shrill and boisterous voices. Miriam looked after them as they slipped into booths across the way.

"Did you get my letters?" he asked.

She looked at him surprised.

"No," she said. "Did you write?"

"No," he said. "I started letters many times and never could put down what I wanted to say. I decided finally I had to come and tell you myself."

She looked down for a moment at her hands, the marvelously gentle hands that made every touch seem a kind of caress.

"It was just as well you didn't write," she said. "There wasn't anything really to say."

"Are you sure?"

There was an instant of strained silence.

"Listen, Alex," she said quietly. "Let's not suffer through one of those nostalgic here-we-are-once-again reunions between old lovers. I'll always be grateful to you. The year we had together was one of the loveliest of my life. But it's over now. The way you wanted it over three years ago."

"I didn't want it over, Miriam," he said. "Not really. But there were all the other things. My mother waiting for me to marry so she could live with us. You don't know what that would have been like. I lived with her and my sister for the ten years after my father died. It got so I couldn't breathe. I had to get away and think things out."

"Whatever the reason," she said. "It's over. Let's just talk for a little while now as old friends."

"Are you happy, Miriam?" he asked.

She laughed her melodic little laugh.

"Dear Alex," she said. "Have you come back to salvage me from misery and spinsterhood?"

"I didn't mean it that way," he said, and felt his face flushed.

"I know you didn't," she said gently. "And I didn't mean to sound cynical. I was miserable and unhappy for a long time after you left.

I cried a lot waiting for the phone to ring or for the mail to bring a letter from you. Little by little I began to mend the broken seams of my life."

"Are there different boyfriends or just one?"

"For the last year, just one," she said. "It's not the way it was with you and me, not nearly as crazy and wild. But he's good and gentle and loves me very much. And I love him."

"Do you, Miriam?" he heard the harsh urgency in his voice and was ashamed.

"Yes," she answered quietly. "I love him very much. I know what you're thinking. All the times we told one another that our love would endure forever. But that kind of love exists only in the poems of lovers. Most of us have to make an accommodation with loneliness and with life."

"Does he bring in your tree on Christmas Eve?" he asked. "Do you trim it together with the ornaments we bought? And do you sit in the glow of the lights and drink Lancer's wine from the little long stemmed glasses?"

"It's almost like that," she said calmly. "But not the same." She sat back in the booth, her head erect, watching him.

He was conscious suddenly that the bar had filled, all the stools taken by shadowed forms, a surging clamor of voices and laughter sweeping the room.

"Have you found anybody else?" she asked.

"There have been a few girls," he said. "No one I care about." No one I loved as I loved you, he wanted to say.

"It's good to have someone you really care about," she said. "You know the way I am. I need someone." She raised her arm to look at her watch. "Listen, Alex," she said. "I've really got to go. I'll be late."

"Go ahead," he said.

She started to rise and then stopped and slowly sat down again.

"Don't be angry," she said gently. "If I could stay longer, I would, for a little while anyway. We could have a few drinks together and share all the old memories. But it really doesn't make any sense."

"Nothing much does these days," he said.

"That's true," she said, her voice low and suddenly somber. "When they murdered Bobby Kennedy too, I cried not only for him but for all of us."

"I've felt like that lately," he said. "Nothing makes much sense. I feel that I'm drifting with no port in sight. Because I can't seem to look ahead I think I've begun to look back."

She was silent for a long moment and he had a curious sense of a period being placed carefully at the end of a page he had kept without punctuation.

"I'm sorry," she said. "Alex, I'm sorry. I have to go."

She rose slowly to her feet. He rose to stand beside her.

"That's all right," he said, and shrugged wryly. "Are you going to marry this fellow?"

"We talk about it once in a while," she said. "Neither of us feel anything urgent about it. We live in the same building, different apartments on the same floor. We can be together, and alone when we want to be."

"Convenient," he said. "I had to drive for miles."

She smiled. "You slept over many nights," she said.

"You cooked fine eggs for breakfast," he said.

She laughed. "You mean burned fine eggs. I was a terrible cook and I'm not much better now."

She put out her small, slim-boned hand.

"Goodby, Alex," she said. "When you're back in the city again, phone me and maybe you and Paul and I can have a drink together." She paused. "I've told him about you. I think you'd like him too."

"I'll phone next time," he said.

She hesitated and then she laughed.

"I was going to kiss you," she said. "But it seems foolish. We've shared so many wonderful kisses, you and I, what use is a little peck in public?"

He smiled against the stiffness in his cheeks. "I'll reach into my memories and pick one more fitting," he said.

She reached out and touched his arm in a fleeting, soft caress. Afterwards she turned and walked to the door, holding her lovely head as high and proud as she always walked. He was reminded of the young hitchhiker of that morning, the same calm, certain step. They both accept life, he thought, and I retreat from it.

The door opened and he saw the glitter of the setting sun mantle her head. He felt an urgent longing to run after her, to cry out that he had returned because he still loved her, still needed her. Instead, he walked unsteadily to the men's room, past the stools and booths filled with laughing, drinking men and girls.

The interior of the church glistened with candles, the air drifting slow and warm scents of incense and melting wax. The priest in his gold and brocaded vestments stood before the altar and raised his long pale fingers toward the cross of Christ.

Alex looked down at the bent figure of his mother standing beside him, a twisted form that might have been carved from the trunk of a gnarled tree. She pressed her hands tightly against the railing before them.

In the pews around them he recognized men and women he knew, looking older, more resigned. He had a strange feeling of the years falling away, standing in the church between his mother and father, memories of coffins closed, candles flickering, elegiac chants, and the sweet taste of communion wine.

The choirmaster's voice rang somberly across the church, the chorus of girl's voices following behind. The priest turned and motioned for the congregation to be seated. His mother leaned against him, her hand gripping his arm for support, and lowered herself slowly to the bench. He sensed her watching him and he turned and caught her with a curious tender joy on her scarred cheeks.

When the collection tray came he reached into his wallet and brought out a couple of dollar bills. He felt his mother tug at his arm.

"Don't put in too much," she whispered. When the tray reached them he dropped in a dollar and she put in a nickel and a dime.

At the end of the service he took his mother's arm and led her slowly into the stream of people moving toward the portico. She peered anxiously around her for familiar faces.

"Hello, Mrs. Savalas, you're looking fine. How's your family? I'm not so good, you know. I'm sick. Remember my son, Alex? He's come from California to visit me."

She repeated the same message loudly to several different people, pleased when strangers heard and looked toward her and Alex. In the portico as he tried to lead her from the church, she pulled back.

"We've got to see Father Valoris," she said. "He'll want to see you."

They waited in the rear of the church and he shook hands numbly a number of additional times with people who greeted his mother. She stood close beside him, one hand resting upon his arm, a warm pleasure rampant within the slow, stiff movements of her head, absorbing the exultant moments to be recalled countless times later.

When there were fewer than a half-dozen people left in the portico, the priest came from the nave of the church, his long black cassock swirling about his ankles. Alex's mother tugged at his arm, moving them into the priest's path.

"Father, you remember my Alex?" she said with her voice trembling. "He's come all the way from California to see me."

The priest put out his hand and smiled. Alex took it and mechanically, as he had done a thousand times in the past, bent and kissed the back of the palm.

"A long way," the priest said, "but worth it to bring such pride and pleasure to your mother's face."

"All the way from California, Father," his mother said and there were tears in her eyes.

They shook hands once more, and then as the sexton began snuffing out the candles to darken the church, they left.

The four of them sat and drank coffee around the old walnut, dining-room table. His mother, his brother-in-law, Chester, eyelids heavy and mouth twisted in an effort to remain awake, and his sister, Marika, pale lean-fleshed cheeks, and a sullen curl to her lips.

"Well, I think I'll hit the sack," Chester said. "We got a rough rolling schedule tomorrow." He rose and smiled at Alex, extending his hand. "Maybe I'll see you in the morning."

"I'll be leaving tonight," Alex said. "I have to get an early start to make New York by the day after tomorrow."

"No, Alex!" his mother said with dismay. "Not so soon!"

"I can't, Mama, I'm sorry," he said.

"At least sleep here tonight," his mother pleaded, her voice whining and distressed. "You can start early in the morning.

He shook his head slowly.

"Let him go, Mama," his sister said. "He says he's got business, so let him go."

"I'd stay but I'm a day late anyway," Alex said.

"Well, if I don't see you, Alex, good luck," Chester said. He smiled at him again and stood for a moment thinking of something else to add. He gave up and said good-night and started wearily up the stairs.

His mother rose heavily from her chair and began fumbling at the plates.

"Leave the dishes, Mama," his sister said sharply. "I'll pick them up."

"I just wanted the rest of the cookies," his mother said and she raised the small platter and held it trembling in her palsied fingers. "I'll wrap them so Alex can take them with him. I know they're his favorite."

"Thanks, Mama," he said. He watched her shuffling weary and slow-gaited toward the kitchen. He looked back to see his sister's eyes fastened in his flesh.

"Can't you even stay with her for one night, you bastard," she said in a low, hoarse voice. "You bastard, do you think the lousy fifty bucks you send each month buys you off everything else?"

He looked at her and recognized the marks of her suffering.

"Has it been that bad?" he asked.

She was silent for a moment, her anger fleeing as quickly as it had come.

"What's bad, what's good," she said with a cold grunt. "She's dying slowly, day by day, falling apart. And I have to watch her dying, listen to her whimper and cry when she thinks no one hears. She can't do more than walk a few steps and can barely dress herself anymore. One of these days she won't be able to get out of bed and I don't know what we're going to do with her then."

"Maybe you can find a woman to come in and look after her," Alex said.

"A woman costs money," his sister said.

"I'll try to send more," Alex said.

"Sure," his sister said. "You send some more,"

He rose then and walked into the kitchen where his mother stood packing the cookies in a small box. He reached around her and picked one up and popped it into his mouth. He whistled in pleasure to please her.

"Delicious, Mama!" he said. "I'll finish them before I'm out of Chicago." He paused. "Listen, I think I'll stay tonight. I'll sleep up in the attic if it's okay but I'll have to leave first thing in the morning."

Her face crinkled like paper, each fold trembling with joy.

"Marika!" she called to his sister. "Marika! Alex is staying tonight. Get sheets for his bed upstairs." She looked back at him. "For one night," she said softly. "It'll be like it used to be. I'll hear your steps and close my eyes and sleep better because you're here."

He lay in his bed in the darkness of the attic, listening to the silence of the house. A branch brushed against the roof and he felt the familiar almost forgotten sound deep in his body. On the street below a car passed and the headlights swept the ceiling of his room with a beam of light. A car door slammed and a dog barked.

Somewhere on the road to San Francisco, the young hitchhiker who was 1 A sat awake or slept in the dark, rocking bus. In their bedroom below the attic Chester and Marika lay together in heavy, burdened sleep. In the small corner bedroom, his aging, dying mother lay comforted by his presence for a single night. And across the city, Miriam's warm, naked body consoled the body of her good and gentle Paul.

The trees made a dry, soughing sound. He settled himself deeper in the covers, turning into himself, remorseful about his mother. He might stay for a little while and try to comfort her. Then he knew he could not stay. We only love those who can still save us, he thought. He turned and faced the wall, thinking of Miriam, wishing it were dawn so he could rise and leave.

Sometimes when men defer marrying until their fifties and sixties, they tend to select a much younger girl. The general reaction to them is that they are reprobates and lechers. I find myself sometimes sympathetic to them, particularly as I grow older. The old King David took the young Abishag to his bed so she might warm his cold bones.

In this story I made Leontis a sympathetic and unselfish man. That isn't impossible in someone over sixty.

THE LEGACY OF LEONTIS

Leontis Marnas married Angeliki when he was fifty-eight years old. She was twenty-four. She had been in the United States only a little over two years. All that time she spent working from dawn to dark in the house of an older brother who had paid her passage from Greece. Her days were endured scrubbing floors and caring for his children. In addition, the unhappy girl did not get along with her brother's wife, who was a sullen and unfriendly woman.

Leontis was not aware at that time of how desperately Angeliki wished for liberation from her bondage. When he visited the house in the evening to play cards with her brother, she released upon him all the smoldering embers of her despair. He would have been ashamed to admit that he mistook her attention for affection and her desperation for passion. He was bewildered and yet wished ardently to believe that a young and comely woman could find him attractive. He could not help being flattered and soon imagined that he was madly in love.

In the twenty-eight years since Leontis emigrated from Greece to the United States, he had made a number of attempts to marry. Several times he almost reached the altar, but in the end these efforts were always unsuccessful. Even when he was a young man the bold girls had frightened him and the shy sweet girls to whom he was attracted lacked the aggressiveness to encourage him. He was without sufficient confidence to make the first move, and as a result always lost his chance.

Sometimes despair and restlessness drove him to women that he paid for affection. As he grew older, however, these visits became much more infrequent, and when he realized they burdened rather than satisfied him, he gave them up.

A year came when he was forced to concede to himself that he would never marry. This caused him a good deal of remorse and self-reproach, but secretly he was also relieved to be spared additional disappointment. His mother, of whom he often said, God rest her departed soul, had affirmed that keeping busy prevented melancholia. He became active in a Hellenic lodge and sponsored the education of several war orphans overseas. He rearranged all the stock in his grocery at least twice in each six months. On Sundays, the hardest day of the week for him to sustain, he rode the trolley from one end of the city to the other. He visited museums and spent many hours at the zoo. He was strangely drawn to the monkey house and quietly marveled at his apparent resemblance to one somber old male in a corner of a cage who seemed untouched by the climate of social amiability that prevailed all around him.

During the week, after closing the store in the evening, he sometimes played cards with fellow members of his lodge. In the beginning, this was his reason for visiting the house of Angeliki's brother. Afterwards, although it took a while to admit it to himself, he went only to see her.

Later, in remembering that time, Leontis often considered how ridiculous his conviction that Angeliki loved him must have appeared to her brother. Perhaps he saw their union as an answer to his concern for the future of his sister. But whatever his reasons, her brother gave his approval and completed the alchemy created by the loneliness of Leontis and Angeliki's wish for freedom.

In the early spring of that year, with the first buds breaking in slim green shoots upon the trees, Angeliki and Leontis were married. But it did not take long for the poor girl to realize she had merely substituted one form of despair for another. He could offer her every advantage but the one of youth to match her own. Leontis knew she must have considered him ancient and unattractive, but his presence in the rooms in which she bathed and slept must have created in her an awareness of her body, and perhaps excited her as well. She could see that he admired and adored her, and at the same time he could not blame her impatience with his fumblings.

She could not comprehend how difficult it was for him to value himself as participant in the act of love. He had too long lived vicariously on the perimeter of life. Yet he desired her fervently and made a valiant effort to play the role of lover. On a number of occasions he did manage to fulfill the functions expected of him. But Angeliki grew petulant and bitter at his inadequacies and began to ridicule his age and appearance. A day came when his own long-suffering patience wore thin, and they exchanged hot and furious words.

"You married me for my money!" he said, and he knew this was not true, but anger selects its own truth.

"No," she laughed bitterly, "I married you because you were young and handsome."

He felt the black bile of despair through his body, and he was tempted to strike her but understood helplessly that she could not deny herself the release of some of her frustration.

"I married you because you were handsome!" she shrieked. "A Greek god with a golden body!"

"Enough," he said, and suddenly his anger was gone and he was only weary. He saw in that moment the absurdity of his delusion and how much more he was to blame than she.

He fled down the stairs. In the store, Thomas Sarris, the young man who worked for him, was stacking cans of coffee. Leontis was ashamed and wondered if Thomas had heard them quarreling.

Upstairs, Angeliki slammed a door, a loud and angry slam. Thomas Sarris pretended he did not hear.

The following spring, a son was born to them. Through the months of Angeliki's pregnancy, observing her body curving incredibly into the shape of a pear, Leontis felt sure the doctor had made a mistake. For a long time he had accepted that he would never have a wife. The prospect of becoming a father had been additionally remote. Not until the moment in the hospital shortly after Angeliki returned from the delivery room was he able to accept the conception as real. He was shocked at the sight of her pale cheeks and her dark moist hair, combed stiffly, in the way of hair on a corpse. Fifty-nine years on earth without awareness of the struggle of birth had not prepared him for the emotion. He could not speak. A great tenderness for his young wife possessed him. He touched her cheeks softly and struggled vainly to find words to explain that he understood the ordeal she had endured alone.

When they brought the baby to Angeliki to be nursed, he was rooted with reverence and wonder. He had seen babies before, not quite as small and wrinkled, but that this baby should be a part of his flesh, a blossom of his passion, filled him with a wild strength. As if in some strange and secretive way he had cultivated a garden beyond the reaches of his own death.

Back at home, Angeliki was a devoted mother and cared diligently for the baby. She was dismayed and fretful at the disorderly abundance of affection Leontis showered upon the child. But he could not help himself. He worked in the store, and whether or not he was alone, a moment came when he was filled with an overwhelming longing to see his son. He would run up the stairs and burst through the kitchen into the room where the baby played. Angeliki would follow him, nagging fiercely, but he paid her no attention. He would bend over the baby and marvel at how beautiful he was. He would kiss the top of his soft head and kiss each of his tiny warm feet. The bell in the store rang endlessly.

Angeliki drove him finally from the room.

"You are mad! I will have you put away. You think of nothing but that baby. Your store, your wife—nothing matters. We will end up in the street!"

He kept a few feet ahead of her, and puffing heavily he hurried down the stairs.

A few weeks before the baby's first birthday they baptized him in the Greek Orthodox Church on Laramie Street. Leontis planned a gigantic party. He had several whole lambs roasted, and fifty gallons of wine, and forty trays of honey-nut sweets. He rented the large Masonic hall and invited almost all of the congregation of the church to attend. It was a wild and festive night, and everyone appeared to marvel at the way Leontis danced. Angeliki at last caught him in a corner.

"What an old fool! You will drop dead in the air. Everyone is laughing at you. They think you are crazy."

But full of wine and lamb and gratitude, Leontis just smiled. He danced and sang for love of his son, and he did not care what others thought.

Now, in that month of his son's baptism, sleeplessness, which had troubled Leontis for years, grew worse. He lay wakeful and still beside Angeliki and stared into the dark, and sweats came, and chills, and strange forebodings rode his restless dreams. He went secretly to his friend Doctor Spiliotis. The old physician examined him silently and spoke without sugar off his square tongue.

"Have you made out a will? If not, go home and attend to it."

"I have a will made," Leontis said. "Thank you, old friend, for the advice."

"No thanks to me," the doctor said brusquely. "Thank that heart of yours, which has endured all the abuse you could heap upon it. Many men have weak hearts. They live long lives by taking care. You seem determined to leave as quickly as possible."

"I have lived a long time," Leontis said. "Looking back, it seems to me there is nothing but time."

The doctor looked down and stabbed fiercely with his hand through the air.

"I only treat physical ailments," he said. "They have specialists now for sickness of the mind. For aberrations of old men who marry strong young girls."

"You should have been a diplomat, old friend," Leontis said.

"Understand me, Leontis," the doctor said. "The time is past for jokes. Unless you go to bed at once and rest for a month to six weeks, I do not think you have long to live."

In that moment, Leontis understood the tangled emotion a man feels who hears sentence of his death. At the same time, it seemed his decision was clear.

"Who will attend the store?" Leontis asked. "Who will walk my son in the park in the afternoons? Who will sit with my family in church on Sunday mornings?" He paused for breath. "And if I go to bed, can this insure I will live a long time?"

"We can be sure of nothing on this earth," the doctor said.

"Then I will wait in the way I wish," Leontis said.

"Get out," the doctor said, but the affection of their long friendship softened his words. "I will send you a wreath, a big one, fit for a horse. It will be inscribed 'Athenian Fool.' "

"Save your wreath for someone less fortunate," Leontis said. "I have lived long enough, and I have a son who will carry on my name."

With the knowledge of his impending death, a strange calm descended upon Leontis. Recalling his sixty-odd years as dispassionately as he could did not permit him any reason for garish grief. He knew that except for his son there was nothing in his life worthy of exultation or outrage.

He was certain of Angeliki as a devoted mother who would love and attend the child. To provide them with economic security in addition to the store, he had been purchasing bonds in considerable quantity for years. Therefore, only the possibility of Angeliki's remarriage to a man who might mistreat the child caused him anxiety.

He began carefully studying the clerk in his store, Thomas Sarris. A young man of strong build and pleasant manner. On a number of occasions, Leontis had noticed him discreetly admiring Angeliki when she entered the store. For an instant, the thought of Thomas Sarris or any man replacing him as father to his son brought a terrible pang to his body, but reason calmed him. Thomas was not wild, as were many of the young men. He did not wish to be more than a good grocer, but he worked hard and would care for his own. He would know how to sweeten a girl like Angeliki and remove the memory of her bitterness in marriage to an old man.

He spoke cautiously to Thomas one afternoon.

"How old are you, Thomas?"

"Twenty-eight," Thomas said.

"Twenty-eight," Leontis repeated, and kept busy bagging loaves of fresh bread so that Thomas would not notice his agitation. "How is it you are not married yet? Many young men are in a great hurry to marry these days."

Thomas easily swung a heavy sack of potatoes from the floor to the counter.

"I have not found the right girl."

"Are you looking?" Leontis asked.

"I will be ready when I find her," Thomas said. "But I am intent on getting myself established first. Get a store of my own."

Leontis felt his pulse beat more quickly.

"Do you like this store?" he asked in what he felt was a casual voice.

Thomas shook his head enthusiastically.

"A wonderful store," he said. "A fine business. I would give anything to have one like it someday."

Leontis turned away so that Thomas would not see the sly and pleased smile that he was sure showed on his face.

From that day he brought the baby and Angeliki and Thomas together. He invited the young man to dinner and afterwards encouraged him to play with the baby. He was gratified when Thomas was gentle and tolerant with the child. And the presence of the young man seemed to act as a balm upon Angeliki. She spoke more softly and laughed easily, and there was a strange sparkle in her eyes. Sometimes, in the course of those evenings, it seemed to Leontis that Angeliki and Thomas and the baby were the family and he the intruder. Awareness of this jolted him, and forgetting for an instant that this was his design, he would flee with the child to another room. He would sit in the dark, holding the child tightly in his arms, and with the bitter knowledge of their separation roweling his flesh, he sometimes cried, softly, so that Angeliki and Thomas would not hear.

Summer passed and autumn swept brown crisp leaves along the streets beside the torn scraps of newspaper. In the morning, opening the store, Leontis felt the strange turning of the earth and endured the vision of the sun growing paler each day.

He knew that it was too late, but he suddenly took great care not to exert himself and called to Thomas to move even the smallest box. More and more often, he left the younger man alone in the store and spent most of the day upstairs with Angeliki and the baby. In the beginning she reproached him for neglecting the store, but after a while she seemed to sense his weariness and left him alone. He sat and watched her work about the rooms and listened to the baby make soft squealing sounds at play. Sometimes Angeliki brought him the baby to hold, and they would sit together by the window, looking out upon the winter street.

One afternoon when it rained and the dark heavy sky filled him with unrest, he spoke to her for the first time of what was in his mind.

"Angeliki," he said. "If I died, what would you do?"

She looked up and paused in sewing a button on the sweater of the baby.

"What is the matter with you?" she answered sharply. "What makes you talk of dying?"

"I am getting older," he said. "It should be considered."

"I will not listen to nonsense," she said.

"Would you marry again?" he asked. "I would want you to marry again."

She did not answer, but bent again over her sewing.

"Thomas is a fine young man," he said. "He works hard in the store. He is gentle with the baby. He would make a fine father and husband."

Angeliki snapped down her sewing.

"What nonsense is this?" she said impatiently. "I have better things to do than sit here and listen to you talk nonsense." She rose to leave the room, but a slight flush had entered her cheeks at mention of the young man.

There was a night he woke with a strange pain in his chest. He looked fearfully at the clock on the stand beside the bed, as if in some senseless way he hoped to arrest time. He was about to cry out, but the pain eased almost as quickly as it had come.

Later the baby cried in his sleep, a thin wail that echoed in the silent room. Angeliki got up and brought the child to their bed and placed him between them. In another moment, her breathing eased evenly again into sleep.

Leontis turned on his side and comforted the child and fell asleep with the warmth of the child within his arms. A noise within his body woke him. His eyes opened as if his eyelids were curtains on all of life. He cried out in despair.

Angeliki sat up in bed beside the baby.

"Leontis, what is the matter?"

He was bathed in a terrible sweat, and his heart seemed to be fluttering wings like a trapped bird to escape from the cage of his body.

"Leontis!" she cried. "Leontis!"

He knew he was dying. Not fear or anxiety, as he had known many times in the past months, but knowledge, swift and real as if seared in flame across his flesh.

"Leontis!" she cried. "You must not die before you forgive me!"

He touched the baby's face. He felt his nose, small and warm, and his eyes, and the soft strands of his hair.

"Forgive me!" she shrieked. "Forgive me!"

Her hands were on his face and then they were lost within the crest of a mighty wave that tossed his body. He tried to hug the boy with all of his soul, and the last great swell exploded from his eyes.

An editor once at *Chicago Review* asked me to contribute a story for an issue they were doing on writing in Chicago. Since literary magazines pay off in subscriptions, I leafed through some rejected stories, thinking they would be grateful to accept even less than vintage Petrakis. They promptly returned the story I sent them with thanks.

Slightly nettled, I pulled out another rejected story but, feeling uneasy about the possibility of a second peremptory rejection, rewrote it. They published "The Prison" happily. And the story was later included in the O. Henry Awards Prize Stories collection for that year.

There may well be a moral here. . . .

THE PRISON

Harry Kladis met Alexandra when he was forty-five and she was forty. For twelve years he had worked with his father in their small candy store. She was a librarian at the neighborhood branch. He admitted to himself that she was not very pretty and a little older than he would have wished but he was drawn to her by the soft abundance of dark hair that she wore to her shoulders and by an air of shyness he suspected concealed loneliness as distressing as his own. One night after she had been coming into the candy store for almost three months, he mustered the courage and asked to take her out. He was so pleased when she accepted that he insisted she take three pounds of her favorite chocolate mints as a gift.

On their first date they walked for hours and talked endlessly. In the beginning they tried shyly to suggest they were accustomed to dating many others. After a while this posturing seemed foolish to both of them. He told her about a girl, handsome and raven-haired, that he had lost to a bolder man years before. She told him of a salesman, tall with sensitive eyes, who held her devotion until, transferred to another territory, he ceased to answer her letters. These melancholy recitals drew them together. They were delighted to find they both enjoyed concerts and chop suey with black pekoe tea and almond cookies. After a month of seeing each other several evenings a week they accepted with grateful happiness that they were in love.

Two weeks before the day scheduled for their wedding, Harry's father died. Returning from an evening with Alexandra, Harry found the old man in the back room of the store where he had suffered a stroke while mixing a batch of fresh milk chocolate.

They recognized it would have been unseemly to marry so close upon death and they delayed their wedding for a few months. Harry wished to sell the store as soon as possible. He had studied accounting some years before and considered taking additional courses to qualify himself for that profession. But his mother insisted he keep the thin security of the store that was all her husband had left to provide for her old age. The first weeks after the funeral seemed merely to sharpen the blades of her sorrow.

"My father and I were all she ever cared for," Harry said to Alexandra. "He is gone now but she wonders what will happen to me if I sell the store and cannot make a go of accounting."

"You will be a good accountant," Alexandra said. "I have my job to help out. It will be better for your mother in the long run."

"I should have made the decision years ago," Harry said and he was ashamed. "I never really cared for the store but I have let the years slide by." He turned away to conceal his distress. "Just a while longer," he said. "I don't want to press Mama in her grief now. Just a little longer."

But he could not make chocolates as well as his father and business fell off. The price he might have received for selling the store declined as well. He worried and worked for longer hours. At the end of six months from his father's death they postponed their wedding once more.

His mother's continued despair confused him and made him unhappy. They tried to include the old lady in the things they did but she did not care for music and could not stand the sight or smell or chop suey. In desperation to appease her relentless grief they spent most of their evenings at home with her. She talked ceaselessly of the past and of joining her husband in death to remove herself as a burden on Harry. He spent the evening assuring her of his love and devotion. The only moments he managed alone with Alexandra were during the brief period when he walked her home. Then bedeviled by the evening of his mother's lament, he had little to say. When he returned home, he had to listen to his mother stitch the final ornament on the hours before he could flee to bed.

"Sitting in with me instead of being out with her," his mother said and a long sigh came wracked from her flesh. "She must resent me and blame me."

"She does not blame you for anything, Mama," Harry said. "She has never spoken a single word against you."

"I want you to marry," his mother said. "I want you to be happy." She looked in dismay at her son. "You were our only child. You are my life now. I would swear to die tonight if you thought I did not want your happiness."

"Stop it now," Harry said. "When Alexandra and I are married, you will live with us and we will look after you."

The old lady shook her head somberly. "You were two years old when your father's sister Sophoula died," she said. "The last ten years of her life she lived with us. I bathed her and fed her and cleaned up her slop. I would say my prayers at night and ask God to forgive me because I hated her on my back and wished her dead." She paused and with her dark dried fingers made her trembling cross. "There were nights I would hear her calling to me," she said. "I would hold my ears and make off I was asleep. And she would call in a voice like a bird for a long time." She bared her teeth in a harsh and cold smile. "My sins have come home to roost. I am the old woman now."

"What more can I say, Mama?" Harry asked. "As long as I live I will love you and look after you. And Alexandra will love you as I do."

The old lady looked at him silently for a long time. He felt himself reduced to the condition of a child unaware of reality and the grim shades of life. She rose slowly and heavily to her feet.

Harry kissed her goodnight with tenderness. For a moment she clung to him fiercely. He felt her fear of death and loneliness riot through his own flesh.

Winter passed into spring. The hours of daylight grew longer. From blossoming gardens in the park came the aroma of new flowers. Within the foliage of trees sounded the shrill-throated songs of birds. In the twilight the moths writhed their wings about the street lamps. The young lovers whispered and laughed in the sheltered groves beyond the walk.

With the coming of spring, Harry and Alexandra felt their spirits rising. Sunday afternoons they spent looking for an apartment with an extra bedroom. They talked confidently of the future. The season filled them with new strength.

On the last Sunday in April they found a bright apartment not far from the park and only a few blocks from the library and candy store. Alexandra was enchanted with it but Harry could not subdue his apprehension. He could already feel the dark attendance of his mother. And closing their bedroom door at night would not shut out her brooding presence.

Afterwards they walked silently in the park. They passed old men with bony faces who sat on benches like withered roosters soaking up the sun, old men who bore the marks of neglect and impending death.

"We will take the apartment!" Harry spoke in a furious effort to break free. "We will go back and take it."

"You did not want it," Alexandra said quietly. "We have been searching for a place like that for weeks and when we found it you did not want it."

He fumbled helplessly for her hand and felt her slim-boned fingers against his palm. "In every room I could feel my mother," he said. "Like all the curtains were drawn and the shades pulled down."

"She cannot live alone," Alexandra said. "We have to work it out."

"She is sure we will come to hate her," he said. "Maybe she is right. I love her and feel a terrible pity for her. I love you too and I don't know what to do."

They paused before a deserted bench and sat down. He put his arm around her slim shoulders and drew her close.

"When I found you I had given up hope of love," she said quietly. "I had put that dream away like a flower pressed between the pages of a book." She moved her head slightly and he felt her breath against his throat. "Now I brush my hair as I did when I was a girl. Every mirror makes me realize I am no longer young. I want you to love me and find me beautiful. I want you to love me before I grow old."

"We will work things out," Harry said and for a moment tightly closed his eyes. "We won't lose each other. We will work things out."

Summer passed. The hours of daylight grew shorter. Dusk and dark advanced as the autumn nights closed in. The earth stirred and waited for the winter.

His mother grew more feeble. She could not bear to be alone and in the afternoon had a neighbor woman help her to the store. She sat in a corner and watched Harry as he worked. In the evening the neighbor returned and took her home so that she could prepare Harry's supper. She sat watching him silently as he ate.

Afterwards he helped put her to bed. She was driven with fear that death would claim her while she slept so she delayed sleeping as long as possible, holding Harry's hand, and talking aimlessly of the past. There were moments when she looked at her son with a strange burning pity. "There is no answer for us on this earth," she said and made her cross. "God save you by taking me soon."

After she slept Harry went to his bed on the couch in the next room and lay awake for a long time. Finally weary and tormented by his thoughts, he fell asleep.

In December of that year Harry and Alexandra parted. They had been seeing each other less frequently as the weeks passed, each meeting marked by a silent grievance and rebuke. They were lonely away from one another and yet miserable when they were together. He made the suggestion, trying to hold back his tears, and she mutely agreed.

That night Harry did not go home. He knew his mother would be in terror at being alone but he remained all night in the store and mixed more chocolate than he would be able to use in months. He kept all the lights burning and tried furiously to keep busy. In the dawn when weariness finally overcame him, he sank down on a chair and laid his head on the table smelling of sweet chocolate. In that moment he envied his father who was dead.

For almost three years Harry did not see Alexandra. From an acquaintance he knew she still worked at the library. He was often tempted to walk by the library in the hope of catching a glimpse of her. He was afraid she might see him and this kept him away.

He saw her often in his dreams. Her thin mournful face and the long hair about her pale cheeks and her slim fingers quiet in her lap. In the morning he woke unrested and faced the day with a burden on his heart.

His mother grew a little stronger. Now that she had him to herself she made fewer demands upon him and let him alone. They never spoke of Alexandra.

He had always been careful about his diet but as time went on he ate as much as he wished and gained weight. When he shaved in the morning he was repelled at how suddenly he seemed to have aged. He was not yet fifty but he felt much older.

More and more the pattern of his life assumed the dimensions that had governed the last years of his father. He rose early and went to the store. He worked through the day and in the evening went home to eat the supper his mother prepared. Afterwards he sat and read the paper while she rocked silently in her chair. When she was in bed he smoked a cigar as furtively as his father had done because she had always complained about the rank odor. He had trouble sleeping and after a while began using sleeping pills that a doctor prescribed.

In the beginning of the fourth year after he and Alexandra separated, his mother died. A cold had plagued her for several weeks. She ran a high fever and had to be moved to the hospital. The fever blazed up and down in spurts while she struggled fiercely to live. A priest came and dispensed the last rites. She died late one night in her sleep.

After the funeral Harry returned to the flat alone. He walked slowly about her bedroom. Every possession of hers, every article of clothing or spool of thread seemed to belong to someone he could hardly remember. He felt suddenly as if she had been dead for a long time.

He went for a walk. Without awareness of direction he found himself across the street from the library. In a panic that Alexandra might see him for the first time in three years on the day of his mother's funeral, he fled back home.

In the next few days he kept thinking about Alexandra. He yearned to go to her and yet shame kept him away. He studied himself in the mirror and mourned how seedy he had become. He determined desperately to diet again and brushed his hair in a way that concealed the growing patch of baldness.

After closing the store in the evening he detoured on his way home to pass the library. He stood hidden in the darkness of the small park across the street. When she came out and started to walk home he knew that he still loved her.

One night that he stood beneath the shadow of the trees a longing to talk to her overcame his shame and fear. When she emerged from the library he crossed the street and called out her name.

It was a strange moment. She did not seem surprised to find him there. He was stunned at the sight of her and the changes that three years had made. She looked much older than he remembered, the last traces of youth gone. He trembled knowing that he too had changed and that she might see her own ravages reflected in him.

They walked home together as they had done so many times in the past. He was careful not to walk too close beside her. For a block they were silent and then they spoke a little. She had become head librarian. He mentioned a concert he had attended a few months before.

They paused before her building. He was about to say goodnight and try and muster the courage to ask to see her again.

"Would you like some tea?" she asked quietly.

For a moment, choked by gratefulness, he could not speak. They walked slowly up the stairs. He sat in her small parlor while she heated water in the kitchen. Everything appeared the same. The rows of books and records in the corner, the photograph of her dead parents, the small plaster bust of Beethoven on the mantel. The room even retained the delicate scent of her powder and he leaned back slightly and closed his eyes. He felt for an overwhelming moment that he was back where he had always belonged.

She brought in the pot of tea and set the cups upon the small table. She poured carefully and filled a plate with a few almond cookies. He had not eaten them in years.

"Do you still like chop suey?" he asked gently.

She shook her head. "Not any more," she said. Her hands, pale and slim-fingered, moved restlessly about the cups of fragrant tea.

"I don't care for it any more either," he said. He was silent a moment, wondering if he had suggested too much.

When he finished his tea he rose slowly to his feet. He wanted to stay longer and yet was afraid to ask.

She brought him his coat. ''You have gained weight,'' she said.

He fumbled hurriedly into the concealment of the coat. ''I have started to diet again,'' he said.

''Your cheeks have no color.'' she said. ''And you are growing bald.''

He made a mute and helpless gesture with his hands.

''Do you find me changed?'' she asked and a certain tightness had entered her voice.

''Hardly at all,'' he said quickly. He was sorry the moment he uttered that naked lie.

''Three years have passed,'' she said and the words came cold from her lips. ''I was not young when you first met me. I am much older now.''

''Alexandra,'' he felt a furious need to console her. ''Alexandra,'' he drew a deep breath and then could not control the wild tumble of words. ''Can you care a little for me again? Can you let me love you once more?''

She made a stiff and violent motion of her arm to silence him. He was shocked at the fury blazing suddenly in her eyes.

''Three years are two words,'' she said. ''Two words easy to say. But three years are a thousand lonely nights and a thousand bitter cups of tea and a thousand withered flowers.''

She raised her hand and struck him hard across the cheek. ''For the thousand lonely nights!'' she said and the words came in flame. ''For the thousand bitter cups of tea! For the thousand withered flowers!'' She struck him again more savagely than before.

He turned then and fled. He went quickly out the door, down the stairs to the sidewalk, across the street into the darkened doorway of a closed store. He stood there seeing the dark reflection of his face in the glass and felt his heart as if it were about to burst. He began to cry, the tears running down his stinging cheeks. And he did not know in that terrible moment of despair whether he was crying for Alexandra or for himself.

I enjoyed writing this story. Although it may have echoes of my earlier work, it was written less than a year ago. I found it reinforcing that I can still write a humorous story and that it can be enjoyed by others in a period when the ritual of courtship no longer has any rules.

One of the letters I received after the story was published queried whether there were still marriage brokers on Halsted Street. While I cannot provide an address and a phone number for Apollo Stambulis, I'm certain that the Greek aptitude for transforming commonplace experiences into epic events still flourishes. I recently heard of a Greek meat man in the Southwest so carried away by the quality of his product that he bypassed the Government gradings of 'Choice' and 'Prime' and stamped his beef, 'Superb.'

THE SIEGE OF MINERVA

Let me state from the beginning that I have been a respected businessman on Halsted Street, that crossroads of culture and superb cuisine existing in the midwestern metropolis of Chicago, for more than thirty years. No one has ever questioned my integrity or my abilities before these scurrilous rumors surfaced about my failure with Victor Zervas and Minerva Poulos.

I might have chosen to ignore these slanders since hundreds, even thousands of my satisfied clients would eagerly negate the accusations of malfeasance. But one must not endure the swinish slurs of avocado-brained louts in silence. I have therefore decided to reveal the full facts of this extraordinary case which will also appear in the 23rd printing of the *Stambulis Primer of Triumphant Courtship* (Parthenon Press, Paperbound, $9.95, plus $2.00 postage and handling).

To begin at the beginning. Victor Zervas appeared in my office on a Saturday morning last September. He was in his early to middle forties, dressed in a stylish, pin-striped, double-breasted suit of Hong Kong silk with a bright yellow shirt bearing the crest of one of those miniature animals so much in fashion now. His appearance suggested taste and substance in keeping with the usual quality of my clients. This initial favorable impression was further confirmed for me when we shook hands and I noticed a number of gold rings on his fingers.

"Mr. Stambulis," he said earnestly. "I didn't make an appointment because the matter was urgent. I am Victor Zervas."

"Appointments are wise because of the heavy volume of my business," I said, "but you are fortunate that I just happen to have had a cancellation."

"Mr. Stambulis," he began again. "I've been told by certain people whose opinion I respect that you are the finest marriage broker in the city of Chicago."

I fluttered my fingers in a modest disclaimer although only my detractors limit me to that amount of territory. While I waited, discreetly silent, I could see that Zervas was snared in the grip of an intense emotion.

"Mr. Stambulis," he said finally, "I have never married because I have been intent on other pursuits. When she was alive, my blessed mother, God rest her soul, would tell me Victor, be patient but remember that you may never find a girl to match all those qualities you admire in me." He paused. "She was right, of course, but I have continued to look. Finally, right here in your parish, I saw her for the first time several weeks ago during a Church picnic. I haven't been able to think about anything since then." He fervently made his cross. "Now I wish you to approach her for me."

"Who is this paragon of beauty, Mr. Zervas?"

He released a long, poignant sigh as if even the mention of her name ravaged his tongue.

"The Widow, Minerva Poulos."

I confess the name made my own ears resonate. The Widow Minerva was one of the ornaments of our parish by reason of her superlative physical accoutrements that combined the most salient and loveliest features of Irene Pappas and Melina Mercouri. Her husband had been the victim of an untimely and fatal accident several years earlier when his produce truck collided with an Amtrak Zephyr. After the customary period of mourning, a number of other men presented their proposals to his widow, either in person (always a calamitous blunder) or through third-parties, but all were decisively rebuffed. Some said she still mourned her late husband who had been a strapping Spartan, while others suggested she only waited for an extraordinary suitor. She was a sterling challenge, and I felt my pulse quicken at the prospect of the hunt.

"Let me commend you for seeking my help, Mr. Zervas," I said. "The Widow Minerva's threshold is littered with the bones of rejected suitors."

"I think of her night and day," Zervas said in a trembling voice. "A friend introduced me to her briefly at the picnic but before I could utter a word, she seemed almost to leap away. If she were any ordinary woman, I am certain she would respond to me favorably. But she seems fierce, and distant as a Goddess!" He made a gesture of resolve in the air. "I am determined to have her as my wife!"

"Slowly, my friend," I said. "Confidence is important but arrogance breeds misfortune. What is important is that we plan the proper strategy." I paused. "First, there are some formalities so I will have all the required information at my disposal. You will notice that I am still recording all such information by hand instead of using one of those abominable computers." From my desk I removed one of my business questionnaires, a form designed for me by a professor at the Illinois Institute of Chiromancy.

"Name?" I asked.

"You already know that," Zervas said a little impatiently. I gave him a reproving look. The success of my service was based on certain fundamental procedures which could not be disregarded.

"Please answer the question," I said gravely.

"Victor Zervas."

"Age?"

"Forty-five, but, physically, the equal of a man of thirty."

"Height?"

"Five-feet, eight-inches," he said, "but proportioned so well many people take me for at least six feet."

"Weight?"

"One hundred and eighty trim and muscular pounds."

"Teeth?"

He stared at me perplexed.

"What about teeth?"

"Are they real or false?"

"Is that important?" Zervas asked peevishly. "We're not asking her to purchase a horse!"

"My dear friend, it is extremely important!" I said. "During the wedding night of a marriage I had arranged some years ago, it was concealed that the groom had a glass eye. He had removed it in the dark and popped it into a container of some solution in the bathroom. When his bride saw it, she let out a shriek and fled home to her parents who wanted the marriage annulled. Therefore, you can see that we must accurately list the portions of your body that retain the original equipment."

"I have twenty-five of my own teeth," Zervas said. "Nine of them have gold fillings that cost me more than $8000."

"Excellent!" I said. "Are you planning to have any of the missing teeth replaced soon?"

"Is that necessary?" he asked. "I can eat like a tiger."

"As you wish," I said, "but from experience I know any suitor should be as complete as possible." I paused. "If you don't currently have a dentist, my first cousin, Socrates Cardaras, is one of the best in the city. I will be happy to arrange an appointment for you."

"Perhaps later," Zervas said. "Let's go on now. What else do you wish to know?"

"Business?"

"I am the sole owner of the Macedonian Coffee Company," he said, "left to me ten years ago at the death of my sainted father. I have tripled the company's assets since then."

"Excellent! What would the approximate net worth of the company be at present?"

Zervas puffed out his chest. "Very near a million dollars."

"We have sufficient information!" I said crisply. "I will be pleased to offer your proposal to the Widow Minerva."

Zervas nodded fervently. "Explain to her what a catch I would be," he said. "Tell her that countless mothers have sought me as a bridegroom for their daughters. Explain I am not only wealthy but intelligent and charming. Tell her . . ."

"My dear Mr. Zervas," I said. "My procedure in these matters has been carefully developed through years of experience. To court a woman properly is to undertake a journey as hazardous as the voyages of Odysseus. Trust me."

Zervas nodded silently and rose. He paused a moment before the framed diplomas of my graduations from the North Halsted Street High School and the Plato Lardakis School of Business Management. He nodded approvingly and turned to me.

"How will you first approach her? What will you do as a start?"

"I know the answers to such questions," I answered gravely. "When I have to explain them to someone, I do not know the answers. Do you understand?"

He seemed slightly puzzled but nodded as evidence of his faith in my judgment. I clapped him reassuringly on the shoulder.

"You are in the devoted care of Apollo Stambulis now," I said. "Remember that marriage is the ultimate, glorious union of a man and a woman, divinely sanctioned and ordained as an essential link in the great chain of God, country and family."

"Magnificent!" Zervas said. "I can understand why you are so highly regarded."

Although I shrugged modestly once more, I agreed wholeheartedly with his canny observation.

For the following four days I sent the Widow Minerva lovely bouquets of roses with my engraved card. I generally sent flowers for only one or two days, but I recognized she might require further pampering. On the morning of the fifth day, I phoned her.

"Yes?" She had a strong, brusque voice.

"Mrs. Minerva Poulos?"

"She is speaking."

"This is Apollo Stambulis of the Apollo Matrimonial Service. I trust you've received my flowers which were sent at the request of my esteemed friend Victor Zervas . . ."

With my customary alertness I realized the line between us had gone dead. Thinking we might have been inadvertently cut off, I dialed again. She didn't speak but I heard her hoarse breathing.

"Mrs. Poulos, I believe we were cut off. As I was saying . . ."

"Say nothing to me," she said curtly. "Your flowers went to the hospital. Don't send any more and don't bother me again."

That time the slamming down of the receiver nearly shattered the drum of my ear.

I had not attained my position of eminence in the community, nor had I survived in a time of sexual promiscuity by being faint-hearted or easily discouraged. Women are like fortresses that must be scaled. If the gate on one side is barricaded too strongly, the assault must be made from another direction (Maxim #23 in the *Stambulis Primer of Triumphant Courtship*; Parthenon Press, Paperbound, $9.95, plus $2.00 postage and handling).

I made a decision to use an impressive intermediary and chose, as I have a number of times, Father Loukas, priest of our parish church. My contributions to the various church charities were considerable and he wouldn't wish to alienate me. But when I told him who the lady was, he sounded apprehensive. Finally he agreed with evident reluctance to go and see her. An hour later he phoned back.

"Apollo?"

"Yes, my dear Father!" I said eagerly.

"She wouldn't listen."

"What do you mean she wouldn't listen!"

"I barely got the first words about you out of my mouth and she asked me to leave."

"She asked her spiritual advisor to leave! Does she realize she's affronting God?"

"She was quite willing to speak to me about God. It was only when I brought up your name that she asked me to leave."

"Eccentric, obdurate woman!" I said.

"Well, I have done what I could do," the priest said. "I was afraid this might happen. By the way, Apollo, you know that we're having a shortage in our coal offerings this year. I was hoping . . ."

"I will send a check," I said crisply.

After hanging up I made a note to charge the contribution for the coal offering on my fee for Victor Zervas.

Having devoted a considerable span of years to the perilous forays of matchmaking, I had experienced, of course, some titanic struggles. Yet I had never lost faith in my noble purpose which was to transform a poet's vision of courtship and love into a reality shared by the blessed men and women I had coupled. But, soon after beginning my enterprise for the consent and heart of the Widow Minerva Poulos, I realized I was facing the most Homeric challenge of my illustrious career.

All my customary successful overtures were thwarted. Flowers were sent on to hospitals or returned to the florist, phone calls were ignored (she even reported to the phone company that I was harassing her!) and all my letters, written with a rhetorical grace and flair, were returned to me unopened. Meanwhile, Zervas grew more desperate and impatient, his own confidence shredded. About two weeks after his initial visit, he came to my office. I discerned at once the man was disturbed and distraught.

"I cannot stand much more!" he cried. "The whole city knows I am being rejected! My friends, business associates, even my employees, I see a smile on their faces and think they must be laughing at me! I have never known such humiliation and shame! You must do something!"

"Believe me, Mr. Zervas, I am trying to do something," I said. "Do you realize that before I undertook to press this most difficult suit there had not been a single failure to besmirch the glorious pennant of my matchmaking service? My pride and reputation are at stake here as well as your own!"

We stared at one another, resentment and agitation evident in our confrontation.

"Forgive me, Mr. Stambulis," Zervas said in a more subdued voice. "That woman's obstinacy has unsettled me. Doesn't she understand the honor I am offering her by asking her to be my wife? What in God's name can be wrong with her?"

"Since our Lord is also a male, Mr. Zervas," I said soberly, "That is not a question He might be able to answer."

He emitted a heartfelt and despairing sigh.

"What is important is that we must not lose heart," I said sternly. "In my years of valiant battles in the cause of love, I have learned that apparently insurmountable obstacles require monumental measures. Our glorious Hellenic tradition has also taught us that at the moment when all seems lost, the miracle occurs!"

At that instant, as if aided by the shades of the vaunted ancestors I had invoked, I was provided one of those revelations, an apocalyptic disclosure worthy of the Oracles at hallowed Delphi!

"I have it!" I cried.

Zervas looked at me with quivering anticipation.

"You must kill yourself!"

His eagerness changed swiftly to horror.

"My God!" he wrenched out. "Isn't that overdoing it?"

"I don't mean really killing yourself!" I hastened to add. "But we must give the impression to the Widow Minerva that you have done it. You must go into seclusion, at once. I will provoke rumors through the city that you have done away with yourself. I will then go with her with a final communication from you. It will say you have decided to kill yourself for unrequited love!" My voice trembled, my spirit caught in the majesty of the conception. "Your letter will bid her farewell, will wish her well, and . . . and inform her that you are leaving her all your fortune as a legacy of your devotion!"

Zervas stared at me, numbed by the recitation, struggling to assemble his scattered wits.

"One moment, Mr. Stambulis," he said in a hoarse whisper. "Won't she be furious when she sees me reappear?"

"We will say the Doctors were able to save you in the nick of time! Meanwhile, she will have understood the extent of your love and your generous heart! Even a goddess could not help being moved!"

The last restraint to Zervas' enthusiasm broke free.

"Genius!" he cried and grabbed my hand to squeeze it tightly. "Sheer genius! Your reputation is totally deserved!"

"I know," I said. "Now, my friend, go and make plans for your disappearance. Let those around you see you melancholy and despondent. Slip away quietly. Let me know where you are but be discreet. I will, meanwhile, be implementing our grand strategy!"

Within the next few days, everything proceeded as we had planned. Victor Zervas disappeared and I mentioned to Mrs. Bratsas, the fiercest jaw in the parish, the possibility of his self-destruction. Her vigorous mouth did not fail me, the news spreading instantaneously through the parishes of the Diocese. The speculations about Zervas grew more violent and bleaker with each transmittal.

The phone call I expected from Father Loukas came after he had heard of the tragedy. He was remorseful that he had not pressed the Widow Minerva harder in our cause. When I informed him I had a final communication from Zervas to the Widow, to be delivered and read by me to her in person, he vowed he would obtain a meeting for me with her. He would tell her he'd relinquish his clerical collar if she refused!

An hour later he phoned me back to tell me I could see her. I tried to disguise the rampant triumph I felt in my heart. As soon as I was off the phone I dressed in my black Hart, Schaffner and Marx suit reserved for prominent wakes and funerals and, with a taxi, hastened to her house. Ringing her bell, I composed my face into a demeanor of sorrow.

She opened the door for me, a handsome and regal woman, her face stern and unwelcome. I savored the moment, imagining the way she would break down and weep when I disclosed the news of the death of Zervas and his last, thrilling and generous bequest.

"I am seeing you only to keep Father Loukas in the priesthood," she said crisply. "Speak what you have to say quickly."

"May I step inside, please?"

She moved reluctantly away from the door and I entered the hallway. I cast a quick glance at the adjoining parlor but she did not ask me to sit down. Realizing I had to strike quickly, I removed the letter I had so carefully composed from my pocket.

"It is my unhappy task," I said dolefully, "to inform you, Widow Minerva, that our friend, Victor Zervas . . ."

"Not my friend!"

I ignored the rude interruption. ". . . that Victor Zervas has disappeared for some days now. Those of us who knew his despair have feared the worst. This morning two letters were delivered to me that confirmed our most dreadful fears. My letter told me he had no other recourse than to kill himself. His last wish was that I deliver and personally read the other letter he addressed to you."

She made an impatient gesture toward the door.

"Widow Minerva!" I said shocked. "Would you deny a dead man his last, sad wish?"

Without waiting for her approval I began reading the letter.

"My dear Widow Minerva Poulos: There is a divine order, which, beyond the order of human justice imposes itself on all men. For this reason I respect your rejection of my entreaty for your hand and your heart. But on an earth where I cannot call you my beloved, I do not wish to live."

I was captured by the beauty and emotion of the words and felt a vagrant tear threaten to flow from my eye. I looked at her quickly to savor the effect the letter was having upon her.

"How much more?" she asked. O heartless woman!

"Therefore," I resumed reading more grimly, "quietly and without wishing to distress any of my numerous friends, I have determined to end it all. I ask only that you do not remember me with disfavor or bitterness. I could not help loving you anymore than a plant can help looking at the sun which nourishes it. I loved you, perhaps not wisely, but too well."

"Are you finished?" she asked. Had the woman no fragment of soul?

"One final favor I wish to ask of you," I went on, stifling my indignation. "That you allow me to bequeath to you all of my estate which comes to a total of nearly a million dollars, my business, my stocks, bonds and several parcels of real estate in Miami Beach. You are to have this modest fortune for anything you wish. For world travel, for your happiness, perhaps to establish a sanctuary for foundlings and waifs. Let this last bequest stand as a tribute . . ."

"Mr. Stambulis . . ."

" . . . to the deep and abiding adoration . . ."

"Stambulis! Stop!"

The words snapped off in my teeth. I stared at her in amazement.

"Enough!"

"Widow Minerva . . ."

"Enough! Do you hear? Enough!"

"But you don't understand . . ."

"You are the ones who don't seem to understand!" she cried. "I wanted nothing to do with that buffoon while he was alive and I want nothing to do with him in any other existence!"

"Widow Minerva!" I said indignantly. "This poor devil has gone to his death loving you! He has gone to the heart of the universe to seek the peace provided for those who die for love! He is a saint!"

"He is a goat!" she said and her fury was awesome to behold. "An arrogant, insensitive bumpkin, a clod, an ass who will blubber through eternity as he driveled through life!"

"Mercy!" I gasped. "Mercy!"

"No mercy!" she cried, waving her hands like warclubs in the air. "I wanted no particle of that cretin alive, asleep, suspended in purgatory, in heaven or in hell!"

"Blasphemy!" I cried hoarsely as I backed toward the door. In a moment she had opened it and pushed me out. I stumbled onto the virago's porch as she slammed the door behind me. Words failed me and I could only shake my fist in mute outrage at that devil's daughter!

Of course, anyone reading this somber tale will understand the superhuman efforts I exerted on behalf of my client. They might imagine, as well, the way Zervas took the news. When I phoned him to tell him he could return from the dead, he was overjoyed, thinking our brilliant enterprise had been successful. Later, in my office, without repeating the precise expressions the Widow Minerva had used about him, I tried firmly to convey to him my feeling that she wasn't worthy of him. I suggested the names of several other ladies I have had in my files for a considerable time. He pledged to think about them but by the way he staggered out of my office, I knew his Hellenic pride was sorely stricken by the Widow's rejection.

I must also admit that my own confidence was battered. I had never failed before and this was not merely failure but rampant and ignominious defeat. For the first time in my active and triumphant career, I contemplated retirement and a move to my sister and brother-in-law's condominium in Ft. Lauderdale, Florida.

When I had about decided that was the most sensible course of action for me (so low had my spirits fallen) I was phoned by a young man who had been referred to me by an older lady of our parish. He spoke of his desire to marry a mature, respectable young woman. I was pleased at his forthrightness and good sense. A little while later he came to my office for the appointment we had set up. Not until I looked him square in the face did I realize the poor fellow's eyes were locked in a gaze that excluded everything but one another! I had mated certain infirmities before but this was an impediment of classical proportions!

My sporting blood was roused at once and I agreed to service his request. Asking him to sit down, I pulled out one of my forms.

"Name?"

"Anthony Pragastis."

"Age?"

"Twenty-nine."

"Height?"

"Five feet ten."

And so on. And as I filled in the form, the fellow eagerly responding to my queries, I had once more a conviction of my mission. A man's good will may be ineffectual in saving him from misfortune but with renewed courage and imagination, he might become again master of his destiny.

"Teeth?"

"All of my own . . ."

"Splendid!"

Perhaps a solitary failure was needed to remind me that I was mortal and not a deity. Meanwhile, the eternal and majestic battles of wooing and courtships go on. And I, Apollo Stambulis, stand poised in the vanguard of those battles, a commander of the forces of romance and a general in the armies of love!

Some years ago I witnessed an intemperately dull-witted television interviewer asking his guest, the novelist and artist, Henry Miller, whether he ever thought of death. The octogenarian Miller, displaying commendable patience with his obtuse host, wryly replied, "All the time."

If I don't think of death all the time, it does occupy more of my thoughts as I grow older. That must be a natural consequence of the ascending years but one also ponders the way one has lived, about words spoken and unspoken and deeds committed or neglected. A sage once wrote that for a wise man a single lifetime should be enough since a stupid man wouldn't know what to do with eternity.

My father died in 1951 when I was twenty-seven years old and I felt unsuited for the responsibilities his death left upon me. As time passed I began to assess and draw upon the small strengths his life had bequeathed to me. I think every parent would like to believe they can leave such a legacy.

The moral might be that if the way one has lived one's life doesn't provide such a legacy, then eternity won't be much help

BETWEEN SLEEP AND DEATH

The last time Peter had seen his father was in February of the year after the heart attack. Another teacher agreed to take Peter's classes at the college in San Francisco where he taught history and he had flown to Chicago. Going directly from the airport to the hospital, he had entered the white, aseptic room and found his father awake and subdued, his graying hair and bearlike head resting in resignation upon the pillow.

"Hi, Pa." Peter bent to kiss him and felt the rough stubble of beard on his cheek.

"Everytime you see me the last couple of years, I'm in the sick-berth hotel," his father said. "You think someone is trying to tell us the old man is through?"

"They won't keep you down, Pa."

"Sure, son, sure," his father spoke without conviction.

"When you're up and around, Ma will get some of her lamb and pilaf into you," Peter said. "We'll be jogging together again by spring."

"Lamb and pilaf won't heal my heart, liver, or kidneys," his father said. "Everything in me is running down, Pete. I feel strength hissing out of me like air escaping from a balloon."

"Come on, Pa! Is this the immigrant who started by pushing a cart forty years ago and built a business that has two stores and three trucks?"

His father nodded, accepting the praise for those early labors. One of his hands tugged wearily at the sheet, raising the edge to his throat.

"That was a long time ago, Pete," he said. "I was a champion then."

When his father was discharged from the hospital, Peter spent a week with him at home. He might have remained longer, but the house was dismal and tense, his mother and sister fussing constantly with his father about diet, medications, and exercise.

For an hour every afternoon, Peter would walk with his father. Before they left the house, his sister would wrap a scarf around his father's throat, binding him to his ears. She'd make him slip his shoes into galoshes.

"It's not raining, daughter," his father said testily.

"For the cold, Papa," Olga said. "They will keep your feet warm."

His father sighed as they started for the door.

"Now, don't walk too fast, Andrew," his mother warned.

"How can I walk too fast, Despina?" his father asked her patiently. "I got on so goddamn much clothes, I can hardly move."

"Don't swear, Andrew," his mother said.

On the porch his father placed his arm in the circle of Peter's arm and they'd descend the porch steps to walk slowly along the street. When they came to the cluster of neighborhood stores his father had patronized for years, he made Peter cross the street to avoid passing in front of them.

"You know all those shopkeepers, Pa," Peter said. "They're good friends."

"I don't belong with them now," his father said. "All those nights I drank with Gortiz, ate with Stathis, played barbut with Roussos . . . all that belongs to the past. When I come around now, I scare them like I already smell of death."

Peter started to protest.

"You think I'm just morbid, son? I tell you I think they scheduled me to die in the hospital this last time. A clerk in Accounts Receivable slipped up and pretty goddamn soon they'll catch the mistake and send a corrected invoice."

"You feel that way, Pa, because you're still recovering," Peter said. "When you get better, your spirits will improve, too."

They walked on in silence for a while, passing a lot where a store had been demolished, a flock of winter pigeons with faded plumage foraging among the rubble. His father took a packet of nuts from his pocket which he opened and scattered. With a rapid scurrying across the stones, the birds gathered for the feast.

Staring at the pigeons for a moment, Peter looked up and caught his father watching him.

"Don't tell Mama and Olga I said those things," his father said quietly.

"I won't, Pa, but brace up, will you? You're not finished yet."

"All right, all right," his father shrugged wryly. "I'm just telling you that whatever happens to me, you shouldn't mourn. I got this reprieve, time to think and put all the years I lived into place." He paused, a calmness entering his voice. "Remember, son," he said. "Between a man sleeping and a man dead, there is only a wink."

On his last afternoon before returning to San Francisco, Peter went up to the bedroom where his father was resting to tell him goodbye. He kissed his father's cheek, smelling the scents of the lotion he used after shaving.

"I'll see you in a couple of months, Pa."

"Sure, Pete, sure. Maybe Mama and me will take a flight down to see you later this year, eat some crab together at Fisherman's Wharf."

As his sister's fiancé, Arnold, who was taking him to O'Hare Airport, and he drove away from the house, Peter looked up at his father's bedroom. He saw the old man's body framed in the window. Peter waved quickly and thought he glimpsed his father waving back.

Through that spring and summer, Peter wrote home regularly and phoned his father once a week. Their conversations were spare and strained, his father assuring him with a false heartiness that he was feeling better. Olga wrote him that his father remained quiet and weak, passing his days as if he were simply waiting.

Peter kept planning to go home again, but there always seemed valid reasons to delay. In the fall he justified another postponement by pledging to remain a full three weeks at Christmas. So, in November, when Olga phoned him the news that his father was dying, he felt guilty and remorseful because he had not made the earlier visits.

On the day he flew from San Francisco to Chicago, the sky was layered with dense clouds that obscured the wing tips of his plane. Crossing the mountains, the sky cleared. Looking down on the ranges and valleys of Colorado, he felt awe in a magnitude that seemed to proportion a solitary human grief.

They descended in Chicago and he emerged from the plane into the terminal, seeing the dark, encrusted day through the long glass windows. In the baggage area he claimed his bag and took a taxi. When they pulled up before the brick bungalow he had last seen in February, he stared up at the second-floor bedroom window, senselessly hoping to see his father standing there again.

His sister opened the door, her meager-fleshed face red and swollen from crying. He hugged her tightly.

"How is he, honey?"

"He's still alive," she said. "But Dr. Samos doesn't think he'll last much longer. Even with the oxygen, his heart is failing."

"Shouldn't he be in the hospital?"

"He didn't want to go. The last thing before he slipped into the coma was to make us promise we'd keep him at home."

"He's fooled everyone before," Peter said. "Maybe he'll pull through again."

"I'm afraid this time he won't," she said, and began to cry softly again.

In the kitchen Arnold was finishing a steak. He held the bone in his hands, tearing with his teeth at the shreds of meat. When he rose to shake hands with Peter, his fingers were sticky.

"Have you eaten, Petey?" Olga asked. "While you go up to see Papa I can fix you something."

"Maybe I'll have something later," Peter said. "Is Ma with him now?"

Olga nodded. "We got a day and night nurse for him, too," she said. "But Mama sits with him for hours. Uncle Leo comes and goes too, sitting in the room until he's ready to collapse. Watching him suffer is as hard as watching Mama. I made him take a walk a little while ago."

He followed Olga from the kitchen up the back stairs. On the second floor they entered an oppressive vapor of antiseptics and medications. As Olga paused before his father's bedroom, Peter heard the oxygen hissing inside.

"I'll tell Mama to come out," Olga whispered.

She slipped into the room and after a moment his mother emerged. Her face was slack with grief, her lips quivering, and as she came into his arms he smelled the old, familiar scents of coffee, flour, and bread.

"Thank God, Peter," her voice was low and hoarse. "Thank God you made it here in time."

Peter entered the shadowed room. The white figure of the nurse glistened against the darker walls. He walked to stand beside the bed, looking down upon his father's head resting stiffly within the pillow. His gray hair was mussed, sweat beaded across his forehead. Below his closed eyes, a small mesh mask was clamped over his mouth and nose, the tube extending to a tank beside the bed.

Seeing his father inert and helpless, shrunken and smaller than the big man he remembered, Peter felt his own heart huddle within his father's frame. Their battered and straining hearts were joined, both aching with a frantic need for air. Yet, even as Peter grieved, he felt an unsettling relief because it was his father's time to leave the earth and not his own.

Later, Peter sat with his mother and Uncle Leo at the table in the kitchen. His mother sipped her coffee slowly, her head poised warily and fearfully as if she were listening for some sound. Once, as she started to rise, Uncle Leo caught her arm.

"Despina, please," Uncle Leo pleaded. "Olga and the nurse are with him now. We'll go up again in a while."

His mother fetched up a sigh from deep within her body.

"Such a good man," she said with fervor. "God should grant him a few more years to enjoy his family, to see grandchildren." She looked accusingly at Peter then shook her head in remorse.

"He had a good wife," Uncle Leo said. "A smart son who is a teacher, a loving daughter. Some of us are not even that lucky."

Uncle Leo was ten years younger than his father's sixty-eight years, a small, dapper man who dressed neatly in shirt, tie, and black suits. He had a pale, narrow face and a small, well-trimmed beard. His father had put Leo through college and then given him work as a bookkeeper in the business. He looked after him, teasing and bullying him gently. That Leo can't fart without asking me, his father would say. Andrew, don't talk about your brother that way, his mother would answer. He is my baby brother and I love him, his father would laugh, but the truth is the truth. He is a sparrow in a world of hawks.

In his late forties, Uncle Leo had married a dour, dominating woman who quickly lost patience with him. During the four years his marriage lasted, before his wife deserted him, Leo continued to come to his brother's house like a refugee.

Olga descended the stairs and entered the kitchen. His mother stifled a cry.

"He's all right, Mama!" Olga said quickly. "The nurse wants the medicine from the refrigerator."

"You shouldn't leave him alone!" his mother cried. "There should always be one member of the family beside him if he wakes up."

She crossed the kitchen swiftly to start up the stairs. Olga got the medicine from the refrigerator and hurried up after her.

"The poor women," Uncle Leo said. "It is hard on the poor women. When your grandfather Digenis died, your grandmother's hair turned white overnight."

He fumbled his fingers together and clasped them nervously. Peter noticed then, as if he were seeing them for the first time, how slender and frail they were, unlike his father's big, strong hands.

"But for the men it is hard, too," Uncle Leo said. "You are his son and I am his brother and we both understand he had such a strength. From the beginning we knew he was the head of the house. Every generation has a guardian, you see, one member of the family like a sentinel who keeps the spirit of the generations. Whatever misfortune I endured, I could always come to him for counsel and support. He'd tease me a little, never with malice, and say, Leo, try to understand the ways of life and men . . . that's what he would say.

Something struck the glass of the kitchen window, a falling branch or the collision of a flustered bird that flew to their light. Uncle Leo stared at the window uneasily and then rose and crossed to the window. He stretched on his toes and caught the cord of the shade, pulling the sash to the sill. For a moment he stood with his back to Peter, a small, frail figure in his neat dark suit.

"This world will be a lonely place for me when Andrew is gone," he said softly.

Peter went up to the attic room that had once been his haven. He lay, still dressed, across the spread that had an odor of mildew, staring out the window at the reflection of streetlamps. Beneath the eaves he heard the stirring of pigeons, the familiar cooings and snufflings he remembered as a boy. Those sounds compressed time for him and he recalled the mornings, so long ago, when his father came upstairs to wake him. He'd be awake already but unwilling to relinquish the warm nest. As his father entered his room, he'd close his eyes, making off he was asleep. He'd feel the mattress creaking and sinking under his father's weight and then the big hand fumbling across the quilt until it found his knee, stroking the bone and flesh gently. When Peter opened his eyes, good morning, son, his father would say. Time to face the new day like a champion.

He dozed a while, unsure how long, and then woke startled from a dream. He rose anxiously from the bed and walked down the stairs. On the way to his father, he passed his sister's bedroom. She was sitting in an armchair beside his mother, who was sleeping on the bed. Olga rose and came quietly into the hall.

"I finally got her to come out and rest," she whispered. "Uncle Leo is with Papa now."

When Peter entered his father's room, the nurse sitting in the corner raised her head quickly as if she had been napping. In a chair close beside the bed, Uncle Leo sat erect and motionless. Peter whispered to him that he would sit with his father for a while. Uncle Leo rose stiffly, staring a moment longer at his brother's face before walking wearily from the room. Peter sat down in the chair that still held the warmth of his uncle's body.

The hissing of the oxygen rose and fell in waves, echoing like whispers from the hidden corners of the room. Recalling again the mornings when his father woke him with a caress, he leaned forward and with his fingers found the outline of his father's leg, following the contour to the hard knob of knee. He stroked the bone and spare flesh lightly, repaying a debt, feeling a futile hope that his father might know.

An alien sound intruded suddenly upon the air, the measure and flow of oxygen altered, a faltering of the tempo. His father's face seemed to swell slightly from the recesses of the pillow, a wind quivering across his cheeks. Then, noiseless and swift as a specter, his life slipped away.

Shocked at how quickly death had come, Peter called the nurse. She bent over his father's body, her fingers moving rapidly over his mouth and eyes.

When Peter entered his sister's room, her head snapped up. For a moment she stared at him and then her wail woke his mother. She struggled from the bed, a shriek bursting from her throat, and hurried from the room. Peter and Olga followed her and his mother had flung herself across his father's body. She cried his name over and over as her flesh tugged urgently and wildly at his flesh.

Afterward, exhausted and silent, she sat in the chair beside the bed, staring at his father's dead face. His sister cried softly in one of the shadowed corners of the room.

He found Uncle Leo asleep in an armchair in the parlor, his head slumped wearily to one side, his cheek rumpled and red. Peter touched his shoulder gently and his uncle opened his eyes.

"Uncle Leo," Peter said quietly. "Papa is gone."

"Oh, my God!" his uncle cried. "Oh, my God! My brother is dead!"

"His last words were for you, Uncle Leo," Peter said, and as his uncle rose from the chair, he grasped him by the arms as he had so often seen his father do. "He woke just before the end and spoke Mama's name and your name, as if to let you both know how much he loved you."

Uncle Leo nodded gratefully, trying to control his trembling. Holding tightly to Peter's arm, they walked up the stairs.

After a while Peter walked downstairs, passing through the hallway to the front of the house. He opened the door and stepped out onto the porch. The night was sharp and chilled, forerunning the cold of winter. The last dried autumn leaves were scattered on the steps. On the roofs of houses across the street, tracings of stars lightened the summits of chimneys. From beneath the eaves of their own house a pigeon took flight with a noisy flapping of wings. Afterward, the earth hung motionless, as if the night were holding its breath.

His father was dead. He felt that loss, and the sorrow of knowing a treasured part of his life was gone. Yet, he also felt strangely consoled. A storehouse of generations, a family's journeys, memories, and dreams, wellsprings of love and devotion had passed in the interval between sleep and death to him.

He stood on the porch a moment longer and then walked back into the house.

This story, unhappily, is based on true experience. Just after the war, when I owned a shabby lunchroom, harried by fear of bankruptcy and collapse I bought a crate of turkeys that had died a natural death. They cost only twelve cents a pound, and my chef, an unwilling conspirator, boiled them for a day and a night. When the wretched creatures were finally palatable, we garnished them with cranberry and a mucilaginous gravy. I served them for a full week, only varying the menu descriptions each day:

Monday:	Roast Young Tom Turkey
Tuesday:	Turkey and Noodles
Wednesday:	Hot Turkey Sandwich
Thursday:	Turkey Croquettes
Friday:	Turkey Hash
Saturday:	Chicken à la King

That was the only week in months my lunchroom showed a profit, but the fearful anxiety that one of our patrons might drop off the stool and expire on our floor has, I am certain, shortened my life.

Fortunately, we suffered no mishap that week. But every Thanksgiving since then, when I sit down at the dinner table to a succulent and butter-basted turkey, I suffer a fleeting but virulent pang of guilt.

PA AND THE SAD TURKEYS

Some damn fool once said that all a Greek had to do to make money in a restaurant was to enter partnership with another Greek and watch the cash register. The guy that started that rumor better stay away from my Pa.

Our place wasn't classy enough to be called a restaurant. It was a drab lunchroom in a factory district near the railroad yards. We had six tables and twenty-six stools. They were all filled for an hour over lunch, and the rest of the day and night a customer might think the place was a graveyard.

There were three of us as partners, and that was a mistake. Pa and Uncle Louie had been partners for a number of years. When the army drafted me, Pa forgave me for having left college after one year, and, in a flurry of patriotism, he and Uncle Louie cut me in for an equal share of the business. They wanted me to have something to come back to a few years later. When I returned in a month with a medical discharge for a bad knee, Pa was sorry, but by then the papers had been signed.

Not that I wanted to stay in the lunchroom forever, but I was still developing my character and had nothing special that I wanted to do yet besides make a fortune playing the horses. The lunchroom was near a reputable bookie, and I had to spend the time between races somewhere. I worked out in front as a waiter, and Pa and Uncle Louie worked in the kitchen as chefs, dishwashers, butchers, and anything else that came up.

Business was terrible and getting worse. About three in the afternoon, when we hadn't seen a customer in two hours, Pa would stamp out of the kitchen and begin. "May the fiend that sold us this place fall in a sewer," Pa said. "May his back swell with boils and his lying tongue turn black."

"Take it easy, Pa," I said. "That won't bring in any business."

Uncle Louie came to stand smiling in the kitchen doorway. He and Pa were brothers, but they weren't a bit alike. Pa was big with a barrel back and the thick neck of a bull. A heavy head of hair, iron-gray at the temples, came down over his forehead until it almost merged with his bushy eyebrows. I loved him, but I had to admit he resembled a gorilla, with a disposition to match.

Uncle Louie was an amiable idiot. I don't say that with any intended disrespect. I loved him too. He was a good-natured gentle little man who always smiled. That might seem commendable except that Uncle Louie carried smiling too far. Tell him about a terrible auto accident with the occupants smashed and bleeding, and Uncle Louie would listen carefully and smile and shake his head. Working with Pa in the kitchen would have driven a normal man crazy. Uncle Louie was insulated.

Pa fixed me with a baleful eye. "Lucky for me you went one year to college," he said. "Tell me, how did you manage four years of education in that one year?"

Uncle Louie smiled broadly.

"Cut it out, Pa," I said.

"Sure," he said and shook his head violently. "I will cut it out when you stop playing the horses and start thinking of a way to save us. This place is a graveyard. You hear me, hoodlum, a graveyard, and you are standing around with a shovel."

"Shut up, Pa," I said. "Here comes a customer."

Pa stared in disbelief as a leather-jacketed baggage handler shuffled in the door and sat down at the counter. Uncle Louie scurried back to the kitchen.

I brought the customer a glass of water. Pa elbowed me aside and handed him a menu.

"Coffee," the man said.

For a moment Pa's face twisted in a silent snarl.

"With or without a toothpick?" Pa asked, and he stood above the man with his hairy arms spread wide on his hips. The man looked up as if suspecting a joke, but Pa was grim.

"Have you had lunch?" Pa asked.

The man gaped at Pa for a moment and then numbly shook his head.

"What are you waiting for?" Pa said. "By skipping a meal you do injury to your stomach. Regular eating habits assure a sound body." He shook his head sadly. "Your appearance is unhealthy. When did you last see a doctor?"

The man nearly fell off his stool in shock and outrage. He stumbled to the door and, with his hand on the knob, turned and spoke in choked indignation. "You must be nuts!"

The door slammed behind him.

"Nice going, Pa," I said. "That should help pick up business."

Uncle Louie stuck his head out the kitchen door. "Thomas," he said to Pa. "I was waiting to hear an order. Where is the patron?"

"Coffee!" Pa said. "At a time when I am faced with eviction for nonpayment of rent, that lout comes in and orders coffee."

"He doesn't care about our troubles," I said.

"Who does?" Pa said and laughed in a show of frivolity. "Does my horse-playing son care? My educated son who spent one hard year in college and got a degree in the Daily Triple."

"The Daily Double, Pa," I said patiently. "Get it right."

"Thank you," Pa said. "I am happy you are around to correct me. I am so happy I wish I could die now in the middle of my joy."

"Don't expire yet, Pa," I said. "The Oscar Mayer man is due in for the meat order for next week."

"No order," Pa said somberly. "They have refused us further credit unless we put up cash. Not a bone without money.'

"I'm sorry, Pa," I said. "I'm broke."

Uncle Louie ducked into the kitchen. He might have been simple, but he knew when to disappear. Not that he had any money either, but he didn't want to put Pa to the trouble of asking.

Pa laughed again without mirth. "In this way does it end," he said. "Next week my doors will close for good. People will whisper all across the city that Thomas Lanaras has failed. The icebox has nothing left but three small pork chops."

"One chop left, Pa," I said apologetically. "I got hungry late last night."

He fixed cold furious eyes on me.

"Can't we have a macaroni and spaghetti festival next week?" I asked.

"Do me a favor," he said slowly. "Don't think. Don't talk. Don't make a suggestion." He walked stiffly to the kitchen. In a moment I heard him wailing to Uncle Louie.

Sam Anastis came in about four-thirty. He was a renegade wholesale meatman specializing in animals that died natural deaths. He had the wide hot smile of a professional con man, a high-pitched shrill voice, and he always looked back over his shoulder at intervals as if afraid he was being followed. He carried a brown bag that he held tightly as if it contained some peerless treasure.

I lifted my nose out of the racing form. "Pa," I called out. "Sam Anastis is here."

"Tell him to drop dead," Pa shouted from the kitchen.

Sam Anastis laughed heartily. "What a sense of humor that man has," he said brightly.

"He's a riot all right," I said.

Sam Anastis walked on small quick feet to the swinging door and opened it a little. "Mr. Lanaras," he called out gaily. "It is me, Sam Anastis. I want to talk to you."

"Got to hell, Sam Anastis!" Pa roared.

Sam Anastis laughed shrilly. When he could catch his breath he shook his head at me. "What a man," he said. "Always kidding."

He opened the door slightly again. "Mr. Lanaras, please come out now," he said. "Sam Anastis has something for you at a price. I could have sold to any of a hundred restaurants, but when this golden opportunity came my way, I thought of you."

Pa said something shocking in Greek that called in question the parentage of Sam Anastis.

"All right, sir," Sam Anastis grinned slyly. "All right. I'll have to take my proposition to Mr. Botilakis. How he will laugh when I tell him I offered it to you first."

He finished and stepped back quickly. A moment later Pa came violently through the swinging door. Uncle Louie followed smiling behind him. If there was anything could set Pa's teeth on edge, it was mention of our archcompetitor, the Olympia Lunchroom on 15th Street, run by that black-hearted Macedonian, Antonio Botilakis.

Pa pointed a big warning finger at Sam Anastis. "I give you thirty seconds," he said. "At the end of that time I personally will kick you from here into the gutter. Now begin!"

Sam Anastis wasted ten seconds trying to decide whether Pa was serious. When he realized Pa was, he hastily opened the bag he carried and drew out something long and scrawny. "Look!" he said triumphantly. "Look!"

"In God's name, what is it?" Pa asked.

Sam Anastis looked hurt. He appealed to Uncle Louie. "You know what it is, of course."

Uncle Louie furrowed his brow. He smiled sympathetically at Sam Anastis. "It looks familiar," Uncle Louie said brightly.

Sam Anastis looked heartbroken. "It is a turkey," he said. "A genuine milk-fed purebred turkey. A wonderful specimen."

"Of course," Uncle Louie said. "A turkey."

Pa looked incredulous.

"That is a turkey?" he asked.

"It is some kind of bird all right," I said. "I think I can make out a wing."

Sam Anastis laughed, and Uncle Louie laughed with him.

"Like father like son," Sam Anastis said. "Both always clowning."

"If that is a turkey," Pa said somberly, "it has been hit by a truck."

"No!" Sam Anastis exploded in protest.

"Why is it so dark?" I asked.

"I'm glad you asked," Sam Anastis said. "This turkey was raised on a farm in Florida. Healthy sunshine all year round."

He made off to hand the bird to me.

"I don't want to touch it," I said. "I don't want to catch whatever it was that killed it."

"I was in Florida once," Uncle Louie said.

"Sam Anastis," Pa said, "I have known you for ten years. I knew your father. In the old country he was arrested three times for trying to sell the Parthenon to tourists. For you to come in here and suggest I buy that bird is an action so arrogant even he would not have dared."

"What is the matter with this turkey?" Sam Anastis asked in a grieved voice.

"What did the autopsy show?" I asked.

"In Florida it was very pleasant," Uncle Louie said. "I spent much time on the beach."

"Get out," Pa said, and he waved his big fist toward the door. "Go sell that abomination to Botilakis."

Sam Anastis backed toward the door still dangling the turkey.

"You are making a terrible mistake," he said shrilly. "I have a crate of these fine birds. You can have them for twelve cents a pound. At twelve cents a pound your profit will be enormous."

Pa stopped short. "Twelve cents a pound?" he asked.

"We stayed at a big hotel," Uncle Louie said. He smiled warmly. "The windows looked out on the water."

"Pa," I said warningly. "Forget it. Serve those birds and the police will put us away for life."

Sam Anastis took a step forward.

"Any chef can fix an attractive bird," he whined eagerly. "These birds are a real test. A lot of boiling to tenderize the meat. Plenty of seasoning to lend aroma. A good thick gravy. Believe me, these birds are a challenge I would be proud to accept if I were a chef."

"Get out, Sam Anastis," I said. "I'm only a sad horse player, not a murderer."

"Wait," Pa said. "Let me examine that bird more closely."

"A turkey," Uncle Louie said. "Of course."

Pa took the bird and turned his nose away. He pressed the bony thigh. "There is meat here," he said. "And there. And there. There is considerable meat on it."

"What did I say?" Sam Anastis shrieked. "A lovely bird and for the price a steal. I make nothing on the sale, but I hope to keep you as friends always."

"How much will the crate come to?" Pa asked.

"Eighty pounds," Sam Anastis said quickly. "Exactly nine dollars and sixty cents."

"I'll give you seven-fifty," Pa said.

"I contracted for twelve cents a pound," Sam Anastis said, outraged. "I gave you the best possible price. I saved them for you. Now you make a ridiculous offer."

Pa shrugged. "Forget it," he said and turned away.

"Wait!" Sam Anastis cried. "It has been a long day. My feet hurt. I'll take it."

He started quickly to his car to get the turkeys before Pa changed his mind.

"Pa," I said. "You must be nuts. Poisoning people is no joke."

"Shut your face about poison," Pa said. "This is a miracle which has been provided to save us from bankruptcy and disgrace."

"Maybe they will let us work in the prison kitchen," I said.

"Zipper your mouth!" Pa said. "You have no faith. Uncle Louie and I will fix those birds. We will fix them so they would be fit to serve on the table of a king."

Sam Anastis came in struggling with the crate.

"Where?" he gasped.

"In the kitchen," Pa said, and there was a wild gleam in his eyes.

That night after closing, the lights blazed in our kitchen. Pa and Uncle Louie placed great pots of water to boil on the stoves. When the kitchen was shrouded in steam, they threw in the turkeys. They boiled them all night, the two of them fretting around the pots like a pair of mad chefs. The smell was awful.

On Saturday morning it was hard to get an order out of the kitchen because Pa and Uncle Louie were working frantically over those birds. Some of the smell from the night before still lingered, and when customers wrinkled up their noses and complained, I told them a gas line had broken.

We did a light lunch business because it was Saturday, and then the place emptied again. By sometime that afternoon the first batch of turkeys had been out of the ovens a couple of hours and the second batch was in. Pa came out and sat at one of the tables with a pad of paper and a pencil, mumbling to himself as he figured out the menus for the coming week.

"Monday will be roast young tom turkey," Pa said. "Tuesday, turkey and noodles. Wednesday, hot turkey sandwich. Thursday, chicken à la king. Friday, turkey hash," He finished, pleased at his sagacity.

"You forgot chicken croquettes," I said.

"Shut up," Pa said.

I buried my head back in the racing form and wondered how I might sneak out to make a bet in the fifth race at Tropical Park.

Everything was quiet. No other sound than Pa mumbling and a mail truck rumbling past in the street outside. I heard the swinging door from the kitchen, and I looked up.

"Pa, look!" I said. "Look!"

Uncle Louie stood in the doorway. For the first time I could remember he wasn't smiling. There was a look of incredible distress on his face, and he held his hand across his stomach.

"Louie, what is the matter?" Pa asked.

Uncle Louie tried to speak, but no sound came. Before our eyes his face seemed to darken and his cheeks seemed to swell. He made another valiant effort to speak, and only a deep mournful croak came out.

"Louie!" Pa hollered. "In God's name, what has happened?"

"Pa!" I shouted. "I bet he ate some turkey!"

When he heard the word "turkey," Uncle Louie stiffened as if he had been shot. Then he stepped forward, placing one foot down carefully, and followed it slowly with the other. He made one final mighty effort to smile. When that failed he spun around like a top, once, twice, propelled by some relentless force, and then he collapsed on the floor flat on his back.

"He is dead!" Pa wailed and ran to him. "Louie is dead!"

"A stomach pump!" I shouted. "His stomach must be emptied!" I rushed to the phone.

Pa knelt weeping beside Uncle Louie. "Speak to me, my beloved brother," Pa beseeched him. "Speak to me, companion of my youth. Speak!"

Uncle Louie stared in anguish at the ceiling.

I got Doctor Samyotis, who had a little office on the boulevard about a block away, and he promised to come at once. I rushed over to where Pa cradled Uncle Louie's head just in time to hear a terrible rattle rise out of Uncle Louie's throat.

"His death cry!" Pa shouted. "Get a priest!"

"Take it easy, Pa," I said. "The doctor will be here in a minute."

"Too late," Pa wailed. "My brother will be gone."

"Don't give up hope, Pa," I said. I opened Uncle Louie's collar. He sure looked awful.

The door banged open, and Doctor Samyotis came in. He took one look at Uncle Louie. "In the kitchen," he snapped. "Carry him back there."

Pa and I picked up Uncle Louie and carried him into the kitchen.

"Put him on the table," Doctor Samyotis said. "Get a pail. The ambulance is coming."

We set him down, and I felt a little sick myself. I left Pa to help the doctor and walked back to the front. A truck driver had come in and was nonchalantly sitting at the counter.

"We are closed," I said.

"I just want a bowl of soup," he said.

"We are closed," I said. "Get out."

"Whadyumean closed?" he said. "I just want a bowl of soup."

From the kitchen Uncle Louie wailed a terrible cry of anguish and doom.

The guy made it to the door in a single leap. I locked up and sat down to wait. I was worn out.

In a few minutes the ambulance pulled up in front of the store. I unlocked the door, and two white-coated guys came in with a collapsible stretcher. I waved them into the kitchen.

In another few moments they came out carrying Uncle Louie. He was covered with a blanket to his throat, and a towel was wrapped around his head. All that showed was his mouth, and poor Uncle Louie wasn't smiling.

Pa came out with Doctor Samyotis.

"Doc," I asked, "will Uncle Louie be all right?"

"He will be all right," Doctor Samyotis said. "Just sick for a while."

The attendants loaded Uncle Louie in the ambulance. A small crowd of railroad workers gathered around outside and peered in through the plate-glass window.

Pa started to get his coat. Doctor Samyotis stopped him. "You stay here!" he barked. "Go bury those turkeys!"

Pa stared shamefaced at the floor.

The doctor walked out and slammed the door. The ambulance pulled away.

A few guys still stared through the window. Pa made a fierce face through the glass, and they scattered. He came back and sat despondently at one of the tables.

"What have I done?" Pa said, and he rocked back and forth like a mourner. "What have I done?"

"It wasn't entirely your fault, Pa," I said.

He shook his head somberly. "He might have died," he said. "Poor Louie might have died."

"It would have been worse if it was a customer," I said. "We might have gotten sued."

"Shut up!" Pa said. "You have no family feeling."

I didn't say anything more because I knew how stricken he was about Uncle Louie.

At that moment the front door opened and Sam Anastis came in as if he had sprung out of the earth. He stood beaming his hot wide smile at us. I was afraid to look at Pa.

"Greetings," Sam Anastis glowed. "I was passing by and thought I would stop and inquire how went the turkeys? Are they roasted yet?"

I finally looked at Pa, and his face was impassive, but there was a blue vein swelling in his forehead and his cheeks were gathering red with blood.

"Welcome, Sam Anastis," Pa said in a strangely gentle voice. "What a friend you were to bring those turkeys to me."

"What did I tell you?" Sam Anastis trumpeted. "I made nothing on that sale, but for friends like you I don't care."

He saw Pa approaching. For a moment a cloud of uneasiness swept his face. Then it was too late. Pa reached him, and I held my breath. But Pa just clapped him softly on the shoulder.

Seeing Pa close enough to feel the heat shaking off his cheeks made Sam Anastis realize something was wrong. He tried to smile away his fear, but by that time Pa had his arm and began to walk him back to the kitchen.

"Come and see the turkeys, Sam Anastis," Pa said. "I will make you a little sandwich."

Sam Anastis looked shocked. He had an iron-clad rule against eating anything he sold. "I have just eaten," he laughed weakly. "I am not a bit hungry. I never eat this time of day."

By the time they got to the kitchen door, Sam Anastis was dragging his heels. Pa graciously all but lifted him through the door and turned back to me. "You!" he barked. "Call Doctor Samyotis!"

I went quickly to the phone and dialed the doctor's office. He wasn't back yet, and I left urgent word with the nurse for him to come. For Pa's sake, I hoped he would make it in time.

As I hung up, a terrible cry of lament and despair sounded from the kitchen. I got my coat and hurried out the door. I didn't want to go all through that again. Besides, if I hurried, I might still get a bet down in the last race at Jamaica.

When I was very young I thought that love, the bond shared by Heathcliff and Cathy in *Wuthering Heights*, endured even after death. As I grew older I understood that love contains only the façade of eternity. When we lose someone we love to death, after a time of mourning, driven by physical and emotional needs, we move again to the virginal experience of another love.

That isn't unfaithfulness, simply the rhythm of life. Still, we must allow a place for those haunted men and women who might indeed be able to love only once.

CHRISOULA

She could not live the remainder of her life in mourning. For a while she would wear her widow's black raiment and grieve for her man murdered in the summer of his life. When she could no longer bear her cold and solitary bed, she would find another man to love her, a man, perhaps, she too might love. That was the way of the flesh and of life. But for as long as she lived, Petros would always remain, for her, the first of men and the best.

Yes, he was a man who could not tell a tale without dazzling lies. He held before him the vision of fair-seeming but false glories. He scorned that which was seemly and good, and blindly pursued that which was graceless and evil.

But he was also tall, raven-haired, with black eyes that gleamed like those of a gypsy. His lips glistened as if he had just bitten into a ripe, sweet plum. She had only to look at his lips and be filled with desire. His arms and shoulders were as powerful as a gymnast's and yet his waist was lean as that of a boy. To watch him enter or leave a room was a delight. He walked in a lithe, strong stride as if he were on his way to or returning from a festival.

He was a man of swift movement and strong beat, untamed and reckless and unafraid of anything on earth. He courted Chrisoula as a princess might be courted with a radiant grace. He brought her flowers, sang to her at night under her window while her sisters giggled and peeked from behind the blinds. He would eat dinner with her family on Sunday evenings and to her father's distress would jump up several times during the meal to regale them with a story that he acted out with fervence and skill. There were times he seemed a marvelous child adrift in a world of adults and at other moments, when they were alone, a mature man. He was twenty-five when they married in the autumn of that year and Chrisoula was twenty-two.

On the night before the wedding, her father took Chrisoula into the basement of their house, away from the ears of her mother and sisters.

"You love this man, I know," her father said. "You love deep in your blood in the way of our people. I am resigned to this love and understand nothing I say or do can spare you the grief you will endure. Go then and marry with my blessing. But when you take this man as your husband, forsake all thought of serenity, a peaceful house, a consoling old age."

"I love him, papa," Chrisoula said. "I will endure what must be endured."

"You will endure," her father said sadly, "but you cannot imagine how much. This man lives out of his time and his place. Centuries have passed him by. The stars and the rivers and the mountains will call him back."

"I will help him, papa," she said. "My love will protect him from harm."

"It is not enough," he shook his head wearily. "One can more easily destroy than save with love."

He reached out to her then and with his fingers touched her cheek in a mute and consoling caress.

For a little while that autumn, Petros and Chrisoula lived as God must have wished men and women to live. They made a refuge and a haven of their three small rooms that looked out upon the street of shabby tenements and dingy stores. When they ventured out to shop for food and wine or to walk in the last fragrant twilights of October, people moved like shadows about them and sounds seemed to come from a distant world.

At night they lay naked together, watching from their bedroom window the sky like a moon-splashed sea and the stars glittering rings and circles of light.

"Do you know why I love you?" Petros asked.

"Because I am a peach and a pomegranate," she said. "Comely as the bride of Solomon with breasts that ravish your eyes."

"You are an insufferable woman!" he laughed. "You take a man's songs from his mouth before they are spoken!"

"I only tell you what you have told me before," she said and kissed him.

"That was before," he said. "Each day and night I love you differently. I savor your face when you laugh, cry out, or in your moments of melancholy."

"My darling," she whispered.

"Listen to me," he said, and his voice trembled. "I have seen many marvelous sights on this earth, a storm in the mountains, a ship under sail on an azure sea, a bride dancing at her wedding. But the naked loveliness of my beloved is the supreme sight of all."

She reveled in his endearments. delighted to feel him asleep beside her, their legs side by side, her toes touching his ankle. Above all she loved the moments of their passion, his fingers pressing her shoulders, his lips curling upon her breath. She felt then the shudders which began as ripples and rolled into great waves across her body. It was as if they rode the crest of a wild sea, their bed a tossing ship, the ceiling of their room a boundless sky.

Sometimes, afterwards, she would cry, the tears rolling slowly down her cheeks. He would hold her tightly and kiss her eyes.

"You foolish little girl," he said. "When you should be the happiest after we love, you cry."

"You are the foolish one if you do not understand why I cry," she said. "After a moment so exquisite I cannot help but think of us as old, someday emptied of youth and passion, withered leaves falling to the earth to die."

"We mustn't waste time brooding about death," he said. "There is too much life to be lived." He leaped from the bed to stand like a naked young god above her.

"But if by some quirk or mischance I should die," he said gravely. "Ornament my body with basil and mint in the way my mother adorned the corpse of my father, and scatter the petals of flowers across my eyes . . ."

"Petros!" she cried, and her blood ran cold. "Petros, stop!"

"Make the house rock with your widow's grief for a while," he laughed, "and then find a hardy man for your lonely bed."

"Damn you, stop! Damn you, damn you, stop!"

He came quickly to kneel beside her on the bed.

"I am sorry," he said, and he was shaken with remorse. "I was only teasing. I am sorry, my beloved, forgive me." He kissed her temples and kissed her eyes. "Love is stronger than death," he whispered, "and our love will live forever, setting eternity ablaze with its burning song."

She took him then into her arms, holding him as a mother holds a child unaware of the grim shades of life. She held him until he had fallen asleep, her naked breasts a plumed pillow for his fine dark hair.

When they married, Petros was working as a bread truck driver, one of many jobs he had worked at through the last few years. He had been a bartender, counterman, had driven a produce truck, and loaded bags of potatoes at the market. After their marriage none of these jobs seemed to satisfy him. He was conscious suddenly of the responsibility of marriage. Chrisoula's father reluctantly offered him a junior partnership in his grocery business, but Petros scorned the offer as a gratuity. He grew vexed and sullen.

"There are many women on this street whose bodies have aged through too much work and too many children," he said. "They might have been lovely once but the years have hollowed them out. They can no longer laugh or sing. I will turn the saints out of heaven before I let that happen to you."

"I am young and strong," she said. "Don't worry about me."

"On my route in the stores where I deliver bread," he said, "I see the wives of other men in fine clothing, driving fine cars. Why should my wife have less than these women? Am I less a man than their men?"

"I have you," she tried to comfort him. "Those wealthy women would trade all their possessions and their sad husbands for someone like you."

He shook his head impatiently. "I am your husband now," he said. "I must look after you, provide you the things which people respect."

"People will respect us if we are true and live well in the eyes of God," she said.

"Chrisoula, will you listen!" he cried. "It is not what you are willing to settle for, but what I feel you should have."

"Petros, be patient," she pleaded. "We have our love, the days and nights we share together. The rest will come. Be patient, my darling."

"To hell with patience," he said, and closed his heart like a stone against her.

For several weeks afterwards, Petros brooded. He was late coming home from work and told her he had been looking for other employment. She knew by his breath and the sodden glint in his eye that he had spent the time in the taverns.

There was an evening in November, a sharp cold night, when she heard him shouting from the street below. She opened the window, shivering slightly in the cold air, and saw him standing on the sidewalk below with a man she recognized as Antonio Gallos.

"We are coming up!" he cried. "I am bringing Mr. Gallos up! Take out the glasses and the wine!"

He tugged Gallos by the arm and they entered the doorway. Chrisoula closed the window, confused and suddenly frightened.

Antonio Gallos was well known in their neighborhood. As a child she had heard her father curse after Gallos had driven past them in his great glittering car. He was a fat, heavy-jowled man who wore diamonds on his fingers, and expensive tailored clothes wasted on his obese frame. He owned a candle company and a bakery. He owned, as well, three gambling parlors packed all day with men wagering on the horses, dice and cards. The candle company and bakery he maintained as a facade of respectability which fooled no one since they all knew the gambling parlors provided him his wealth.

She took off her apron, started nervously to smooth back her hair and then angrily stopped. She walked to the door just as it burst open and Petros entered.

"Come in, come in, Mr. Gallos!" Petros motioned him over the threshold. Gallos entered wearing a fine black cashmere coat and a white silk scarf, in sharp contrast to Petros' jacket and cap.

"This is my wife, Soula," Petros said. "I told you she was a beauty, didn't I? Soula, this is Mr. Gallos."

Gallos stood staring at her, blinking slightly in approval. The skin of his face was sallow, his nose long and thin, his lips meager and colorless.

"Please come in," Soula said and avoided asking for his coat.

"Give me your coat, Mr. Gallos," Petros said and glared at her.

Gallos drew off his gloves slowly, and his hands were small, his fingers blunt and unsightly. On two fingers of each hand he wore sparkling diamonds.

Petros helped him off with his coat and Gallos walked into the small parlor and sat down heavily on the faded cushions of the couch. He drew his shiny pointed shoes back carefully from a threadbare section of carpet.

"I have brought Mr. Gallos home to meet you and to have a glass of wine," Petros said, a sullen anger beginning to stir in his voice. "Mr. Gallos has honored us by offering me a fine position."

"I'm sorry, there is no wine left," Chrisoula said. "We finished the bottle last night at dinner."

"No wine!" Petros cried in dismay. He made a gesture of apology to Gallos. "A house without wine is a body without blood. I will go downstairs and buy some."

"Never mind, Petros," Gallos made a small delicate shrug of his shoulders. "We can have a glass of wine together some other time."

"I beg your pardon, Mr. Gallos," Petros said, his voice rigid with pride. "In your house and in your business, you command and I will obey. In my house, as my guest, I will command. You will please wait just a few moments. Soula will keep you company. I will go just a few doors down the street and return instantly."

Then he was gone, rocking the door closed behind him, his feet beating a hurried descent.

For a long, stiff interval the room was silent.

"The weather seems to be turning colder," Gallos said finally, and looked down at his shoes.

"Yes," Chrisoula said.

He nodded. "To be expected, of course, this time of year."

"Mr. Gallos," Chrisoula said. "What work will Petros be doing for you?"

He brushed a speck of lint from his trousers and frowned as he looked toward the window. "A number of duties relating to my business," he said.

"Which business, Mr. Gallos?" she asked quietly.

He looked at her startled and blinked. A slight, uneasy smile trembled the thin flap of his upper lip.

"You are a handsome woman, Mrs. Zervas," he said, "and a blunt one too. I admire that quality in a woman. My blessed mother was like that, God rest her departed soul. Kept my poor father off balance all his life." He stared down at the rings on his fingers. "It is well known that I operate several gambling rooms in this neighborhood. But I maintain them as honestly as I can. I provide people a place for the excitement they find in gambling. This Christmas I will have been in business here forty years." He sighed. "Frankly, I am tired. After all, I am not as young as I used to be. And I find fewer and fewer men I can trust. Would you believe, Mrs. Zervas, that everyone steals from me? My managers and dealers and ticket writers and runners." He fumbled his fingers nervously together in his lap. "There are those who say that I operate outside the law. That is completely false! I am in perfect harmony with the law. I have one captain, three lieutenants, six sergeants on my payroll. Every Christmas more than a hundred policemen receive baskets from me with turkey, ham, cheese and fruit, and bottles of good wine. Their families enjoy a pleasanter Christmas because of my generosity."

"Forgive me, Mr. Gallos," Chrisoula said. "What role will Petros play in all of this activity?"

He did not answer for a moment. He stared anxiously at the door, as if eager for Petros to return. He looked back at Chrisoula.

"I have been watching Petros for quite a while," he said earnestly. "I admire his energy and his courage. He is bright and quick and people are drawn to him. I believe he is honest. What I wish him to do for me is to keep a close check on all phases of my business. Collect the monies from my managers, keep an eye on my dealers and runners. Satisfy my customers that they are being treated honestly. You need not worry about Petros if he works with me. I will look after him and he can go far with me."

"We may not wish to go your way," she said.

He nodded slowly and then sighed. "Long ago when I was young," he said, "I tried to be fair and good and make a living for myself in some conventional occupation. But I was ugly, sin enough, and worse than that, innocent. Yes, I admit my ugliness and my innocence. You see I can speak as bluntly as you. But I quickly learned that society is composed of thieves. Whether in mahogany-paneled offices on La Salle Street or in my gambling rooms, all steal in one way or another from others. He who steals the most achieves the greatest wealth and success."

"That is not true, Mr. Gallos."

"Please, Mrs. Zervas," he cut her off with a quick nervous flutter of his fingers. "Allow me to finish, I beg you. Petros will be back in a moment and I may not have another chance to explain this to you." He rubbed his palm gently in a caress across the rings on his other hand. "I want Petros to prevent others from stealing what is mine. It is as simple as that. In return, I will pay him well, and, who knows. I am childless and not well. After I am gone the business must belong to someone."

"No," she said, and felt a sliver of fear pierce her heart. "No!"

"Yes!" he said, and for the first time a force and conviction entered his voice. "Yes! In this life there are only victims and masters. Petros will always remain a victim driving a bread truck."

At the bottom of the stairs the street door closed with a bang. Gallos jumped as if the noise had startled him.

"Remember what I say," he spoke in a hurried whisper. "Don't make your husband a wound to fit another man's arrows . . . help him fashion arrows of his own."

The door opened and Petros entered carrying a full case of wine on his shoulder. With ease he swung the case to the table. He reached in and pulled out two bottles of wine and held them high over his head. "Wine for my darling and for my new employer!" he cried. "Soula, the glasses!" His voice trembled with excitement. "The glasses so we can drink to the future!"

Chrisoula rose and started to the kitchen for the glasses, fighting the despair that curled like a black snake in her body.

For the next few months, through the coldest part of winter, Petros supervised the handbooks for Gallos. He made sure they functioned in accord with Gallos' wishes. In return for this protection, Gallos was generous. Petros brought home more money each week than he ordinarily had earned in a month of work. After a few futile efforts to convince him that what he was doing was wrong, Chrisoula gave up and kept silent. And each week the money increased. Petros bought new suits for himself and new dresses for Chrisoula which she secretly returned.

When she refused to move from their small apartment to larger, more lavish quarters, Petros had all the old furniture carted away and replaced it with new chairs, bureaus, a table and a large, gaudy and expensive couch. One afternoon he drove home in a new car and she rode with him in it while he chattered as excitedly as a child.

Sometimes lying beside him at night, watching the pale winter moonlight sweep the ceiling of their room, feeling his body warm and quiet against her flesh, she rested within the serenity and love they had in the early months of their marriage. But in the morning she woke to another day filled with foreboding.

For all her despair, Petros was happier than he had been in years. Each triumph fed his vanity and his pride. Because of his energy and effort, Gallos prospered, and opened two additional handbooks, the first such expansion in more than twenty years. Petros tasted the respect and envy of other men and found it a savory wine. They called him the young crown prince and it was rumored that Gallos was as fond of him as if Petros were his own son.

The marauders came from across the city, lean, hard men with the souls of maggots. They had heard of Gallos expanding his gambling and came for his spoils. They bombed one of his handbooks, and, in terror, Gallos wanted to give up. In his old age he feared for his useless life. But Petros scorned their threats. When two of them came to Gallos to present their ultimatum, they found Petros waiting for them instead. He took on the two of them, laughing with excitement as his powerful arms beat them into a bruised and bloody retreat. He regarded the fight as part of a jubilant game, a game in which the contestants were honorable men.

That night flushed with the heat of his triumph, he celebrated in a circle of admiring, shouting men while Gallos ordered case after case of wine for the hordes to toast the young prince of his realm.

Chrisoula waited for him to come home. She walked through the rooms, her shadow rising and falling in frantic sweepings along the walls. She marked each passing minute as if it were an hour. When she could endure waiting no longer, she went down to the street.

The night was bleak and cold, a smell of snow riding the air. She followed his triumphant trail from one tavern to another. In the last one, they told her he had left a few moments before to go home. He had convinced the neighborhood florist who had been drinking in the tavern to unlock his shop a few doors away so he could assemble a cluster of bright flowers to carry home to his wife.

She hurried the blocks back home and at the corner of their street, she saw him almost before the entrance to their door. She cried out his name, her voice shrill and clear across the frosted and silent street. He turned and waved the massive bouquet of flowers. Her heart flew out to him and she started to run to his arms.

She saw the lights of a parked car suddenly flash on, veiling Petros in a strange luminous mist. As he turned around, the car surged forward. A fearful cry from Chrisoula's throat was lost in the stuttering thunder of the shots.

For a moment Petros seemed to leap off the street, a great spring to carry him over the roofs of the buildings, a stunning and impossible effort to escape. Then, as if his heart had burst, he fell back to the earth and the flowers scattered in the wild wind of his wake.

When she reached his body and saw the blood, she screamed a great tearing apart of her flesh. She fell across his chest and kissed his mute limp mouth. Shouts and lights broke the night around her. Two men sought to pull her away and with her fingers curled like claws she went like a hawk for their eyes.

They let her alone. She knelt beside him and stared at his face, startled and shattered in death. A few flakes of snow fell and glistened on his temples and in his hair. She picked up petals of the strewn flowers and put them gently on his lips and over his eyes. The snow fell on the flowers and gave his face a misted and serene beauty.

Only when her father came would she allow Petros to be taken from her, to be washed and anointed and dressed. And in the old way of their people to be decked with basil and mint.

In the sunless and damp room of the dead, the old women mourning and whispering like black crows, she knew he was gone. At the cemetery with the people standing like faceless statues around his grave and the cry of a bird falling shrilly from the sky, she knew he was gone. And for weeks afterwards in her solitary bed, her breasts and loins chilled as if death had become her lover, she knew Petros was gone and would never return.

The weeks passed into months and then the winter was over. The first traces of new green grass appeared in the vacant lots. A single tree, stunted in the shadow of bricks and mortar, sprouted a few fragile buds. In the twilight the air was shaken with fragrant wind from warmer land.

Each day the sun grew stronger. From the dismal buildings the old men emerged like moles to sit on their stone steps blinking in the glaring light. Children cast off their garments of winter and shrieked joyously in play.

With the renewal of spring, Chrisoula felt the resurgence of her body. She walked the sunlit streets conscious of the bold staring eyes of men. At night she lay restlessly in her solitary bed, watching the haunting waves of the moon, hearing the husky laughter of couples passing in the darkness of the street below her window. Spires and towers moved through her fantasies. When she slept fitfully and wakened, the pillow which had been beneath her head was clasped tightly against her breasts and loins.

She came to understand in the lonely passage of those long spring nights that the time of love was brief and that vows of eternal fidelity faltered before the yearnings of her body. There was nothing the dead could offer the living but lament.

So she cried softly for Petros. Then she slept and dreamed of the wild laughing lover she would someday bring to her cold and dormant bed.

Even in my early, unpublished stories, I showed a preoccupation with aging and death. From my reading of Jack London's *Martin Eden,* at age thirteen, I also gained an awareness that a time might come in any life when sleep would not provide the needed rest and death could be a liberation. That was the theme of this story.

For reasons that escape me now, I also named the character of Death in this story Matsoukas. In my later novel *A Dream of Kings* I used the same name for the forceful, life-loving, and sun-possessed Leonidas Matsoukas, operator of the Pindar Master Counseling Service, who always acted as if he were immortal.

There may not be a contradiction here. Without life, there could be no death. Without death, life would be endless and meaningless. So life and death may not be polarities, but an integral, undivided whole.

MATSOUKAS

On Saturday evening Lambos kept his small grocery open an hour longer than his usual closing time. This enabled his regular customers to buy a carton of milk or a loaf of bread for Sunday morning when he did not open until noon.

That Saturday evening near the end of November was a cold and desolate night, the black and mottled streets deserted of all living things except a prowling tomcat gliding furtively through the glow of a street lamp before disappearing again into the dark cave of an alley.

Only a fool would brave the wind and the cold, Lambos thought, and his legs ached as they always did by the end of his long day. He yearned suddenly for his bed in the quiet small room above the store. He turned the key in the door and snapped off the main lights leaving only a tiny bare bulb above the window and another dim light in the rear of the store.

Across the street a tattered awning flapped in the wind. A patch of moonlight broke abruptly upon a sheet of newspaper floating over the curb. The beam of a passing car swept the pyramids of cans in his window. A corner of a wrapping-paper sign on which he had lettered with black crayon and taped to the window had come loose and he bent and pressed the tape back into place, feeling the glass cold beneath his fingers.

He was startled by the figure of a man watching him from the sidewalk outside his window. Lambos peered through the glass to identify him but the small bulb did not allow sufficient light. Deciding unhappily that he was a customer expecting the store to be open, Lambos snapped the lock back and opened the door.

The small bell tinkled as the man entered, a gust of icy wind swirling about his legs. Lambos shivered and closed the door quickly. When he turned around the man was standing almost concealed in shadow. Lambos could only make out that he was small of build wearing a gray topcoat too light for the weather and a battered felt hat pulled rakishly to one side.

"I was just closing," Lambos said in annoyance. He turned to open the overhead lights.

"Don't bother," the man said and it seemed to Lambos the words came flippantly from his mouth. He turned and peered over the counter at the shelves of canned goods. "Do you carry Meyer's clam chowder?" he asked.

"The supermarket in the next block," Lambos said brusquely. "They carry everything. I carry what my customers buy."

The man walked past the glass counter that contained several varieties of cheese. He halted before the small barrel of briny pickles. "These are my favorite," he said with a pleased wave. For a moment the light shone full across his face that was shaped like a total moon with small bright eyes above the pinches of scarlet where the cold had marked his cheeks. His mouth was so wide when he smiled the corners cut almost to his nostrils giving him a droll and absurd appearance. Almost midnight, Lambos thought bitterly, and I get a clown.

"One pickle," the man said. "Mark it down." He reached into the barrel and raised a single dripping pickle and with measured relish bit off the end.

"I will remember," Lambos said. "Something else?"

The man chewed the pickle slowly punctuating each bite with a loud smacking of his lips.

"A man shouldn't eat pickles this time of night," Lambos said. "They cause heartburn."

When there was still no answer, Lambos felt a sudden uneasiness. He looked toward the battered register in which he kept change and a few bills. As if understanding, the man laughed softly. "Don't worry about that, Lambos," he said.

"You know my name?" Lambos asked in surprise. He peered more closely at the man again.

The man finished the pickle and drew out a handkerchief to wipe his fingers. "You have never seen me before, Lambos," he said with a jaunty wink, "but you and I have had an appointment for a long time."

"Maybe you are right," Lambos said soothingly, "but it is late now, friend, and I wish to close up. If there is nothing else . . ."

Instead of moving toward the door, the man walked to the end of the counter. He sat down on a wooden crate and indolently crossed his legs. "That supermarket has ruined you, hasn't it?" he asked cheerfully.

"My business is no business of yours," Lambos bristled, forgetting his decision to humor the man. He turned his back on him and picked up the broom and began sweeping a patch of floor in agitation. He heard no sound but the whisking of the strands of straw against the bare wood. He ceased sweeping and turned to stare helplessly at the man who had not moved.

"My name is Matsoukas," the man said and his mouth twisted in a weird and expansive grin.

Lambos saw a glimmer of hope. "Are you Greek?"

"What else?" Matsoukas said.

"If you are Greek," Lambos said, "you know it is not polite to enter a man's store at closing time and eat a pickle and sit around like you are in a coffeehouse."

"Think of me as a friend," Matsoukas said, "who has come to help you find rest."

"Five minutes after you are gone, friend, I will be in bed," Lambos said.

"You need a much longer rest," Matsoukas said. "A rest sleep for a single night cannot provide." He lifted his shoulders in a wry shrug. "Actually I've been putting this visit off. I should have come a year ago."

"Who are you?" Lambos said. "What do you want?"

The cold eyes measured him and the great mouth taunted him silently.

Lambos loosed a hoarse cry and walked as quickly as his legs would allow behind the counter. He reached into the box where he kept a hammer and raised it violently above his head.

"You are a crazy man!" he shouted. "Now get out of my store!"

Matsoukas pointed to the hammer and shook in a spasm of silent and sardonic laughter. "Cuckoo, cuckoo, cuckoo," he snickered when he could get his breath.

Lambos lowered the hammer slowly to the counter. "I don't understand," he said helplessly.

Matsoukas leaned forward and his face entered the ray of light. The mask of the clown was strangely altered, as if the surface were a dried and wrinkled crust stretching over something more ominous beneath.

"I will make it clear," Matsoukas said with disdain. "Your heels are run down, your cuffs shabby, your pants so stiff with odors even the moths ignore them." His voice was the jagged edge of a broken mirror. "Your veins are scurvy roads that run through the ruins of your body. You endure a solitude reserved for beasts and saints. It is time to throw in your soiled towel."

Lambos stared at him numbly trying to find some sense in what was happening. "Are you sure you are Greek?" he asked finally.

"My name is Matsoukas."

"A name means nothing."

"Mine does," Matsoukas chuckled.

"What does it mean?"

"What I want it to mean."

"I don't want to listen to you any more," Lambos said.

"You are not listening now," Matsoukas said harshly. "Protoplasm is a sticky business. Better to have it over and done with."

"Are you a doctor?" Lambos shook his head fitfully. "You want to take my temperature and give me a prescription? I have a cabinet full of powders and pills."

"It is too late for pills," Matsoukas said. "I am here to unchain you from your barrel of pickles. Wise up."

"Who are you?" Lambos cried. "Tell me who you are?"

"Who I am doesn't matter," Matsoukas said loudly. "It's who you are that counts."

"Who am I?" Lambos asked loudly.

"I can sum up your life in one breath," Matsoukas said. "First a suckling baby, then a child answering his name, a youth with pustules on his face, a man searching for love, a husband in the misery of unhappy marriage, a father dreaming of eternity and resurrection," his baleful eyes flayed Lambos with scorn. "Now you are a sick and spindly-legged old man, wife and son dead, and not a single reason why you shouldn't be too. Wise up."

"Leave me alone." Lambos put his hands desperately to his ears.

"Admit what I say is true," Matsoukas said. "Is there anyone left to mourn you? Is there anyone left to love you?" He made a gesture of impatience. "I can't waste much more time here." He rose from the crate and walked in agitation to stand at the window staring silently into the street.

"Listen to me," Lambos pleaded. "Will you listen to me?" When Matsoukas did not turn around, Lambos began to pace the store. "How can you know what I am?" he said. He started around the counter and turned and walked back, dragging one foot slightly behind him. "Twenty years I was married," he said, "and then long after I had given up hope I could ever be a father, we had a son. All my life seemed different then." He passed beneath the light and bumped the edge of the counter and nearly fell. "I saw him growing into a fine man, raising a family of his own, my grandchildren. I saw my old age as green and warm. But from his tenth year he had a sickness in his body. For two years they kept him alive by giving him blood. He grew thin and his flesh bruised and blue and then he died. For two years I watched and measured each pulse of his dying. Not a day or night when I would not have died in his place." He paused and stretched his arms to the ceiling of the store and spread his dry stiff fingers, and then he cried out, a terrible cry of loss and despair. At the window Matsoukas stirred uneasily.

Lambos walked wearily to the same crate Matsoukas had used a short while before. He sat down and let his face drop slowly against his cupped hands. He closed himself into the nest of his palms, alone for a moment with the heavy beating of his heart. "I am afraid," he said softly. "I am afraid."

Matsoukas turned then from the window. He walked to Lambos and then slowly and awkwardly put out his hand and touched Lambos gently on the shoulder.

"Listen, Lambos," Matsoukas spoke in a strangely altered voice. "Your heart is scarred by loneliness and sorrow. Your body is a wound from which your life falls like drops of blood. Your burden is hopeless and it will grieve no one if you lay it down."

Lambos closed his eyes tightly for a long moment. When he opened them he noticed that moonlight had entered the store. It shimmered across the worn wood of the floor and swirled mist in the corners.

"It is easy to accomplish," Matsoukas said. "Merely believe and say, I want to die. Think of night eternal across your body." He paused and drew a fitful breath. "I'll tell you something I don't ever bother to tell anyone. Grief and despair belong to life. False dreams and vain hopes belong to life. Death is peace."

It seemed to Lambos in that moment as if the sharp and mournful world around him began to soften. The edges began to dissolve, shelves and counters and walls fading slowly away.

Lambos nodded slowly and rose. He hesitated for a moment and then reached again for the broom. He swept the last of the litter into a pile and picked it up with a piece of cardboard that he threw into the basket in the corner. Then he fumbled at the apron that bound his waist.

"When I was a boy I had such dreams," Lambos said. He looked sadly around the store. "Now at the end there is so much I do not understand," he sighed, "perhaps if I had not been such a simple man . . ."

"Only the simple and the great may be sure of dying in their own way," Matsoukas said. "The rest die in imitation."

Lambos folded his apron and placed it upon the counter. He stood uncertainly for a moment as if there were something he had forgotten to do. "Will you stay with me now?" he asked and tried not to show his fear.

"Each man must enter death for himself," Matsoukas said. "But do not despair, Lambos. Go up to your bed and lie down and close your eyes and you will sleep as you have never slept before. I promise you that."

Lambos walked to the foot of the steps. He looked once at the door and then turned back to Matsoukas.

"And God?" he asked softly. "Where is God in all of this?"

"If you have not found the answer to that in all your years on earth," Matsoukas said gravely, "how can you expect to have the answer now?"

Lambos placed his hands on the railings for balance and started slowly up. He heard the tinkling of the bell above the door and felt a sudden gust of wind about his legs. He looked back and beyond the glass of the window saw the arm of Matsoukas raised in a shadowed farewell.

He walked up a few more steps. The chill of stone crept into his body and he thought of tombs and the comfortless earth. He remembered his son and tried to go higher but his one leg trembled so badly it would not hold him.

"Matsoukas!" he cried.

There was no answer from the store below him. The steps he had passed were shrouded in darkness. He looked once more up to the door and felt himself suspended on a frail bridge over the void. He slipped to one knee.

"Matsoukas!" he cried in anguish. "Help me!"

Then he remembered. Grief and despair belong to life, Matsoukas had said, false dreams and vain hopes belong to life. Death is peace.

He pulled himself to his feet and holding to the railing with both hands began to drag himself up. Strangely his fear was gone and he felt a strength such as he had not felt in many years. He smelled the fragrance of his unmarked youth, the childhood of his life. He felt with certainty that he was going home, mind and body and heart back to his beginning.

His voice echoed in a long joyous cry down the stairs. Below him the shelves and pyramids of cans, the racks of bread and the paper banners, snapped squarely and forever into darkness.

This story also relates to the elements of aging and death I wrote about in "Matsoukas." An act of infidelity may not always stem from a lack of love between a husband and wife but be a product of the anxieties that develop in us as we grow older. Feeling life slipping irrevocably past, one reaches out in panic for additional moorings.

I was not trying to justify the husband's unfaithfulness but to make it a little more understandable.

END OF WINTER

The first snow fell early in November. Almost at once the weather turned cold. Wind howled in the night and shook the house. The oil furnace ran from dark to dawn almost without stopping, but the rooms were still cold. Della and I got up several times during the night to make sure the boys were covered.

In the morning I was the first one up and shaved and woke the boys for school. While they dressed, Della made their lunches and cooked breakfast. We ate together and I left for work about the time the boys headed for the school bus. Della waved to us from the door and the dog next door barked as she always did.

The boys were eight and six years old that winter. Della was pregnant again, we had found out for sure from the doctor just after Labor Day, so we had the winter to go with the baby to be born in the spring.

The pattern of our lives ran much the same as it had for years. In the evening we ate supper and then watched a program on TV—Disneyland or one of the better western stories. I enjoyed them, too. Then, while Della finished the dishes, I put Tom, the six-year-old, to bed. I washed him and tussled with him on the bed. I read him a story and took pleasure in his wonder at the world opening before his eyes. Ralph would come up and wash himself and then the three of us would lie together in the darkness for a few moments recounting the events of the day.

Once a week Della and I went out. A baby sitter came in and we went to a show or a play. Sometimes friends visited us. We drank Martinis or Manhattans and played charades and laughed about many things I could not remember the next day. After they had gone Della and I went to bed and made love.

I know that winter my job in advertising was no more beset by aggravations than it had been in other years. I had been promoted in the summer to brand manager and while it increased my responsibilities it allowed me more freedom as well. I enjoyed my work most of the time and still looked forward to the evenings at home. If the routine of supper and baths and stories weighed sometimes on my back, much more often I was aware of the warmth and laughter.

So in a way I find it hard to understand why that winter, after almost twelve years of marriage, I should have been unfaithful to Della for the first time.

A girl who worked in our offices. Not a girl obviously suited to infidelities the way Norma was, tall and blonde with lithe long legs that gleamed like satin, or elfin-eyed little Dolores who worked in the art department and was always smudged cutely with paint and whispered promises to all the men at the office Christmas party.

Pat had shining black hair the color of Della's. Both had large dark eyes and clear skin. They looked alike except Pat was about 24, the age Della was when we were married.

I remember that afternoon in November when I first suggested to Pat that we have dinner together. She had brought some copy into my office for my approval and stood waiting beside the desk. She had been with the firm about a year and I knew little about her except that she had been married young and then divorced. She had high small breasts and fine ankles. I was conscious of her as attractive, but I swear more than that drew me to her. There was a dream of candlelight and lost springs about her. A fleeting memory of youth as a time of promise. The shadow of some unfathomed sadness about her eyes. Suddenly I felt the stirrings of desire, but not of the flesh alone. A wish to see behind the mask of her face, to share her laughter, and know her well enough to push back the dark errant curl of hair fallen across her forehead. I mentioned dinner to her then, my tone jesting, to provide a retreat if she seemed offended. She was silent for a long moment and I knew she understood the truth. In the way she watched me, coolly appraised me, I knew she had decided to accept.

She met me that night in a small café on the edge of the city. I waited at a table by the window as the snow fell softly across the bare trees in the park across the street. I thought of the years with Della and of the children at home preparing for bed. I thought of the unreality of the moment sitting in a strange café, miles from my house, watching the snow fall and waiting for a strange girl.

When she came to the table she startled me. The snow glistened in her hair and her cheeks were bright, flushed with night and cold.

"I'm late," she said, and her voice was low and husky and her red lips moved easily about her teeth as she spoke.

"I was watching the snow," I said.

I took her coat and saw the soft pale skin of the back of her neck. The waiter came and we ordered wine and then sat watching one another.

"When I walked up," she said, "you looked as if you had forgotten I was coming."

"I was watching the snow," I said, "and fell into some kind of trance."

"Were you hoping I would not come?"

"I'm glad you did."

"I wanted to," she said. "I am not much good at poses. I can't show outrage if I don't feel outrage."

"I guess you thought I was like the rest," I said. "Another married man with problems looking for a young shoulder to cry on."

She watched me silently for a moment.

"I have no problems," I said. "I love my wife and children. I am not unhappy in my job."

"Then why are you here?" she asked softly.

That stopped me for a moment.

"I don't really know," I said. "I thought of a lot of things when I came into my office today. Maybe I fooled myself. Perhaps I'm here because you're very pretty and I want to touch you."

"That is why I came," she said quietly.

She must have read something in my eyes and she laughed softly.

"I told you I was no good at poses. Does that shock you?"

"A little," I said.

The waiter brought the wine and seemed to give us a look that implied censure. She raised her glass and the wine gleamed red.

"There are many wolves," she said, "behind every office door. They leer and pinch and pat. I don't think you belong among them. You are unaware of all the frantic machinations that go on in the office by men trying to get girls to go to bed."

"How can you be sure I'm not like all the others?" I said.

"I can't be sure," she said. "I think I am right. I think that's why I came. To be made love to by a man who has been faithful to his wife for twelve years is like love-making in a strange land."

So we ate a little and drank more wine and left the café. I sat with her in the front seat of her car with the heater going. We watched the snow falling around us in the deserted park. The scent of wine was about us, aroma of walnuts and richly laden tables. I kissed her lips and tasted ripe sweet fruit.

I touched her body, gently, almost shyly at first and then more rudely as the warmth became flame and still unlike the passion I remembered in the first years with Della. Because even in desire I could not forget those years or the children that waited at home. So there was this sadness as we made love, a sweet and burning sadness, and all the while the snow kept falling out of the darkness.

In the next few months I saw Pat several times a week. I lied to Della of meetings with customers after hours. Of accounts in jeopardy and old college friends in for a few hours between trains. The trust built through our years together helped her believe. After the first night it was easier and I did not think as often of the children.

Pat and I went dancing sometimes in little cafés outside the city and afterwards made love in the car. Other evenings we would spend in her small apartment with the glistening lamps and the Pullman kitchen and the bed that came out of the livingroom wall. We made ham sandwiches, thick with lettuce and tomatoes, and listened to her hi-fi as we ate them and afterwards went to bed. Sometime after midnight I had to get up and dress to leave. She would be warm and sleepy within the sheets and her lips soft as I kissed her goodby. Then I drove through the dark midnight streets to my own dark house. I undressed quietly in the bathroom and looked in on the boys and climbed gently into bed beside Della. She stirred restlessly and moved against me in the bed, warm as Pat had been warm, flesh that was mine where Pat's was borrowed. I would lie awake for a long time listening to the stillness of the house, hearing Della breathing softly in sleep beside me, finally falling asleep myself for a few moments and waking with a start not sure in whose bed I really was.

There were nights when my life of lies and deception bred anger in me at Della and the children. I put the boys brusquely to bed, quick to slap or reprimand. Again there were nights I made love to Pat roughly as if to revenge myself for the injustice upon my family.

The weeks passed into months and the swell of Della's body curved like the arc of the moon. In awareness that her flesh would soon become sluggish and shapeless, she demanded love more fiercely than she had in years. Afterwards we lay together and she would be pleased and feel in some way we were drawing closer together.

"I'm storing up love," she said. "For the baby. I'm taking love from you and holding it for the baby."

I would touch the warm flesh of her throat and stroke the slight swell of her body and feel a strange pain in my chest.

"I am scared about this baby," she said. "I wasn't with the others, but I am scared with this one."

"You will be all right," I said.

"I think I will," she said. "But I am older now. It must be harder when you are thirty-six, not as easy as when you are younger."

"It will be all right," I said.

"Tom was coughing today," she said. "I want to take him to Doctor Vaughn on Friday."

"All right," I said.

"Flora Seaman called today," she said. "They want us for dinner on Sunday. I called Nora. She can come to stay with the children, if you want to go."

"We'll see," I said.

She rose from the bed and went into the washroom. I watched her, not sure of just what I felt, but something bred of remorse and a shattering of my flesh.

There was a night in March I spent with Pat. She cooked supper for us in her apartment and then barefooted in slacks and a blouse came to lie at my side across the bed. The music from the record player in the corner drew together the small warm room.

"Almost two weeks since you last came," she said. "In a little while you will not come at all."

I touched her ear, the delicate lobe I had gotten to know so well.

"I have been busy," I said. "One of the boys has had a bad cold that keeps hanging on. He waits for me to come home in the evening." I paused a moment under great tenderness and moved closer to her on the bed. "I miss you when I do not come," I said.

"I miss you too," she said.

We were silent for a while listening to the music.

"I can see it ending," she said. "The little love that kept us warm this winter. There is something sad about love when it is over."

"Why do you say over?" I said. "Nothing is over yet. We will have the spring and the summer. Things will be the same."

She shook her head.

"For a little while you feel a part of you has been lost," she said. "You look into faces on the street to find someone, something that is gone."

"Was your first love like that?"

"That was different," she said. "That hurt in a way terrible to remember. I was seventeen when I married him."

"Where is he now?"

"He is remarried," she said. "To a woman in Dallas who had three children." She laughed softly. "I would tell him he could not accept responsibility, so he showed me. But before that I wrote him long letters. Shameful letters in which I begged him to take me back. He never replied."

She uncoiled off the bed like a cat with warm and supple grace and came to sit on my knees. I put my arms around her waist and felt the warmth of her flesh through the thin cloth of her blouse.

"We should not stay in," she said. "It is not good for you and not good for me. You think of your children and your boy who is waiting for you to come home and I think of my first love and how far he is from me now. We should go somewhere far out of the city and dance and kiss each other in the shadows of a booth and make our love in the car."

"Tuesday night," I said. "Next Tuesday night we will do that. Tuesday night for sure."

I stood up and tucked my shirt in my trousers. She came once more into my arms, her dark eyes searching my face.

"In a little while it will be spring," she said. "And in the springs to come will you remember this winter?"

"I will," I said. "I will."

When I got to the street I seemed to smell from far off the faint early scents of spring. The shade of her window was pulled slightly to the side and she stood there with her body shaded against the light. I waved and could not be sure she waved back or not.

When I got home I knew something was wrong. I came in the front door and hung my hat and coat in the hall closet. I saw light in the kitchen and felt a quick sense of dread.

Della sat dressed at the kitchen table. I stood for a moment in the doorway. She knew I was there, yet for a long moment she did not look up. I walked to the table and sat down and saw her cheeks pale and still moist and knew she had been crying.

"Wally," she said, and she spoke softly in almost a whisper. "Wally, don't lie to me now. I promise not to cry anymore or become angry. I want to talk to you. I can take almost anything, but don't lie to me now."

I sat there and did not answer.

"There was no meeting tonight," she said. "Lawrence called for you. And then I thought of all the other meetings late at night that you have attended the last few months. All the other things that suddenly fall into place. Then I knew it was a girl."

Her face was naked and her flesh tight across her cheeks.

"Yes," I said. "Tonight and all the other nights. Yes, there is a girl."

She must have expected to hear me say that, but still her face loosened as if the bone beneath the skin had suddenly broken. I was sorry I had not lied, that for a little while I had not indulged all the heated denials.

"Do you want a divorce?" she asked.

"Del," I said. "It was just a girl. I don't want a divorce. It didn't mean that much to me."

"It means that much to me," she said. "Maybe I want the divorce." her voice rose just a little. "Do you think you are a rooster who can come swaggering back from another henhouse and find everything in order in his own roost?"

"Del," I said.

"Do you think because I'm pregnant now," she said, "and because I have the children that I'm helpless? Do you think you can make me swallow your dirt because I'm helpless? Do you think that?"

"Del," I said. "I don't think that."

"Why?" she said. "I've been sitting here for almost three hours frantically trying to reason why, why? Is it that I'm not a good wife? I don't wash enough clothes or do enough dishes? I make too many demands? I nag too much? I don't keep myself neat? Why?"

"Del," I said, and struggled for the right words. "My God, Del, it was none of these things. Something happened to me. A bad and restless winter. It wasn't right, but it had nothing to do with you."

She laughed a hard little laugh that echoed strangely in the kitchen.

"Has she been the first?" she said. "Has this one been the first or have there been others?"

"I swear the first," I said.

She watched me then.

"What are we going to do?" she said. "What is it you want to do now?"

"I don't know," I said. "I mean there's nothing to be done. I will not see her again. I would have stopped soon anyway. I want you to believe that."

We sat silent for a long time.

"Like a telegram with word someone close has died," she said. "A world suddenly coming apart. I was angry, but I'm not angry now. I am bewildered and confused. I don't know what this means to me." She put her hands across the full swell of her abdomen. "I don't know what this means for this one in my body or for the boys upstairs. I'm scared and I should still be angry, but I'm only scared and mixed up."

"Del," I said and got up from my chair. I went to her but she shook her head.

"Not now," she said. "Don't touch me yet. I want to believe you. I want you to tell me you still love me and we can go back to the way it was. Then I'm ashamed because it means I have no pride. I'm ashamed and scared and alone."

She stood up and walked out of the kitchen. After a moment I turned off the lights and followed her upstairs.

We undressed in the dark bedroom and did not speak. I went to the bathroom and when I came out she was lying still under the sheets.

I walked to the boys' room across the hall and checked them and came back. I sat on the edge of the bed and moved slowly beneath the sheets careful not to touch her.

"I know what you want," she said softly. "I know what you want."

The house about us was quiet and the room shadowed and still.

"You want the love we had," she said. "You want us young as we used to be."

She moved helplessly beside me and I felt the length of her leg along my own flesh. I took her into my arms and held her tightly against the trembling that swept us both.

There was a sound of coughing from the boys' room. I got out of bed and went to them and Tom coughed again, harshly in the darkness. I pulled his covers about his throat and felt the flesh of his cheek flushed and warm.

I went to the window and closed it a little. The night was cool and all the earth was still. Far off in the dark huge sky the timeless stars glistened.

In that moment a great sadness burned my body.

I wrote this long story during the late 1960s, with the agony of Vietnam poisoning so much of our spirits, and bitter confrontations between students and police taking place in the streets. No other story I have written came from as vulnerable a part of me as this one.

I make a confession now I have never made before. Earlier drafts of this story had the principal character a middle-aged writer going through the anguish of wondering what his role in the struggle should be, distraught because he could no longer conceal from himself how much of his early hopes and ideals he had forsaken for spurious comforts and liberal aphorisms.

In later drafts, that naked exposure became almost unbearable and I lost my courage and masked the principal character by making him a priest.

Looking back on that decision now, it doesn't seem too implausible. During the Middle Ages many writers became priests, and, in our own tumultuous times, priests, in turn, become writers.

THE WAVES OF NIGHT

That Sunday morning in late March, Father Manos rose, as usual, before daylight, not shivering quite as much as he had on previous Sunday risings for months. He walked to the window and pushed aside the curtain to peer out. Darkness still covered the sleeping city, misted stone and brick peaks of buildings, a single ring of light under a corner lamp. For the first time it seemed to him he could hear the heart of the earth beating faster, a thin promise of early spring, a forerunner of green feast and fruitfulness in the weeks ahead.

He washed and dressed briskly and left the house, walking the deserted streets to his church as the fragmented dawn glimmered across the roofs and parapets of the city.

The shops he passed were shadowed and silent, the taverns that had throbbed with revelry a few hours before, padlocked now, their muted neon signs creaking gently in the stillness. A tomcat emerged from an alley, fur ruffled and wary, idling its way home after a night of errant and promiscuous love. I will expect you at confession, Father Manos thought wryly, as the unrepentant rake glided by.

Even inside the church, sombrous and damp with the chilled shadows of the night, he seemed to feel the stirring of the earth beneath his feet. Then, with a laugh, he realized that it was the old sexton, Janco, raking up the coals in the basement furnace. Soon the old man would come up and begin lighting the candelabras before the icons of St. John the Baptist, and the Holy Mother with the Child-Christ. In another few hours the great chandelier would be lit and the light representing the stars in the sky would shine down upon the nave full (well, almost full) with the members of the congregation.

It was his custom in these quiet and serene moments to pray. He knelt before the Royal Gate of the Sanctuary, the portal decorated with the icon of Christ as Shepherd. He prayed for the end of the war in Viet Nam, for the starving children in Biafra, for the welfare of the poor, for the general condition of the country. He prayed for the wellbeing of his parishioners, for the perpetuation of the faith, and, finally, he spoke a prayer of gratefulness for the plenitude of his own life.

He was fifty-nine, in good health although somewhat overweight, and with (some exceptions, unfortunately) a good parish. It was true there were a few of the wealthier parishioners with an unholy penchant for distressing him. There was the peculiarly Greek conception of the priest having to spin like a dervish to fit the parishioner's vacillating moods and needs. He had, over the years, managed to balance these unreasonable demands in a way that produced a minimum of resentment. The blessed St. John himself could not have accomplished more.

Not all the priests in the city were as fortunate. Father Peter of St. George's Church was caught between two rabid factions in his parish, one seeking to banish him and the other to retain him. Father Theodore of St. Dionysios was also in trouble although it was common knowledge that he gambled and drank. But many of the weaknesses which the priests developed were not really their fault. The young priests came from Pomfret and Brookline, eager to serve their flocks and God, but their years of prayer and study provided no inkling of what they would find in their new parishes. The malicious, envious individuals, the myriad groups in reckless rivalry, the constant bickering, the vanity of the wealthy and the resentment of the poor, all took their toll.

Our priests are forced to wear the masks of clowns and fools, the savage Father Grivas of Holy Trinity Church often cried. He responded by affixing a single fierce and unrelenting demeanor to his own face, ignoring the angry threats of his trustees to petition his removal. That he was able to remain in the pulpit and serve as priest was simply due to the fear in which they held him. They regarded him as a ruffian, capable of murder if he were crossed or betrayed.

Wasted effort and lost energy, Father Manos tried to counsel him. He met similar problems with a more subtle and political response. He did what he could and if this were inevitably less than was expected of him, he apologized earnestly for his infirmities.

Playing their hypocritical game, Father Grivas would storm at him, but Father Manos saw no reason to whirl in a tempest of anger and bitterness when some amicable diplomacy could smooth issues out.

The sexton, Janco, came up from the basement into the church. He was a crooked-limbed old man who moved in a disjointed scramble of elbows and knees, his speech all but limited to mumbles and grunts. He lived in a room in the basement of the church and did not require more than a few dollars a week for food. Father Manos supplemented the meager wages the trustees gave the old man with a little money from his own salary, but he found him an ordeal. Now he directed him in the lighting of the Kandilia and patiently pointed out several pews that had not been swept. By that time the first of the black-garbed, stony-faced old women appeared bringing a Prosforon, the offering bread he would use in making communion. Another old woman brought in a small plate of Kolyva, the boiled wheat garnished with raisins and almonds, a reminder that the dead will rise again as the wheat which is buried in the earth sprouts out and bears fruit.

When it was time for him to dress for the service, Father Manos entered the Deacons' door into the anteroom adjoining the Sanctuary. He slipped on his Stiharion, the long tunic that covered his body from the shoulders to the feet. He put on the stole, belt, cuffs and the felonion, the scarlet vestment cape, kissing each holy article before adding it to his person. By the time he had finished tying the cords and ribbons, the first young acolytes appeared in the anteroom on the opposite side of the Sanctuary, slipping noisily into their white altar gowns. He caught the eye of one of them and waved sternly for silence.

"Good morning, Father Manos," Elias, the choirmaster said, as he entered the anteroom.

"Good morning, Elias," Father Manos said.

The choirmaster, a handsome man with pomaded hair that glistened in blue-black swirls, changed into his cassock.

"Looks like a good turnout this morning," he said. "They should fill the collection trays."

"Let's first fill their souls," Father Manos smiled.

The choirmaster left the anteroom and a few moments later his strong and resonant voice chanted across the church.

Father Manos entered the Sanctuary. "Blessed is our God, always now and ever . . ." he whispered. He adjusted the Evangelion and the candlesticks on the great marble Holy Table. He motioned the young leader of the acolytes to silence all movement and speech and then he took his place before the closed panel of the Royal Gate. He folded his hands gravely.

In another moment the old sexton, his brittle, awkward frame harried as usual, rushed past the acolytes into the Sanctuary, crossing himself clumsily, taking up his place at the Royal Gate. When given the signal he would slide open the panel and Father Manos would stand revealed in the total firmament of the church, all eyes drawn through the charismatic union of crosses, icons and candles to him. It was a moment that he had always, secretly, and he admitted honestly to himself, vainfully cherished, imagining the resurrective effect of the sanctified light across his colorful and brocaded vestments. Behind him the great Holy Table and large wooden crucifix on which the carved, life-sized body of Jesus Christ was nailed, heightened the effect.

The sexton crouched with his skinny arms against the panel, his scrawny old rooster's neck twisted toward the priest. Father Manos nodded somberly. The old man grimaced in a violent effort to match the high solemnity of the moment and slid the panel open slowly, making certain as Father Manos had often warned him, to keep his own figure hidden. The glitter of the church burst across the priest's head. He raised his hands slowly. The congregation filling the benches in uneven rows rose with a sound of woodwinds for the beginning of the Mass.

At the end of the service he divested himself of his vestments, the young acolyte helping him. He put on his black cassock and walked from the anteroom to stand on the Soleas, the elevated section of floor between the Sanctuary and the main part of the church. He felt the pangs of hunger rumbling in his stomach and quickly appraised the number of people waiting to see him. There were about five or six, no more than usual, but he had somehow hoped to be spared even that number today. Then he sternly admonished himself for his impatience. Lantzounis would wait, would indeed expect to wait. The luncheon his good wife prepared for them would be even more delicious when they finally sat down to eat.

He motioned toward the group. Hesitantly, the first man walked forward. He was a poor visitor, he said, from another section of the city, asking for a little money to buy food and clothing. He had the uncertain manner and nervous demeanor of the chronic alcoholic. Although there was a contingency fund that would have allowed Father Manos to give him a few dollars, he brusquely promised instead that one of the church organizations would send the man a basket of food and some articles of used clothing. The man left unappeased, mumbling a disappointed thanks. Father Manos was pleased to see a second man among those waiting leave with him.

The second parishioner to come up was a man in his late fifties, stocky and broad of build, with thick grey hair. Father Manos had seen him in church a number of times but could not recall his name.

"I am George Yalukis, Father," the man said in a harsh, anxious voice.

"I know you, Mr. Yalukis."

The man nodded gratefully.

"You know my son, Sam, Father," Yalukis said. "He played baseball in the GOYA tournament last year."

"I remember Sam," Father Manos said. "A fine boy and a splendid athlete."

"Father," Yalukis leaned forward slightly and lowered his voice. "I don't know what to do. Last week Sam got notice to go into the army. He's been 1 A and passed his physical. But he won't go. Says he'll go to jail first."

"Why won't he go, Mr. Yalukis?"

"I don't understand him, Father," Yalukis said. "He talks about the war in Viet Nam being wrong, things like that."

Father Manos shook his head somberly.

"These are difficult times for a young man, Mr. Yalukis," he said. "No youth wants to go to war but to serve one's country is a solemn obligation and responsibility. If he refused and went to jail it might ruin his life, place a stain upon him for as long as he lives."

"I know, Father," Yalukis grimaced as if he were in pain.

"Try to explain that to him." Father Manos said. "Explain how serious the whole matter is, the catastrophic results. Meanwhile I'll say a prayer for him as well as for you and your family."

The man stood staring mutely at the priest. What does he expect of me, Father Manos thought uneasily. What more can I tell him now?

"Father," Yalukis looked shakenly down at the tips of his shoes and then raised his head. "Can you come over with me to my house now, to talk to him? He came home today to see his mother, not me, but he won't stay long. If you could come and talk to him . . ."

Father Manos wavered. He found it more and more difficult to communicate with many of the young people in his parish, particularly the militant and unreasonable ones. He might go with Yalukis to talk to Sam but would probably accomplish nothing if the youth's mind were already made up. Yalukis, obviously a strong-willed and stubborn man, had probably totally alienated his son. How could the priest be expected to pacify him?

"I'm sorry, I can't come now," he said regretfully to Yalukis. "I have another appointment. But tell Sam I want to see him, ask him to come to church and see me tomorrow."

Yalukis shook his head silently and patiently as if he were resigned to his fate. He bent and gripped one of the priest's hands and kissed the back of the palm. He turned and started walking slowly and dejectedly down the center aisle.

For a moment watching his retreating figure, Father Manos felt pinches of remorse. There were so many problems he was helpless to resolve, one aging man trying to administer to a parish of more than four hundred families. Did they want his blood as well as his flesh and bone?

He sighed and looked up at the small windows in the dome of the church. The sky gleamed a vibrant blue through the panes of glass. It seemed to him a bird winged past with a shimmering grace. The winter had been long and hard, he had felt it like a cold stone in his body, but the spring was coming. There would be sun to warm his bones and the scent of flowers in the gardens and the laughter of children on the walks.

"Father Manos?"

He turned back to the church and a young woman stood at the foot of the steps of the Soleas. He recognized Angela Fotakis, a plain, pale-cheeked girl over thirty. Her father, Kostas, was one of the wealthiest men in the parish, owner of four large resplendent restaurants, a substantial contributor to the Coal and Easter offerings.

"Yes, my dear?" Father Manos said.

"Father, my parents are waiting outside," she said. "I've only got a minute." She stared up at him with watery eyes. "They have found a man willing to marry me. He's old... more than fifty." She paused, stricken suddenly by what he might feel to be rudeness.

Father Manos smiled to console her. "Don't fret," he said. "My graying hair and arthritis have made me immune to the vanity of thinking over fifty is young."

"I'm sorry, Father," she said. "I know I'm past thirty now. I know what they tell me is true, that no other man may be found who wants me if I wait. But I hoped... at least... for someone just a little younger."

"I know the man your parents are considering," Father Manos spoke earnestly, and with a measured degree of caution because of her father. "He is a good man who will be a good provider. If he is not as young as you wish, that is, after all, not his fault." He took her hand between his palms, felt her fingers tense and chilled. "There are worse things than marriage to an older man. You could marry a young wastrel, a drunk, someone who would beat you. Would youth compensate for cruelty? I know, my dear. We have several cases like that in our parish now." He felt the disquieting rumble of hunger widening in his stomach. "You think about it a little more. Measure the benefits against the disadvantages. I'm sure your good parents would not make you do anything against your will. Let me know what you decide. If you think the aspect of the man's age too distressing, come back and see me. I'll promise to talk to your father."

Angela nodded slowly, her face still pensive and sad. He reached out and patted her cheek gently. She smiled faintly and turned and started toward the narthex.

Father Manos hurried back into the anteroom and slipped off his cassock and put on his suitcoat and coat. He noticed a button hanging precariously on one sleeve. Iota would have to sew that on.

He emerged from the anteroom again. "Janco!" he called, and his voice echoed across the silent church. When there was no answer he called again more sharply, "Janco!" An instant later the old sexton came stumbling out of the shadows.

"I'll be at Mr. Lantzounis' for lunch," he said. "Remember we have a baptism for four o'clock. See that everything is prepared. I'll be back a little after three."

The old man nodded dolefully. His face seemed incapable of cracking a smile. Iota at home and this grim old devil here, Father Manos thought. They were enough to age a man before his time.

But sitting at the head of the bountiful Lantzounis table, Father Manos felt young and ebullient. The platters were heaped with grape leaves stuffed with rice and meat, broiled chicken in a lemon-butter sauce, tureens of creamy avgolemono, leafy green salads with black olives and chunks of white feta cheese and loaves of warm, crisp-crusted bread. There were, as well, several decanters of chilled retsina wine.

He bent his head and blessed the table and the family, his palate quivering with anticipation. When he raised his head the silence was broken by an eruption of amens and hands moving swiftly through the stations of the cross.

"Eat, Father!" Mrs. Lantzounis cried. "Eat and drink now and relax." She was a cheerful, incredibly obese woman with a roll of fat around her neck so thick it resembled a collar of fleshy fur.

Father Manos patted his midsection. "I have too much weight here now," he said. "Iota starts me dieting every week."

"You're just right, Father," Lantzounis said. "Let me refill your glass." He was a tall, handsome man with strong arms and dark, curly hair. It was common gossip throughout the parish that Lantzounis had a mistress, a young Spartan girl who worked in the office at his meat packing plant. But looking at his poor wife, Father Manos thought, how could one blame him? The rule against adultery must still be tempered by justice. That was the difference, he had always felt, between an enlightened priest and a clerical fanatic.

Sixteen-year-old Caliope Lantzounis whispered into the ear of her sister, Aspasia, and then broke away to giggle shrilly.

"What's so funny, young lady?" Lantzounis snapped.

"Leave the child be, Cleon," Father Manos smiled. "At her age all of life is a source of mirth. I laughed often when I was sixteen." He looked at Aspasia, slender and lovely and dark-eyed. "And at eighteen."

"Have some more wine, Father," Mrs. Lantzounis said. With his mouth full of grape leaves he could not answer but motioned eagerly to his glass.

The wine warmed him and he saw the great bulk of Mrs. Lantzounis flitting with the grace of a nymph around the table, filling plates over again, and pouring endless glasses of wine. The hunger of his stomach was fully appeased. He could feel the wrinkles filled out with the warm, savory food. He managed to stifle a belch and decided, regretfully, that he had eaten enough.

The girls rose in a few moments to help pick up the dishes. They wore print dresses with frilly skirts, modestly miniskirted. As Aspasia bent beside him to pick up his plate, her skirt rose up her legs and he caught a glimpse of her bare white flesh above the hem of her silk stockings. He felt a sudden frivolous impulse to pat her slender bottom.

The urge was disquieting. It is the wine, he thought. The barriers that age and the habit of abstinence had erected crumbled like faulty dikes under the flow of the juice. It was true that what had once troubled him a great deal, now bothered him rarely. He was immensely grateful for the quietude of his body, something achieved after considerable hardship. Even now it was never completely dead. There were vagrant moments when it returned to trouble him and he found himself pricked by the most carnal thoughts.

There was the magazine he had confiscated from an eighth grader in the parish school some months before. In the privacy of his office he had leafed through the pages and was shocked at the photographs of totally nude women in incredibly suggestive poses. His first reaction was one of outrage against the publishers and then he considered sending for the boy to give him a thrashing. But he remained rooted in his chair, the magazine in his hands, his feelings suddenly changed. A curious lassitude settled over his limbs. He saw the breasts of one woman, not as young as some of the others, a certain maturity in the proportions of her flesh, in her dark prodigal nipples. To sleep at night, he thought, against such breasts. To feel the warmth of them against my back in frozen winter. He stared then at his hands, at the fingers and the palms. They seemed dessicated and bloodless like the hands of the saints in the icons. He imagined them caressing the breasts of the woman in the magazine and he groaned and snapped the magazine shut and tossed it into his bottom drawer. But the vision continued to burn him and he opened the drawer and took out the magazine and using all his strength he tore it into pieces too small to tear any more. he threw them into the wastebasket beside his desk. He looked down at the torn pieces and felt a curious and plaintive sense of loss.

"Father?" Lantzounis' voice startled Father Manos from his reverie. "What were you thinking of?"

Father Manos looked into the laughing face of Aspasia staring at him with a certain intuitive wisdom and he felt a rush of blood to his cheeks.

"The wine," he said loudly, in an effort to cover his disorder. "The wine has made me drowsy."

"A cup of coffee then," Mrs. Lantzounis said and she emerged from the kitchen carrying a silver coffeepot and Caliope followed her carrying a great silver tray laden with powder-sugared kourabiethes and honey-nut baklava.

"Mercy!" Father Manos cried with such vigor that they all laughed with him, their voices blending into a happy and harmonious warmth.

Father Manos returned to church some time later than he had planned and found the parents with the child to be baptized waiting. He donned his robes quickly and assembled the relatives and friends in the baptismal corner.

The baby was a girl of about eleven months, a fair and plump child with a fuzz of golden hair. The godfather was Spiro Marketos, President of the Board of Trustees of the church, a man who had made a fortune by speculating in real estate.

Father Manos found him a pompous and insufferable man always determined to have his own way. On a few occasions they had quarreled but for the most part they observed a certain wary truce. Because Marketos was the godfather, Father Manos would be obliged to attend the celebration dinner following the baptism, although he had no more desire for additional food and drink. He also knew, unhappily, that Marketos was fascinated with the sound of his own voice, punctuating his tedious speeches with countless "now in conclusion's" and never ending.

The moment came during the ceremony to immerse the baby under the water in the baptismal font. It was a time for Father Manos that contained all the mystery and beauty of faith. That this naked, squirming pullet of flesh, only some months removed from her mother's womb should now be receiving the sacrament of baptism and anointed with oil in the sign of the cross, filled him with fervent satisfaction. He tried to remember, holding the baby in his arms, the number of infants he had baptized in the past thirty years. A few of them endured the ordeal silently but most screamed shrilly in outrage, thrashing their small limbs violently. He had learned to hold them firmly and gently, without fear, and dunked them for a second, completely under the water. He enjoyed the pleasant murmurs that came from the watchers as the body of the infant emerged from the water, dripping and breathless, to be enfolded in the warm, fleecy towel.

When the baptism was over, Father Manos congratulated the parents and relatives. Marketos looked at him with a certain bovine haughtiness. "You are coming to the reception, of course?" His tone suggested no other action would be tolerated.

"I am coming," Father Manos said and within himself sighed.

He sat at the table of honor staring out upon the half-dozen tables grouped together in the private diningroom of the luxurious Regis Hotel. The pleasure of eating and drinking he had sustained earlier in the day had vanished and he found the presence of so much food suddenly repugnant. He reproached himself for not having eaten less earlier and left a margin of space. He sipped his champagne without savor. Simple good Greek wine would not do for any child that Marketos baptized.

". . . now in conclusion," Marketos said, for the fifth time, and it seemed to Father Manos that the buffoon had been talking for hours. "I want to relate to you how I came to baptize this lovely baby. Her dear mother, daughter of one of my closest friends, the distinguished owner of the Salonika Laundry, came to see me. She had already been to church to visit Father Manos . . ." Marketos paused and looked toward the priest, half perhaps for confirmation and half to ascertain whether he was paying attention. Father Manos sat up a little straighter and nodded although for the life of him he could not remember when the girl had come to him.

"I could discern at once the young lady was troubled," Marketos paused to allow the audience time to absorb the sensitive attunement of his perceptive powers. "She told me there was a young man she wanted to marry."

God have mercy, Father Manos thought, that was more than three years ago. No wonder I couldn't remember. Will the simple flit never stop?

". . . now in conclusion." But by then the voice of Marketos faded into an intermittent mumble and the stain of wine spilled on the tablecloth nearby made Father Manos remember the wine glass the girl's father had shattered when he learned the boy she wanted to marry wasn't Greek. For a year the father had not spoken to his daughter, remaining angered and embittered. Not a trace of Marketos all that time but Father Manos had argued and pleaded the cause of the young people. Now the father sat beaming on the other side of Marketos, all rancor and animosity forgotten, the son-in-law's managership of a lucrative Ford agency helping to obliterate the parental wrath. All the hours of anguish they caused me, Father Manos thought, and now they sit here like lovers, their souls entwined in each other's arms.

He was conscious of a sudden oppressive silence. He looked up startled to find Marketos glaring at him, the eyes of everyone else in the room on him as well. I listen to him faithfully for forty-five minutes, Father Manos thought unhappily, and the moment my attention lapses, the booby quits.

"Our esteemed Father Manos works too hard in his spiritual duties," Marketos said with an edge of malice in his voice. "He finds it hard to remain awake, or perhaps I speak too long, is that it, Father?"

The crowd laughed goodnaturedly and for a fleeting moment of bravado, Father Manos considered saying, yes, that is true, Marketos, you go on and on like a cracked old record and say nothing. But his courage subsided quickly into the rigid propriety of his position and he rose to his feet.

"Forgive me, Mr. Marketos," he said gravely. "I was carried away by your eloquence and moved by your recollections. When you spoke of the day Demetra came to the church to see me, I was reminded of that fateful hour myself, my own feelings as she informed me of her wish to marry this fine young man . . ."

The parents beamed. Demetra clapped her hands in delight and embraced her husband. The guests joined in applause. Marketos sat down to nurse his defeat. Father Manos could not refrain from a sly feeling of triumph. O I can play your game, he thought gleefully, when you cross lances with me, you nincompoop, you had best bolster yourself with a sturdy rod shoved up your starched backside.

Then, ashamed of his vengeful incontinence, he lowered his head and with sincerity invoked the benediction, wishing the guests, the parents, the grandparents, the baby, and yes, even Marketos, a long and fruitful life.

At eight o'clock that evening there was a meeting of the Daughters of Sparta where he spoke concerning the needs of the Boston orphanage. At nine, a half-dozen members of the picnic committee met in his office at church to discuss plans for the Hellenic Federation picnic in July. By the time they had finished a little after ten o'clock, Father Manos was exhausted and Rexinis, one of the members, drove him home.

He walked wearily up the steps of the house he had left near five that morning. He took off his coat in the hallway and went into his study. He sat down in his armchair and bent burdensomely to untie and remove his shoes. He wiggled his toes, unbuttoned his trousers and leaned back in his chair uttering a deep fervent sigh. He yearned suddenly for bed and for sleep.

There was a brusque knock on the door of his study and without waiting for his answer, Iota entered. She was the withered, almost bloodless old lady who tended house for him, an ancient crone with hard blue veins webbing her parchment flesh.

"A call for you, Father," she said and blinked in annoyance at the open buttons of his trousers. "They phoned the church just after you left."

He sighed again, a vexed, loud sigh, not caring that the old lady heard and pursed her thin lips in disapproval. He rose heavily and walked to the hallway for the phone. He had been pleading for a year for an assistant rector to replace young Deacon Botsis who had been transferred to a parish in Atlanta. The trustees were reluctant to pay another salary and the only concession they made was to allow him a priest to help him during the Christmas and Easter holidays. Meanwhile he felt his life being shortened by the excessive burdens and demands of the parish.

The call was from the floor nurse at the Mercy Hopsital with a message from Peter Kramos. His nine-year-old son, suffering from leukemia, a boy that Father Manos had visited several times in the hospital and twice given communion, was dying and not expected to survive the night. His father requested the priest to come.

Father Manos slipped his swollen feet back into his shoes and buttoned his pants while Iota called for a cab. He felt a surge of pity for Kramos and his wife, the anguish of parents losing a young child. At the same time he could not help thinking there was nothing he could really do besides join them in their suffering. He had been witness to death many times over the years, felt it a blessing for the aged and incurably ill, a cessation to their suffering. But there was nothing more shattering than the death of a child and at such times he whirled in a helpless desperation to find words to console the bereaved parents.

Carrying his small bag containing Bible and chalice for communion, he walked down the steps to the cab. They drove through the darkened streets. By the time they reached the hospital and he paid the driver, making sure to get the receipt he would turn in to the parish treasurer at the end of the month, his weariness had been submerged under a determination to meet the ordeal ahead.

He was taken by a nurse to the eighth floor. As he came out of the elevator he recognized the boy's uncle who had come to the end of the corridor to grieve alone. His face was stained with tears and when he saw Father Manos he bent and pressed his lips fervently against the back of the priest's hand. Father Manos embraced him silently and walked down the corridor to the boy's room.

The child lay almost lost within the huge bed, only his thin, frail face visible, a thatch of dark hair against the stark whiteness of the pillow. A white-coated doctor stood at the foot of the bed and on either side were the parents. Mrs. Kramos with her hands pressed to her mouth to stifle her moans. Peter Kramos staring down at his son with a mute and terrible grief.

Father Manos looked at the doctor who slowly shook his head. The priest moved closer to the bed, pausing a moment to console the mother. He placed his bag on a chair and removed the chalice for communion. He read a brief prayer and then raised the chalice and with the tiny golden spoon forced a little sip of the bread and wine between the boy's blue lips. The liquid bubbled for a moment from the child's mouth, running a thin scarlet line down his chin. At that instant the child shuddered, his mouth opened, his small teeth glittered in a frightful grimace. After one short shrill explosion of breath, he died before their eyes.

Father Manos almost cried out in shock at the abruptness of the end, only moments after he had entered the room. If the taxi had been delayed even five minutes, he thought frantically, the child might already have been dead when he arrived. Then he remembered the father and mother and looked at them with stark compassion. The doctor had moved from the foot of the bed and bent over the boy. The mother stared uncomprehending at her son. The father took a step closer to the bed and stared down in disbelief. He pushed the doctor aside and put his big hand against his son's frail throat, his fingers touching the boy's flesh in some taut and ghastly effort to revive him. A low hoarse moan broke from his lips and he put his mouth down over his son's mouth and screamed against the pale still lips.

The mother wailed and Father Manos embraced her, the tears burning in his own eyes. He led her from the room while the doctor tried to draw the father off the body of his son. The uncle hurried past Father Manos and the mother to enter the room.

Father Manos helped the sobbing, shuddering woman up the hall. She tried once to turn and go back but he urged her gently and firmly toward the small waiting room at the end of the corridor. He made her sit down and tried shakenly to console her.

When he looked up, the doctor and uncle were bringing Kramos into the room. His face was still shattered, his eyes anguished, the image of the boy's dead face torn across his cheeks. Father Manos left Mrs. Kramos and went to him.

"God bless you in this moment," he said fervently. "God sustain you, my dear friend . . . provide you the strength to endure your terrible loss . . . may God console you with his balm of compassion . . ."

For an instant Kramos stared at the priest as if he were not really seeing or hearing him. Then his face seemed to break apart. He opened his mouth and with a kind of horror Father Manos saw the scream trying to break free. Then Kramos lashed out his fist and struck the priest in the face.

It was a terrible blow. The priest felt his senses cracked apart and as he fell, he cried out in shock and fear. He landed sprawling on the floor, the room rocking wildly around him. His arms flew up in a weird broken flutter of his fingers. He saw the face of Kramos swooping down to attack him again.

The doctor and uncle grabbed Kramos. In his wild fury to get to the priest he dragged them along. His wife screamed and ran to fling her arms around her husband's throat, dragging the weight of her body against his lunge. For a few moments their arms and bodies held him, the three of them barely enough, while in terror and panic Father Manos scrambled to his knees looking vainly for a way to escape.

"Goddam you priest bastard!" Kramos screamed. "Goddam your God! Goddam animals who let my son die!"

They struggled to hold him while he screamed and raged and another intern and orderly came. They dragged him from the room into a vacant room across the hall and closed the door which could not shut out his screams.

A nurse and doctor came to Father Manos where he still huddled on his knees. They helped him to his feet and he heard the solacing voices dimly and to every question he could only shake his head. They washed his face and offered him a bed to rest in, but he begged for a cab to take him home. They took him down to the lobby and called a cab and a nurse offered to accompany him but he insisted on riding home alone. He did not remember getting out of the cab or paying the driver. He fumbled in his pocket for the key and could not find it. He rang the bell. The sound echoed back shrilly and he looked back fearfully behind him at the shadowed street. When there was no answer from inside the house he knocked loudly and urgently against the wood.

Iota finally opened the door, drawing a robe about her gaunt body, mumbling complaints about being awakened. He hurried past her up the hall to his bedroom. He entered and closed and locked the door. He sat on the side of his bed and for a long time did not move. Iota knocked on the door and spoke to him. He did not answer. After a while, still grumbling, she left him alone.

When the rooms about him were silent, he rose and undressed. In his underwear he slipped into bed. He pulled the blankets to his throat and shivered. He slid his hands down across his stomach and gripped his genitals. He held himself tightly in a trembling frenzy. Great waves of cold followed by surgings of heat swept his flesh.

"O God," he whispered. "O God, why . . . O my God, why?"

He could not have slept more than a few moments when something startled him, a strange bursting within him and he cried out in terror. He felt sleep abandon him as if it were a soul leaving the body of someone dead. He flung off his covers and rose and left the room. He had a sudden fear of being left alone and he made deliberate noise in the kitchen hoping Iota would wake and come to scold him. At that moment he would have been grateful for even her skinny shanks in their cotton stockings and the sour line of her bloodless lips.

He returned to his bedroom for his robe and then back in the kitchen heated some milk. He sat at the table sipping it, the silence whirling in circles that grew tighter around him. He looked at his hands and was suddenly conscious of them in a way he had never been before. The myriad lines of the palm that laced together in a weird and disturbing pattern, a dark vein pulsing beneath the pale skin of his wrist.

He walked to the bathroom, relieved himself, and felt a burning in his organ. He let water run into the basin and soaked his face with a cloth. He saw his reflection in the glass, the raw ugly bruise that discolored his cheek.

He stared at his face silently for a long time and then felt another sweep of terror rack his flesh. It started in the small of his back, a knife between the ridge of his buttocks, and traveled up as if a frozen blade were rending his body. His mouth opened, his tongue and teeth appeared, and then he screamed . . . not very loud, but thinly and shrilly striking the tile walls and falling back upon him. He put his hands to his ears and felt them as if they were wounds.

I am going mad, he thought. This is the way it must begin.

When the first light of dawn broke over the city he looked up from his Bible with an exhausted relief. He leaned back in his chair and for the first time in hours dared close his eyes. When he opened them the light had spread, glinting across the bedposts and the bureau. He rose wearily and left the room.

In the kitchen, Iota turned from the stove to confront him sullenly.

"What's the matter with you?" she asked sharply. "You rushed in last night like the devil was chasing you and I heard you moving around all night. I couldn't sleep a wink."

"I'm sorry," he said. He stared at her waiting for her to identify the bruise. But she looked at him without a sign that she noticed anything unusual. "You want eggs or oatmeal?" she asked shortly.

"Nothing," Father Manos said, and turned away uneasily, his fingers rising to touch his tender, swollen cheek.

He started toward the bathroom, his muscles sore and cramped from sitting up through the chilled night. He felt the ache with a grim relief, a physical pain that had its origin in something he could understand.

When he moved before the vanity mirror, he hesitated with apprehension. The bruise was clearly there, a raw, red-black blemish that marked his face like a leper's taint.

The remainder of the reflection that stared back at him was familiar, the soft and ordinary face he had known for many years, changing only as age changed it. Yet he saw it now with every vestige of dignity and grace stripped away. The thinning gray hair that he wore long and brushed to cover the area of scalp that was balding. The arched, wry line of his eyebrows above the sockets of his indecisive eyes. The small brush of ridiculous mustache under his nose. Every wrinkle and fold, dreary and common.

For a while he considered remaining at home. But as the morning wore on and he could not sit or rest, he dressed and left the house for the church. He kept his head lowered and his collar up in an effort to conceal the bruise.

In the church he went at once to his office and closed the door. The parish secretary was visiting her mother in Denver, but Janco had heard him entering and brought him several messages from people who had called. As he handed them across the desk to him, Father Manos waited again anxiously for the old man to see the bruise. But the sexton merely stood waiting for some command, shifting from one crooked leg to the other. The phone rang again and with a peremptory motion of his head, the priest signalled the sexton to take another message. Then he fled into the church.

It was dark and sorrowful in the nave, only a few forlorn candles flickering before the icons. He walked through the Deacon's door to the anteroom and from there into the Sanctuary. He stood motionless for a moment in the dry, ascetic air, absorbing the Evangelion, the Blessing Cross, the candlesticks, the Ark for the Sacrament of Communion.

He went to the small basin and washed his hands. Before the Oblation table he began to prepare the communion. He cut out the middle square of the Prosforon and pierced the bread with the lance. He poured water and wine into the chalice and cut the square of bread into tiny pieces, for the Holy Virgin, for the Saints, for the Bishop, for people living or dead, for himself. He put the pieces of bread into the chalice and spread the coverlet over it. He kissed it and prayed to God to accept and sanctify it. He removed the coverlet and with trembling hands raised the chalice to his mouth. The wine tasted warm and sour on his tongue, trickles seeping into the pockets of his cheeks.

Through the configuration of his arm and the chalice he saw the wooden cross on which the Saviour, Jesus Christ, was crucified. He stared up at the pierced palms and at the anguished countenance and felt a burning in his soul.

"O my merciful God," he whispered to the figure on the cross, "tell me thy name." He held the chalice numbly in his fingers, his voice faint and shaken in his ears, "I pray you, tell me thy name."

He waited in an entombed silence, feeling the pounding of his heart. From the rear of the church came the sexton's hoarse voice summoning him. He was reluctant to leave the Sanctuary, moving further back into the dense shadows for concealment. The sexton came to the anteroom door and called him again and he walked out to answer the call.

The hours of that day passed unlike any he had ever experienced before. He spoke to the visitors who came to his office, feeling his features altering stiffly from frown to wan smile, hearing the words he spoke echoing as if from far away. He was conscious of talking with his head lowered, one cheek turned aside, his fingers raised often to conceal the bruise. Yet no one seemed to notice it, or if they did, made no sign. And the mystification of that veiling fed his disorder.

When the last visitor left, he rose and in the doorway of his office saw the narthex empty. Through the single lone paned window in the corner he marked the fading light and his terror of the night came storming back.

In his office he noticed on his calendar that he was to meet Father Grivas for dinner at the Hellenic Cafe that evening. Earlier in the week he had planned to cancel the dinner with the savage priest but he was grateful now that he had not. He phoned the Holy Trinity Church, afraid Father Grivas might have forgotten about the dinner, and asked him if they could meet a little earlier, as well. The other priest's harsh voice agreeing filled him with a measure of consolation.

Father Manos instructed Janco to lock up and then hurried through the twilight streets. Entering the Hellenic Cafe, a shabby grocery and restaurant, he passed the counters filled with dark green and black olives, ripe white cheeses, and crisp crusted breads. He usually paused to enjoy the plethora of food, often buying some to take home with him. Now he walked directly into the shadowed back room. There were a dozen booths lit only by candles that masked the drab and faded cloths. He sat down wearily in one of them, grateful for the shadows and the dimness. When a lean-hipped waiter with a soiled apron tied around his waist came for his order, he asked for a bottle of retsina. As the waiter left the booth, Father Manos saw the other priest.

Father Grivas came striding through the shadows, pulling off his coat on the way. His hair hung shaggy and unkempt over his clerical collar. He had a swarthy, pocked face and a full-lipped mouth that he twisted into a sardonic grimace of greeting.

"It's been a long time," Grivas spoke in a rumbling voice, "since I've heard anybody so eager to see me."

The waiter reappeared with the bottle of retsina, Grivas stared up at him in irritation. "Don't just stand there, boobhead," he said. "Bring another glass." As the waiter walked away, he added, "That one would make a great Deacon." He stared sharply at Father Manos.

"You don't look well," he said. "Did you have a meeting with your damn Board of Trustees?"

"I didn't sleep well last night," Father Manos said. He kept his face averted slightly in an effort to conceal the bruise even though he was not sure the other priest could see it. At the same time he felt a swift, compelling yearning to reveal his terror. He restrained himself with an effort. Like a child, he thought for a vexed moment, like a child I will blurt out all my absurd fears. "It's nothing," he said impatiently. "Insomnia that bothers me now and then."

The waiter returned with another glass. Grivas filled both glasses with the wine. He handed one to Father Manos. "Drink up," he said, "and then drink some more. You'll sleep soundly tonight." He dismissed the waiter with a sharp cutting motion of his hand. "Get lost until we want you," he said.

They sat together drinking for a long time. Some men they knew entered the restaurant, ate dinner, and then left. Instead of eating dinner themselves, they ordered another bottle of retsina. Father Manos was aware he was drinking too much, that other patrons were staring at them, but after a while he didn't care. The wine warmed him, relaxed his body, seeped into the dark, hidden hollows of his distress.

Across from him, Grivas drank steadily, pausing only to order still another bottle when the second one was empty. Although a wilder glint entered his eyes, he showed no other visible trace of the amount of wine he had consumed.

"They are plump and well-fed, shallow and mundane," Grivas said.

"Who?"

"Who else?" Grivas curled his heavy lip with contempt. "You know damn well who I mean. Our blessed brothers in white collars, wallowing in their sties."

"They haven't done you any harm," Father Manos said.

"Just seeing and hearing them harms me enough," Grivas said stridently. He refilled his glass. The wine spilled over the rim and sloshed across his fingers. He raised his big, hairy hand to his mouth and with his tongue recoiling swiftly between his teeth, licked his fingers. "But the fault isn't theirs alone," he said. "They reflect the nescient cretins who make up their congregations. Forced to pander to every idiot who throws a stinking dime into the tray, they become freaks themselves, lambs who live with snakes so long they learn to shed their skins."

He made a move to refill both their glasses. Father Manos tried to stop him with a half-hearted gesture that Grivas brushed aside.

"You are a relentless man," Father Manos said slowly. "Relentless and cruel. A shade of compassion would make all these frailties bearable."

"I have compassion for them," Grivas growled. "The compassion Herod had, and that is more than they deserve."

With a sudden resignation Father Manos remembered he had heard all these denunciations many times before. He raised the glass of wine to his mouth and took a long swallow. The liquid flowed down into his body, into caverns where his organs lay inert and still.

"I tell the bastards where to go!" Grivas struck the table with his heavy fist and the glasses jumped. "Gluttonous swine wallowing in food while millions starve! Pimping merchants obsessed with spoils while children burn in Viet Nam! Coming to me on Sundays to absolve them of their filthy, necrophilic sins! I'll send them to hell! Let them ask for absolution there!"

"Grivas," Father Manos said, and suddenly he did not care how he might sound to the other priest, "Grivas, something is happening to me."

Grivas fell silent, his chest still heaving in agitation. His harsh breathing grew calmer and he stared at Father Manos with a wary curiosity.

"I don't know what it is," Father Manos said. "I have the feeling it began with a nightmare but I can't be sure." He looked for a long moment at Grivas, then slowly turned his bruised cheek into the candlelight.

Grivas looked at him silently.

"You see nothing?" Father Manos said. He put his hand to his cheek and felt the tender swollen scale of the wound.

"What should I see?" Grivas asked.

"Nothing," Father Manos said, and shook his head, and felt a flare of panic rising in his gullet. "I'm afraid I'm losing my mind."

For a long moment Grivas did not answer. When he finally spoke, his voice was a shade less harsh.

"Why shouldn't you lose your mind?" Grivas asked. "You wouldn't be the first priest who did, especially in these times. I know one cleric who has twice slashed his wrists and another who tried to conduct his Sunday services stark naked."

Father Manos closed his eyes and held them tightly shut. He fumbled for his glass of wine and raised it to his chilled lips.

"I'm weary and alone," he said. He opened his eyes and stared across the table at Grivas. "The God who was with me as a child, who grew with me as a man, as a priest, He's suddenly hidden from me now."

"Some modern priests think God is dead," Grivas said with a shrug. "That's the new faith now."

Father Manos shook his head slowly. "I don't think He's dead," he said in a low, shaken whisper. "I think He's examined my spirit and my heart and found them wanting. He has turned his face from me because I'm not worthy. He is no longer my rock."

Grivas looked down with an uneasy shrug. "I don't know what's happening to you," he said. "It could be many things. Despair, loneliness, fear and trembling. A man can go on mouthing the clichés for just so long and then a part of him caves in."

"I'll go and see a doctor," Father Manos said, and he clutched at that thought as if it were a raft in the whirlpool of his soul.

"Go ahead," Grivas said. "He'll probably find something wrong to reassure you, but your trouble won't be over then." He finished the last of the wine in his glass, the end of the third bottle and wiped his mouth roughly with the back of his hand. "I think you're a moderately decent man who has suddenly awakened to the absurdity of the whole charade. The pious frauds and bleating hypocrites that you try to anesthetize with candles, incense and dull sermons."

Father Manos felt a sudden ripple of anger in his body, welcomed it for the assault upon his despair.

"Are you any less of a hypocrite?" he asked, feeling the words bitten through his teeth. "Are you any less a fraud than the worst of priests? Tell me that, Grivas!"

"I'm as bad as any of them," Grivas said quietly. "With one difference. I admit my worthlessness and accept my hell. I don't fool myself with false hopes and futile dreams of sacrifice or service. Like the poor priests trying to find meaning in their lives who march with the blacks in Mississippi and get their heads broken by rednecks, or the priests who march into draft boards and pour blood on the files in protest for Viet Nam and for that Christian exercise are sentenced to rot for ten years in some filthy prison with cutthroats and thieves. Leave your pulpit and raise your voice and they'll burn you or crucify you." He paused, a wry grin twisting his lips. "But that might be your salvation," he said. "Join the marchers and protesters. There's always room for a benign, gray-haired martyr."

Father Manos looked shakenly at Grivas. "Once I marched in such a group," he said slowly. "With Blacks into a white neighborhood. They screamed and cursed us and the Rabbi walking beside me was struck with a brick. I panicked and ran. I was sick for three days, told everyone it was the flu, but it was simply terror." He shook his head wearily. "I'm afraid," he said. "I've grown old, soft and afraid."

"Screw them all!" Grivas said, his face dark with a rush of blood. "Let them devour each other! In the end we may leave the earth as clean as it was before Adam and God's curse!"

Father Manos stared at him in shock and wonder.

"How do you live, Grivas?" he asked. "How do you endure your days and nights despising yourself and all other men?"

Grivas looked at him without answering. He rose soddenly to stand swaying for a moment beside the booth and then clutching his coat, turned and walked unsteadily toward the exit. At the door he paused. After a moment he started back to the booth, reached it and bent forward, putting his hands on the table for support. His face was close enough for Father Manos to smell the rank pungence of wine, close enough to see the marks of suffering like dark etchings around the priest's eyes.

"I live on my hate," he said, and the anger and bitterness were gone from his voice, a terrible anguish in their place. "Hate alone keeps me alive."

After Grivas had gone, Father Manos remained at the table for a little while. His knees trembled and he was afraid that if he tried to walk, he would fall. Finally, he rose and left the restaurant, surprised how quiet and desolate the streets were. He was anxious to reach home and the pavement tossed under his legs as if it were the deck of a ship on a stormy sea. He looked vainly for a cab, peering with apprehension at the occasional car that rumbled past as if it contained parishioners who would recognize him. A drunken priest, he thought helplessly, a drunken priest who will fall into a gutter where they will find me in the morning.

But he did not fall down. After a while the night air, cool and damp with the faint scents of spring, cleared his head. He raised the collar of his coat about his ears and walked with his head lowered, charting the path his steps would follow. At each corner he raised his head to take a renewed measure of direction.

Then he stood before the house. He walked up the steps with a silent, grateful prayer that nothing had happened to him on the way. He found his key and fumbled it into the lock and opened the door. In the dim hallway he was assailed at once by the staleness of the rooms around him. The thin mist of cologne the old lady sprayed under her fossiled arms and upon her withered breasts. His own odors, dry, thin scents of prayer and flat, rheumatic spoor of aging, useless flesh.

He went to his bedroom and pulled off his topcoat and suitcoat together. He unbuttoned and removed his collar and took off his shoes. He pulled up the blanket from the bed and lay down and covered himself with it. He lay curved on his side, his head bent forward, his knees drawn up almost into his stomach. Dear God, he thought, merciful God, let me sleep.

Whether because of the wine or his exhaustion from the night before, he slept. He woke with his head buried in his pillow and could not be sure the length of time which had elapsed. For a moment he was stung by the fear it might still be night. He kept his eyes tightly closed and raised his head slightly to listen for some familiar sound. When he heard nothing he tensely opened his eyes a slit and with a spasm of gratitude opened them completely. The rim of window around his shade was bright with sunlight. He rose quickly from the bed, remorseful at his terror of the night before, ashamed when he remembered drinking with Grivas.

The shower spray struck his naked flesh with a piercing satisfaction. The water ran in torrents down his legs and into the drain, flushing the crust of despair from his body. As he was dressing, Iota knocked brusquely on the door of his room. He asked her cheerfully to prepare eggs and toast for his breakfast.

His mood of ebullience carried him into the afternoon. A steady stream of parishioners came to see him on various problems and the hours passed quickly. Late in the afternoon a young man and girl came to see him about plans for their marriage. Happiness radiated from their pores and for a while he basked in their joy. After they had signed the necessary papers he walked with them through the narthex to the outer door of the church and outside on the stone steps. They waved to him from their car and he raised his hand in a final flutter of farewell. He saw his fingers outlined like the claw of a skeleton against the darkening sky and the first streaming shadows of twilight. He could not believe that the day was already gone and he felt his flesh tighten in a sudden, haunted distress. He turned and fled back into the church.

He spent the evening at home with the television playing loudly, for the first time not minding the inane noise and chatter. Finally, Iota asked him to lower it. She was peeved at him anyway because he had not eaten any of the dinner she had prepared. He tried to engage her in conversation to postpone her going to bed. But she told him she was tired and went to her room.

He went to his own bedroom and brought his Bible back to the parlor. He sat down again and began to read. The words blurred before his eyes. He made an effort to concentrate, speaking the verses out loud. They echoed with a stark hollow ring back in his ears.

He closed the Bible and leaned forward in his chair. He listened for sound in the silence of the house. His tongue felt dry, his throat tight, and he rubbed his palms in quick nervous flutters across the cloth of his trousers. The table, chairs, curtains, all seemed washed in a strange, eerie light. Even a bowl of unripe plums on the table caught the cold sparkle, their yellow glow glaring into his eyes.

He closed his eyes, felt them seal his flesh like the lid closing on a coffin. A great scream burst somewhere deep in his body. He slipped from the chair to his knees and then, unable to help himself, pitched forward to the floor. Prostrate and exhausted, his body swept by waves of trembling, he began feverishly to pray.

On Saturday morning he sat in an anteroom of the Archdiocese waiting for his appointment with the Bishop. He huddled in his chair, his head down, faintly hearing the voices of people around him. He felt a tugging at his sleeve and looked up, startled, into the thin, pale face of the Deacon.

"You can go in now, Father," the Deacon said. "His Grace is waiting."

Father Manos rose and followed the Deacon toward the large double doors. The Deacon opened them and he passed into a huge chamber and the doors closed behind him.

Bishop Okas rose from behind his dark-oak desk and crossed the room, his robe sweeping about his ankles. "How are you, my dear Father?" he said. He extended his hand, almost in apology, as if knowing yet regretting that ritual required he do so. When Father Manos bent and kissed the back of his palm, he withdrew his hand quickly as if the gesture of obeisance somehow embarrassed him.

The Bishop was a young man, still in his early forties, with a face and a body made lean and spare by prayers and fasts. He had a mustache and a small trim black beard. His face might have been that of any ordinary parish priest but for the way, Father Manos had noticed before, it radiated a capacity for love and devotion, suggesting a grace that came through fulfilling God's will.

"Thank you, your Grace, for consenting to see me this quickly," Father Manos said. "I know how busy your schedule is."

"Not at all, Father," the Bishop said. "I am always delighted to see one of my brothers in Christ." He motioned to a chair. "Please come and sit down."

Father Manos sat down on a stiff-backed armchair and the Bishop sat down across from him, spreading and smoothing his black cassock across his long, lean legs. His eyes, large, dark and intense, stared somberly at the priest.

"What is it, Father?" he asked softly.

Father Manos raised his hand to hesitantly touch the bruise on his cheek. He had ceased expecting that it was visible to anyone but him, yet now, in the Bishop's consecrated presence he had a quiver of hope that the wound might be seen and healed.

"Something has come to me in the night," he said, and even the words filled him with foreboding, and he made an effort to keep his voice from becoming shrill. "I'm filled with a terrible fear." He shook his head in bewilderment. "I have never known anything like it before."

Bishop Okas listened earnestly. It seemed to Father Manos that a flutter of compassion swept the younger man's face and he was ashamed of his confession. As if sensing his discomfort, the Bishop leaned forward and reached out to touch the priest on the arm in a gesture of consolation. How beautiful his fingers are, Father Manos thought, long and slender and so pale they were almost white. They might have been the fingers of one of El Greco's saints, stretched toward an unfathomable, unreachable height, toward a vision visible only to the spirit.

"I have been a priest so long," Father Manos said. "Spoken so many benedictions, performed so many sacraments. And now I shrink and tremble and fear. Is it because I have failed God? Nothing is clear to me anymore. The night brings phantoms and demons. I feel my soul cry out."

The Bishop stared at him silently. He looked once toward the ceiling and for an instant his finely curved lips were visible within his silky beard. Then he rose, unfolding his body to his lean, full height. He stood with his back to Father Manos.

"Life is a jungle," he said softly. "All around us is murder, avarice, brutality. The jungle is tangled and thick and the animals scream in the dark." He turned slowly to look down at the priest. "But a road runs through that jungle, a rough and stony road that seems to fall away in places, or is sometimes hidden, yet it is still there. The road of faith."

His eyes blazed with a lucent fervor. "You are older than I am, Father, you have been on this road longer, have more reason to grow weary, more reason to feel anguish. These are times more wicked than the time of Sodom and Gomorrah. A bitterness rises through our lives, a nausea, a mist of melancholy, things that sound a knell." His voice fell to a sibilant whisper. "He who loves his neighbor burns his heart, and the heart, like green wood, in burning groans and distils itself in tears. We must understand, Father, that the evil of our suffering can be cured only by greater suffering."

Father Manos looked down at his hands, the soft, trembling fingers, the backs scarred with spots like the back of a toad.

"We can no longer save Man from himself," the Bishop said. "We can only keep the faith alive until He returns, for He must return. Meanwhile we must have a passion for God. It must possess us and fill us with such fire that we are conscious of nothing else. God can keep us in sight of the road. God! Only God! And if we remain on the road, the Church will survive, and our Saviour will return to redeem us!" His voice rose slightly and he clasped his hands together and extended them to Father Manos in mute and quivering entreaty. "Let us pray together, Father," he said, and he slipped to his knees before the priest.

The sight of the Bishop kneeling before him swept Father Manos with a fit of trembling. He reached out and clasped the Bishop's fingers and then slipped to his knees on the floor beside him.

"O my God," Bishop Okas whispered. "O my God, help your servant who is in sore need of your light and consolation. Help him, my God, do not forsake him now in his hour of need."

He lowered his head toward the floor. His cassock spread like a mantle about their ankles. His slender shoulders trembled. "Abandon despair," he said. "Abandon anguish. Give yourself freely to God's spirit."

"I will," Father Manos said.

"God is love!" Bishop Okas said.

"God is love," Father Manos said.

"God is light!"

"God is light."

"God is eternity!" Bishop Okas cried.

"God is eternity."

Tiny beads of sweat had formed on the Bishop's forehead, a vein pulsed in his temple, dark with a rushing through of blood. A small bubble of saliva ran from his mouth into his beard. He swayed slightly and let out a great long sigh that seemed to surge from deep in his body.

Father Manos reached to him and bent and kissed the lovely and slender hands again, feeling the flesh moist and warm, a scent of some fragile, delicate greenhouse flower rising from his palms, a flower able to thrive only in compounds of heat and filtered light.

Bishop Okas turned his head slightly and for a moment their eyes met.

He must see me now, Father Manos thought. He must recognize the wound I bear now, in this moment, this unmatched moment when our souls have been joined in a solemn and tender benediction.

But Bishop Okas made no sign that he had seen anything but his own visions. He turned aside and rose to his feet, smoothing down his cassock. Father Manos rose slowly and made his cross and left.

That night, again, he did not sleep. But the frenzy and terror of the preceding nights altered now for him into a strange resignation. In his darkened room he floated upon the waves of night, watching the moonlight curl around the shade of his window, hearing the floorboards creak. In the passage of that night he recalled the years he had lived, unrenowned and unmemorable years marked by futile words, wooden gestures, faltering faith. What had happened to his dreams of life with purpose and fulfillment? He felt his soul poured out like water, his bones out of joint, his heart like wax. He heard a bough blown against the house and raised up his head and quietly prayed for death.

Before daylight he dressed and walked through the darkness toward the church. He heard his short, stiff steps echo on the pavements as if he walked in a great hollow chamber. At the rim of the sky darkness and light raveled their threads.

He unlocked the heavy church door, swung it open, and entered the darkened narthex. He walked into the silent nave and sat down in one of the pews. He sat for a long time staring into the shadows until the shades of dawn lit the ceiling of the dome and seeped down into the hidden corners, unveiling angels and saints, winged and fluted seraphims. The Royal Gate of the Sanctuary energed glittering from the darkness. From there, blinded in his vanity and pride, he had taken the name of the Lord vainly. If he did not murder, his silence condoned the murderers. If he did not starve the poor, he comforted those who ate while the poor hungered. If he did not burn the innocent, his complacence sanctified the burners.

After a while he rose and walked to the anteroom. He began dressing himself in his robes and vestments for the beginning of the service. He heard the first of the young acolytes entering the anteroom on the opposite side of the Sanctuary. Then the choirmaster entered.

"Good morning, Father Manos," he spoke cheerfully without looking at the priest.

"Good morning, Elias," Father Manos said.

"A lovely, early spring morning," Elias slipped into his cassock. "Winter will be over soon now."

"Yes, Elias," Father Manos said. He walked into the Sanctuary, crossed himself, and took up his place before the closed panel of the Royal Gate. He heard the choirmaster begin his chant, the rustling and murmuring of people moving into the pews, the whispering of the acolytes in the anteroom. And in those moments that he listened and waited he understood he would hold his bond to the earth and to his church until it was God's will to sever him from them. He would live joylessly watching the coming and going of the seasons. Yearning for death and peace he would be burdened with mortality, each year like ten he had passed before, the long thin drawing out of his soul to cover them.

But in those years remaining to him he would seek to build again the shattered temple of his faith, seek to renew that vision of something surpassingly fair which had haunted him in childhood, make the words of his mouth and the manifestation of his spirit acceptable in the sight of God.

And if he still failed because he had lived too long with hypocrisy and deceit, then he would bear the bruise on his face and soul for as long as he lived. When he died, he would have nothing to render the Lord but the thin, futile ashes of his suffering.

The old sexton entered the acolyte's anteroom and came in his broken-gaited jog into the Sanctuary. He crossed himself hastily and took up his crouched position before the panel, twisting his face fearfully and anxiously toward the priest.

For the first time in all the years the two of them had waited together before the panel, Father Manos recognized the sexton's terror. He suddenly understood how each Sunday morning the simple act of pushing aside the panel was a pillory and an anguish for the old man, an endlessly repeated ordeal wherein he might commit some terrible indiscretion before his priest and his God.

"Don't be afraid, Janco," Father Manos said softly, and he reached out to clasp the old man's bony shoulder in a gesture of consolation.

The old sexton gaped up at him numbly for a moment and then slowly, awesomely understood that the priest had recognized and forgiven him his fear, had touched him in absolution. He bent renewed to his task, his crooked, twisted shoulders shaking.

Watching the old man begin to cry, Father Manos felt tears breaking slowly from his own eyes.

He bent his head and as the panel slid open, he saw the tears glitter into specks of flame on the scarlet cloth of his gilded vestments.

I knew a blind girl once, and although we were not lovers, she helped me renew a delight in touch and a wonder in life. Many readers have written me they found this story moving, but a dear friend, whose son has been blind almost from birth, who taught herself Braille and who teaches classes to the blind, felt the story was not totally realistic. She told me the blind are not as graceful as I portrayed the girl to be, and she should know.

If my portrait of the girl is not as authentic as it might be, the writer is a genuine and impeccable creation. He is the fool I was, the fool I am, and the fool I will always be.

THE EYES OF LOVE

Autumn came and passed quickly that year. Almost overnight the last dry, brown leaves burned in the twilight street fires. The nights began to turn cold, and in my basement flat the steam sputtered and hissed through the overhead radiators. I pushed my bed away from the window in the bedroom and pulled a woolen blanket from the shelf in the closet.

I didn't really mind the winter. I preferred it to the false faces of spring and summer, the ephemeral masks of buds and flowers that concealed the desolation underneath. The season I liked best of all was autumn, when the air smelled definably of death, and the declining days wore their proper raiment.

I was a writer of stories and a couple of novels that had been reviewed well in the *New York Times*. They produced a small spasm of activity in the book-review columns and a sparse display with my picture in one of the downtown book stores. Then, like the tide coming in across a beach littered with debris, the cut-glass fragments of my fame were once more submerged in anonymity.

But writing was still the only thing I wanted to do, even though I had realized years before how senseless was a writer's dream that he could, within the pages of a book, cultivate a garden beyond the darkness of his death. In addition, the stories provided me a meager living and saved me from forty hours a week in another man's vineyard.

Each day I rose early in the morning and slipped into worn sneakers and old pants. I enjoyed a pot of hot, rousing coffee and then wrote at my typewriter till afternoon, when the children broke loose in squealing joy from school.

There was a basement flat similar to my own across the narrow court, and it was occupied by a piano teacher I had never seen. Each day after school her students banged out a shrill and discordant series of scales. To evade their wretched hammering I walked down to the corner tavern and lingered for a couple of hours over beer.

In the twilight I returned to my flat and shaved and dressed in more formal clothes. I ate a steak in a neighborhood restaurant and marinated it with a glass or two of red wine. When I sold a story and had a new check in my pocket, I treated myself to a full bottle of good wine. Then, with my normally somber nature submerged beneath the laughter of the grape, I would ardently search out some young lady in a tavern and tempt her to join my celebration. This was a kind of gaiety that could not survive the sober dawn, and in the morning I had a mountain of a head and a tongue like the moss on a rock.

It was on such a night in that autumn, preparing for a small celebration because the check for a sale had been meager, that I passed the piano teacher's flat. Through a partially raised shade I saw that she was a young woman with dark, long hair sitting on a bench before an upright piano.

Later in the evening, after I had consumed a half-bottle of wine, I thought of her again. She had been attractive and young. Each afternoon her talentless students drove me from my rooms, and that seemed a legitimate grievance on which to base a visit. I took along what was left of the bottle of wine.

When I reached her apartment, the shades were all drawn closed. I thought she might be asleep or out and then I saw a shadow of movement along the rim of a shade. I rang her bell.

In a moment the door opened just a few inches and I heard the jangle of a chain.

"I beg your pardon," I said, and couldn't see her face. "I live in the basement flat across the court. I was just passing and felt it was time to introduce myself."

She was silent and wary for a moment. "It's a little late, isn't it?"

"We are artists," I said amiably. "You a musician and I a writer. We understand that time is the greatest irrelevance of all."

I couldn't be sure in the shadows but it seemed to me she smiled. "I have heard you typing for hours at a time."

"I have heard your students at their lessons," I said. "An unusually talented group."

"I'm sorry if they disturb your work."

"Not at all," I said, "but I would be interested in knowing whether they use hammers on the keys?"

She laughed a pleasant sound that dispersed some of the wariness.

"My name is Pete Zachary," I said, "and perhaps we could visit for a few moments."

She hesitated a moment longer and then made up her mind. She closed the door and drew off the chain and then opened the door again. With a triumphant swagger I stepped inside her apartment.

I followed her into the living room. There was only a small lamp burning on a table in the corner, and most of the room was draped in shadow. The upright piano took up almost one entire wall, and on a couch across from the piano reclined a gray, furry cat that regarded me with ominous yellow eyes.

Off the living room was a small kitchen similar to my own with a table and two chairs and an assortment of plates and glasses in an open cabinet. There was a large shelf along the wall decorated with several heads of sculpture, carved and polished heads of men and women, that seemed suspended without bodies on the wall.

"My name is Andrea," she said, "and the cat is Emily." At the sound of her name the cat rose and stretched indolently and then leaped with a sinister warning to the floor.

"Pleased to meet you both," I said and sat down.

Andrea sat down on an ottoman across the room from the lamp so that she was darkly concealed in shadow. From as much as I could discern, she was an attractive girl, slender-bodied with good legs. Her hair framed her face and the skin of her cheeks gleamed pale in the shadows and gave an impression of ghostly beauty. But the most striking thing about her were her hands. They were pale, paler than the hue of her face, and the fingers flowed from her slim wrists as if they were long-petaled flowers.

"What kind of things do you write?"

"Short stories mostly," I said. "A couple of novels that did nothing. My creations disappear into the water like small pebbles or finish on a table of remainders at forty-nine cents apiece."

"Are you a beatnik or an angry young man?" she asked with a trace of humor in her voice.

"I'm not revolting against a thing," I said, and the wine loosened my tongue. "All is vanity and vexation of the spirit. Nothing is worth fighting about." I shook my head. "What about you? What makes a young, attractive girl become a teacher to a bunch of piano butchers?"

"That is the way I make my living," she said, "and they're not all butchers. One or two are even very good."

"Things are tough all over," I said and then realized I was still clutching the half-full bottle of wine. "I was taking some wine home. Would you like a small glass?"

"No, thank you," she said, becoming wary again. "But you have a glass if you like."

I walked toward the cabinet. "This place is laid out exactly like mine," I said. There was a lamp on the cabinet and I switched it on to locate a glass. I poured an extra glass and carried it to her.

"You really should try a sip," I said. "It's good sauterne." She raised her head as I reached her. The lamp I had turned on glowed light across her face. She stood staring at a point just beyond my shoulder, not looking at the glass or me, and I realized that she was blind.

I was fiercely shaken and, as if she understood, she spoke quickly to cover my disorder. "I will try a sip," she said and raised her hand to take the glass from me without a trace of fumbling.

"I'll have a glass myself," I said, "and then I'd better leave. It is late, and I shouldn't really have disturbed you." I drank my wine quickly.

I hesitated a moment and then walked toward the door. She rose from the ottoman and followed me. We stood for an instant by the door. "I am sorry about the students," she said softly. "I'll make sure my windows are closed."

"That's all right," I said quickly. "Don't worry about me. I'm through writing by then anyway."

I opened the door and walked out. She was a dark, slender figure against the light, her face concealed again in shadow.

"Goodnight, Pete," she said in a calm and pleasant voice.

"Goodnight, Andrea," I said. She closed the door quietly.

Instead of returning to the bar, I went home. Coldly sober by that time, I mourned the impulse that had sent me to her door. If the world were full of grief and affliction, there was no need for a man to search it out. I felt sorry for her, but there was nothing I could do. I went to bed.

In the first total snap of darkness as I closed the lamp, I wondered what her life was like, denied the sight of faces, figures, fruits, and flowers, the red of a sunset, and the green of grass. After a while I was grateful when I could make out dim familiar objects in my room. But there was also a strange serenity about her that I found moving in recollection, the loveliness of her pale, slim fingers and the softness of her voice. It took me a long time to fall asleep.

The rain started the following Friday night and kept falling all day Saturday until late afternoon. I wrote for a while and then sat by the window smoking a cigarette, watching the water strike the streets and sweep in swift currents to the sewers.

I was hungry, and there was nothing in the place to eat. I put on a raincoat and an old felt hat and ran to the corner to a Chinese restaurant. I ordered a large carton of chow mein and carried it straight to Andrea's door as if I had meant to do that all along.

She answered the door in slacks and blouse, a thin yellow ribbon holding back her fine, black hair. I had the feeling even before I spoke that she knew it was me.

"Andrea," I said. "I've got enough chow mein for two. You interested?"

She smiled and motioned me in quickly out of the rain. I hesitated. "I'm dripping wet," I said.

"Give me your things," she laughed. "I'll hang them in the bathroom to dry."

While she took my wet things inside, I unlaced my sodden shoes and stepped out of them.

"Bring the chow mein in here," she called from the kitchen. I crossed the room, and on the couch Emily somberly turned her head and looked at me with her baleful yellow eyes.

We carried two plates of chow mein back to the living room.

"If you don't mind sitting on the floor," Andrea said, "we can use the coffee table under the window."

"I always eat better on the floor," I said.

She sat down, folding her legs lithely beneath her. I sat down across from her. The window was a square of gray light, and the rain cracked against the panes of glass.

I watched her as she ate. Now that she was visible in a better light, I saw that she was very lovely. The ribbon held her hair, but a single strand had come loose and hung down across her cheek. Even as I noticed, she raised her hand and swept the fallen lock back into place.

"This is wonderful," she said between swallows. "Much better than the hamburger I was going to fry."

Emily came slowly from the couch to sniff the plates. She rubbed her furry back in silent appeal against Andrea's leg.

"Do you think it would bother her?" Andrea asked.

"She may never drink milk again," I said, "but forever after demand pekoe tea with fortune cookies."

"I'll chance that." Andrea laughed and gave her what was left in her plate.

"I'm sorry about the other night," I said, "busting in here like I did half-tanked."

She smiled slightly and bent her head to conceal the smile. "You were so surprised," she said. "You came in here like a jolly bulldog and left like a remorseful Chihuahua."

"I was full of wine," I said ruefully.

She drew up her legs and clasped her arms around her knees. Her face changed under a pensive and solitary withdrawal.

"People are always much more sensitive about blindness than the blind," she said. "When you are blind you get used to it."

"How long has it been for you?" I asked.

"About twelve years now," she said. "I spent eight of those years in an institute for the blind. I came out four years ago and took some college work back home and then came to Chicago and started giving piano lessons to support myself."

"What do they teach you in an institute?"

She smiled pensively again, and her nose twitched in recollection as if she had bitten on a sour plum. "You learn to find the end of a piece of meat with your fork and cut it off with your knife. You learn about social graces and adjustment to society. You learn to try never to fumble because any fumbling you do will make people pity you and remind them you are blind." She paused and grimaced. "But all that sounds very scientific and orderly. What it comes down to is that you learn what it is to be a donkey in a world of horses."

"The things most people take for granted," I said, "must be the things you have to learn all over again."

"The beginning is the worst," she said and she seemed to be listening to the sound of the rain against the glass. "It happened to me when I was ten years old after meningitis. Emily Dickinson wrote of dying, and years later when I read her poems I understood that is the way it is; as if a fly came with an uncertain, stumbling buzz between the light and you, and then the windows close, and then you cannot see." She shifted her body slightly on the floor. "Do you know Emily Dickinson's poems?"

"Some of them," I said.

"I have all her poems in Braille," she said. "They don't consider her too fashionable anymore, but she does well for me." She stroked the cat, who raised her head and stared ominously at me. "Emily here is named after her." For a moment she did not speak. "Now what about you?" she said. "Have you been writing long?"

"Since the Korean War," I said. "I was going to do a great war novel, better than Shaw and Mailer, but it never worked out. I worked on a newspaper for a while and wrote stories at night. About four years ago I sold my first story and published my first novel about a year later. I've managed to make enough by writing to eat and pay the rent and get drunk every once in a while."

"On wine?" she asked.

"On wine," I said. "It's more genteel than Scotch or gin."

"Don't you have a girl?" she asked.

"I was engaged to a girl right after the war," I said. "She broke it off because her parents felt I was indolent, lazy, and shiftless because I wouldn't take a steady job. She agreed with them, and they were all right."

"Where is she now?"

"Who knows? Married to another poor slob and making his life as unhappy as she would probably have made mine."

"You sound so old and weary," she said.

"In this gilded age," I said, "you don't have to grow old to feel weary. Even the young perch on their ash heaps and wait like Job for the next disaster." I paused to light a cigarette. "Where you from?"

"A little town in Kansas," she said. "My father was a pharmacist there and lived with my mother in a frame house with a long porch that I was born in."

The room had grown darker, and I could barely make out the white fabric of her blouse. The rain grew faint and left only the sound of water gurgling in the gutters.

"How did you happen to come here alone?" I said.

"Whenever my mother kissed me I could feel the tears on her cheeks," she said. "And every time my father walked into my room I could sense his grief and despair. They loved me very much, but they were full of pity and wouldn't let me live. I write them that I am living with three other girls, happy, friendly girls, who take good care of me."

"You've got guts," I said.

"I'm not at all brave," she said with a trace of scorn for herself in her voice. "I'm not always cheerful either. I left home simply because I couldn't bear their pity. There was even a boy who took me to dances, and his nobility rose like wind from his pores, and everybody in town praised him for dating a poor, blind girl."

"You're a good-looking girl," I said. "Maybe you weren't fair to him."

"There have been a few others like him," she said defiantly. "Men intent on a quick moment of pleasure and willing to concede that sometimes a woman has no need of sight. But I don't need that kind of love."

A silence settled between us. The room was completely dark by then. I felt a vague unrest and moved to rise.

"Let me turn on a light," she said. "You'll stumble and fall."

She rose and crossed the dark room swiftly and switched on a lamp. The light hurt my eyes for a moment. She stood there, slender in her slacks and blouse, her face a pale oval within the frame of her hair.

"Will you read me something you've written?" she asked.

"Sure," I said, "but don't expect Emily Dickinson."

She brought me my coat and hat, and we stood a moment by the door.

"You're tall," she said slowly. "You have a strong voice, a little weary sometimes, but with a good tone. What do you really look like?"

"You'd never mistake me for a movie star," I said. "My face is what a pulp writer would call weatherbeaten."

"I can imagine you any way I wish," she said. She smiled and extended her hands toward me. Her fingertips made a soft and subtle contact with my cheeks. I had never known that a woman's hands could be that gentle. They touched my temples and moved across my eyes and slipped down my cheeks. "Your eyes are set in deep hollows," she said, and there was a look of waiting and listening on her face. "I think your nose is too broad. Your upper lip is full, and you have a sharp cleft in your chin and you need a shave."

The touch of her fingers carried a pressing warmth through my body, and I felt an urgent longing to touch her. I bent and kissed her then, first on the forehead, lightly and with gentleness, and then with urgency, hard on her lovely lips. When I reached out to hold her, she pulled away.

"What do you want?" she asked, and a strange hardness had entered her voice. "What do you want?"

"Andrea," I said, "listen . . ."

"Do you love me already?" she said, and there was no mistaking her baleful mockery. "Is it desire you feel without love, or just pity for the poor little blind music teacher?"

"I just wanted to kiss you," I said. "Emily Dickinson would have understood."

A shadow of remorse swept her face, and then she shook it off, "Thanks anyway for the chop suey."

"Chow mein," I said.

"All right," she said and relented slightly with a trace of a smile.

"Some day this week." I said, "I'll borrow a car and we'll go for a drive."

She was silent for a moment. "Maybe," she said finally. "We'll see."

I had never put credence in the myth that love might begin at first sight, by a look or by the touch of a hand. And I had always mocked those sonnets of passion that mediocre poets wrote in flame. But that winter, those days and nights of cold and snow, I woke in the morning without a sense of burden in the beginning of another day. For the first time in years I could endure the twilight becoming darkness without a wavering of my spirit.

Andrea and I took long walks together in the park. We sat closely together on a bench beneath the black trunk of a cold, bare tree. When she listened raptly to the scurrying of a squirrel, or ran her hands along the hard, frozen bark of a tree, or felt a change in the wind I could not hear, it was as if we were both young again, on an earth that still retained its magic. When I was with her it was strangely true that all things recaptured their edges, became sharp for me where they had been blurred.

"Andrea, do you believe in God?" I asked her one day in the park.

"Yes," she said quietly.

"Blindness has not made you bitter?"

"If I had not become blind," she answered softly. "I might have lived my years taking the earth for granted. My blindness has made me search again to discover all things anew. Is not God somewhere in this search?"

There were evenings in her flat when I lay on the couch while she played a melancholy sonata or a gay song that echoed the wild whirling of figures in a lovers' dance. We ate and drank together, and the stain of wine glistened upon her lips, and it was true that she came upon the desert of my days as if she were a flower.

But there was always a wariness in the hours we spent together, an evident fear in her at what was growing between us. When I tried to kiss her she drew back in guarded restraint, so that I grew apprehensive, too, and all that winter did not speak of the way I felt. Until one night, one night when I could not contain myself any longer, I broke the silence that held us apart.

She had moved from the bench of the piano and had come over to where I lay on the couch. She sat on the floor with her head near my knees, and the moon fell across her face, a white and glistening vision. I touched her hair, felt the fine strands tingle beneath my palms, and understood how aware she had made me of touch. The thought of having her as my wife suddenly possessed me with a wild sweetness such as I had never known.

"I love you, Andrea," I said.

She withdrew her head from near my knees. Her open fingers which had been lying on the cloth near my hands flew back to her lap.

"There is an old folk legend," I said, "that speaks of a blind man joined with one who is lame. They journey together until they find the healing waters and are both restored."

"I don't want to talk of love," she said. She rose from the floor and went to stand beside the window.

"Are you going to spend the rest of your life alone?" I asked. "In this little flat, in these dark rooms, teaching piano to unhappy children?"

"I can look after myself," she said. "I don't need anyone to look after me."

"We all need somebody," I said.

"I can look after myself," she said, and the words came ripped from her flesh. "I don't need pity."

She moved away from the window, away from me, into the darkness at the other end of the room. She sealed herself against me, retreated into silence that she wore as if it were armor. And I was left alone in the beam of the futile and bright moon that seemed to be hanging just above the roof of the building across the street.

I did not see Andrea for several weeks after that night. I wrote hard, harder than I had in years, and drank much more, and spent a good deal of time walking alone in the desolate park. I felt her everywhere, and yet pride and anger kept me from her door. In the afternoon, when the children played their scales at her piano, it filled me with a fierce melancholia. Sometimes walking past her flat at night I paused in the darkness and waited for a quick, furtive glimpse of her within the basement rooms.

The first traces of spring appeared in the city. Great winds swept the streets at night, and in the parks and gardens the earth stirred and waited. I listened to the wind shake the panes of my windows and knew Andrea must have been listening to the wild wind as well. In the morning the sun felt a shade warmer. Then, one day in early April, a sparrow perched on my sill and in the quick flutter of its jubilant step I knew the spring had come.

Near the end of April on an afternoon, while leaving my flat to go for a beer, I passed a small moving truck parked outside in the street. As it pulled away I noticed an upright piano secured with rope and cloth. Under a sudden apprehension, I looked at Andrea's windows, and the shades were up and the curtains were gone. I went down the stairs and tried the door. When it opened I walked inside. I called her name, and there was no answer. The furniture was gone, and the rooms were empty. I turned in despair to leave, thinking of ways to pursue the truck, when a small, furry body moved beside the stove in the kitchen and caught my eye. Emily came slowly over to look at me, and I knew that Andrea would be back.

I waited until twilight fell. The street lights went on and threw sharp beams of light through the uncurtained windows across the bare wood floor. I found some milk in the icebox and poured a saucer for Emily, but she rejected my offering.

It must have been some time later when I heard the car outside. I looked out the window and saw the taxi from which Andrea had emerged. A moment later she entered the apartment. I made no sound, and yet she knew at once I was there.

"Pete," she said, and I couldn't understand whether there was sorrow or gladness in her voice.

"You were running away," I said bitterly. "I understand you now. When you say you don't want pity it is really pity that you want. You want to remain alone because then people will always pity you."

"You have no right," she said, and her voice was a thin, tight whisper, "no right to say that to me."

"Emily has more courage than you," I said savagely. "She at least goes prowling in the midnight alleys and comes back in the dawn with her fur ruffled and shreds of skin under her claws. But you are afraid of love."

She twisted her body as if to flee, and then something made her turn back, and the sight of her cold white cheeks swept the anger from my heart.

"When I found you my life was nothing," I said. "You taught me a new way of seeing a tree and a flower. A new way of understanding the earth and hearing the wind. You taught me that all life is connected by the touch of a hand. Don't take that from me now."

For a long moment she did not move. She seemed to be holding her breath. Then she walked slowly to where I stood and raised her face to mine and lifted her hands to my cheeks. Her breath came out in a long shaken sigh. She did not speak, but for the first time touched me in a fierce caress. She touched my eyes and touched my lips and her hands trembled with love. And for the first time since I was a child, I cried again for the great wonder and beauty of life.

On rereading, this story doesn't impress me. I have allowed it to remain in the collection because if critics are looking for weakness and fallibility in my work, they might fruitfully probe this story. On the other hand, if they are enthusiastic about all the other stories in the collection, then, in the name of decency and through a recognition that no human being is unflawed, they might simply ignore it.

THE RETURN OF KATERINA

In April of that year, Paul Brademas had been dead two years. His widow, Katerina, lived with his father, Lycurgus, in a small apartment above their tavern.

After his son's death, Lycurgus wished to sell the tavern. He was almost sixty himself and wearied of the long hours on his feet. In addition he did not think it proper that a young attractive woman such as Katerina should work in the smoky room of boisterous men.

But Katerina insisted they keep the tavern which brought in a good profit. When she worked hard there was little time left to brood upon the death of her husband. She also felt it provided Lycurgus a meeting place for a few old friends with whom he could sit in the evening.

In the beginning Katerina's grief for her husband was a wild despair. For a while the memory of their lovemaking was something she could recall at will. At those times she felt her breath become short and her breasts grow taut. And so strong was the love she held for him that she could almost feel again his hands across her body and the strength of his arms about her waist.

But time passed and the seasons changed. In the winter the snow piled in drifts before the tavern. Katerina would rise early to clean the walk before the old man rose. When he came downstairs he would grumble that shoveling was man's work and take the shovel from her hands.

In the spring of the second year after her husband's death, a strange restlessness possessed Katerina. She was no longer satisfied to recall her husband in dreams. She walked in the glittering twilight and felt envy growing in her heart at the sight of lovers in the park.

She visited her husband's grave and placed fresh flowers upon the mound of earth. In those moments under the sighing trees she wept and swore eternal love. She waited for some sign that he had heard and understood but the earth made no gesture of redemption.

In the evenings in the tavern she no longer took pleasure in the wild laughter of the men. She became snappish and cross. Her temper flared quickly and she acquired a reputation for an acid tongue. Lycurgus was concerned for her and tried to ease her labor in different ways thinking that perhaps she was working too hard.

After closing he sent her to bed at once and swept the floor himself and locked the door. The only person left inside was his old friend, Zakinthákis, veteran of ten thousand drinking bouts and three wars. A wise rascal of a man who counted his life of fighting and wenching well spent. Lycurgus disapproved of his friend's morals but enjoyed his company.

After counting the cash Lycurgus took a final glass of mastiha to the table for himself and another for Zakinthákis. They toasted each other solemnly.

"I am troubled over Katerina," the old man told Zakinthákis. "Nothing seems to please her. She has grown as peevish as an old woman."

Zakinthákis looked into his glass of mastiha and a faint zestful smile curled his thin lips. He admired the fine lush body of Katerina and knew the reason for her distemper. He wished he could still have been the one to comfort her.

"When Paul was alive," Lycurgus said sadly, "she was not like that. They loved each other dearly." He wiped a stray tear from his eye. "It must be her grief," he said. "She still mourns for him."

Zakinthákis sipped at his mastiha and marveled at how a man could have lived as many years as Lycurgus and still understand so little about women.

"Grief is a terrible thing," he said somberly, and within him he laughed because he knew that when he died a thousand women would grieve for him . . . but not for long. Then because the long evening of drinking had dulled him slightly, he spoke without thinking. "She needs a lover," he said.

Lycurgus sat shocked and rooted to his chair. His lips moved and no words came. Then he found his voice and let out an angry roar.

"Devil!" he shouted. "Lecher and animal out of darkness! Have you lost your mind?"

Zakintháкis realized his mistake and sighed. He rose heavily to his feet to leave. Lycurgus followed him raging to the door.

"You dare speak of my son's wife in that way!" he cried. "Get out, you stepson of some unholy devil!"

Long after Zakinthákis had left, Lycurgus still paced the tavern and hurled curses upon his friend's head. Each time he considered the outrage, his blood flamed anew.

Finally he turned off the last lights and went upstairs. Outside the bedroom of Katerina he listened for a moment at her door. There was no sound from her room and he went to bed.

For a long time he could not sleep. The murmur of the night came through his window. He was restlessly aware of his age and his inevitable death. The years had swept by so quickly. He had never traveled, never cared for cards or drink, and had been shy with girls. A day came when he married because he could not bear his loneliness any longer. His wife had been a dark and thin woman who wore black for mourning all her life. Rarely would she suffer Lycurgus to caress her and from one of these uncertain, unsatisfying unions their only child had been born. But the child was little comfort to Lycurgus because of the domination of the mother. In the boy's seventeenth year, his mother died, accepting death as gratefully as a suppliant. Lycurgus could not grieve for her and accepted joyously the return of his son. When Paul married Katerina he wept for their happiness and for his own good fortune. He envisioned the day that grandchildren would scamper around him. But then the young man had fallen sick, and after a short shocking illness had died. As if his mother, dark and brooding from the grave, had called to him to join her.

Lycurgus tossed in helpless despair. Then he remembered Katerina in the room beside his own. Her nearness was a comfort to him, and he slept.

Spring passed into summer. The heat came early in the day and twilight brought no relief. Along the street on which they lived men and women sat before the stores, fanning themselves until long past midnight. The boys and girls ran by squealing to slap one another's bottoms in the dark alleys.

After closing the tavern Lycurgus and Katerina walked for a while in the park. On the grass in long uneven rows, men, women and children slept under the sky. A great sound of whispering, like the drone of countless crickets, rose from the dark and hidden groves.

Back in their flat with the open windows providing no relief from the heat, Lycurgus lay awake in the dark listening to Katerina in her room. He heard her talking to herself, and though he could not make out the words he heard the bitterness in her voice. Once he thought he heard her weeping, and because he felt she wept for the dead, he cried with her, silently, so she would not hear.

On a night in August a group of strangers came to the tavern. They were loud and bold young men, blond Norsemen, and they drank great quantities of beer. Countless times during the evening Katerina carried trays of beer to their table. They laughed and teased her and a bright flush of pink appeared in her cheeks. They finally left, holding one another up, and the bawdy sound of their voices could be heard rioting from the street.

The next night one of them, a blond young giant with big hands, returned alone. He sat in a corner and did not sing or carry on. Katerina served him several times and lingered at his table.

From that night on the blond stranger came every evening. Whenever he could, Lycurgus served the man whose light pale eyes seemed full of menace. Lycurgus was reminded of tales he had heard as a child of the villages raided by the pillaging Turks. The burning of houses and the screaming of women.

An evening came when several hours before closing, Katerina told him she was not well. He suggested she go at once to bed but she wished to walk alone for a while and he let her go. It was not until she had left that he noticed for the first time in several weeks that the blond stranger was not at his table in the corner. A cold fear enveloped him but he remembered Katerina's sacred allegiance to her dead and suppressed his apprehension.

Summer passed and the first winds of autumn swept the scent of burning leaves along the street. The days grew shorter and there was a strange still beauty in the crisp nights.

With the passing of summer, Katerina took on a new grace. Lycurgus marveled at the change. She had thrown off the terrible melancholia and once again enjoyed the laughter in the tavern. Her black hair gleamed lustrous and alive and her body once more appeared lithe and supple. He heard her sing in her room at night.

In the morning as she cooked him breakfast, he basked in her radiance and marveled at how beautiful she had become once again. He watched her eat with pleasure, the ripe soft lips parting slightly and the small pieces of food going between them. Her cheeks were as soft and unblemished as those of a child and the color of her flesh was the cool, transparent whiteness of the foam on new milk.

When they had finished she rose from the table and carried the dishes to the sink. She spoke softly with her back to him.

"Papa, I am going away," she said. "I am going to the country for a little while. Now when the leaves are changing and the earth is so beautiful."

"Going away?" Lycurgus said in alarm. "Katerina, you cannot go away alone!"

"For just a little while," she said gently. "I am weary suddenly of the city and the noise and the disorder."

"It is not right that you go alone," Lycurgus said. "We will close the tavern. We will go away together so that I can look after you."

"I wish to go alone," she said, and then she added quickly, "You do not like to travel. You would come only because you are concerned for me." She bent over the dishes in the sink. "Zakinthákis can help you in the tavern. I will be gone only a little while."

"Zakinthákis!" the old man cried. "I would sooner ask help of the devil!"

"Then find someone else to help you," she said and there was a firmness in her voice.

She left the following Friday and was gone for almost two weeks. Lycurgus missed her terribly. At night he could not bear to go to their rooms and stayed downstairs in the tavern long after closing. In loneliness and desperation he accepted the return of Zakinthákis and drank with him for hours.

"She could have waited until I died," he complained bitterly to his friend. "She could have taken her vacation then."

Zakinthákis merely sighed.

At the end of the second week Katerina returned. On a night after Lycurgus had closed the tavern and sat drinking with Zakinthákis.

He had turned off most of the lights and when he heard the door he thought he had forgotten to lock it and that some patron had entered. Then he heard her voice speak his name and a great gladness leaped in his heart. He rose quickly from the table.

"Katerina!" he cried. "Katerina!"

It was not until then that he saw she was not alone. Only when his eyes became accustomed to the shadows about the door, did he recognize the tall blond stranger.

A terrible distress ran riot in his body. He wanted to cry out but no sound passed his lips. He stared at the silent figure beside Katerina. Never had he hated a man more. He would not let himself think but only let the hot flow of hate sweep over him in waves.

"Papa," Katerina said, and her cheeks gleamed pale in the shadows. "This is my husband, Edwin Larsen."

Then Lycurgus cried out. A cry of pain and anguish. A cry for his dead son and for deceit and the fiendish heart of a woman. He burned suddenly under a white hot flame.

"Thief!" he said to Edwin Larsen, and smoke and fury curled off his tongue. "Vandal, bastard out of darkness!" His voice rose. "I should have killed you the first night I saw you!"

"Papa, try to understand," Katerina said. "I loved Paul very much. You know I loved him." Her voice rose and broke. "But you cannot love the dead forever."

"Not forever!" Lycurgus said and he spoke to her in angry bitterness. "Only two years and you forsake his memory."

"I loved him," Katerina said. "When he died I could have died with him. But I lived and in the summer I saw the new buds spring to life on the trees and heard the lovers whispering in the dark groves."

"Silence!" Lycurgus cried. "I do not wish to hear your shame!"

Katerina turned and reached back for her husband and brought him into the light. "Papa," she said, "Papa, do you want me back? Tell me now. If you want me back I will come back."

Lycurgus looked back from her to the stranger. "Alone," he said. "I want you back alone."

"I cannot come alone," she said. "I am married now."

"You are married to my son."

"He is dead," Katerina said.

"I do not want you then!" Lycurgus cried. "I do not want you then!"

Through a mist of grief he saw her turn. Slim beside the tall Norseman, she walked to the door. Her steps made a slight fading sound as she reached the street.

When he could hear her no longer he turned fiercely on Zakinthákis. "Get out," he said. "Leave me alone."

Zakinthákis moved slowly to the door. He paused with his hand on the knob. "I am going," he said. "I will tell you something first, old friend."

"Leave me alone!" Lycurgus cried.

"You do not weep for your son," Zakinthákis said, and his voice was filled with pity and sadness. "You weep for yourself."

And in that instant after the door closed and he was left alone, in that moment of dark revelation, he heard his voice cry her name in the silence. "Katerina!" and only the raven-winged vision of his wife heard and returned to comfort him.

None of us can fully understand what it means to lose a spouse we have lived with for many years unless it happens to us. I have an intimation of such loneliness, however, when Diana is away for a few days. Descending from my study to the darkened, silent rooms of our house suggests the dimensions of an irretrievable loss.

This story also has to do with lust. The less sensitive young might prefer that senior citizens exemplify celibacy and tranquility of appetite. But the surge of life and desire isn't the exclusive province of youth. I had a couple of friends considerably older than I am and both these men remained randy to the end of their lives. One died at seventy-eight and the other at eighty-one.

In a way I find such constancy of prurience heartening.

THE LAST ESCAPADE

"I'm ashamed to talk about it, even to you," his sister Naomi said. "But I'm at my wit's end about what I'm going to do with him. I had to phone you to come."

When he'd received her urgent message, he imagined it concerned their father, who was seventy-four and widowed six years since the death of his mother. He lived alone in an apartment a few miles from where Naomi lived with her husband and children. Several earlier conversations with his sister had hinted of his father's involvement with a girl. He had avoided talking to Naomi about it in the past but now he asked her if that was the problem.

"Not just a girl!" Naomi exclaimed. "A child! Keith, she's barely twenty years old! He met her . . . ," she lowered her voice so the children playing in another room would not hear, " . . . in a massage parlor!"

"Maybe he just wanted a massage," Keith said.

"Oh for God's sake, Keith, spare me your academic wit! This is the most dreadful crisis we have ever had with him!"

"After all, he's in pretty good health," Keith said. "Maybe he still has an active sex drive."

"I don't want to hear about his sex drive!" she said. "I don't even want to think about what they do together! It's too disgusting! I'm sure he's giving her money and she hasn't any shame about cheating a senile old man."

"Are you sure he's giving her money?"

"He admitted it! A few times when I tried to talk to him about the danger of what he was doing, he grew impatient and flip with me and told me brazenly, he was paying her rent, gas and light!"

"That means she's not living with him."

"Oh God, don't even mention that possibility! If he did anything as stupid and outrageous as that I wouldn't let the children visit him again!"

"All right, Naomi," Keith tried to speak patiently. "He's seventy-four years old and he's involved with a twenty-year-old girl he met in a massage parlor. The whole business is a little sordid, I admit, but it seems to have been going on for some time. You mentioned it to me when I was here at Christmas. What makes it a crisis now?"

She rose from her chair and went to peer nervously into the dining room. The children had gone outside and she returned and sat down, leaning closer to speak to Keith in a shaken whisper.

"The girl had a baby two weeks ago!"

"Is he the father?" Keith asked.

"Don't be ridiculous!" Naomi said. "Honest to God, Keith, sometimes I think there is a streak of simpleness in you in spite of your degrees!"

"Well, other men his age have children," he protested. "There's that senator from the South, Strom Thurmond . . ."

"The baby isn't his!" she snapped. "He admits that much. He must have realized how shocked I was and he laughed, you know the nasty way he can laugh sometimes, and then he brazenly told me he has been impotent for years! Can you imagine a man saying that to his own daughter? That proves he's senile!"

"Whose baby is it?"

"God only knows! One of the men she's been sleeping with, probably, some other fool she met in the massage parlor. A tart like that will never really know!"

"But if the baby isn't his child, why are you so concerned?"

"He is acting like the father!" Naomi said. "He was with her at the hospital during her delivery! My God, what if someone who knew me had seen her there?"

"A hospital is better than a massage parlor."

"Keith!"

"I'm sorry, Naomi."

"You don't seem to understand the gravity of what is taking place," she spoke in the older sister's voice he remembered her using with him for years. "Our seventy-four-year-old father, stumbling into his dotage, has taken up with a twenty-year-old girl who has had a baby! His vanity makes him act like he is the father. Can't you just see us together on holidays? Bruce, the children, you and me, Father, his twenty-year-old girlfriend and the baby!"

"Maybe he felt obliged to help her," Keith said. "Now that she's had the baby, perhaps he won't have anything more to do with her."

"In his senility he won't be that sensible," Naomi said. "More than likely he will be reliving his own years of early marriage, pushing the baby on walks in a buggy he bought. It won't bother him that people will think he is the great-grandfather of the child."

Keith couldn't become as agitated as Naomi but he understood her concern. His father lived on a pension from the Colony Insurance Company and his Social Security and didn't have to touch the money he'd received from the sale of their house when his mother died. Some of that money had gone to Naomi when she and Bruce bought their house and his father had given Keith ten thousand dollars while he studied for his doctoral degree. The money belonged to his father to do with as he wished, but they had a responsibility to make sure the girl didn't cheat him out of it.

"What do you think we should do?" Keith asked.

"You should go and talk to him," Naomi said sternly. "You are his son and maybe you men understand this kind of perversion. Try to make him understand that what he is doing is shameful and obscene! My God, if he is impotent, what do they together?"

He started to explain there were other diversions but Naomi cut him off with a sharp wave of her hand.

"I don't want to hear the gory details!" she said. "I just want you to talk to him!"

"All right, I'll go over and see him now."

"You better phone him first," she said. "You might find the two of them in bed." She fetched up a sigh that quivered her plump body. "Oh my God, I'm only grateful that poor Mama isn't alive to suffer this shame!"

But if his mother were still alive, Keith thought, his father would probably have never gotten involved with the girl.

He phoned his father, who seemed delighted that Keith was in town, and agreed to see him at once. He left Naomi's house after promising her he would return that evening to report to her exactly what his father had said.

The children were playing on a neighbor's lawn. As Keith walked to his car, seven-year-old Cathy sprinted over to give him a hug. Keith tousled the child's hair and told her he'd see her later.

His father lived in a pleasant residential neighborhood north of downtown, in a three-room apartment he had rented after his mother's death and the sale of their house. Keith helped him move into the apartment and understood that his father's adjustment from a large house with his mother to living alone would be difficult. He pledged he'd visit him several times each year. Somehow, his own academic and social schedule always prevented the visits. He saw his father on a few holidays and on his birthdays, which he and Naomi always spent with him. Because Naomi lived in the same city, she saw his father more often than Keith but he knew neither of them had been as diligent about their visits as they should have been. As Keith drove up to park beside his father's building, he resolved that when the business of the girl was settled, he would drive in to see his father more often.

His father opened the door of the apartment and greeted Keith with a warm hug. Keith looked quickly for evidence of deterioration but his father seemed unchanged from his last visit. A tall, wiry man with gray, thinning hair and a slight paunch, the changes in him over the years seemed slight except for his ruddy complexion growing paler and his flesh more translucent. His eyes retained that keenness that had made him one of the best regional directors Colony Insurance ever had on their staff.

"Want a beer?" his father asked.

He nodded and was grateful when his father walked to the kitchen, giving him a moment to assemble his thoughts about the best way to begin. When his father returned with the beer, he took several quick swallows.

"That sure tastes good," he said. He stared nervously at his father who sat down and smiled benignly at him. "I haven't seen you in a couple of months and I just decided to drive up," he said. "The weather was nice . . ."

"Keith-O," his father interrupted him gently. "You're a bright young man with degrees in Literature and English and I know you're a fine teacher. But you were never any great shakes as a liar. I've been expecting you to come. I knew your sister would call you as soon as she heard about the baby."

"You always could see through me, Dad," Keith smiled, a little flustered. "Naomi did call me. She's just concerned and hasn't been able to talk to you herself. She asked me to come and see you."

"Fair enough, son," his father said. "Your sister is a wonderful woman but she can never see beyond her outrage." He paused, raising his hand to brush at his hair. "I want to talk to you too. I think you'll appreciate some of the irony in what has happened to me. I began a relationship with the basest of intentions and now I am reliving the anxieties of early fatherhood."

His father paused again, as if assembling the words to go on. From the street below a car backfired several times, the sound echoing loudly through the apartment.

"The girl, Sally," his father said, "is kind of a simple child without any wisdom about the men she becomes involved with. Now she has a baby." His father's voice was calm but when he reached to the endtable beside the chair for his pipe, Keith saw his fingers trembling. He knocked the bole gently against an ashtray. "When I first saw that red, wriggling naked, little body I was sorry for it . . . really sorry and sorry for his mother, who was still such a child, and sorry that I wasn't younger."

"If you were younger, would you marry the girl?" Keith smiled, as if to reassure his father that he was joking.

"I think I would have had more sense than that," his father said. "But if I were younger I could have helped her and kept an eye on the two of them." He paused. "We've never really had that serious a relationship. I know she doesn't really love me in the way a woman loves a man and she has deceived me about needing money for her rent or to fix her car. She might even be giving some of the money I give her for those expenses to some man. She's foolish in that way."

He tapped fresh tobacco into his pipe, a familiar gesture that reminded Keith of his years of growing up. He suddenly noticed things about his father, how his sweater was torn at the sleeve and stained at the waist, things his mother would never have allowed. His father caught him staring at him and sighed.

"I'm sorry if I'm hurting and disappointing you and Naomi," he said. "And I didn't plan for this to happen. I was lonely and feeling, you know, kind of horny . . . no matter what the young think, that can still happen often at my age. I had walked past the massage parlor at least two dozen times and, one day, I simply walked inside. I almost walked right out again except for a pleasant, matronly lady who talked to me about how natural my visit was. I gave her some money and then I went into a small room with a table like doctors have in their examining rooms. I started to unbutton my shirt, the woman had told me to undress, and then this girl came in. She was very young and blond and, when she smiled, she didn't have very good teeth. She was wearing a kind of little toga and when I saw her I started buttoning my shirt again. She must have been used to old men having second thoughts because she finished unbuttoning my shirt. When she started to unbuckle my trousers, I told her I'd do it. I felt I was exposing myself in a school yard full of children. I was conscious of how old I was and my skinny legs and I panicked. I told her I had something to do and pulled up my pants and beat it out of there like a bulldog had its teeth in my ass."

Keith was suddenly conscious that he had been listening to his father as if he were hearing him for the first time in years.

"I would never have had the courage to go back into that massage parlor," his father said, "but about a week after that first aborted visit, I was shopping in the Dominick's on Laramie and, in the produce section, I saw her. My first impulse was to run but she looked straight at me over a stack of tomatoes and recognized me. I was sure it was her when she smiled because of her bad teeth." He shrugged wryly. "We had a cup of coffee together in Burger King and talked about many things. Finally, she asked if I'd like to have her visit me and I said yes . . ."

His father drew slowly on his pipe, exhaling a tiny swirl of smoke.

"I wasn't really expecting she'd show up the following night," his father said, "but I cleaned the apartment anyway and bought crackers and cheese and a bottle of wine. She did come, dressed like a young college girl on a Saturday night date. We talked about the Cubs and the Sox and the small town in Kansas where she grew up and the first boy she loved, who left her to join the Air Force. She was a sweet girl, a little naive and simple, like I said, but uncommonly sensitive for twenty. And then, after about an hour, she got up and came over to me and gently sat down on my lap."

He paused, staring uneasily at Keith.

"Does this disgust you, Son, or make you angry?" he asked. "Would you prefer I didn't tell you anymore?"

"You don't have to explain anything to me," Keith said quickly, even as he was conscious his palms were growing moist, "but I don't mind you talking."

His father nodded with what seemed gratefulness.

"I knew that after I told Naomi about the baby, she'd call you to come and see me," his father said. "I didn't know if I'd have the courage to tell you these things and I practiced them, not because I was lying, but because I wanted to tell you honestly the things I feel, the things she made me feel. Even that first night, when we went to bed and she did a few things she thought would please me, they weren't pleasing. I was tense, frightened, ashamed. I thought of Naomi and my grandchildren and your mother. The way she would shake her head and say, 'Alfred, Alfred,' when I did something she thought absurd. All I wanted the girl to do was to get up, get dressed and leave. It wasn't until after she was gone that I recalled the wonder of the experience. The room had been dark except for a glow from the streetlight. For just a few moments she might have forgotten and thought she was truly with her lover. I thought I could tell when those moments came because there was something different, more tender and less practiced, when she touched me."

His father's voice had grown hoarser and he reached over and turned on the lamp. "Do you want another beer, Keith?" he asked. "Or shall we make a pot of coffee?"

Keith shook his head. He stole a glance at his watch, surprised that it was already five-thirty.

"There isn't much more to tell," his father said. "That was about a year ago. She'd visit me once or twice a week. Sometimes we just sat and talked, you know, the way she might have talked with her own father," he grimaced, "or her grandfather. Sometimes she'd ask me for money for her rent or for repairs on her car. She had to have some dental work done and the dentist told her he could cap her bad teeth. She didn't ask me for that money but there was such a naked pleading in her voice and eyes, like a little girl begging for something she wanted more than anything else in the world. I had the dentist fix her teeth and paid him myself."

Keith didn't ask how much that work had cost but his father understood.

"It cost about fifteen hundred dollars," his father said, "but she looked so much better and was so delighted. When she came to see me, right from the dentist's office after he'd finished, she told me she smiled at everybody she passed on the street." He laughed softly. "If I thought her gratitude would make her come to see me more often, I was mistaken. Sometimes I wouldn't see her for a couple of weeks. And then, during one visit, she told me she was pregnant. She had told me before of the men she'd been involved with, one bastard after another, so even if she'd known who the father was, it wouldn't have made any difference. She had been living with one fellow and one day he kicked her out. Just like that. Then she met a mechanic who kept beating her up. She came over once with a black eye and a swollen cheek. I really bawled her out then, the way I might have if she'd been my granddaughter, and she cried a little. She broke up with him too. I'm not sure how. Maybe she found the sense to leave him."

From the street a siren wailed, the strident sound sweeping through the room. His father waited until the noise had passed.

"I don't think she has anyone now," his father said. "She's fascinated with the baby. He's like a new toy to her, a living toy, but she loves him too. I felt some of that love when I waited in the hospital with her and first saw her with the baby. He was such a beautiful little boy and in some strange, foolish way I thought of the boy belonging to me too. Since then I realize how absurd the whole business is really. She's not related to me and the baby isn't mine. But I enjoy seeing her and look forward to their visits. In the few times the three of us have been together, I feel happier than I have felt in years."

There was a long silence, his father not talking. Keith tried to think of something to say. "What is going to happen to her?" he asked finally.

"I don't know," his father said slowly. "The baby is enough for now but the day will come when she'll take up with another man, another bastard no doubt, she doesn't seem able to choose any other kind. She's young, and I suppose she'll make it through, but I worry about the baby."

He stared at Keith, who grew uncomfortable under the intensity of his father's gaze.

"You know, son," his father said quietly, "I don't want to make excuses but the whole thing came about because of loneliness. I am not blaming your sister or you. You live four hundred miles away and she has her life with Bruce and her children. But when a man is alone as he grows older, you have to understand that his days and nights are different. He doesn't have the expectations he had when he was young, or the dreams, or planning for the things he hopes to do. He wakes up in the silence of the dark room and can't help thinking that it's just another night moving him closer to death. Oh, I know, there is the senior center nearby and movies and television. But I find that gathering of old people depressing and television is full of idiotic comedies and the movies show films that have nothing to do with the life I lived. I am grateful when you and Naomi and the children and I enjoy holidays and birthdays. But those celebrations pass quickly and then there are empty, lonely weeks again." His father shrugged. "I said I didn't want to make excuses but I guess I just did."

"You might go and live with Naomi," Keith said, "or come down to Carbondale with me. You know I'd love to have you."

"I'm sure you would, Son," his father smiled. "But that wouldn't work. Naomi is nervous around me now and if she had me around, day and night, no matter how hard I tried, she'd go over the brink. As for living with you, Son, when you brought a girl home to spend the night, would you ask me to go to a movie or to spend the night in the YMCA? No... loneliness is a misery but when a parent lives with a son or daughter, there can't help being feelings of resentment and guilt."

"We'd never feel that way about you!" Keith said earnestly.

"I'm not saying that would be true about you or Naomi," his father said, "but it might be about many sons and daughters, even good and loving ones. I have lived alone six years since your mother's death and I'm grateful now that she died before me. This life might have been harder for her to endure because she was a woman. Can you ever imagine your mother walking into a massage parlor? I tell you something, Son, something I have come to understand in these last years and I don't say it bitterly but because it's the truth. The old are not really loved. They are tended and cared for and turned so their chairs face their favorite channel but, in our hard-sell society, they have nothing to sell anymore but a reminder that not even youth and beauty endures."

His father rose and motioned to the clock.

"It's almost six o'clock," he said. "Naomi is probably expecting you for dinner."

"Come to dinner with me," Keith said. "Naomi told me to ask you to come back with me."

"The hell she did," his father laughed. "She's so mad at me these days that she might poison my salad. You go ahead and have your dinner and, if you get a chance to talk to her alone, try to make her understand the things I told you about the girl and me."

Keith rose and hesitated a moment longer. He started to tell his father that he'd stay in town and they'd spend some time together. Then he remembered the date he had with Marcie in Carbondale the following evening.

"Let's eat together this evening anyway," he said. "I'll call Naomi and tell her you and I are having dinner together. I'll drive back to Carbondale later tonight."

His father gave his arm an affectionate squeeze.

"You stop squirming and go ahead now," he said reassuringly. "You really listened to me and I think you understand but it's got to be uncomfortable for both of us. I am relieved I got it out but I don't want to talk about it anymore and we'll strain talking about other things. Maybe on your next visit we'll spend more time together. If you didn't mind, maybe I could have Sally bring the baby up here for you to see. She likes to feel respectable and that would please her, but only if you didn't have any objections."

"That would be fine with me, Dad," Keith said.

"There's one more thing, Son," his father said. "You know I've got some money saved. Not a great deal, but money that will go to you and Naomi when I'm gone. I may want to make some provision for the baby, some money for his schooling and for other things. I hope you and Naomi will understand and won't try to cut the child out. I'm not asking you to give it all up, just to share some of it."

"It's your money, Dad," Keith said. "You do what you want with it."

"I'll leave most of it to you and Naomi," his father said. "I just feel sorry for the baby and would like to provide for him too."

On an impulse Keith moved back and embraced his father. He smelled the scents of his tobacco and the odors of food and stale coffee grounds on his sweater. He remembered then how clean his mother had always kept his father's clothing.

When he had walked down the stairs and reached his car he looked up toward the apartment windows. He wasn't sure whether his father was standing at the window, but he waved anyway. He climbed into his car buoyed by a sense of resolve he would explain everything his father had told him to Naomi.

But with every block he drove through the gathering twilight, the futility of explanation to his sister overwhelmed him. He imagined her outrage and the way she would make it appear as if he had failed her. His determination weakened until he turned his car away from the direction of Naomi's house and drove toward the Interstate. He'd phone her from a gas station and tell her he'd forgotten an important appointment he had in Carbondale for early in the morning. If she wanted to know what his father had told him, he'd say someone was waiting for the phone and he couldn't talk.

The small, shabby lunchroom I mentioned earlier was in a factory neighborhood near a railroad station. A young girl came in one night when I was about to close. She told me an unhappy story about having come from downstate Illinois to meet a young soldier so they could be married. She had waited all day in the station and he never appeared. Feeling sympathetic to her, I took her home to spend the night with my wife and myself in our small apartment. The next day, I bought her a bus ticket for her home and took her to the station. She promised to send me the money. I never heard from her again, and to this day I'm not sure whether she was telling me the truth.

ROSEMARY

"I must be nuts," Korshak, the white-haired railroad guard sitting at the counter, said. "Every meal I eat in here brings me a month closer to death."

"The complaint department is out the kitchen door and down the alley, third can from the right," Nick Manos, the lunchroom owner, said. He was a stocky, strong-bodied man in his late thirties, a soiled apron tied about his waist. He had dark unruly hair, a somber face, and even when cleanly shaven, his cheeks appeared shadowed.

"Ain't nothing wrong with this food," a tall, lean baggage handler named Noodles said, "long as your insurance premium is paid up."

Nick sighed. He scribbled on a pad and tore off a check that he put down in front of Korshak. "Eighty-six cents," he said.

The guard shook his head. "A shame I got to pay for a meal like that," he said sadly.

"You ate it," Nick said.

"I couldn't imagine it would taste as bad as it looked," Korshak winked.

"How much do I owe you, Nick?" Noodles slid off his stool.

"Sixty-three cents," Nick said. He shrugged wryly. "Sixty-three cents and eighty-six cents. If I ever get a customer with a check over a buck, I'll give him the place."

"He would want change," Korshak said sagely.

Noodles placed a few coins beside his check. "Guess I'll wash up later tonight after work," he said, and gave Nick a broad leer, "and drift around over to the Poinsetta Hotel."

"Better stay away from there, Noodles," Korshak warned. "That place full of tarts is due for a raid soon."

"Why don't you find a nice girl?" Nick said.

"Are there girls like that?" Noodles smirked.

"There are decent girls around," Nick said. "You meet one and get to know her and stop chasing whores."

Noodles laughed rejecting the advice and walked out to the dark street. Korshak brought his check to the register and put it down with a dollar bill. Nick rang up the amount and returned his change.

"About time to close up," Korshak said.

"Twenty more minutes," Nick said. "Just in time, too. By the end of the day this place becomes a prison."

He waved Korshak good night and walked along the counter to pick up the last dishes. He carried them to the kitchen and placed them on the shelf beside the battered metal sinks.

He stood for a moment over the sinks seeing the whole shabby and squalid lunchroom reflected in the rancid water. The place had been owned by his father for twenty years until his death six years earlier when Nick inherited it. He had made a few halfhearted efforts to scrub the floor and paint the walls. Then he gave up and consoled himself he could really do nothing with the aged stains of gravies and soups on the floor boards, the strong smells of wilted vegetables, the crusts of dried hard grease on the stove, the scarred and unmendable counter and stools. He planned to hold the place just long enough to build a small stake and then dump it for whatever he could get. But without his father's capacity to salvage and utilize scraps, he barely made enough on which to live and a little more to give his mother who lived with his married sister. In addition, as time went on he found himself forced to work longer hours every day in an effort to achieve even that meager return.

He dipped his hands savagely into the dishwater and saw his blurred image among the particles of food and whorls of grease floating on the surface. He considered draining the sink and running in fresh water but decided against the additional delay.

When he finished the last dishes, he drained the water and dried his hands. He carried a broom out to the front to sweep the floor. He was surprised to see a young woman sitting at the far end of the counter.

"I'm sorry, lady," Nick said. "I didn't hear you come in."

"I heard you working in the kitchen and didn't want to bother you," the girl said. "All I want is a cup of coffee."

He filled a cup of coffee from the urn and carried it to her. The only women who patronized his place in the shadow of the trucking depots and the railroad terminal were the assemblers and coilers from the factory across the street. They were beefy-armed, robust-breasted women with huge rumps that engulfed the stools. This girl was slim and no more than twenty-three or twenty-four. Her face was pale, her features even and small, her eyes large and dark. Her hair was dark brown and long and she wore a narrow band of black velvet across her crown, a band studded with tiny stars.

The band was strangely familiar and then as if the past were a crust that suddenly shattered he remembered a girl he had known when he was a young boy. He could not remember her name but they had skated together in the winter on the frozen ponds, whirling and laughing, their arms holding one another, their breath joining swift spirals of mist in the cold clear air. She had worn a short red skating skirt, white stockings, a fur-collared jacket, and in her hair a black velvet band studded with tiny stars.

Still unsettled by nostalgia, he finished sweeping the floor and then wiped the pie case. He closed at ten and when he looked at the clock again it was a few minutes past that time. The girl was smoking over her coffee, lost in reveries of her own. He walked to the door and flicked the switch that turned off the light above the sign outside and darkened the row of small lights in the window. When he turned back she had risen from the stool.

"Time to go," she said. With a nervous flutter of her fingers she crushed the tip of her cigarette into an ashtray. She wore a dark cloth coat and she tugged the collar higher about her throat and stared with foreboding out at the street. He felt sorry for her.

"I won't be leaving for a few minutes yet," Nick said. "Have another cup of coffee on the house before I empty the urn."

She looked at him gratefully and then nodded slowly and sat down. He brought her another cup of coffee and watched her begin to sip it. The coffee moistened her lips and they were full and well curved with a tiny cleft in one corner. She caught him staring and he turned brusquely to finish his work. He emptied the urn and put in a fresh bag for morning. She finished her coffee and brought him the cup and saucer. Then she fumbled in her purse for change. He waved her money aside.

"It's on the house."

"Thank you."

"You live close by?" he asked and was startled by the loudness of his voice. "I mean it's late and do you have a car?"

He sensed a sudden distress about her. She was silent for a long moment before she answered.

"I don't live in the city," she said. She stared through the plate-glass window at the railroad station looming above the roofs of the buildings across the street. "I was supposed to meet someone earlier today. A soldier who was coming from out of town, too. I was to have met him at two this afternoon." The illuminated clock in the tower of the station had black hands shining at twenty minutes past ten.

"He could have had his leave canceled," Nick said. "That happens, you know."

"I knew by late afternoon he wasn't coming," she said slowly. "I waited even though I knew he wasn't coming."

A truck rumbled past on the narrow darkened street and the old wooden floor quivered slightly under their feet. A gust of wind whipped a shred of newspaper against the window. It hung there a moment and then whirled off.

"You know anybody in the city you can phone?" Nick asked. "I mean do you have any family or friends here?"

She shook her head. A slight tremor swept her shoulders. He wondered uneasily if she were going to cry.

"I'll walk over to the station," she said, "and wait for a train back home. I think there is one in a couple of hours."

"Just wait a minute now," he frowned and stood thinking for a moment. "I'm just closing. I'll walk you back to the station. This isn't the neighborhood for a girl to walk around at night."

He walked quickly to the kitchen, pulling off his apron on the way. He made sure the back door was locked and got his coat from the locker. He snapped off the remaining lights, completely darkening the lunchroom except for a small bulb that threw an eerie beam over the desolate counters and stools.

She moved aside and he opened the door. A gust of cold air chilled their ankles. He locked the door and they started walking toward the railroad station.

"I'm glad to get out of that place," he said. "My father owned it, worked it eighteen hours a day for twenty years until he died."

"Do you work it that way, too?"

Another truck rumbled by sweeping their bodies with twin beams of light. From the railroad yards a bell tolled a sharp harsh sound. He shivered and pushed his hands deeper into the pockets of his coat.

"I made the old man a promise to stick it out and I've got my mother to support. But I have other plans. A good friend of mine has been writing me to come help him run a big fancy hotel in Denver with several hundred rooms. He wants me to manage the restaurant and bar. I'm planning to go soon."

At the corner he took her elbow and through her coat felt the firm young flesh of her arm. He was seized by a flutter of unrest in his stomach. They walked up the stairs to the station and he noticed her legs were long and slender in sheer nylons and high-heeled pumps.

They entered the large station waiting room, gray walls and concrete floors and worn benches, the air stale with old smoke and rancid steam from the radiators. The waiting room was almost deserted except for a few soldiers and sailors sleeping on some of the benches, duffel and sea bags cradling their heads. A porter swept a mop across a segment of the concrete floor with a weary flinging motion of his arms. Beyond the waiting room were the ticket windows, all closed but one, a bald man suspended within the lighted square.

"There might be a message for you with the agent," he said.

She nodded slowly and he watched her walking toward the ticket window on her slender legs, her back slim and straight. He wondered whether the soldier and the girl were lovers and jealousy bit his flesh. He moved toward a bench away from those occupied by the sleeping servicemen and after a few moments she joined him.

"There's no message," she said. "I didn't think there would be."

She spoke softly and calmly, sorrow apparent only in her voice, and he admired her restraint.

"When does your train leave?" he asked.

She opened her purse and drew out a small red ticket stamped for Champaign, Illinois. "In an hour and a half," she said.

"I'll wait with you, if it's OK."

"You don't have to stay," she said. "You must be tired. I'll be all right now."

He shrugged. "I'm used to it."

She sat down at the end of the bench and he sat down beside her, making sure a few inches of the bench was visible between their bodies. They sat without speaking for a few moments. He stole several glances at her face, noting the strange weary and uneasy lines around her mouth. He felt a flare of idignation at the man who let her wait in the station alone.

"Do you like stations?" she asked.

"I don't know," he said. "I don't have any feeling about them one way or another."

"I love to come and just sit in them," she said. "I do it sometimes even when I don't have anyplace to go. I make believe I'm going on a trip, or that I have just returned, and that family and friends are going to meet me. You ever noticed how happy people who travel are?" He shook his head.

"It's usually true," she said. "They're going to visit friends or relatives or going on vacations. For a while there may be separations but then the reunions are joyful."

"I never thought of it that way," he said. "I guess you're right."

"It isn't always true," she said quietly. "Sometimes there is unhappiness, too. And then there are the soldiers and sailors like those asleep over there. They have to go where they are sent, from one camp to another, and then perhaps overseas, away from their families and sweethearts for a long time." She shook her head. "Some of them are just kids."

"You're not much more than a kid yourself," he smiled.

She answered with a brusque short laugh.

"I mean it," he said. "How old are you?"

"Twenty-three," she said. "And you?"

"Thirty-six," he said and felt foolish because he had cut a year and then regretted he had not severed several more. "I'm thirty-six and still unmarried," he shrugged wryly.

She studied him for a long moment and he grew uneasy under her gaze.

"Someday a fortunate girl is going to get you," she said.

He looked at her sharply, wondering if she were mocking him.

"It's true," she said gravely. "When you offered me the second cup of coffee so I could stay inside a little longer and when you walked me here to the station because you were concerned something might happen to me, I knew you were special."

"That was nothing," he said.

"You were kind," she said slowly. "Kindness is rare and when you have it you are someone special."

"That's enough about me," he said, and his voice came out strong and jubilant. "You know I don't even know your name?"

She smiled and he felt the two of them drawn closer.

"Rosemary," she said.

"That's a lovely name."

"Some people hate their names," she said, "and wish they had been called by another. But I have always thought Rosemary sounds like a flower."

He nodded and spoke softly under his breath. "Mine is Nick," he said. "Not much of a name but I'm stuck with it. Actually it's Nicholas."

"I like Nicholas better than Nick," she said. "But I suppose everybody calls you Nick?"

"Nick and a lot of other things," he laughed. "Most of my trade are railroad workers and baggage handlers and truck drivers. Rough, maybe, but good guys."

"They must like you," she said. "They must come to talk to you if they have troubles."

He remembered her grief and it sobered his pleasure. He looked at the young sleeping soldiers.

"Sometimes it helps to talk," he said. "But you don't have to talk about your friend if you don't want to."

"I don't mind talking about him," she said quietly. She put her hands together in her lap and he saw how meagerly the flesh hinged across the wrists.

"I'm not bitter or angry with him, either," she said. "In the beginning after we first met, he wrote me almost every day. Beautiful letters that I will always treasure. In the last two months he wrote me only twice. I felt he had met another girl, loved her as he had once loved me, and I wrote asking for the truth. At first he denied it and then we agreed to meet in the station today, to talk over what we were going to do." She spoke softly, her voice barely more than a whisper, and he leaned slightly closer to hear. "He must have felt this way would be easier than having to tell me," she said. "I don't blame him, and I'm not bitter. Shall I tell you why?"

He nodded although he found it hard to understand why she should not have been angry.

"Even if I had known it would end like this," she said, "waiting for hours in a station and taking a train home alone, even if I had known, I wouldn't have given up a single hour of the time we had together, the letters, or the dreams." He saw her face with its spare flesh stretched tightly over small bones, a redness in the corners of her eyes. "True love is worth any sorrow and any grief and I will remember as long as I live that I had such love for a little while."

He heard the anguish in her voice and the loneliness and he was moved. He closed his eyes for a moment, locking himself in darkness.

"I understand," he said. "I had a love like that once, too. A girl I was going to marry years ago. She became ill and died." He opened his eyes and looked at her. A quick and tender compassion for him swept her face.

"It happened years ago," he said. "I think I loved her in the way you speak of because I have never been able to feel the same about anyone else since. I think of her now at different times during the day but mostly at night, after a long tired day in the lunchroom, at night when I can't sleep and wonder what my life would be like if she had lived."

They were both silent for a moment and then she moved her hand from her lap, slowly, bringing it to rest on his wrist, her slim fingers touching his arm lightly in consolation. The moment passed and she drew her hand away. He was embarrassed and grateful when the hoarse almost unintelligible voice of a man sounded over the loud-speaker announcing the arrival of a train. A soldier on one of the benches raised his head like a startled bird and then lowered it slowly to the bag on the bench. A redcap emerged from a baggage room and walked leisurely toward the gate.

"Maybe you're hungry," he said cheerfully. "The refreshment counter is closed but they've got vending machines in an alcove. I can get you a sandwich and a Coke if you like, or maybe some candy."

"I'm not hungry, but thanks," she said and smiled. He smiled at her and felt his weariness lifted like a rock from his back.

"You know it's strange," he said. "Strange the way we've met. Do you know what I mean? It's almost like fate, you coming into the lunchroom just a few minutes before I closed and coming back here together and talking like this."

"I believe in fate," she said, and smiled again. "Maybe there's something here neither of us can understand." She looked down at her fingers in her lap. "Both of us sharing a grief and a memory of love," she said gravely.

They fell silent and he looked with concern at the clock. There was so little time before her train. Yet Champaign was only a few hours away and he imagined himself driving down for a weekend. He felt a quick sharp excitement through his body.

"Rosemary," he said. "This may sound crazy because we just met tonight, and I know how you feel about this young man, and I'm a good deal older than you . . . but I wonder if I could write to you . . . just a letter or two in the beginning . . ."

He was interrupted by a noisy outburst of voices in shouts and laughter. A group of half a dozen men had entered through one of the gates, loudly roistering their way through the station.

"Some of the guys from the yards," he said resenting the distraction, "on their way for a beer." He turned back to her feeling a flurry of panic because he might have assumed too much, pressed too quickly against a still raw grief.

"You don't have to write me back if you don't feel like it," he said. "But I'd like to write you a few letters so you can get to know me better. When I go to Denver I can write you what my experiences are and whenever you feel like dropping me a short note you can let me know how you are, too."

The men drew closer and he recognized a casual patron or two and one nodded and the other waved his hand in a brief greeting. Then the lean wry face of Noodles emerged from the group, as he fell a step behind the others when he spotted Nick.

"Hi ya, Nick, boy," he cried loudly. "Skipping town to evade the Health Department?" He noticed the girl and fell silent. A surprised and twisted smirk crossed his cheeks. "Hello, Netta," he said. He winked and pursed his lips. "Take good care of Nick, will you?" He grinned and rolled his eyes. "He's a buddy of mine." He moved off after the men who had reached the door. They all left the station.

For a moment Nick did not move. There was a stunned fumbling in his head and a whirling of sound in his ears. Sweat erupted across his back and chest. He rose from the bench and he felt himself trembling.

"Jesus Christ," he said, and the words came slurred from his lips. "Jesus Christ."

She looked up at him with her face shocked as his, her cheeks white as gravestones, her lips frozen.

"Are you crazy?" Nick said hoarsely. "Is this some kind of goddam joke?"

She shook her head numbly and a great shudder swept her body.

"I didn't mean any harm," she said, and the words stumbled in a frantic whisper from her lips. "I just came in for a cup of coffee and you were nice to me and I just started making things up. . . . I swear to God I didn't mean any harm."

He felt an outrage at her deceit, and even more anger at his own gullibility. She had tricked him, cheated him into exposing himself, duped him into pleading. He reached down and snatched the purse from her side. He snapped open the clasp and reached in and drew out the ticket.

"What the hell did you buy the ticket for?" he cried in a low harsh voice. "Ride there and ride all the way back so you could carry the trick right through to the end! Have me see you off, have me put you on the goddam train and wave goodbye so that you could laugh all the way to Champaign and back! You must be nuts!"

In a wild eruption of fury he tore the ticket into shreds and threw the pieces on the floor at her feet.

She stared down at the floor as if he had torn her up as well. She bent slowly and picked up one of the fragments. He saw the band of stars in her hair and felt a furious urge to tear it from her head. She looked back up at him with her face like a mask of death.

"You goddam lying whore!" he said. He twisted away from her and hurried from the station.

He wandered the dark cold streets around the depot for a long time. A wind carrying the chill of the frozen lake whipped his flushed cheeks. Anger died slowly in little spasms within him. He passed the lunchroom and looked with a sudden loathing at the shadowed interior, the dingy counters, the battered coffee urn. In less than five hours he would be back in that prison again.

He walked to the boulevard that ran parallel to the park. He passed under the gaunt trees, his shadow sweeping the deserted benches that glittered under the swaying street lights. The wind blew scraps of newspaper around the base of the stone monument erected to some heroic dead. He shivered and the station clock struck twelve, the resonant peals lingering in the desolate night.

He climbed the stairs to the bridge over the maze of tracks, rested his elbows on the ledge in the center, and listened to the banging of freight cars being shunted in the dark yards below. He looked up, trying to make out the clarity of a star against the darkness of the sky but suddenly the frail paleness of Rosemary's face intruded before his eyes.

He closed his eyes tightly for a moment and when he opened them he stared at the buildings gleaming in the distance, lighted tiny windows still resembling remote stars. Something closer caught his attention and over the bare frozen branches and boughs of trees a mile or so away he saw a clearing with a glistening pond of ice. He could just make out the small dark forms of a boy and girl skating together, the two of them alone on the pond. They moved as if locked by their arms, skimming in circles around the pond until the girl broke free and whirled gracefully.

He leaned forward on the bridge imagining he could hear the shrill whistling of her skates on the ice, almost see her face sparkling with the joy of her flight. He felt his heart straining to join her, to share her delight. He was seized suddenly with trembling.

He left the bridge, retraced his walk leaving the park, and hurried back to the station. He walked up the stairs and entered the doors, with his blood pulsing. When he saw she was gone, the bench where they had been, empty, he almost cried out.

Confused and uncertain what to do next, he thought of finding Noodles. Then he recalled the Poinsetta Hotel where she might have a room.

He walked quickly down to the street again, passed the lunchroom without a glance, crossed the boulevard entering the settlement of small dingy hotels, dim smoky taverns, and strip joints masquerading as clubs. When he saw the misted amber sign of the Poinsetta Hotel, he ran until he reached it. He entered the lobby short of breath. A night clerk with cheeks like granite and eyes like chips of stone sat behind the desk reading a newspaper.

"Is Netta here?" Nick asked.

The clerk raised his head for a moment. A slight stiff curl of his lips denied the name. He looked back at his paper.

"I'm not a cop," Nick said. "I work right here in the neighborhood. I know her."

The clerk kept his eyes on the paper.

"Listen," Nick said desperately. "Noodles is a friend of mine. He told me to ask for her."

The clerk studied him for a long hard instant. He motioned finally toward a house phone around the side of the desk. He left his chair and as Nick picked up the receiver, he plugged in a line at the switchboard. There was a buzzing in the receiver and Nick held his breath. When he heard her voice, a small fire cut the darkness.

"This is Nick," he said. "Nick Manos."

She did not answer.

"I want to see you, please," he said. "I want to come up for a minute."

There was another tight moment of silence and then he heard her voice, quiet and without emotion.

"Room 314," she said.

He hung up the phone and walked toward the elevator. The door was open and he entered, pushed the button for three, and the doors closed. The elevator creaked and whined up.

On the third floor he emerged into a faintly lit corridor. A phonograph wailed a scratchy tuneless melody carrying from a nearby room. He peered closely at one of the numbers and then saw a feeble square of light at the end of the corridor. He walked slowly toward it.

The door was open and Netta stood inside a narrow room lit only by the gloomy light from a tiny lamp on a bedstand behind her. He could make out the bed, a dresser, and an armchair. Her face was shrouded in shadow and she wore a quilted robe that hung to her ankles. Her feet were bare, slim and white on the darker carpet, the toes like small shining shells.

He hesitated a moment and then stepped into the room. He closed the door behind him. Almost at once he breathed the scent of some strange perfume, an odor of withered flowers or musty leaves.

"There is something I want to tell you," he said, and his words whispered like an echo. "I've been walking around for a long time and I had to come and tell you I'm sorry. I'm sorry for what I said."

She stood concealed in shadow and silence and he tried to see within the shrouded hollows and circles of her face.

"There is something else, too," he said. "I'm not stuck in the lunchroom because it was my father's dying wish. I'm stuck in it because I'm lazy and worthless and don't know what else I want to do. I don't have any ambition and I don't have any hope."

The silence tightened and drew thin between them. She did not move or make a sound. The spread on the bed reflected tiny metallic points of light.

"I don't have any friend in Denver who owns a fancy hotel," he said, "and who wants me to handle the restaurant and bar. The only job I been offered in the past five years was to take bets for a bookie who hangs out in the men's room of the railroad station."

He had a sense of the wretched months and years moving past his lips, falling with an ache from his flesh. He looked down at the scuffed worn tips of his shoes.

"The girl I might have married years ago," he said. "She didn't get sick and die. She became pregnant and I would have married her but I was afraid that the kid wasn't mine. She had an abortion and couldn't stand the sight of me afterward. I don't know where she is now."

His voice fell away and he finished in a futile silence.

For an instant it seemed something stirred under the shadowed flesh of her cheeks. Then she moved around and walked a few steps to the other side of the bed. She turned back to him.

He saw her face in the gleam of the lamp and she appeared a stranger. The flesh puffed slightly about the eyes, the skin of her cheeks gray and sallow, the hair dull and lank. But it was her eyes that were altered the most, hard cold buds suspended between the womb and the grave.

"I'm a whore not a priest," she said, and the words came frozen and quiet from her lips. "If you want to stick around, it's ten bucks a jump."

He looked at her and tried to answer. The words stuck in his throat. He heard a moan beginning somewhere deep in his body and as it sought to burst from his heart, he turned for the door and fled.

When I consider all the Greek coffeehouses and Greek tavernas I have eaten and drunk in, all the evenings I have spent listening to the singers and watching the dancers through the viscid vapors of saganaki, gyros, and the resinated wine, I am surprised I have not used this background in much more of my work.

If I often use priests as narrators in my stories, I also show an affinity for bartenders. Making the bartenders Greek also gains a dimension. In addition to the philosophical outlook on life they gain from their profession, they are also steeped in the bloodstream of a fertile past. Like the leader in an old tragic chorus, they can draw attention to the parallels and the forebodings.

This story was published in *The Saturday Evening Post* and retitled "A Knowledge of Her Past." When I complained about the change in the title to an editor on the magazine who was also a good friend, he advised me to shut up and cash the check.

I took his advice. . . .

THE BALLAD OF DAPHNE AND APOLLO

You would not have thought, to look at him, that my friend Apollo was a subject for tragedy. He had none of the great mournfulness of countenance that must have marked Macbeth and Oedipus. But calamity is not the divine right of kings alone.

Apollo played the guitar in the tavern of Ali Pasha, where I worked as a bartender. He was in his middle thirties and of average height. He appeared taller because he had a lean and hard body and moved with the grace of a flamenco dancer. He had strong white teeth that flashed in a warm and engaging smile.

In the evening, when the tables in the tavern filled with patrons, he would ascend the low platform in a corner of the large room. He played bright Greek mountain dances that made any feet but my swollen and aching ones itch to leap into the air. He played bucolic love songs of Zakynthos and Thessaly, and old-country island melodies that I remembered hearing as a boy.

Late at night as the smoke grew thicker and the mastiha ran freely down eager throats, a line of wild old men would rise to dance. They would circle and weave among the tables in a brisk Hassapiko or a martial Tsamiko that provided the leaders a chance for precarious leaps and hazardous jumps.

It was on an evening near the end of summer that Daphne first came to the tavern. She entered alone sometime after midnight wearing a raincoat and a strip of silk scarf across her head that she untied as she approached the bar. Her hair as it tumbled free was the rich black shade of fine Calamata olives.

"I would like to see the boss," she said in a husky voice.

I walked to the door at the end of the bar and called for Ali Pasha. In a moment he came lumbering out of the office. He had a great, gross body, the disposition of a hangman and a range of facial expression from bitter to bleak. He also fancied himself a bit of a rake and sported a handlebar mustache with curled and pomaded tips that he pulled fiercely when he grew excited.

"I'm looking for a job," the girl said.

"Only men serve the tables," Ali Pasha said brusquely. "The kitchen staff are men as well."

She swept her hair back impatiently with one hand, exposing a long jeweled earring glittering on her ear. "Do you take me for a kitchen flunky?" she asked. "I am a singer."

"A singer," Ali Pasha said, and a rude leer settled around his mouth. "Where have you sung?"

"Plenty of places," she said. "My last job was at George Spartan's in Cleveland and before that the Hellas in Detroit. Business improves wherever I sing."

He gave her a long, appraising look. She was a handsome young woman with a certain sensual boldness that made me uneasy. He motioned her to a stool. "Sit there," he said. "I will listen to you in a minute."

He walked toward the platform where Apollo sat. I wiped the bar briskly with a cloth. "Would you like a mastiha?" I asked.

"Thanks."

I poured her a glass, which she raised to her lips and drank as swiftly as any man.

"Is that guitar player any good?" she asked.

"He plays a beautiful guitar," I said firmly. "When he plays the songs of the old country, he returns old men like me to our mountains and our islands."

"If he could just make you forget the brandy and cigar stink of places like this," she said with a taunting little laugh, "he would still be the best I have ever heard."

In another moment Ali Pasha returned with Apollo. "This is Apollo Gerakis," he said to the girl. "He plays the guitar for me." He motioned to Apollo. "This girl is a singer."

"Daphne," she said. "Daphne Callistos."

"Daphne," I said. "Apollo and Daphne." The old legend came to my mind.

"What's that?" Ali Pasha asked.

"Nothing," I said. There was no use explaining anything classical to him.

"I suppose we can use a singer," Apollo said as he looked carefully at the girl. "Can you sing the songs of Pontus and Epirus and Crete?"

"I know them all," Daphne said. "The lullabies and the love songs and the laments."

"One thing you should know," Apollo said. "The salary here is next to nothing. I exist on tips which are tossed into a box while I play. We would have to share what tips we get."

"I've worked that way before," Daphne said.

"Never mind salary and tips," Ali Pasha said. "Let's hear her sing first."

She gave him a final amused look and walked with Apollo toward the platform, removing her raincoat on the way. She was sheathed in a black dress that fitted her body tightly. Ali Pasha uttered a low, hoarse curse.

When they reached the platform, they stood talking a moment, and then Daphne moved alone into the beam of muted light. Apollo struck the first chords of a lament and the men at the tables quieted slowly.

A lament is a morose and melancholy song, and Apollo played them with feeling. But as she sang I had the strange sensation I was hearing a quality of despair I had never heard before. Her voice, haunting and mournful, led us down the path where the stream of woe pours into the river of lamentation. At the tables men stirred, and a wind of pleased muttering swept the room.

When she finished the lament, Apollo changed the tempo to the lilting melody of a festive mountain dance.

Daphne placed her hands on her hips and threw back her head, and her voice, suddenly bawdy and vibrant, assaulted the room. At one of the tables near the bar an old man sleeping off too much to drink raised his head like a startled bird. Her ardor paid homage to the woodland spirits of fertility and abandon. In such a way must the wild nymphs have sung in the festivals of Dionysus before the satyrs playing their pipes made of reeds.

When she finished, a storm of applause rose from the roomful of men. She walked with a careless insolence past the tables, and many called to her and blew her kisses. She came back to the bar, and Ali Pasha showed his teeth in hungry admiration. "You sing all right," he said grudgingly. "The truth is, I don't really need a singer. It is an expense I might not be able to afford."

In another moment Apollo joined them. "You are very good," he said.

"The boss doesn't think I'm good enough," she laughed.

"Never mind the lousy salary," Apollo said. "I think you will fill the box."

"Out of which you'll take your half," Ali Pasha snarled. He spoke to the girl with a crooked attempt at a winning smile. "If you want to work, you can start tomorrow night at eight."

She nodded calmly as if the outcome had never been in doubt. She turned to leave, and Ali Pasha spoke slyly. "A good-looking woman like you will be a pleasure to have around."

She looked at him as if her eyes were knives severing little hunks of his flesh and made a motion of good night to the rest of us as she pulled on her raincoat. We watched her as she walked to the door. Ali Pasha tugged fiercely and silently at the tips of his mustache, and walked back into the office.

I dimmed the lights in a signal to the customers that we were preparing to close. Apollo sat down on a stool at the bar.

"I wonder where she comes from?" he said slowly.

"She is from disaster," I said, "and on her way to catastrophe." Then, because he did not seem to be listening, I reached across the bar and shook his arm. "Forget her," I said. "Don't get involved with her."

"She is not all that brass she puts on," he said. "When she sings, she sets dreams to weeping. I remembered that it has been a long and lonely summer. I am tired of playing my songs alone." He pushed off the stool. "Hurry and clean up, Janco," he said. "I'll buy you a cup of coffee on the way home."

He walked toward the platform for his coat and guitar. I snapped off the lights above the bar. The waiters were beginning to clear the tables, and customers were moving in reluctant groups to the door. An old man who had been sleeping on his arms was disturbed by the clatter and moaned hoarsely.

"No more auditions tonight," I said in a vexed voice. "We don't need another singer."

After Daphne started to sing in the tavern, business became much better almost at once. Ali Pasha, merciless in his greed, set up additional tables that barely left room for the cursing waiters to squeeze by.

When Daphne sang an unhappy ballad or a lament, she had the old men weeping for the grand days of their lost youth. When she sang a dancing song from Macedonia and suggestively rendered the lyrics of a shy man and his bold wife, the old men went wild with delight. When the graybeards finally rose to dance, they exhausted themselves to demonstrate their unflagging virility, and leaped off the floor like drunken and festive roosters.

Ali Pasha couldn't take his eyes off her. When she sang, he gripped the tips of his mustache in anguish. She held him off by a fury of blazing defiance in the same way she held off the countless other males who stampeded around her at the end of each evening. She provoked my grudging admiration in the ruthless way she cut them down.

But Apollo confused her. Against him she raised defenses that were not needed. He pursued her with a gentleness that was a source of wonder to her. Slowly, almost against her will, she must have felt herself drawn to him. Perhaps he stirred in her a memory long lost in the tide of dark days, a dream of fair love.

There was a day in the beginning of October when rain fell until evening and left a brief scent of freshened earth across the city. Late in the evening Apollo came looking for Daphne and seemed distressed. A while after that, one of the waiters relieved me at the bar, and I slipped out the kitchen door to smoke a cigar and get some fresh air.

Daphne called my name from the shadows.

"What are you doing out here?" I asked. "Apollo is looking for you."

"Let him look," she said defiantly. "He is as bad as all the rest."

"Is he?" I asked quietly. I sat down on a crate and with a sigh raised my burning feet to rest on another.

For a long moment she did not answer. I drew a cigar from my pocket and struck a match, and in the brief flare of light I saw her pale and weary face.

"Perhaps he is," she said. "Perhaps he isn't. But there are times when I am sick and tired of all men."

"The fate of a handsome woman," I said.

She laughed mockingly in the darkness. "I only feel comfortable with you, Janco," she said. "Why is that?"

"My arteries and my bad feet," I said wryly. "You sense correctly they have immobilized me for any pursuit."

She fell silent again. Above us the rain clouds had disappeared and the stars glittered.

"Wasn't Apollo the name of a god?" she said.

"He was the god of life and light," I said. "And he loved Daphne above all other women."

"I knew the story as a child," she said quietly, "I don't remember now except that it was sad."

"Daphne was the daughter of Peneus, the river god," I said. "Apollo was seized with love for her, but she yearned to keep her freedom. Many lovers sought her, but she spurned them all.

"Apollo loved her and longed to have her as his own. She sensed he was different from all the others, but she was afraid. She belonged to the unspoiled woods and to the untamed rivers. He followed her relentlessly and told her not to flee from him as a lamb flies before the wolf or a dove before the hawk. He was the god of song and the lyre and played a mighty melody of love."

"A guitar player," she said softly. "Playing a sweet and sad guitar."

"She tried not to listen to him," I said. "She was innocent of the meaning of love. But he would not let her alone. Her strength began to fail, and she called upon her father to aid her, to change her form, which had brought her into danger. Scarcely had she finished pleading when a stiffness seized all her limbs. Her hair became leaves, her arms became branches, her feet stuck fast in the ground as roots. Apollo touched the stem of the tree and felt her flesh tremble under the new bark. And he wept for his lost love. 'Since you cannot be mine,' he sang, 'I will wear you for my crown. I will decorate with you my harp and my lyre. My songs will make you immortal.' "

When I finished, she moved restlessly from the shadows and for an instant stood in the strip of light before the door. "The legend does not tell the truth," she said, and there was a black and bitter edge to her words. "Do not believe she fled because she was innocent and cared nothing for him. She fled because she had known many men and did not deserve the kind of love he offered. She knew if they loved each other they might both be destroyed."

"It is only a story that belongs to the past," I said wearily. "A bit of foolishness for children and old men."

She went in the door, and after a moment I followed.

It was not long after that night that Apollo and Daphne became lovers. I do not know why she changed her mind. Perhaps even the daughters of gods have moments of mortal yearning. And the legend does not tell us whether in that unhappy chase the two of them did not pause for a moment together, perhaps in an hour of twilight when the darkening of the woods made them feel keenly the burden of being alone.

No one told me they became lovers, but I knew by the radiance that came from them when they were together. Sometimes when they had finished their last song after midnight they came to the bar, and I served them little glasses of wine.

"Is she not beautiful, Janco?" he said, and there was the intimacy of possession in the way his fingers touched her hair. She accepted his touch, and I saw their faces stir with the soft wind of each other's desire.

"Is he not mad?" she said and laughed her husky laugh, animated and deepened by affection.

"He is a guitar player," I smiled. "You are a singer of sad love songs. This gives you both a head start on madness."

"When I was a boy," Apollo said softly, looking at Daphne, "I had dreams of conquering cities and of ruling men. Dreams of loving countless fair and dark women." He paused, and the words came shaken from his throat. "I have found them all," he said. "In my love I have conquered cities and rule all other men. In my love I have spanned the oceans and circled the earth. In my love I possess countless fair and dark women."

"He is mad," Daphne said, and in her eyes there was a longing to believe him. "He is trying to make me as mad as he is."

"The mad are sane," I said, "and the sane are mad. Only love can harness both."

She raised her glass of wine and watched me as she spoke. "Legends are stories that belong to the past," she said, and a shadow swept her cheeks. "Is that not true, Janco?"

"That is true," I said quickly. "A bit of foolishness for children and old men."

She accepted my assurance recklessly and held tightly to Apollo's hand. "Then I drink to the future," she said. "A future that will make stories of its own."

"I drink to that," I said and spoke from my heart.

I am sure the ugly trouble began with Ali Pasha. When he could not have Daphne, his soul festered in rancor and wished to destroy that which he had been denied. He whispered in low malevolent tones to the waiters, falling silent when I came near. They followed the dark spoor and, like coyotes that feed on what the wolf brings down, added their own venom to the pot. Rumors and suspicions and whispers about Daphne and her past spread furiously through the tavern. There were sidelong smirks and muted laughter when Apollo passed the tables.

When he understood something of what was going on, he twisted in frustration and rage, but could find no adversary visible. I think he wished mainly to protect and defend her, and yet the baleful laughter nourished disorder. He knew that the shadows of her past concealed much he did not relish, and he began to brood over what could not be forgotten.

I fought to help him where I could and yet protected Ali Pasha as well. I knew that if Apollo suspected the origin of the vile whispering there would be violence. Ali Pasha kept a loaded gun in the top drawer of his desk and was coward enough to use it if he were attacked.

Under the taunt of these aggravations Apollo one night flung a patron violently from the platform when he sought to slip a folded bill into a pocket of Daphne's dress. There was a roar of catcalls and jeers. The man who had been shoved shrieked for the police. Ali Pasha hurried him into his office to conciliate him. A moment later Apollo came raging to the bar, followed by Daphne.

"He meant nothing," Daphne pleaded to calm him. "That was a good tip, and he meant no harm."

"Let him choke on his good tip!" Apollo said. "I should have smashed him. I saw him paw you. I should have smashed the pig!" He twisted on the stool, all the weeks of provocation and helplessness fused into explosive direction. "I have to sit there and watch them hour after hour," he said. "Drunken pigs who think their grimy dollar entitles them any liberty."

"Listen, please," Daphne said in a low, soothing voice. "I can tell when one is a bad apple. I would slap that kind down myself. Mostly they are old roosters with cut claws showing off for applause from their friends. They mean no harm."

"They harm me!" Apollo said. "I do not want the woman I love pawed by pigs!"

Her eyes began to flash fire of their own. "You forget one thing," she said. "I am a singer of bawdy songs in a tavern. In Cleveland and Detroit I earned my tips this way. This is the way I earn my bread."

"To hell with that," Apollo said, and his cheeks shook off heat. "To hell with earning your bread that way."

"Don't tell me how to earn my bread," she said, and the words came bitten from between her teeth. "From the time I was ten no one cared whether I had bread at all. I have made my own way and asked no favors and earned my bread. Don't tell me now what is right. Don't sit in judgment like a god over my life."

"What kind of woman are you?" he asked savagely. "Not to mind being pawed by a hundred men!"

She stepped back as if he had struck her. Then, without another word, she turned quickly and almost ran to the door. He made a sudden frantic motion with his hand to call her back and then changed his mind.

"Go after her," I said quietly. "You were not fair, Apollo. She cares a great deal for you. Don't let her grieve alone!" I looked uneasily at the closed door to the office. "Ali Pasha will be out in a minute."

"To hell with him," Apollo said. But the circles of anger around his mouth loosened slightly, and then he slipped off the stool and started after Daphne.

A moment later Ali Pasha came out of the office embracing the patron whose outrage seemed to have softened. "Give this gentleman two bottles of mastiha." Ali Pasha's voice dripped unctuous tones. "Drink them, sir, with my compliments."

After the mollified rooster walked away clutching his bottles, Ali Pasha quickly dropped the mask of civility. "Mark that down," he snarled. "Those two bottles come out of the guitar player's tips. Charge him the retail price." He glared around the room. "Where are he and the girl?"

"Out for the air," I said.

"You tell them when they get back," he said, spitting the words from beneath his flaring mustache. "You tell lover boy that one more outburst like that and he and his prize paramour can both clear out." The sweat glistened on his swarthy face. "Who the devil does he think he is to protect that tart?"

"He is only a man in love," I said slowly. "A poor man goaded and tormented by dirty rumors and vicious lies spread by animals who only feel at home in the dark."

The blood left his face as if I had struck him.

November came, and the hours of daylight grew shorter. Dusk and dark advanced as the winter nights closed down. For the first time that I could remember I dreaded the coming of winter. The bleakness of the earth mirrored a desolation gathering in myself. I tried to validate this as the ominous premonition of an old man who did not have long to live, but I knew it was really because of my grief and despair for Apollo and Daphne.

The ugly whispering and mocking laughter had slowly faded away. Even Ali Pasha tired of the brutal game. But the baleful harm had been done.

Apollo could not forgive or forget the measure of mockery Daphne and he had endured. He tasted a bitter cup of brooding that would not let him rest. Each night that Daphne sang he devised in fury that the room secreted her former lovers, and he held himself tense and ready for violence. She sought to soothe and reassure him, but he was beyond reason. When they could bear no more, they raged loudly at each other and did not care who heard. At other times they fought in dreadful silence.

In those dissembled moments when they sought to tear from the fabric of the nightmare a pattern for survival, they drew me with frenzied gaiety into their plans.

"Can you see me tending house?" she asked, and laughed a quick, shrill laugh. "Janco, can you honestly see me in an apron?"

"I see you clearly," Apollo said. "I will come home weary in the evening—"

"And Daphne will greet you with a song and a dance," I said, smiling.

"She will greet me with a tableful of food," he cried. "Roast chicken and white pilaf and salad garnished with Calamata olives and ripe mezithra cheese."

"Where will this splendid meal come from?" Daphne asked.

"You will cook it," Apollo said. "As my mother cooked for my father."

"Fine," Daphne said mirthfully. "I will cook for you as your mother cooked for your father. Fine."

"You will cook it," Apollo spoke with confidence. "And we will invite Janco to dinner several nights a week."

"I will work hard to learn," Daphne said. "You might both be surprised at how good a cook I become."

"I think you will become a fine cook," I cried. "And when you achieve this mastery, Apollo will create a ballad about your prowess in the kitchen."

There were those other bleak and furious moments when he stormed past the bar into the office, and she followed as if she were tied to his flesh. I could hear their voices through the thin panels of wood.

"You are a madman," she told him. "You are blind and mad."

"I see enough," his voice trembled. "The way that sailor looked at you. The things you promised when you sang to him."

"It is only you I care about," she cried. "Don't you understand that?"

"You knew him from before," he said.

"I have never seen him before tonight."

"You lie!" he said savagely.

"I'm not lying!" she said. "I'm not lying!"

"There were other men," he said. "You cannot deny there were many other men."

"What can I say about that now?" she said, and a terrible pain rang in her words. "What can I do about that now?"

There was a day in the beginning of December when I got to the tavern very early in the afternoon and found it deserted except for Daphne on a stool at the bar.

"You are hours early," I said smiling. "Are you that attached to this place?"

"I am leaving, Janco," she said quietly. "I came to say goodby."

I could not answer. A sadness settled upon me. After a while I said, "Where will you go?"

"I don't know," she said. "I don't care."

"He will follow you," I said. "He will not let you go."

She did not answer or move for a long moment. Then she slipped off the stool and turned and stared gravely across the shadowed room with the chairs piled upon the empty wooden tables. "These places are all alike," she said bitterly. "When you have sung in one you have sung in all. They are graveyards one moment and circuses the next moment. They all have the smell of damp cellars that never see the sun."

"If you went away for a little while," I said. "For just a little while and then came back."

"That would do no good," she said. "You know that."

She walked a few steps, and her shadow rose and swept along the wall behind her as if seeking a place to rest.

"In the world outside," she said, "there are countless people who love and marry and bear children. They live one day like the next. I have never envied them before." A stricken wonder came into her voice. "I try to remember the moment for me when there was no turning back. I try to remember the moment such a dream was lost to me forever. I cannot." She shook her head wearily. "All my life seems a long, bawdy song."

She came slowly to where I stood and kissed me. Her lips were cold against my cheek. "I could not say goodby to him," she said. "I say goodby to you instead."

"Will you leave him a letter?" I asked. "A message?"

"Everything has been done." She shook her head. "Everything has been said." She walked toward the door of the office. "I will fix my face and go," she said. "The first waiters may come soon."

She stood for a moment in the doorway. Her face, suddenly stained with tears, had imperfections, but no face is faultless, and still she glittered in that moment with some strange beauty. "So the legend is right in the end," she said. "Daphne and Apollo are lost to each other."

"Not really lost," I said. "They have loved each other. He will never forget her. He will wear her love for his crown and will decorate with her memory his harp and his lyre."

"You are a foolish old man," she said softly. "Life to you is a song and a harp and stories that belong to the past."

She closed the door behind her. I turned wearily to prepare for the evening, trying to ease my distress in the movements of habit, the opening of bottles and the wiping of glasses. A few moments later I heard the sound of a shot.

A cold wind from the grave swept my body, and I went quickly through the door to the office. She was sitting in an armchair with her head limply to one side and the tumbled waves of her lovely hair almost hiding her face. There was a small stain of blood on her breast above her heart and at her feet the gun of Ali Pasha from his drawer.

I made my cross and closed my eyes for a moment and cried out then, a terrible cry from the marrow of my bone, for Daphne and Apollo and for the earth which had lost their love.

The winter seems to last forever. March is still a cold and dreary month. Sometimes the snow falls softly during the night, and in the morning the earth is frozen and buried. I walk shivering to work, and when I breathe, a quivering mist rises like smoke from my mouth.

The tavern is not the same. Ali Pasha carries a dark burden of guilt and drinks savagely and alone. The wild old men still dance, but without the vigor they had before, as if they are only sad and futile ghosts. Apollo still plays the guitar, but he is changed as well.

Many come to hear him play in the evening. I swear there are tears off his strings, and his songs are great white stars that set dreams to weeping. And as I stand behind the bar late at night and listen, it seems to me that I am back in the mountains of the old country under Homer's glittering moon. Parnassus stands behind dark mountains. The olive groves and the ruins of columns lie among the age-old trees. The sea and Piraeus are white with light. Under the stars the shepherds sleep beside their flocks.

When I have to sit down because my ankles are swollen and my feet hurt, I return unwillingly to reality and know I am only an old man. A foolish old man to whom life is a song and a harp and a legend that will never die.

This is a grim story, and rereading it still chills me.

THE JUDGMENT

Elias Karnezos entered the United States as an immigrant from Greece in 1919. He was twenty-six years old, the son of a farmer from a village near Tripolis, in the Peloponnese. He was short, stocky, with robust arms and shoulders, strong hands, and thick black hair. His good health and ebullient spirits made him confident he would achieve success and make a fortune in the new land.

A friend who had emigrated from the same village a few years earlier, working as a bellboy in a Chicago hotel, obtained a job for Elias as a shine boy in a neighborhood shoe-repair shop. Elias shined shoes zestfully while singing songs of his village. The old shoemaker liked him and began teaching him the rudiments of his craft.

When conventions were quartered in the hotel where his friend worked, Elias joined him as a bellboy. From his paycheck and tips, he sent money home to his parents and to repay the debt he had incurred for his passage to America. Whatever remained after deducting for rent and food, he spent in roistering with a group of young sports. They gambled, danced, drank, and visited whores with jocular enthusiasm. Some of the first words Elias learned in English remained his favorite ones: "Sonofabitch!" "Goddam!" "Jesus Christ!" He never used these words in anger but simply as explosive and fervent expressions of his excitement and delight.

When the old shoemaker died, the owner of the store gave Elias the job with a substantial raise. Elias bought several new suits and a wide-brimmed Borsalino like those worn by gangsters of that period. He gained a reputation as a dandy and a generous man with friendship and money.

Among the cronies with whom he gambled were two brothers named

Varvari from a village not far from his own in Greece. Playing poker in their apartment, he saw Katina, a younger sister the brothers had brought a few months earlier from Greece.

The girl was sixteen, tiny and slim-boned, with a somber face. She had never attended school and could not read or write. At the pleading of their parents the brothers had reluctantly brought her to America to have her educated and married. But they found it simpler to utilize her as a menial. She scrubbed, cleaned, washed, and cooked for them and their friends without complaint. She was shuttered by shyness and paralyzed by ignorance and terror. Her brothers ridiculed her constantly, mocking her ignorance by tossing newspapers and magazines at her and demanding she read them aloud. When they grew surly because they were losing in the games, they pinched her and threatened her with beatings.

"Why don't you leave the poor girl alone?" Elias cried indignantly.

"Sticking up for her is a waste of time," one of her brothers sneered. "She's dumb as a sheep and hasn't as much meat on her skinny frame as a starving chicken."

Katina knew Elias was defending her and fled with flushed cheeks back to the sanctuary of the kitchen.

In the following weeks, on visits to the apartment, Elias found excuses to enter the kitchen. It took him a while to overcome Katina's shyness and fear. One night he brought her a small box of sweet chocolates and saw her laugh with pleasure for the first time. He noticed then with surprise that she was a pretty girl, her hair black and lustrous, her features delicate, her eyes bright and alert. And she was so tiny that, despite his own short stature, he felt huge and tall beside her.

Her brothers thought him crazy and wavered between encouraging his interest to get Katina off their hands and avoiding the dire prospect of losing their indentured servant. The fact that Elias did not seem concerned about the traditional old-country dowry decided the brothers to accept his proposal of marriage to their sister.

Elias and Katina were married in a small church ceremony. He wore a rented tuxedo too small for his brawny shoulders and she wore a cheap white gown grudgingly paid for by her brothers. On the first night of their weekend honeymoon in the hotel where he worked as a bellboy, Elias took his bride's virginity with gentleness and patience. Despite her fear and shock at the sight of her blood, he was surprised at the fierce passion in her small, slim body.

They lived in a shabby, two-room apartment overlooking an alley a block from the shoe-repair shop. For the first few months after their marriage he came home after work every night to the dinner Katina prepared. But he found her meekness and silence oppressive, and in the monotonous hours of the evening he ached with nostalgia for the revelries of the nights before his marriage. He began meeting his cronies again, explaining to Katina there were shoes to be repaired after hours in the shop. When she did not question his excuses, he discarded even that flimsy pretense, slipping easily back into his routine of drinking, gambling, and visiting the jovial, bountiful whores who laughed and shrieked in his arms.

When he arrived home late at night, stinking of wine and the colognes and powders of other women, he climbed heavily into bed beside Katina. He heard her fitful breathing.

"Katina?"

She did not answer.

"Katina, I know you're awake."

She did not move. He reached under the covers and groped clumsily with his fingers for her naked body under the cotton nightgown, a maudlin gesture of remorse and affection. She twisted violently away from him, and untroubled within his drunken euphoria, he fell soddenly asleep, unaware of the tears of shame and fury Katina cried into her pillow as he snored.

Katina's life resumed the pattern of her labor in the service of her brothers. She scrubbed, washed, and cooked for Elias and the friends he brought home. In addition, she received him into her body for the occasional spurtings of passion he salvaged from his whores.

Elias could not understand that Katina's inability to read and write locked her into a dark obsession with her own grievances. Although she had feared the cruelty of her brothers, their brutalities seemed trivial to those she now endured. She felt betrayed, her rage at Elias compounded of her own unsatisfied passion and the way he selfishly surfeited his needs. She began resisting his caresses, subduing her desire in a corset of tightly laced hate.

"What the hell's the matter with you?" he would say in aggravation. "You're stiff as a carrot! What's wrong with you?"

"Leave me alone!"

"What the hell is wrong?" he cried.

"Ask your whores!" she said hoarsely.

Stung by the justice of her condemnation, he would turn away from her in the bed.

"Goddam women!" he would mumble under his breath. "None of them understand a man needs a little fun. . . ."

At other times, however, when drinking dulled his guilt, he forced himself upon her. They warred with their bodies, his strength pitted against her spirit. Though she was determined to deny herself any pleasure, there were moments Katina's body betrayed her will and she cried out with a wild, unwilling joy. Afterward she bathed and scrubbed her breasts and thighs as if they had been defiled.

In the second year of their marriage Katina became pregnant. She accepted the doctor's diagnosis with resentment and distress. But as the baby grew within her body, she felt herself softening, curling warm and alive, the world less grim and forbidding.

Elias was jubilant. He sang loudly as he pounded on the last, cut down his drinking, reduced his gambling, and subdued his whoring except for a few infrequent lapses when desire drove him wild. On those occasions he did not linger after he was relieved but would hurry to dress.

"Where you going so fast, honey?" a whore named Anneta, who was fond of him, asked.

"I'm going to have a son," Elias said, as if that anticipated event explained everything.

In the evenings after work he went home to Katina eagerly. He treated her with an awkward, uncommon gentleness as he watched her tiny belly rise and swell. At night in bed when he felt her stirring restlessly to find a comfortable position, he spoke to her softly.

"Are you all right?"

"I am all right," she answered quietly.

"Do you have any pain?"

"I have no pain," she said.

"Can I get you anything? A glass of water or some tea?"

"I am all right!" she said impatiently. "Go to sleep!"

In the silence that followed he slid his body carefully closer to her, gently touching her bare foot with his own toes. He was overwhelmed with gratefulness when she did not pull away.

The baby was born in the spring of that year, a dark-haired, brown-eyed boy they named Peter. When he beheld the infant in Katina's arms for the first time, Elias cried with pride and joy. In that sacred moment he swore he would never touch a whore again.

Their lives mended in the delight of their son. After each day's work Elias rushed home to play with the baby. Katina scolded him for his ardor but enjoyed the baby herself, her days filled with the wonder of his beauty and his growth.

The following year, Katina gave birth to a baby girl. Almost a year to the day after that birth, in the same month that Elias purchased the shoe-repair shop for his own business, Katina gave birth to a second daughter, their third child. For all three children she was a devoted and capable mother, unhindered by her inability to read and write.

Contented in his home and family, Elias worked vigorously, and his business prospered. He bought a second shoe-repair shop and then a large dry-cleaning business. He had more than thirty employees working for him, joined a fraternal lodge and a businessmen's association, bought a new car, the first he had ever owned, and learned, not without some minor mishaps, to drive it.

For a while Katina firmly refused to allow the children or herself to ride with Elias, but when her apprehension lessened, she looked forward to their drives into the country on Sunday afternoons. Another favorite pastime was when they invited a score of friends to the park on summer weekends. Elias would buy a whole lamb and roast it over a charcoal fire and a spit, drinking and dancing and singing until it was time to eat.

And every Sunday morning they dressed the children and themselves in their best clothing and went to the Greek church. Standing stiffly beside Katina as they held the children in their arms, Elias felt his family blessed and sanctioned by God.

When Peter was three years old, the girls about one and two, an epidemic of influenza struck the city. All three children became ill, but only their son suffered complications. In the space of two nights, despite the frantic ministrations of a doctor and a nurse, the boy died.

In the anguish that followed their son's death Elias sought to comfort Katina, feeling a mother's loss even a greater calamity than his own. Yet he could not console himself. During the day he would suddenly burst into tears. Every small boy he passed on the street cut like a knife into his heart.

Katina, tearing at her hair in grief, came to feel the boy's death was a punishment for her acquittal and acceptance of the corruptions and debaucheries of Elias. By forgiving her husband's lechery, she had had delivered upon her a terrible retribution. She swore she would live the remainder of her life seeking to protect her daughters and herself, convinced that, in the end, God would exact damnation on Elias. Katina made her decision to mourn and remember, and to suppress every small pleasure and joy.

"What can I do?" Elias cried. "Sit in a dark room, day and night, remembering the boy?"

"Say your prayers and go to church!" Katina cried. "Light candles! Ask God's forgiveness!"

"Candles won't bring me back my son," Elias said bitterly.

"He is with God now."

"He doesn't belong to God!" Elias said. "He belongs to me!"

"Wait!" Katina cried. "Wait! God will answer your blasphemy!"

"I'm not saying nothing against God," Elias said. A resignation and despair swept his spirit. "I'm only saying that goddam candles won't bring me back my son."

In a frantic effort to anesthetize his sorrow, he invited friends to dinner several evenings a week. He spent money lavishly on wine, lamb, olives, and cheese. He sat at the head of the table, shouting for his guests to eat and drink. His arduous efforts at gaiety faltered before the somber presence of Katina. Sometimes she spoke a few words to one of the guests, but mostly she remained silent and unsmiling, casting her mournful shadow over the gathering. The uncomfortable guests would leave soon after dinner.

Sometimes at night, their daughters asleep, Elias and Katina in bed in their darkened room, he'd make an effort to embrace his wife. She pulled away as if the touch of his body had burned her.

"Let me love you a little," he pleaded. "It will be good for both of us."

"Never again," Katina said, her voice cold and relentless. "Never again for as long as we live. That is what God has decreed."

"How do you know that?" he cried in a low, hoarse whisper. "Why should he want that from us?" When she did not answer he turned away from her, trying to separate and calm the waves of fear and desire that swept his body. He remembered the oath he had taken, after the birth of his son, never to touch a whore again. He saw the balance of his life, cold and unloved.

"Sonofabitch," he murmured softly. "Sonofabitch."

Upon his small daughters Elias lavished all the generosity and affection his wife rejected. Despite her disapproval, he bought them frilly expensive dresses and small ermine coats. He spoiled them rampantly, loved to have them come running into his arms when he entered the door in the evening, their fingers eagerly searching his pockets for the gifts he always carried.

In contrast to his indulgences, Katina taught the girls the crafts of cooking and sewing, sternly pushing them to their books and studies, although she had no comprehension of the things they were studying.

When Elias sought to help the girls with some facet of their schoolwork, she turned on him resentfully.

"You think that's the way it really is?" she said scornfully. "You think because you can read, you know what's going on? You know nothing about life and the way people really are! You are a fool!"

To reinforce her argument she drew upon all the flotsam that floated unmoored in her head. Ignorant of the barest fundamentals of the knowledge in books, she lived in a teeming cupboard of superstition, myth, village theology, memories, fears, rumors, and the gossip of neighbors.

If Elias tried to argue with her, she'd burst into a rage. The girls would flee to their room and Elias would shield himself behind a newspaper, trying vainly to understand the reason for her vehemence and fury.

The years passed. The girls grew into dark-haired, dark-eyed young beauties. Katina was a vigilant tyrant, refusing to allow them to attend dances at school or parties in the homes of friends. The only organization she permitted them to join was the choir of the Greek church. On the holidays, she allowed them to invite a few friends into their home, but she subjected every boy who entered to so baleful a scrutiny, he fled, vowing never to return. When her daughters complained, Katina silenced them with angry, ominous warnings.

"All men are animals!" she cried. "Seeking to destroy girls, turn them into sluts! That won't happen to you while I'm alive!"

In the year their eldest daughter graduated from high school, Elias suffered a disastrous fire that totally destroyed his dry-cleaning shop full of the clothing of his customers. His insurance covered only a fraction of their losses, yet he felt his honor required he pay the full amounts. When he had fulfilled this obligation, he was almost penniless, left with a single small shoe-repair shop, a shoemaker, a shine boy, and himself.

These reversals reinforced Katina's conviction that Elias was a shallow and indulgent man who accidentally managed some success that, in the end, his stupidity caused him to destroy. He, in turn, began to believe she was right in calling him a blockhead and a fool.

Within a year after their graduations, both daughters left home to be married. For the first time in twenty-five years, Elias and Katina were alone.

Elias aged quickly. Although he was only in his middle fifties, his thick black hair was mottled with strands of white. Futility cut deeper creases into the flesh of his cheeks and darkened the hollow circles about his eyes. He sought desperately to salvage his shattered business under a persistent burden of failure and defeat. He let the shoemaker go and returned to the last himself. But the years had dulled his fingers, and his poor workmanship was the final blow that caused him to close his business. They moved to a smaller apartment, grimly reminiscent of the dark rooms they had lived in during the first years of their marriage. Elias managed to pay the rent and buy food on a small insurance annuity he had taken out years before.

He looked for work but there was nothing for a man of his years without any special skill. He retreated to spending his hours before the television set, waiting for the visits of his daughters and the small grandchildren that had been born in the past few years. When they came to see him, he hugged them playfully, tickling and kissing them with delight. Katina shrieked that he would hurt them, confuse them with his insensate shouts. He'd make an effort to ignore her but, finally, pained and subdued, he'd let the children alone.

When they sat at the table, he slipped into the bountiful role he had always loved, urging food upon the children, wine upon his sons-in-law. Everything he did incurred Katina's displeasure.

"Shut up, old man!" she cried. "You think everybody guzzles and eats like you do! Not a dollar in your pocket and you still eat and drink like a pig!"

"Goddam, leave me alone," he'd say weakly and shake his head in resignation.

When he began to recite a story, some episode out of his past, his eyes would glitter and he'd laugh gaily. At some point in his excited recounting, Katina entered like a chorus.

"He was your good friend, that one, wasn't he? As long as you had money in your pocket and wine and food on your table. Where is he now?" She mocked him. "Where are all your other friends? Now that you have nothing but the pants you wear each day and the pants you wear on Sunday, where are all your friends? Answer me that, old fool!"

In order to evade Katina's nagging, he began leaving the house each morning, gathering with a few other old men in a coffee shop a couple of blocks away. They passed the hours telling stories of their youth.

Through the owner of the coffee shop, Elias heard of an old Italian shoemaker in the neighborhood who wanted to sell his small shop and return to Italy to die. Elias visited the shabby, narrow store, the fixtures decrepit, the machinery ancient. But the old shoemaker was willing to sell out for five hundred dollars, and the rent was only fifty dollars a month.

Elias borrowed two hundred and fifty dollars from his elder daughter's husband as a down payment on the purchase price and promised to pay the shoemaker the balance within six months.

When Katina learned of what he had done, she shrieked at him in fury and denounced her daughters for aiding him in his folly.

"Just wait a few months and I'll show you!" he cried. "I'll be on my feet again in no time! Jesus Christ, watch if I don't show you!"

Once more he rose with renewed hope at dawn and walked briskly to his shop, feeling a delight in turning on the lights, putting on his apron, starting the machinery. Yet, despite working from dawn until seven or eight o'clock in the evening, he barely made enough money to pay his rent. Rather than confront Katina's scorn, he borrowed a few dollars from one of his daughters and gave it to his wife at the end of the week as if it were a profit.

In the winter of that year, the wind and snow sweeping through the desolate streets, he sat huddled for warmth beside the small coal-burning stove, wearing his coat to conserve on fuel, staring through the window, vainly waiting for a customer to appear. Sometimes a whole day passed without a single person entering the store. The few pairs of shoes he repaired stood forlorn on the counter. At the end of the day he locked and shuttered his shop and despondently walked the few blocks home to the dinner Katina had prepared for him.

A new distress rose to plague him. His vision began to blur and the few customers who brought him work complained about the poor quality of the repair. Apprehensive of complaining to Katina, he kept the knowledge of his failing sight to himself for months. Only when he finally slashed his fingers on the shoe machines did he ask one of his daughters to take him to the doctor. An examination disclosed he had ripened cataracts in both eyes.

He entered the hospital for surgery, a dreadful period of darkness, sustained only by the faith that he would be able to see again. When the bandages were finally removed, his vision remained clouded by the failure of his eyes to heal properly. He sat for hours before the television set, watching the screen for that instant when the blurred faces and figures would once more come into focus. Instead of improving, his sight grew slowly worse. Each time one of his daughters took him back to the doctor for re-examination, he pleaded for help.

"Goddam, Doctor!" he cried. "Maybe something, some new medicine can make me see better. I can't work or read a paper! A man can't live like this!"

He could not accept the doctor's explanation that there had been incurable damage to the retina of his eyes, that although he might not become totally blind, his sight would slowly diminish and he would have to exist in a world of shadows.

With that irrevocable diagnosis, Katina ceased to nag him, fed him patiently, tended his needs without complaint. He was so grateful for her kindness, he was often moved to tears.

"I'll get better, Ma," he promised her fervently, holding tightly to her hand. "They'll find some medicine, some new treatment. You'll see, I'll find another store, get a new start, look after us both once more."

He marveled how calmly and stoically she accepted his plight. He praised her constancy and devotion to his daughters.

"Jesus Christ, that woman has become an angel," he said. "The way she takes care of me every minute. That's what she is, an angel."

But as the weeks passed and his hope faltered, his anguish grew and the bonds holding him to life weakened. There was a night he woke with a strange heat burning through his body. He started to call to Katina, who slept in the bedroom across the hall, then slipped again into a fitful sleep. In his fevered dreams he saw the faces of his father and mother, the fields and groves about his village, the ship on which he journeyed to America. He saw the cronies of his early revels, the glittering bodies of whores, the laughing, carefree black men who worked for him, the mountain of shoes he had mended. He saw the countless wine casks he had emptied, the lambs roasting on the spit, the dancing friends who had shared his joy. He saw the cherub's cheeks of his son, the flowered mound of his grave, the eyes of his grandchildren glowing in the light of candles on the holiday tables. Above them all he saw the figure of Katina.

He could not be certain whether she was part of his dream or whether he had wakened to find her standing over him, grown to a vast and stunning height, huge and broad as he had once felt when she was small and slim. But he suddenly recognized her as a vengeful, merciless, and satisfied witness to his fate.

In the great flood of water rising to engulf his body, a torrent rushing to clear his eyes, he uttered a single perplexed and bewildered cry, the last sound he made before he died.

I don't know quite what to say about this story. I enjoyed writing it and am particularly fond of the last line:

"In a world of fools, the lout is king. . . ."

THE SHEARING OF SAMSON

In a world where uncertainties abound, a man must depend on common sense. Reason is the only weapon with which to combat the hoary superstition and unbridled hysteria of fools. I tried often to explain this to my friend, Louie Anastis, but the man's incapacity to be reasonable merely confirms my observation that he is a lout.

In order that you might better understand the situation, I should first tell you something of Louie and myself. Before his retirement Louie had been a meatman specializing in animals that died natural deaths. He offered these beasts at substantial discounts to any restaurant owner foolish or greedy enough to purchase them. (I do not mention this fact to slander him but because it is the truth.)

As for myself, Alexis Krokas, until my own retirement two years ago I had been the owner of a restaurant. Nothing fancy, you understand, just a small lunchroom with sixteen stools in a factory district that kept me alive for thirty years until it was time to collect my social security.

Then there was Samson. Samson Leventis. He was our very close friend, a patron of the Parthenon coffeehouse where Louie and I drank mastiha every evening and danced to the bouzouki on Saturday nights. (We managed this feat in spite of Louie's weight and my wretched sciatica.)

Samson was a big man of about forty years, as strong a man as I had ever known. He owned the Zorah Wholesale Produce Company on Halsted Street and could open a crate of produce by shattering the wood with his fist. He had a voice as resonant as a clap of thunder. His clothing consisted mostly of mismatched trousers and coats and he never wore a tie. The most striking thing about him, however, was his thick black hair that he wore so long it concealed most of his ears and curled like a horse's nape over the collar of his shirt.

We were always pleased when Samson joined us and on that night in the spring when he came to our table in the Parthenon, we greeted him warmly.

"Your bottle is empty," Samson said as he sat down. "Waiting too long between bottles causes gas." He called out in his resonant voice and almost instantly old Barba Niko shot out of the shadows with a full bottle of mastiha. Samson filled our glasses.

For a long strange moment afterwards he was silent. Louie and I felt a curious suspense and waited for him to speak.

"My old friends," Samson said finally, "I think for the first time in my barren forty years of life, I am truly in love."

Frankly, I was startled and Louie was stunned. Respecting good sense and reason as I did, I had, of course, remained a bachelor. Louie had been married once for three years and his experience had been a calamity. His wife, a harpy who outweighed him by sixty pounds blacked both his eyes at least once a month and on one frightful occasion even kicked him down a flight of stairs. When he had despaired of ever attaining freedom he received a joyous parole. She deserted him to run away with a Turkish coffee salesman who had the brazen nerve to return to Louie three weeks later and plead with him to take back his wife. Louie hastily put his case in the competent hands of another mutual friend, counselor Pericles Piniotis (the poor devil suffered an untimely death when struck by an ambulance backing up) and achieved a separation. His tragic experience had completely unbalanced him on the subject of women and marriage.

"Well, is nobody going to speak?" Samson cried. "Are you both going to sit there dumb after such news?"

Louie was still so badly shaken he could not answer. I felt it was up to me to observe the amenities. "Congratulations, Samson," I said. "Who is the lucky woman?"

"Not a woman," Samson said fervently. "A goddess."

Louie rose from the table with one hand across his stomach. Samson reached up and pulled him back down. "Sit, old friend, and drink!" he cried. "I know how delighted you must be for me." He caught me watching him and with one of his massive fingers gave me a playful poke in the chest that almost caved in my ribs. "How about it, Alexis?" he laughed. "Does an old bachelor like you know anything about great love?"

"Certainly," I said slightly huffed. "Love is a strong affection for a member of the opposite sex. Like Dante for Beatrice and Abelard for Heloise." I spoke these references modestly.

"Those are Turkish names to me," Samson shook his head. "I'm talking about real love and not fairy tales."

"Those people were real," I said.

"Is that right?" he asked and his interest was quickened. "That Dinty something or other must be an Irishman, eh?"

"An Italian," I said. "He was a man who loved a woman from the time she was a very young girl. He wrote poetry to her all his life and never said a word to her, never spoke to her."

"The only way," Louie said somberly.

Samson stared at me in disbelief. "Never spoke to her? What kind of nonsense is that? Of course he spoke to her."

"No," I said firmly. "He died without ever speaking a single word to her."

"God bless that man," Louie said.

Samson's cheeks quivered. "Where did you hear that?" he asked.

"That is something I learned back in school."

Samson slammed the table with his fist and made bottles and glasses jump. "That makes me glad I never went beyond the fourth grade!" he cried. "That's sheer nonsense."

"Let me tell you about my wife," Louie said. "My first mistake was talking to her."

"What about the other fellow?" Samson asked me. "That Abe something or other?"

"Abelard," I said. "He was a priest who fell in love with a beautiful girl and ran off with her."

Louie made his cross in dismay.

"That's more like it," Samson gave a long low whistle. "A priest too. That took guts. What happened?"

"Her kinsmen became angry," I said, "and sent some men to take revenge on Abelard. They severed certain parts of his body."

"I knew something terrible would happen," Louie said.

"What parts?" Samson asked. "His legs? Arms? Hands?" I shrugged grimly. A look of horror swept Samson's face.

"The butchers!" he cried in outrage. "The bloody butchers!"

"Violence and women," Louie said bitterly.

"In the end," I said, "Heloise became a nun and Abelard went into a monastery."

"Of course," Samson said with compassion. "What else could the poor devils do?" He sat in somber silence for a moment. "My own beloved is a widow whose husband has been dead five years now," he said gravely. "She moved here from Cleveland six months ago to buy the Sorek Bakery on Harrison Street. She bakes the bread and cakes in the kitchen. That's how I first saw her, her face flushed from the heat of the ovens, and flour smudged across her dark lovely hair. I tell you, old friends, I haven't been the same since." He made a gesture of resignation. "It took a week of going into the store before I mustered up the courage to talk to her. You know I am a pretty rough sort, not much for fancy ways, and enough to scare a real lady when I meet one."

"You are highly regarded," I reassured him and Louie nodded quickly in agreement. "You can outdance and outdrink any man on the street. All of us respect you."

"Old warriors like yourselves," he said, "but a woman measures things differently. I've been seeing her for two months now. I go and sit with her in the kitchen while she works. Sometimes she lets me take her to dinner. She seems to like me but she also says I lack appreciation of the finer things, that I dress like a bum, and that I look like a shaggy bear with my hair down my neck." He sighed and rose to his feet to leave. "Maybe I could change," he said somberly. "For a woman such as the Widow Delilah, I think I would do anything." He nodded in farewell and walked slowly to the door.

Louie moaned softly. "Delilah!" he said and struck his fist on the table in a puerile imitation of Samson.

"Do you know her?"

"No," he shook his head in distress, "but in the Bible the mighty Samson was destroyed by the wicked Delilah."

"Don't be a fool," I said impatiently. "The names are mere coincidence."

"Any woman is a calamity," Louie said, "but one named Delilah for a man named Samson!" He slapped his cheeks with his palms in despair.

"Louie, listen to me," I said sternly. "Get a grip on your head."

"We must save him," Louie said. "He is too noble a man to be destroyed by an unscrupulous woman." He paused, breathing heavily. "I must go to see the Widow."

"Just like that," I laughed wryly. "You will go and see the Widow and ask her not to marry Samson because her name is Delilah. She will throw you on your crooked head."

Louie rose and drew himself to his full, plump and quivering five feet and two inches. "I consider Samson almost a son," he said with emotion. "I must make an effort to save him."

I sighed. I knew the density of that man's head and how impervious he could be to reason. "You will make a mess of this affair," I said. "Since you insist on meddling, I will have to go along and prevent you making a greater fool of yourself than you already are."

Early the next morning Louie and I met at the Sorek Bakery. We stood for a moment outside the window laden with frosted cakes and sugared rolls.

"Now let me do the talking," I warned him. "If you have a comment, make it sensible and brief, if that isn't asking too much."

Louie agreed uneasily. We entered the warm little store scented with the aroma of freshly baked bread. A young slim girl worked behind the counter.

"We have come to call on the Widow Delilah," I said. "We do not wish to interrupt her work but we would be grateful for just a few moments of her time."

The girl retired to the kitchen and returned to motion us around the counter. We walked into the kitchen and met the Widow Delilah.

She was a tall and stately woman in her early thirties. Her face was a flawless ivory oval within a frame of thick black hair gathered into a great bun at the back of her head. Her dark eyes had a startling brightness. There were stains of flour upon the apron which rose and swelled across her majestic breasts.

For a moment I thoroughly appreciated Samson's admiration for her. I gave her a warm smile. When I caught Louie watching me with suspicion, I sobered quickly.

"Widow Delilah," I said politely, "this gentleman is Louie Anastis and I am Alexis Krokas. We are very close friends of Samson Leventis. He has spoken of you with great respect. Since we happened to be passing we thought we would just drop in and introduce ourselves."

"We regard Samson as if he was our son," Louie said ominously.

At the mention of Samson, a deeper pinch of red appeared in the Widow Delilah's already flushed cheeks. "I am pleased to meet you," she said in a husky voice and her lips parted as if they were glistening halves of a ripe plum. She raised the tray of bread and pushed it into the oven with a supple grace. She turned back to us wiping her fingers on a cloth. "I am very fond of Samson," she said.

"Are you going to marry him?" Louie asked in a shrill voice.

A startled confusin swept her cheeks. I gave Louie a hard censuring look and spoke quickly. "Forgive Mr. Anastis," I said. "He cares greatly for Samson and sometimes this causes him to speak bluntly."

She made a gentle gesture of forgiveness. "No apology is necessary," she said. "Your concern for your dear friend speaks well for both of you. You will permit me to speak just as frankly. I am very fond of Samson but I am afraid that I could never marry him."

"Never?" Louie asked eagerly.

"Why?" I asked puzzled. "I don't understand."

"My husband, God bless his departed soul, was a good man," she said quietly. "With his insurance I moved here from Cleveland and bought this store. I am lonely, very lonely sometimes and I would not object to marrying again except that it must be to a man interested in music and art, the things that I am interested in. I am afraid I could not endure a rough and disorderly existence."

"Samson is rough and disorderly, all right," Louie agreed with satisfaction.

"He is a strong man, true," I said. "But he has a purity of spirit as well. He appears unruly and fierce but I have never known him to commit an unkind act against any man or woman."

"He never went beyond the fourth grade," Louie said looking at me indignantly.

"The neighborhood children adore him," I said. "After school they stop by his business for a banana or a peach. You may think, my dear Widow, that you know Samson but until you have seen him teasing and cavorting with a group of delighted children, you cannot know the real man."

"He drinks a great deal," Louie said shrilly. "Two, often three bottles of mastiha a night."

"He is a champion of the weak," I went on swept by growing enthusiasm. "When hoodlums threatened Gavaras, the tailor, and poured acid on his racks of clothing, it was Samson who drove them off Halsted Street. Three men he thrashed that day in a fight that will be remembered for years. They have never dared return."

"He fights a great deal," Louie said loudly and wrung his hands fretfully. "Every weekend, sometimes."

"Let us not forget the baskets he distributes to the needy on Christmas and Thanksgiving," I said. "Many families would go hungry if it were not for Samson."

The Widow Delilah listened in silence. When I paused finally out of breath, she raised her hand in a soft gesture of concession. "I did not know all these things about him," she said, and it was evident she was moved. "He is such a loud and boisterous man, one would never conceive of such goodness and gentleness being a part of him as well."

"Most of the time he is pretty wild," Louie said desperately. "Ask the priest what he thinks of Samson and he will make his cross."

"It speaks well of Samson that he has such loyal friends," she said slowly and nodded gratefully at Louie, "such honest friends willing to admit his faults as well as his virtues. I am sincerely impressed." She offered us her hand in a gracious farewell.

We emerged into the street and Louie trembled in agitation.

"She told us she could never consider Samson," I said to reassure him. "How could I malign him after that rejection? Louie, believe me, I am quite sure this woman was speaking the truth when she told us she would never consider Samson."

It was less than a week after our visit to the bakery when we were sitting one evening at our table in the Parthenon. Louie and I had maintained an uneasy truce since speaking to the Widow Delilah. I was sipping my mastiha slowly and scratching my ear when a wild triumphant bellow shattered the darkness of the coffeehouse. Louie was nearly blown off his chair.

The wild bellow rang out again and a big man came stamping between the tables waving his arms like windmills. It was Samson and he came almost at a run to our table. "There you are!" he cried.

The old men from the nearby tables gathered around our own. "Hey, Samson," a graybeard called. "Did you find a pearl in one of your bananas?"

Samson laughed loudest of all. "I don't need a pearl," he cried, "when I have friends such as these two."

"What have we done?" Louie asked fearfully, sensing disaster.

"What have you done?" Samson shouted. "I will tell everyone what you have done! By your loyalty and devotion to me you greatly impressed the Widow Delilah. She regarded me in a new and kinder light. Tonight she consented to be my wife!"

Louie's terrible moan was lost in the roar of approval from the old men around our table but I heard it clearly. Samson started to pull Louie and me from our chairs. "Come with me, old friends," he said. "Tonight I buy drinks for everybody and you will drink the best brandy old Barba Niko has in his cellar."

"You go ahead, Samson," I smiled faintly. "Louie and I will be right along."

He started toward the bar dragging a half dozen of the old men with him. Louie and I were left alone. He stared at me as if I had committed some infamous crime. "You convinced her," he said in a choked voice. "You sealed his doom."

"You are an idiot," I whispered angriy. "A woman isn't convinced by a few words of praise to marry a man unless she intended to marry him all along. She concealed her true feelings. And what if they do marry? The trouble with you, Louie, is that you let one deplorable female sour you on all women. You should have made your wife understand from the beginning that you were the boss."

"Are you mad!" Louie said in a shocked voice. "That monster outweighed me by sixty pounds!"

"Louie," I said more gently, "it depends upon the man. Can you imagine any woman getting the better of a man as courageous and strong as Samson? Can you imagine such an absurdity?" I laughed at how ridiculous the possibility seemed but Louie did not crack even a glimmer of a smile.

"Hey, Alexis! Louie!" Samson shouted from the bar.

I rose from my chair. "Now cheer up," I said to Louie. "Let us go and drink to Samson's nuptials."

"I would rather stop breathing!" Louie said. He rose and fled to the door, waddling slightly under his burden of fat. I went to the bar alone and told Samson that Louie had been overcome by the joy of the announcement and had to leave.

We did not see Samson again for almost six weeks following that night. Two weeks after he came to thank us so jubilantly, the Widow Delilah and he were married in Cleveland. Their honeymoon included a week at Niagara Falls. The first awareness we had of their return was when Delilah phoned us at the Parthenon one Friday evening and invited Louie and myself for dinner the following evening. Louie had still not subdued his resentment and apprehension and was reluctant to go until I convinced him it would be a gross affront to Samson.

The next night we dressed in our Sunday suits and walked to the apartment on Blue Island which had been Delilah's before she married. Ignoring Louie's disapproval I carried a small bouquet of flowers for the new bride.

We rang the bell of their apartment. A moment later Samson's voice answered faintly from the mouthpiece beside the mailbox.

"It is Alexis and Louie," I said loudly. "Welcome back, Samson."

The buzzer sounded and I opened the door and started briskly up the stairs. Louie came slowly and heavily behind me. On the third floor Samson stood waiting in the doorway of the apartment.

"Hello, old friend," he said and his voice sounded low and subdued but there was another apartment on the landing and I thought perhaps a neighbor was ill.

"Hello, Samson," I whispered.

There was a single dim light in the hall, a small bulb on the wall near the stairs and I could not see Samson clearly. I noticed with surprise that he wore a white shirt with a tie looped around his throat as if it were a noose. He seemed to be swaying slightly and when I looked down at his feet I did not see the old cracked wide black brogues he had always worn but a glittering pair of two-tones that tapered to an incredibly sharp tip. Samson swung open the door of the apartment and stepped back to allow me to enter. In the bright ceiling light I saw his head for the first time and I almost cried out in shock and consternation.

The great black tangled forest of hair that had curled over his ears and matted around his collar was gone, shorn from his scalp as if he were a sheep, leaving a short bristling stubble over an expanse of pale flesh. For the first time in twenty years I saw his ears and they were crooked and pointed like the ears of a sad dog and skewered at an incredible angle from his head.

Louie, breathing hard from his ascent, stepped in the door and when he saw Samson, he staggered as if he had been dealt a stunning blow.

"Some slight changes," Samson laughed nervously, and his big hand fumbled uneasily at his head as if in futile search for the mop that was no longer there. "Looks neater, eh?" He spoke with the pathetic eagerness of a child wishing to be consoled.

"Certainly, Samson," I said quickly.

Louie could only stare at him in horror. Fortunately, at that moment, Delilah swept down the hall to greet us. She was dressed in a long white gown, her hair coiled in great thick braids about her head. Somehow the sheared scalp of Samson served to accentuate the vitality of her own abundant locks. From her ears hung silver earrings in the shape of slim glistening knives.

"So good to see you, dear friends," she said warmly. "And what lovely flowers? Aren't the flowers lovely, Samson?"

Samson nodded somberly.

"Shall we go and sit down?" Delilah said. "Dinner will be served in a moment. Samson, put the flowers in water. There is a vase in the kitchen. This way, gentlemen."

Samson started down the hall taking short mincing steps as if he were practicing a dance for the wretched ballet. Louie watched Samson in agony and I had to pull at his arm to follow Delilah.

In a few moments we sat down to dinner at a table covered by a fine lace cloth and set with delicate china and crystal. But in spite of the splendid roast lamb with browned potatoes, the whole meal was a calamitous series of fumblings and admonitions.

"Not that fork, love," Delilah said to Samson, "the other one. Stir with the spoon, love," she said. "Don't hold it as if it is a stein of beer." She spoke gently but with a vein of iron in her voice.

Even Louie and I became apprehensive. Although she did not correct us, she watched us. A number of times I hesitated and let my food grow cold because I could not be sure what bloody piece of silverware to use. Louie seemed to lose control completely once and, missing his mouth with his fork, jabbed a piece of lamb into his cheek.

But I forgot my own discomfort in watching Samson. He sat huddled in misery in his chair, the bright lights burning down upon his bereaved head, not daring to pick up a glass or a fork without receiving an approving nod from Delilah. Every swallow of food seemed to stick somewhere in his throat.

At the end of that cursed meal we were allowed to relax slightly over small cups of sweet coffee. Samson mustered the courage to ask a few questions on his own.

"How are things at the Parthenon, Alexis?"

"Everybody misses you, Samson," I said eagerly. "The dancing is not the same without you. Next Saturday night they are bringing in a new bouzouki player from New York. There will be some wild dancing. Come and join us."

Samson started to nod with enthusiasm and then looked at his wife. Delilah smiled with a slight shrug of regret. "Our Saturday nights are taken for the next six weeks," she said. "Samson and I have reserved tickets on those evenings for the opera."

"The opera!" Louie gasped. "Samson?"

I coughed to cover his confusion. "The opera is very cultural," I said stiffly. "The very best people go to the opera."

Delilah nodded in firm agreement. She shook a gently reproving finger at Louie and myself and with a peremptory movement of her wrist included Samson. "You have all spent far too many nights in the coffeehouse," she said. "There are pleasures far above the bouzouki and bottles of mastiha. There are symphony concerts and the art galleries downtown. I want Samson to learn to appreciate these delights he has been denied up to now. Perhaps the four of us can visit some of these galleries and attend some of the concerts together."

"Certainly," I said, and then I pushed back my chair and rose quickly. "At the moment, however, I have just remembered there is a meeting of our lodge chapter this evening. Please forgive me if I run right off because I am late already."

"I am so sorry you must leave," Delilah said. "I planned for us to listen to some classical records for a while."

Louie rose with a bounce from his chair. "I must go to the meeting too," he said. "Forgive me."

We said goodnight and walked to the door. Samson came behind us. We stood waiting while he hobbled and swayed to join us. We stared at his feet and he smiled uneasily. "They're the latest style," he said. "They're my size too." He looked warily in the direction of the dining-room. "Those damn tips," he whispered. "They're built for men with two toes instead of five." He made a gesture of resignation. "I'll get used to them, someday, I guess."

"If you don't go lame first," Louie said in a choked voice. With a tight forlorn wave of his hand he started heavily down the stairs.

I gave Samson's hand a reassuring squeeze.

"She's a grand girl, Alexis," he said fervently. "She wants what is best for me. I try to go along with her. It's for my own good, you know."

I started down the stairs. Samson hung over the railing. "Say hello to all the boys," he called after me in a plaintive voice. "I'll stop by . . ." there was a wretched pause, " . . . one of these days."

"I'll tell them, Samson," I said, and there was a tightness in my throat. "I'll tell them, old friend."

When I reached the street, Louie waited for me. I expected tearful recriminations but the whole evening had been such a shock, he was apparently having difficulty collecting his senses.

"Just like in the Bible," he said, struggling for breath. "Samson was shorn of his hair by Delilah and lost all his strength. It happened just like in the Bible."

"You are an idiot!" I cried furiously. "Stop talking nonsense! The whole business is sheer coincidence!"

I turned away and Louie reached out and grabbed my arm.

"It will be all right, Alexis, don't worry," he said hoarsely. "Remember what happened when Samson's hair grew back? He pulled down the pillars of the temple and destroyed Delilah and the Philistines." He nodded in a spasm of delight. "It will be all right! Samson will triumph in the end!"

I looked at him in shock. He stood there with his plump cheeks quivering and revelation rising like mist from his pores.

"Louie," I said, and my voice trembled, "Louie . . ." I closed my eyes and had a sudden and bitter vision of those crooked ears and that naked and wretched head. I felt my senses rattled and my reason succumb with a groan.

"Enough, Louie," I spoke in a shaken whisper. "Go to the church and light a candle for Samson. Light one for me too. Ask the priest for a prayer."

"Right!" Louie cried fervently. "At once!"

I turned and started hurriedly away. "Where are you going?" he hollered shrilly.

I did not answer. I assembled my quivering legs and set a furious pace for the Parthenon, staying well beneath the bright beam of the streetlamps.

When reason is staggered by dread and superstition, when sanity is routed by necromancy and spirits from the vasty deep, no recourse remains for a reasonable man but to drown the whole catastrophic dilemma in a bottle of mastiha.

In a world of fools, the lout is king. . . .

My mother was a compassionate woman who devoted a considerable portion of her life to serving needy families and unfortunate individuals. One of those she aided was a lonely little seamstress in her late fifties suffering from a terminal illness. After we had finished a holiday dinner at our family table, my mother would fill a small basket with food for the seamstress, who lived in a furnished room some miles away. I resented having to leave the party and deliver the basket.

Later I found myself reluctantly involved with driving the woman back and forth to the hospital for treatments. When she required drugs for which she could not pay, I used my own money, begrudgingly again, because a free lancer's income was precarious.

When I complained to my mother about the time and expense involved in caring for someone who was, after all, a stranger, she reprimanded me. "You want to write about life," she said. "This dying woman is life."

Of course my mother was right. When the seamstress died, a few weeks later in a ward at the county hospital, moved and remorseful I wrote "Zena Dawn." When I sold the story I recouped many times over whatever that poor woman had cost me in money and time.

ZENA DAWN

There was a sound Zena Dawn heard early in the morning before daylight. In the beginning she thought it belonged to a dream but afterwards there were many nights she lay awake and heard it too. As if a strange wind, restless and cold, swept fleetingly through her room. But her door was closed and a ventilator locked in her single window. There was no opening through which a draft might enter.

Once she heard the sound she could no longer sleep. She drew the spread tightly to her throat and held herself aware of each long and silent minute.

The night is so long, she thought. The night is so quiet. Even a sudden fall of rain against the window comes as a relief. Even the murmur of the pigeons mourning in the cornices and the cry of a prowling cat help me remember I am not alone.

She was grateful for Mrs. Cohen's husband, a baker who rose early, a heavy-bodied man who tried to walk quietly. But his bulk and the absence of carpeting on the stairs defined his steps. His passing raised a shade on the night and soon the first in a series of alarm clocks ruffled the silence with a thin and agitated humming. A baby in the flat above hers wailed a hungry cry for food. Zena Dawn was able to sleep again knowing that the long night was over.

She woke to full daylight and the strong loud voice of Clara calling to her from the basement landing of the building next door. She rose from her bed and slipped into her robe feeling the stiff twinges of pain. She walked unsteadily to the window and raised the shade and waved.

Clara was a rampart-breasted Black woman in her late fifties who owned the junk shop in the basement of the building next door. She lived in three rooms in the back of the store with a half-dozen children she raised alone since her husband deserted her.

"Good Lord!" Clara hollered and her voice carried clearly through the ventilator in the window. "Woman, you going to stay in bed all day? I'm on my third pot of coffee and the sweet rolls from Jenny is dripping sugar. Now put out the cups and I'm coming."

Zena Dawn turned eagerly from the window anticipating the visit which was a morning ritual for them both. She went to the mirror over the dresser and combed her hair. As she swept the strands back from her cheeks she saw how illness had ravaged her face and hidden her eyes in dark and solemn pits. She turned quickly from the mirror and walked to the small table that she covered with a clean cloth. From the shelf above the table she took down a pair of decorative cups and saucers. She had only a moment left to fill a pitcher with milk when she heard the heavy step of Clara on the stairs.

Clara entered like a wild woman clutching a pot of steaming coffee in one hand and a bag of sweet rolls in the other.

"Gangway!" Clara cried. "On the way up here I run over two hags and burned hell out of a third!" She laughed boisterously and went rapidly to the table and poured the hot black coffee into the cups. "Get it while it's hot!" She waved Zena Dawn to the table and briskly opened the bag. "And wait till you taste them sweet rolls."

Zena Dawn sat down and placed the napkin carefully across her lap. "It smells good," she said. "Clara, the coffee certainly smells good this morning."

"You say that every morning," Clara said.

"I mean it every morning," Zena Dawn shook her head earnestly. "But this morning it smells especially good."

Clara tore a sweet roll in half with her big hands and took a large bite. She chewed vigorously and swallowed with pleasure. "Course it smells good," she said. "Clara Sullivan makes the best damn coffee in the city."

From the sidewalk below the window came a shrill cry.

"Can't leave me alone for a minute," Clara said in a vexed voice. She walked from the table and flung open the window impatiently.

"Ma," the voice of her eldest boy called. "Ma, a man here wants to buy the iron eagle. I told him it was two dollar and he say he not going to give no more than one dollar."

"One dollar!" Clara hollered. "You tell that man that eagle belonged to a lady so rich and elegant I be ashamed to sell it for cheap pickings like one dollar. You tell him I rather throw it away or give it to one of you kids for a wedding present when you old enough to marry."

"He hears you, Ma," the boy called. "He putting on his hat."

"Wait!" Clara shouted. "Tell him if he pleased to pay a dollar and a half he can take that fine eagle home right now."

"He going, Ma," the boy said. "He got one foot out the door and the other in the air."

"Tell him to leave that dollar!" Clara screamed and her broad rump shook in agitation. "Get that dollar and give him the eagle. Clyde, you hear me! You make that sale or I beat your seat with a barrel stave. You hear!"

An anxious moment of silence passed and then the boy's voice floated up in triumph. "I got the dollar, Ma. The man got the eagle."

Clara drew her head back in and closed the window down to the ventilator loudly.

"That boy be my death," she said and returned to the table. "I try to teach him all I know and make a trader out of him but he don't know which end is up." She motioned at Zena Dawn's plate. "All that time," she said grievously. "You make only one chintzy little bite into that delicious sweet roll. You got to keep up your strength, honey, you all bones now."

"I'm not hungry," Zena Dawn said. "I love the sweet rolls but I'm just not hungry." She looked anxiously at Clara wishing to please her but unable to make the food go down her throat.

"You had much pain again?" Clara asked in a softer voice. "Did you pass another real bad night?"

"The pain wasn't bad at all last night," Zena Dawn said, and tried to speak cheerfully. "When I fell asleep I had a dream. I was somewhere in the sunshine, Clara, and could smell fresh flowers just as real as if I stood in a garden."

"The way you dream," Clara marveled. "And the things you dream."

"When I was a little girl I used to dream of flowers too," Zena Dawn said. "My father would kiss me goodnight and I would smell the flowers of his shop on his clothes and our house was always full of flowers." She paused and looked shyly at her pale fingers on the cloth of the table. "I've told you so many times before."

"Tell me again!" Clara said. "I like for you to tell me again!"

"Our house was full of flowers," Zena Dawn said. "Roses and sunflowers and chrysanthemums. Clara, it was always so beautiful."

"I bet it was," Clara said in awe. "You were lucky." She clucked her tongue. "Flowers all the time. Imagine that."

"I loved my mother," Zena Dawn said, "but my father was more dear. He picked out my name. He called me Zena Dawn because it sounded like the name of a flower."

"It sure does," Clara agreed earnestly.

"He said my name would always be a charm," Zena Dawn said, "I would have many friends and people to love and I would never be lonely." She grew suddenly pensive. "That was so long ago. Mother died when I was still living at home. But when my father died I was far away and I rode a train for two days and a night to go to his funeral but when I got there they had buried him. And all the flowers were wilted too."

"Eat some of that sweet roll now," Clara said vigorously. "You listen to me and eat some of that sweet roll."

"Bawl me out, Clara," Zena Dawn smiled. "It makes me feel good when you bawl me out. When I get better and can sew again I will make you a dress, a beautiful red dress that you can wear to church on Sundays. I promise you that."

"A red dress?" Clara said pleased. "It's been a long time since Clara had a new dress." She winked at Zena Dawn. "That's the way to talk," she said. "Think on tomorrow instead of what happened years ago."

"It's hard sometimes," Zena Dawn said. "How different we expect things to be. I was married to Theron for only three years when he was killed. He will be dead nineteen years this September. We had so short a time together. And the years have passed so quickly since then."

"We both lost our men," Clara said. "But your man went to heaven and my man just went." She paused and shook her head. "I married a real prize. I waited and thought carefully and then I picked the laziest, most no-count man I could find and I married him. He was big and sassy and loved to slap me across the seat." She laughed huskily in spite of herself. "But he was no good out of bed. He was an evil man that done every sin you can think of and even made up a few more." She sighed with pleasure in the recollection. "One day he up and left me. He left me with six kids. That man was evil and no good but for a long time I missed him. To this day whenever I smell cheap gin I think of him."

She rose from the table and carried the cups and saucers to the small sink. Zena Dawn rose to help her and a sharp quick pain in her body made her cry out.

Clara watched her in concern. "When is the doctor coming back?"

Zena Dawn sat down again and placed her hands with the fingers open squarely upon the cloth of the table. She breathed slowly and fearfully against the pain rippling within her. "He won't be back until the day after tomorrow. He told me to keep taking the pills."

"That's right," Clara said firmly. "Keep taking them medicines. They help you get better and keep the pain from becoming too bad." She peered closely at the assortment of bottles on the shelf. "You got any of them red pain killers left?"

"I've got some left," Zena Dawn said.

"When you run out I send Clyde to get you some more," Clara said.

"I won't let you spend any more money on me!" Zena Dawn said. "You have your own family and all the other things you do for me is enough."

"You just shut up," Clara said with rough tenderness. "When you well enough to begin to sew, you can pay me back." She stared sharply at Zena Dawn. "Any of the relief money left?" she asked. "Now don't tell me no lie."

"Only the rent money," Zena Dawn said. "Mr. Mitchell is coming for that tomorrow."

"Then he be here tomorrow," Clara said grimly. "He come on his black horse and with his black pocketbook open as wide as a whale's mouth. He come blowing his rent-horn like a wild jackass out of hell." She stopped pleased as Zena Dawn began to laugh. "It's true!" Clara cried vigorously to encourage the laughter. "If the Lord took it into his mind to wipe out the earth with forty days and forty nights of rain, just before we all drown, that bastard come swimming by for his rent."

Zena Dawn laughed so hard she had to hold her ribs. Clara watched her with pleasure. "Laugh!" Clara said fiercely. "Laugh! When you most feel like crying, that's the time to laugh!"

"Clara, Clara," Zena Dawn said in wonder as she caught her breath. "How can you laugh when you've got the children to worry about, to feed and to clothe, and the store to run, and me to look after?"

"I got a few more things even than that," Clara said with a tight edge to her voice. "I got a boy whose teeth coming in so crooked they look like they belong in two different mouths. Doctor says he needs wires around them and for the price I swear I could buy ten miles of fence. And I got two feet, two damn feet that raise corns and calluses quicker'n the landlord can raise the rent. And I just got a letter from my daughter, the growed-up one, that married the iceman. He beating her up every Saturday night now and she want to bring her baby and stay with me."

"O Clara," Zena Dawn said in quick compassion. "I'm so sorry for her."

"That's all right," Clara shook her head with a savage resolve. "I told her to come. We make room for her and the baby. Always room for a few more." She brushed the crumbs from the bodice of her dress and looked sternly at Zena Dawn. "Now you do like you're supposed to," she said. "I'll see you a little later."

Zena Dawn was silent for a moment. She struggled for words to encompass the measure of Clara's devotion. Clara cut off her need to speak with a quick wave of her broad-palmed hand.

"There ain't no need to say nothing," Clara said. "As for looking after you, I do that because I want to. Maybe," she shrugged, "maybe because you're a white woman and there ain't no white man nor white woman showed up to help you." She smiled in a gentle jest. "Maybe it's just your fancy name. Zena Dawn. Maybe that's it. You got to live fifty-seven years with a washerwoman name like Clara to understand that." She picked up the coffee pot and started briskly to the door. She paused with her hand upon the knob. "You call me now if you get bad pain," she said. "Just holler by the window."

When she had gone, Zena Dawn felt as if all the light and life in the room had fled as well.

At lunch Clara sent her a bowl of soup and some crackers which she barely managed to finish. Later Clyde brought up the afternoon paper. Zena Dawn read for a while and in the late afternoon the sharp stabbing pain returned. She went quickly to the bed and pressed her arms tightly across her stomach. She held her breath because she could feel the walls crumbling again, the tissue-thin walls that gave way before the bleeding. She felt her life draining out with her blood. She managed to rise from the bed and with a faint cry of despair stumbled to the ledge above the table and took down one of the bottles of pills. With a flare of panic she saw only one was left. She filled a glass with water and flooded it down. She went back to the bed and lay down and pressed her face into the pillow.

She felt a pounding in her forehead, an ache behind her eyes. Her breath rose in little bubbles to pop in her ears.

How lightly I lie upon the springs, she thought, how fragile is my hold upon the earth. A gust of strong wind could blow me away. She turned on her back and stared gravely at the ceiling. It was blue by day but in the twilight all color seemed bled from it, and it loomed over her head as if it were the cold stone of a tomb.

She tried furiously to form the images of memories. Once when I was a child, she thought. But she could go no further. One memory fell upon another. One tumbled quickly upon the next. They would not assemble into any order.

A minute passed and then another. Or was it an hour? She fell asleep. A great starburst of pain woke her. She shrieked and pulled at the sheet. Despair flooded over her. She cried out to her father. The room door opened and Clara stormed in.

"Damn you," Clara said. "I told you to call me. Damn you, white woman, with your fancy name!" Then in quick remorse she raised the slim frail body and held her fiercely to her own great breasts and rocked her gently back and forth.

"Clara!" Zena Dawn cried and she looked in terror at the ceiling. "I want to go to the hospital. Maybe they can help me there."

"Just hold up," Clara said. "There ain't nothing the hospital can do for you that old Clara can't do."

"Don't leave me alone," Zena Dawn whispered. "Clara, don't leave me alone. I am dying and don't leave me alone."

"Only a minute, honey," Clara said in a soft and shaken voice. "Only one minute to phone the doctor and I'll come back and I won't leave you again."

The doctor came a few hours later. He sat beside the bed and briefly examined Zena Dawn. She watched him from her eyes that were crusted by pain. He filled a syringe and gave her a shot. He closed his bag and rose to leave. Clara followed him to the hall outside the door.

The doctor looked tired and out of sorts. "Something might keep her alive a few more days," he said. "But it's better if she goes fast." He turned away and Clara caught at his sleeve.

"She wants to go to the hospital," Clara said. "She thinks they might help her there."

"That won't do any good," the Doctor said quietly.

A sudden anger flared in Clara's voice. "They don't want her to die there," she said. "They want poor folks to do their dying at home."

"Everybody is dying, mother," the Doctor said. "The rich and the poor and the weak and the strong. Everybody is dying a little all the time."

"I know," Clara said and her anger left as quickly as it had come. "God knows that is the truth."

She sat with Zena Dawn through the night. In the dark still hours after midnight she rose at intervals from her chair beside the bed and stretched against the stiffness cramping her body. She went a number of times to the window and listened for a sound from the basement next door.

Zena Dawn stirred uneasily on the bed and Clara took her a little water and moistened her lips. Her face was loose and dark, changed somehow, and her lips trembled in drugged and uneven sleep.

The hours passed slowly. Standing by the window Clara heard the cooing of the pigeons in the cornices. Somewhere a dog barked a sharp sound upon the night. She sat down in the chair and closed her eyes and dozed. Mrs. Cohen's husband woke her as he left for work, his steps heavy and clear upon the stairs. An alarm clock hummed down the long corridor. A baby raised a plaintive cry.

Clara walked to the window and raised the shade. The first faint gray of morning hung across the roofs of the city. A pigeon took flight with a harsh beating of its wings. She peered down at the back of her store to make sure everything was still quiet. She went back to the bed to cover Zena Dawn and saw how still she lay within the folds of sheet. Clara shook her head gratefully and pressed her hands tightly against her breasts.

The back door of the store downstairs opened and the voice of one of her children rose to her. She walked to the ventilator and called that she was coming. She turned for a moment back to the bed.

"You don't worry no more now, Zena Dawn," she said quietly. "You got a place all set for you. Old Clara been paying on a burial plot for you too, right next to me, and you don't worry no more now." She wiped fiercely at her eyes with the back of her hand. "There ain't going to be no more pain and no more bleeding and no more white folks not caring whether you live or die. Ain't going to be no more stale sweet rolls and no more landlord beating on the door come the first of the month. Ain't going to be no more relief checks that run out the end of the second week." She paused and struck her breasts violently with her fists. "You got a place next to me and they ain't going to put you in no pauper's grave nor cut you up. You got a place to rest and long as I live I see there is a flower on your head." She finished and shook her head in despair. "You the lucky one now," she said. "The rest of us got to go on living."

From the store another child wailed for her and a second took up the chorus of complaint. She turned and walked to the door. She looked back once and made a mute final gesture of consolation toward the body of Zena Dawn.

I tend to resist the category "ethnic writer," since it is often used in a pejorative sense or to suggest that the work is limited in domain. Since most of my material is based on a Greek background, the heroes and the history of Greece are important to me. From that past I move to the immigrant descendants of those heroes, small merchants and shopkeepers, who look back with longing toward a golden, seemingly inviolate landscape and time.

If I were a writer of American Indian origins, I would draw upon the rich social patterns and cultural mores of the great tribes. Studying their myths and histories, I know I would unearth the same passion for the perpetuation of a tradition, the same nostalgia, I find now in the Greek. I wrote "The Victim" as an example of what I mean.

A writer must write about the things he knows, utilizing those inherited resources of the generations that produced him. That is only a beginning, however; from there he must contend with love, hate, vengeance, betrayal, and death, those emotions bridging the barriers of race and tongue. In the end, whether the stories involve Greeks, Indians, Jews, Poles, Germans, or the black and white southerners of Yoknapatawpha County, those things that alone can make good writing, as William Faulkner said, "are the problems of the human heart in confict with itself."

THE VICTIM

Standing in the shadow of a pillar beside the tracks on which the steaming train had just come to a stop, Lenny watched the travelers descend from the coaches and then saw his father. From that distance Charley Hawk did not appear changed at all in the seventeen years since Lenny had last seen him. His hair was white and straight as it had been and he looked just as tall and lean. For a moment he was lost behind a rack of baggage and then he reappeared walking with a grave and unhurried gait up the ramp. As he neared the pillar where Lenny waited, he passed beneath a bright terminal light and for the first time his son saw his face clearly, an ancient mask modeled by death for very old age.

His skin was dark brown and tight across the bone and etched with a web of coarse wrinkles. There were pits at his temples that ran along gullies into the shriveled hollow of his mouth. His nose, always big, loomed now like the great scarred beak of an eagle above the crag of his jaw. He was dressed in a shabby and shapeless gray suit, a heavy cotton shirt buttoned at his throat, a pair of battered work shoes on his feet. His only baggage was a shoe box under his arm, tied with a piece of rope.

Lenny stepped out of the shadow of the pillar. The old man stopped and recognized him without a sign of greeting. Lenny saw that his eyes had not changed, they were still dark and savage and unafraid in the shadow of death.

"How you been, Pa?" Lenny made an effort to smile before the austere face and then abandoned it as useless. The old man answered with a brief, barely visible nod of his head.

"I got my car just outside the station," Lenny said. "I thought we could go to my house first and give you a chance to rest."

"Where's Jim's body?" the old man asked and his voice came in a low harsh rumble from his throat.

Lenny tried to meet his eyes and failing, turned away in irritation to smooth a wrinkle from the sleeve of his dark tailored blue suit. "He's at the Indian Center," he said. "We'll have him cremated in the morning the way you want and you can take his ashes back home."

"Take me to him now," Charley Hawk said.

He turned and began walking again up the ramp. Lenny came a step behind him, sneaking glances at the scarred and stony profile, the erectness of the body attached to the old and withered head. Lenny remembered him back on the Dakota reservation incredibly agile and lithe even in his sixties. He had to be close to ninety now, probably one of the last Sioux alive who could remember having hunted buffalo and fighting in the last Indian Wars against the cavalry. Even now that he showed his age he was still the damn stoic Indian, Lenny thought resentfully, more like the useless legends than the legends themselves.

He swung open the door of the car. The old man bent and moved in without a trace of stiffness. Lenny walked around to the other side and got in behind the wheel. He turned the key and with a roar the motor kicked over.

"Two hundred and sixty horsepower," Lenny could not refrain from a defiant show of pride.

Charley Hawk grunted. They drove in silence for a while. Lenny gave up expecting that the old man would ask any questions.

"He died in the hospital," Lenny said finally. "When I got word he was there I went over with my own Doctor but it was too late. He had been drunk and fallen asleep or passed out in some alley. The rain fell on him most of the night. By the time they found him, he was near frozen. He died a day later and that's when I sent you the wire."

Lenny paused and stared with irritation at the face that might have been chiseled out of stone.

"I know you blame me," he said defiantly. "He was always your favorite. You never cared what happened to me. But there was nothing I could do any more. I got him a job, two, maybe three times in the past three years. He couldn't stay sober long enough to hold one more than a week. I didn't even have to help him that much but I did. He didn't want to help himself."

"I knew he was dead," Charley Hawk said and he spoke quietly as if he were talking to himself. "I had a dream that night. A horde of black-tailed magpies attacked a sick and weak gelding. The gelding screamed. He raised his head straight up. The magpies dug in with their claws, picking at his eyes, gorging upon him until they pulled him down."

"Jesus Christ, Pa," Lenny said impatiently. "Your dreams had nothing to do with it. He drank himself to death and there was nothing anybody could have done to save him."

Charley Hawk was silent for a moment and then he made a harsh spitting sound with his mouth. Lenny gripped the wheel tightly between his fingers and pressed his foot down harder on the gas pedal. The car spurted forward and swept swiftly along between the terminals and factories on either side. The old man stared straight ahead, looking neither to the right or left.

"I had the same beginning as him," Lenny said bitterly. "I grew up on the reservation too. I went to the government school and when the war came I went into the army same as he did. Why couldn't he make his way like I did?" He curled his heavy lips and the words flared from between his teeth. "They told us both, 'Big Chief Wampum good only to sit by his tepee on U.S. 66 selling beads to tourists,' or 'keep whiskey away from an Indian, they go crazy on it,' or 'the only good Indian is a dead Indian.' " He drew a hard shaken breath. "He would always lash back, always fight, and that made them torment him more. I laughed with them and made a place for myself. I got a good job and a nice house and a car and money in the bank."

"He was your brother and of your tribe," Charley Hawk said. "You looked out only for yourself."

"Why not?" Lenny said savagely. "The tribe did nothing for me. It meant nothing to me but poverty and hardship, scrawny cattle and barren land. The dingy shacks and the ceremonies that made no sense and the old men living in the past and the old women always mourning. It was different for you. You remember a time when you were free. But I had nothing and had to fight to make a place for myself in the white man's world. I am respected here. People call me Mr. Carey. They don't even think of me as an Indian anymore."

It came out in the rush of words and the moment he had spoken he clamped his teeth together tightly. They drove along residential streets with well trimmed lawns and lights gleaming in the windows of the houses.

"My house is just a mile or so from here," Lenny said and spoke more softly. "You have known only the reservation and the farm. You don't need anyone close to you. But I want to live like a human being and raise my children and see they have shoes on their feet and hear them laugh when their little bellies are full." He looked into the glass of the windshield, seeing the old man's unmoved cheeks reflected in cold panes and circles.

They rode then in silence until the car pulled up before a two story building on a street of shops. Charley Hawk sat in the car until Lenny had gotten out and came around and opened his door. Then he swung his long legs to the curb and rose swiftly. They walked up to the building entrance and Lenny knocked. After a moment the door was opened by a well-dressed man with a brown glistening face and dark black hair.

"This is my father, Charley Hawk," Lenny said. "This here is Bill Cloud who is in charge of the Indian Center. He has made the arrangements for the services and cremation tomorrow."

Charley Hawk nodded. "Where is my son?" he asked.

"He's in the north parlor," Bill Cloud said. "We laid him out there so that any friends who wished could pass and pay their last respects. We got a couple of nice wreaths already. We notified his American Legion post and although he hasn't been an active member for some years they're going to have a rifle squad at the services tomorrow." He waited smiling for the old man to show some approval and after a moment he looked at Lenny. "That's all right, isn't it?" he asked.

"Why not," Lenny shrugged. "Let them give him the full treatment."

Bill Cloud looked uneasily at Charley Hawk once more and then turned and led them down a narrow hall. From some other part of the building came a loud scatter of voices and a burst of laughter. "Some of the younger boys in the recreation room," Bill Cloud said in apology. "I'll ask them to quiet down."

He paused before the entrance to a room that had long drapes hanging from the walls. A few armchairs and a table with a small potted plant and in the center of the room on a low platform, a square plain casket with a candle burning at the head. Charley Hawk stared for a moment at the casket and started slowly into the room. Lenny moved to follow and the old man looked back at him with eyes like knives.

Lenny faltered. Then he shrugged. "I'll wait for you out in front," he said.

"There is no need to wait," Charley Hawk said. "I will stay here until morning."

"That's all right," Bill Cloud said quickly. "There won't be anybody to bother you. I'll just tell those fellows to quiet down." He moved off down the hallway.

Charley Hawk turned again toward the casket. Lenny watched him for a moment from the doorway. "How can you feel anything?" he called harshly after his father. "How can a Sioux whose heart is made of stone feel anything?" He pulled the door closed behind him.

Charley Hawk stood above the casket. The face that lay within the shapeless folds of white cloth was that of a stranger, the rouged cheeks looking like jagged patches of color on stiff canvas. The body lay stiff and straight in death, the wrists springing like broken stalks from the sleeves of his shiny black suit, and the long brown fingers of his hands folded together on his chest.

The old man tried to remember the face of this son as a young man. His skin had been deep rose-brown, his hair so black a blue sheen glinted over it. He had strong cheekbones and a high arched nose and sinewy arms and strong legs.

Now the face seemed muted and blurred, the mouth marked by dissolute circles, the cheeks and throat more grimly scarred than the old sun dance scars on Charley Hawk's chest. He reached out and smoothed a fold of cloth away from his son's cheek and then sought vainly to rub away the stains of rouge. The flesh felt like coarse stone and would not yield to his touch.

He sat down in a chair beside the casket. He could see his son's face in profile and he studied it in wonder for a long time. He closed his eyes and for a moment he dozed, and in his sleep heard a mare whinny and a stallion answer with a great shrilling. He rose with a start and leaned over the casket. After a moment he spoke with his lips close to his son's face.

"I tell you again, my son," he said. "This land belonged to our people long before the white man came plundering and seeking gold. There was nothing in your blood of which to be ashamed."

He moved away and returned, his eyes holding to the dead man's face as if they were teeth.

"You were impatient with the tribe and the land," he said. "You scorned the plow and the seed. The world of the white men drew you and like your brother you tried to become white yourself. But not all eagles can become ravens."

He stood motionless for a long time, the flame of the candle sweeping shadows across his face.

"There are no drums to beat for you now, my son," he said. "No painted shields and lances to wave for you in the air. No songs to be sung at your pyre."

He sat down again beside the casket. He stared at the great veins in the back of his hands, dark and hard, smoke-dried like old meat.

"If I had been born thirty years before," he said, "and you had been born my son then, you might have become a warrior, one of the great men of the tribes like Black Moon or Crow King or Spotted Eagle. You might have ridden a fine buckskin yearling and followed the winter frost cloud of a buffalo herd."

He leaned his back against the wood of the chair. He stared at the white cold ceiling overhead.

"You might have known the scent of sweetgrass and sage burning in the council lodge," he said. "You might have hunted the swift antelope showing their white rumps in flight and heard the fall whistle of the mating elk. You might have taken as a wife a daughter of a chief with bracelets of copper and silver on her strong arms. She would have borne you many sons who would have grown up with deep chests and sinewy arms and they would have ridden the prairies at your side. All this you might have known."

He rose then and slowly went to open the small box he had carried in with him. There were ashes in the box and a long glistening eagle feather and a slim handled knife. He scattered the ashes across his own head and shoulders and he carefully placed the eagle feather beside his son's head so that it rose like a warrior's plume from his hair.

He picked up the knife and ran the blade around his left forefinger until it drew a thin line of blood. Then he sat down and put his hands over his son's folded hands. He leaned his head against the rim of the casket and closed his eyes. He began to chant softly, a chant that became a low terrible wail.

I knew two old men just like the ones in this story and worked for both. I pressed clothes for the tailor who told me I had a heavy foot and suggested a cathartic of castor oil and barley water. I delivered groceries for the grocer who paid me off in dimes, slightly spoiled fruit, and a recital of his laments.

Some years after leaving their neighborhood, driving by again one day, I noticed the stores were still there. I made a vow to stop by to confirm if either one was still alive.

That was one of those vows we never get around to keeping until it is too late.

A HAND FOR TOMORROW

In the fifteen years since the end of the Second World War many changes had come to Bleecker Street. The Quality Delicatessen, which had once specialized in a fragrant potato salad, had been joined with a lunchroom and a small hand laundry to form a glistening supermarket dominating the street. Banners with great red letters and numbers were splashed across the windows, and shiny shopping carts rolled in and out of the parking lot all day. Farther down the street, the little dusty tailor shop of Max Feldman, who claimed at one time or another to have pressed the pants of every male within a mile radius of Bleecker Street, had been demolished along with a radio-repair shop and a candy store to make a bright and gaudy drive-in cleaners operated by his sons.

Of all the stores that had existed on the street before the war, only the small grocery of Kostas Stavrakas remained unchanged except for concessions to the miracles of modern packaging.

Kostas, ignoring the trend to health breads and protein breads and enriched breads, still baked his own loaves as he had baked them for thirty years in the oven in the back room of his store. He carried an assortment of Balkan spices and Greek and Bulgarian cheeses white as the foam on fresh-whipped milk. Although he had accepted the utility of neon lighting and had purchased a small sign to hang in his window, his store stood out at night by appearing almost an island of darkness beside the flaming, garish splendor of the rest of the street.

What little business he did came mostly from the older people who had traded with him for years. As they died or moved away, there was nobody to replace them. In the meantime he did some business in the morning before the supermarket opened and in the evening after it closed.

He did not mind the leisurely pace of his trade. For some years now his legs had been bothering him, and he wore shoes slit along the sides to ease the swelling of his feet. But he could not conceive of existence away from the store in which he had spent thirty years. When his wife was alive, they had planned together for his retirement, but after her death of a stroke, a few years before, this dream had lost relevance. He lived with his married son and wife, who had a two-year-old daughter whom Kostas adored. This family and the store with the warm, familiar scents of spices and cheese and yeasty bread hot from the oven were the boundaries of his life.

The afternoons were long and quiet, and shortly after lunch he would be joined each day by his old friend, Max Feldman, the tailor whose shop had been surrendered to the ambitions of his sons and the cornucopia of progress. They would gravely set up the checkerboard within arm's reach of the briny pickles in the barrel.

"Where does the count stand?" Max asked, and puckered his thin, dry lips and wiggled his crooked ears. "I must be leading by a dozen games this month."

"No more than three," Kostas said. "You have no conception of the difference between addition and multiplication."

Max shrugged that off. "This will be a short, murderous game," he said. "Five, maybe six of Feldman's murderous moves and, pfft! you will be gone."

"Your best game is with your mouth," Kostas said. "If hot air counted, you would be champion checker player of the world."

"Play!" Max cried. "Today I have no mercy!"

They made their first moves and settled down to the game, staring intently at the board. They played in a tight silence until the door of the store opened and a little bell jingled. A gray-haired heavy woman entered. Kostas rose to serve her.

"Don't cheat," he said in a soft warning whisper to the tailor. Max looked outraged.

"Good day, Mrs. Lanaras," Kostas said warmly. "How is your fine son, Thanasi?"

"Still growing," Mrs. Lanaras said, "and eating enough for three grown men. How is your family?"

"Excellent, thank you," Kostas smiled. "At two years of age my granddaughter is as beautiful as Aphrodite. Can I help you?"

"A little cheese, I think," Mrs. Lanaras said. "A half-pound of feta and a loaf of bread. Thanasi takes four sandwiches for lunch."

Kostas packed the items, rang up the sale, and Mrs. Lanaras walked briskly to the door.

"Yesterday as I was coming," Max said, "I saw her and that lummox Thanasi carry two bags out from the supermarket. Bags loaded like that only giants should carry. Here she comes to buy a little cheese and a loaf of bread. Such customers should do you a favor and pass by without stopping."

"She was good to come in for that," Kostas said. "The supermarket has a counter with cheeses from all over the world and varieties of bread. I am grateful she comes in for anything at all."

Max looked for a long, searching moment at Kostas. "Tell me something," he said slowly. "Are you making expenses?"

"Certainly!" Kostas said in a shocked voice. "What kind of businessman do you think I am? Every month a small profit is made here, although I admit not what it used to be."

"What about your son, Nick?" Max asked. "Does he still come sneaking in with a carpenter and an electrician under his jacket?"

"They were in here again last week," Kostas said and smiled, "They took measurements for hours and scribbled a padful of figures. Nicolas is so excited. He wants to do so much. I tell him to wait. When I am dead he can do what he wishes with the store."

Max shook his head somberly. "Believe me, they can't wait," he said. "Don't I know? Twenty-seven years in one location they should let a man walk out, but from my store they shot me like a shell out of a cannon. They came to me one afternoon and said, 'Papa, tomorrow the wreckers will be here.' " His lips curled with contempt. "A drive-in cleaners they wanted. So lazy louts never lift their rumps from the car. A girl they got in a short skirt and naked legs to take the clothing right from the car. Believe me, they can't wait."

"You admit yourself they are making a lot of money," Kostas said.

"Money, money!" Max cried. "Do me a favor and stop talking about money. A little money a man should make to live, but with dignity." He flung his arm up and cut the air violently. "Imagine! A drive-in cleaners with a girl in a short skirt and naked legs to take the clothing from your car!"

The door of the store opened, and the bell jingled again. Nick Stavrakas came in. He was a tall, thin young man with a serious twist to his lips and black curly hair and intense eyes.

"Hi, papa," he said. "Hello, Max."

He stood for a moment balancing on the balls of his feet. He looked up to the ceiling, and a shadow of annoyance crossed his cheeks. "Papa, that light is still burned out. I thought you were going to get Leon to fix it?"

"I forgot to tell him yesterday," Kostas said. "I will tell him for sure today."

"You can hardly see the canned-goods label on the center shelf with the light on," Nick said. "With the light out, the shelf is in total darkness."

"I'll be sure he fixes it today," Kostas said quickly.

Max smiled slyly at the young man. "Tell me, how are all your friends?" he said. "The carpenters and electricians."

Nick frowned at the old tailor. "If you don't mind, Max," he said. "I wanted to talk to papa alone for a minute."

Max sighed and rose slowly from his chair. "I'll take a walk to the park and watch the pretty nursemaids for a while," he said. "There is one Bathsheba who is like a juicy strudel."

"Sit down, Max," Kostas said. "We have no secrets from you." He looked gently at his son. "You have some more estimates?"

With a final despairing glance at Max, Nick pulled a sheaf of papers from his pocket. When he spoke, his voice was vibrant with excitement. "Papa, these estimates are the best yet!" He motioned eagerly with his hand. "This plan would almost triple the area usable and let us stock three times the items we carry."

"How?" Kostas asked.

"By knocking down that wall," Nick said, "opening those partitions in the rear and utilizing all that lost space."

"What about my oven in the back room?" Kostas asked.

Nick shook his head fretfully. "That would have to go," he said. "That takes up space and yields nothing."

Max gave a sharp, pointed laugh and looked intently at the checkerboard. Kostas looked quickly at his friend and tried not to smile.

"Papa," Nick said, and his voice rose a little, "you know that oven is outdated. It costs you forty cents to bake a loaf of bread that you can't sell for more than thirty. In the supermarket, people get their choice of forty kinds of bread."

"Fifty kinds," Max said sagely. "Once I counted them."

"I have been baking bread for families here for thirty years," Kostas said.

"Papa," Nick said excitedly. "That kind of business you can afford to lose. We've got to streamline this store. Do you know that Tony Manteno, the real-estate broker, was telling me this block is a gold mine for business? This block draws a fantastic number of people. We've got to get our share."

"We do a fair business," Kostas said. "We make a fair profit on the items we sell."

"Not one-tenth the business we could if we remodeled," Nick said. "Papa, I've racked my head to plan every step. I tell you we can't lose. We would have our additional investment back in a couple of years."

Kostas did not answer for a moment. "I know there is truth in what you say," he said slowly. "Let me think about it a little more."

"Papa," Nick said in exasperation. "You've been saying that for three years, and you haven't made a move."

Kostas walked from the counter to the window. He stood silently for a moment, looking at the people walking past.

"Thirty years is a long time," he said finally. "Children who stood with their eyes open like big saucers before the jars of three-for-a-penny candy are grown into adults and married, with children of their own. Friends who once came in and sat and smoked and sipped a glass of wine have grown old, and some have died. This store has many memories."

"Papa," Nick said, and a softness entered his voice. "memories are fine, but you can't live today in a dream of the past. You've got to keep up."

"They can't wait," Max said somberly, as if he were speaking to himself. "They can't wait."

Kostas turned back to his son. "All this new business," he said, "will mean additional help. I have always managed this store alone. People who come in expect me to look after them."

"We would need some help," Nick said. "You could begin to take it easy and supervise everything. Sort of keep your eye on the whole operation."

"Tell me," Max asked sharply. "Do you think you might use a girl in a short skirt with naked legs?"

Nick looked at him in irritation. "What does that mean?"

"Nothing," Max said innocently. "I just happen to know where there is one such girl available."

"Nicholas," Kostas said. "We will talk further this evening. We will examine the figures together." He nodded at Max. "This boy has a marvelous head for figures," he said proudly.

"Papa," Nick said, "I know talking about this makes you unhappy, but something has to be done. I've become the laughingstock of the street. Always estimates and figures and plans and nothing more. Think of me."

Kostas looked for a long, silent moment at his son. "I am always thinking of you," he said softly. "Of you and Lucy and Katerina. The three people I care most about in this world."

Nick lowered his head to conceal the flush risen suddenly to his cheeks. "I'm sorry, papa," he said. "I know how much you think of us." He paused for a moment and tasted this defeat and could not resist one final assault. "Look now," he said, and his voice shook under an effort to speak quietly. "I've been in here almost twenty minutes now, and not one customer has entered in that time. Do you call this a business? It's more like a cemetery."

"I am a small grave on the hill," Max said wryly. "Before you leave, water my plot."

Kostas could not help smiling. Nick glared in sudden anger from one to the other. "Laugh!" he said shrilly. "Laugh and sit in this cemetery and play checkers all day. At least admit you aren't really in business. You don't want this place to become a business because it would interrupt your game. You sit in here, and outside the world has changed, and you go on playing checkers and ignoring burned-out lights."

"Nicholas," Kostas said with concern.

"I'm sorry, papa," Nick said. "I'm fed up! I'm your only son and I love you more than anything else in the world, and I swear to God I want what is best for you and Lucy and the baby. I'm full of energy and ambition, and I want to repay you for all the good years and take care of you, and all you can do is sit and worry about playing checkers."

He turned and stumbled once in his haste and then went quickly out the door.

"They can't wait," Max said grimly. "They can't wait."

Kostas returned to his chair and sat down and shook his head in despair. "Maybe we are the selfish ones," he said. "We have forgotten what it is like to be young." He paused and looked around the dimly lighted store, breathing the warm, familiar scents that came from the darkened shelves and the hidden corners. "Maybe the boy is right," he said. "Maybe this place is a cemetery."

Max shook his head violently. "Better a cemetery than a circus!" he cried. "A circus with a girl in a short skirt and naked legs so the lummoxes won't raise their rumps from the car. Big, flashing neon signs and tinsel waving like every day is the Fourth of July."

"They are young," Kostas said sadly. "It seems like yesterday that we pushed their buggies in the park on Sunday afternoons and wiped their running noses and dreamed of their growing up to be President of the United States." He stared at the board without seeming to see the checkers. "Now my Ethel is gone, and your Sarah is gone. The babies are grown into men who live in a world different from the one we remember. And the time goes by so swiftly."

Max pulled out his handkerchief and blew his nose in a harsh trumpeting of sound. "Move!" he said. "It's your move for a half-hour now. You are maybe planning to move sometime before closing? Do me a favor and move, why don't you?"

They finished their third game late in the afternoon. Max dozed a little in his chair, his bald and bony head nodding slightly. Kostas quietly swept out the store. When Leon, the maintenance man, came in, Kostas had him replace the burned-out bulb. A few customers came in for several small purchases.

As twilight fell across the street and Kostas turned on the window light, Nick returned. He brought his wife, Lucy, and their daughter, Katerina, sitting upright in her stroller.

Kostas saw them coming and held the door so Nick could push the stroller in. He looked quickly at his son's face to see what vestige of the morning's disturbance remained. Then he forgot everything in his pleasure at seeing his grandchild.

He lifted her squealing from the stroller. He kissed her warm, soft cheeks and raised her high above his head. She shrieked with delight, and he held her close and poked her gently with his nose.

Lucy, a pretty, slender, dark-haired girl, kissed him on the cheek. "We have lamb and green beans for supper tonight, papa," she said gently. "I fixed them especially for you. Nick and I came to watch the store so you can go home and eat while the food is still warm."

Kostas looked at Nick, and for a moment the young man did not meet his father's eyes. Then Nick managed a slight, repentant smile, and Kostas smiled in warm and grateful response.

"Lamb and green beans?" Max said, coming out of the shadows. "Is there perhaps enough for an old tailor who eats no more than a sick baby?"

"All sick babies should eat as well as you," Kostas said. "They would become well in a hurry."

"Always enough for you, Mr. Feldman," Lucy said. "You go along and keep papa company."

"There is plenty of food," Nick said. "Lucy cooks enough for six men."

"She knows lamb and green beans are my favorite," Kostas said proudly to Max. He patted his daughter-in-law's cheek with tenderness and affection. "I am a lucky man. I have a fine son, and he married a grand girl, and together they produced this incomparable child." He made a face at the baby.

"My sons married monsters," Max said somberly. "Wailing harpies who cook like poisoners. Believe me, every meal at their table freezes my blood."

Nick took the child from his father and returned her to the stroller. He gave her some cellophane-wrapped candy canes to play with. A customer entered, and Kostas started behind the counter. Lucy waved him away. "I'll take care of the store, papa," she said. "You and Mr. Feldman get started now. The lamb will become cold."

Nick went into the back room and returned with his father's jacket. He held it for Kostas to put on.

"Papa," Nick said, and he spoke softly so that only his father could hear. "I'm sorry about this morning."

"It was not your fault you became angry," Kostas said quickly. "Max and I should not have laughed."

"No, papa," Nick said, and shook his head in muted despair. "I've been thinking about it all afternoon. I talked to Lucy for two hours. I been fooling myself for a long time, but I got no right to change you or change the store. Anybody who has worked as many years as you have worked this store has a right to keep it just the way he wants.

"Nicolas," Kostas said. "I am not saying my way is right."

"Let me finish, papa, please," Nick said. "I guess I'm not as smart as I think sometimes, but when I stop and figure it out, a light begins to dawn. I've been bothering you for three years, but you don't have to worry or become upset any more. Starting now, I'm through with estimates and figures. I'm going to leave you alone about the store. That's the way Lucy and I decided."

Kostas looked silently at his son for a long time and then impulsively embraced him. He held him tightly for a moment and then, suddenly self-conscious, stepped away quickly, looking to see if Max or Lucy had noticed. He turned his face slightly and spoke slowly and carefully. "This is my store," he said quietly. "And I have made up my mind what must be done. This place is a disgrace. It was fine for thirty years ago, but it has become a rusty bicycle on a street of fast new cars. Changes must be made."

"Papa," Nick said, and he shook his head in wonder. "What are you saying?"

Kostas did not trust himself to touch the boy again. "I've made up my mind I want to see what you can do for me," he said briskly. "I am not that bad a businessman. I am satisfied you have looked into the matter thoroughly, and I put my faith and trust in you. Don't let me down."

"Papa," Nick said angrily "You're doing this because of what I said this morning. You're doing this because of me. I won't have it."

"Will you shut up about this morning?" Kostas cried. "Am I a child that a few words spoken in excitement cause me to change my mind? I am not married to this old store. It has provided me a living and memories, but it has also given me swollen feet and aching legs. Now go and help your wife and let me go home and eat my lamb and green beans, and in the morning call the carpenters and electricians and make plans for the work to get started."

As he finished speaking, Max came silently to stand at his side. Nick turned on the tailor with enthusiasm. "Did you hear, Max?" he cried. "Papa and I are ready to go ! We are going to make this the finest little store on the street! We'll show them all!" He turned fervently to his father. "Just wait! You won't be sorry! I'll make you proud!" He turned and walked quickly toward his wife.

"They can't wait," Max said softly. "And because they are flesh of our flesh, we give in."

Kostas watched Nick talking earnestly to Lucy. He turned on Max. "The trouble with you, Feldman," he said loudly, "you live in the past. You lack vision. Your sons were right to throw you off the premises. You have a brooding face that invites disaster and despair."

He started for the door, and after a moment of outraged silence Max followed. Lucy and Nick called to Kostas and started toward him, but he waved them away. "Later," he said. "The lamb and beans grow cold. Later."

He fled to the street. Max followed him out, and when he caught up, the old tailor laughed dryly.

"Moses Stavrakas," he sneered. "So I lack vision. I live in the past. You rushed out of that store because maybe in another minute you would have been crying. Ha!"

Kostas glared at him and did not speak. He walked with as quick a stride as his swollen feet would allow, and the tailor had to half run to keep up.

"You know what this means?" Max paused for a moment to catch his breath. "The song is familiar. When all the painting and renovating has been finished, the only old antique sticking out of place is you."

"I know," Kostas said. "I know."

"But do not despair," Max said, and he laughed a dry, ironic laugh. "I will be here to help you. I will teach you to sit in the park and watch the pretty nursemaids and argue politics with the Irishmen who sit like black roosters in the sun. I know the best benches for checkers, the ones shaded beneath the trees. And when the weather turns cold, there is always the public library with newspapers from all the big cities."

"Feldman!" Kostas said wrathfully. "Feldman, go to the devil!"

They walked on together without speaking. They passed under the bright, flashing glitter of the signs and the neon night streaked with multicolored lights. As they approached the great, gleaming festival of the supermarket, Max fell a step behind and fiercely brandished his fist at the long window with flaunting banners. With a violent gathering of his body, he spat on the ground before the store.

This story came out of a gray, desolate period during the last year of my father's life. My wife and I had been married only a few years and had moved into a house with my mother and father. He was ill then and not sleeping well, suffering the slights and arrows of trustees of his church who wanted to eject him for a younger, more vigorous priest. I would come home at dawn from the night shift at the steel mill to find him alone at the table, his briefcase of papers and letters and petitions open before him.

The steel mill and my father near the end of his life were the beginning. From that point, the story wove its own strange and marvelous design. In the end, I was surprised and awed at what had been revealed.

THE WITNESS

That winter seemed to last forever. At the end of March the ground was still frozen. Walking home from a night shift at the mill, I huddled my head into the collar of my jacket and found Pa in his bathrobe in the kitchen with a pot of fresh coffee brewing on the stove.

In the past few weeks he had been having trouble sleeping. Even after taking the pills the doctor had given him, he lay awake through most of the night. Just before dawn he would come quietly downstairs. He would light the oven to warm the kitchen and put on a pot of coffee and wait for me.

I came in cold and tired with the dust of the mill on my cheeks. I wanted only to wash, peek in on my sleeping son and then climb into bed beside my wife, between the sheets that would be warm with her body. But Pa waited for me with a pot of coffee and I had to sit with him for a while.

"Didn't you get any sleep again, Pa?"

He pulled the cord of his robe tighter and turned his face slightly away, because he was no good at deception.

"Better than I have slept in weeks," he said. "Maybe those damn pills are beginning to work."

He poured me a cup of steaming coffee and the sharp aroma pulled at my weariness. "Pa, you made it too strong again," I said, sitting down. "I can tell by the look of it." I was sorry the moment the words were out of my mouth.

"I only put in six scoops," he said. "You told me six scoops was just right."

"Sure, Pa," I said. "Six scoops is right. I just remembered Ethel saying she was going to switch to another brand. Maybe she got one that is stronger."

He walked to the pantry and brought down the canister of coffee. He raised the lid and stared intently at the beans.

"Don't worry about it, Pa," I said. "Sit down and have a cup yourself."

He came to sit down at the table. He dropped two slices of bread into the toaster. Then he raised the pot and poured himself a cup of coffee. His hand trembled slightly because he was old and not well. But his hand still looked big and strong, with the large powerful fingers I remembered as a child. I would get out of school in the afternoon and run to wait for him at the north gate. He would come across the bridge with his crew from the plate mill at the end of the turn. He would see me waiting outside the fence and holler and wave.

He would swing me to his shoulder and the men would laugh and slap my legs. I would ride home high on his back, his hands holding me securely, proud of his strength and his love.

"How did it go last night?" Pa asked as I sipped slowly at the coffee.

"We beat the other two turns by eleven ton," I said.

"No fooling!" His face flushed with pleasure for me. "Who was rolling?"

"The Dutchman," I said. "On all three furnaces."

"He must have been going like hell!" Pa laughed and his pale and tight-fleshed face seemed to flood suddenly with color. Whenever we spoke of the mills he seemed to feel the heat of the furnaces, the glowing slabs bobbing on the rolls.

"You boys still can't touch our record," he said. "I'll never forget that night. Bungo on the furnaces shooting the slabs out like shells from a cannon. Montana on the crane over the hookers. Fuller thinking we were nuts when we gave him the tonnage at four."

He sat up straight in his chair with excitement flashing in his eyes. The doctor did not want him excited, because of his heart and, besides, I had heard the story of that night a hundred times. The stocker with a smashed hand who cried when they took him to the hospital because he didn't want to leave the crew. The way old steel men who had been there swore the crane was a bird snatching up the slabs like a crust of bread. And Pa up and down the length of the mill hustling his crew in a voice that could be heard above the thunder of the roughers and the shrill whistles and bells of the cranes.

". . . And that fool, Barney," Pa was saying, "getting his hand pulped and refusing to go to the hospital. Even taking a poke with the other hand at one of the plant cops who tried to force him off the line."

"Pa, listen," I said. "We both enjoy talking about the mills, but this morning I'm really beat. I run myself crazy trying to keep up with the records set by my old man." I laughed as I stood up and gave his shoulder a slight punch. "Every few days a damn foreman asks me when you're coming back, so they can start breaking tonnage records again."

He smiled up at me then and I saw the thin clean line of scalp under his thick gray hair. "You're a damn good millman," he said. "Better than I ever was, bigger, and a hell of a lot smarter."

"Sure, Pa," I said. "Go tell that to some of the old-timers and they'll lock you up." I arched my shoulders and stretched. "Let's go up," I said. "Maybe you can get a couple of hours' sleep before the kid gets up."

"You go ahead," he said, "and I'll be along in a minute. I'll just rinse the cups and make the kitchen look nice for Ethel when she comes down."

He stopped me when I reached the stairs. "Don't forget the kid's birthday party," he said, and all the love and devotion he felt for Alex was in his warm wink of anticipation. "Tonight is the night."

I stopped for a moment in Alex's room. He was asleep in his crib, looking like some kind of dark-haired angel. He was quick and bright and a joy to be near. I spoiled him a little, but Pa was worse than me. When Ethel cracked Alex across the behind for something he had done wrong, Pa left the room because he could not bear to hear the kid cry.

In the bathroom I stripped and shivered as I washed. I went quickly into the bedroom and slid carefully between the sheets. Ethel stirred beside me and I kissed her soft warm cheek. She moved gently against me, warming my body with her own, until I stopped shivering and fell asleep.

Alex woke me a little before one. His habit was to creep softly into the room and climb up on the bed. If this wasn't enough to wake me, he would bring his mouth to my ear and, like a puppy, begin nibbling at my lobe.

There was a joy in waking to the boy's great brown eyes and clean-child smell. I would hug and tickle him till he shrieked in delight.

Afterward I showered and dressed and went downstairs hungry. I kissed Ethel, standing before the stove, and gently stroked her swollen little belly that pressed up against her apron.

"Potato pancakes again?" I said.

"Don't eat them," she said cheerfully.

"Anything else?"

"Eggs."

"I married a cook," I said.

"We get what we deserve," she said. "My mother used to say, Ethel, marry a rich man and keep off your feet."

"You didn't get that little belly standing up," I said. She took a swipe at me with her dish towel and we both laughed.

Alex came into the kitchen with cookie crumbs around his mouth and wanted another one. Ethel told him no and I winked at him and slipped him a chocolate chip from the jar. He ran out of the kitchen with his prize.

"It's his birthday," I said.

"You spoil him worse than Pa," she shook her head.

"Where is the old man?"

She motioned toward the back yard and the garage. "With Orchowski," she said quietly.

I sat down at the table and she brought me the potato pancakes and several slices of sharp salami.

"They should play in the house," I said. "Find a place somewhere in the house. That small stove doesn't keep the garage nearly warm enough."

She stared at me silently. I ate slowly, without looking up from my plate. We had covered this same ground often before. I kept bringing it up, even when I knew what she would say.

"Mike," she said said wearily, "Mike, what's the use of talking?"

"I know, honey," I said. "But he's not well."

She made a helpless gesture with her hands. In that moment I realized how much of her day was spent in the kitchen cooking for us, washing the dishes, ironing the clothes. The potato pancakes stuck in my throat.

"I know, too," she said, and she spoke softly. "I want to do right, but I want to be fair to Alex, too. Why don't they play in Orchowski's house?"

"You know why," I said. "His son-in-law doesn't like his cigars or his beer."

"They don't have a child like we do," she said. "When they play inside here I can't keep Alex out of their room. Pa hasn't got the heart to lock him out. I don't mind Orchowski's cigars, how bad they smell in the house, but I mind the hollering and the cursing. Honest to God, Mike, you've heard them."

"They're roosters with cut claws now," I said, feeling my cheeks hot. "All they can do is swear and holler."

"I know that," she said patiently. "But curses and hollering are no way to bring up a child." She twisted the dish towel uselessly in her fingers. "This neighborhood is bad enough," she said. "They call it the bush and laugh at the number of bars. When Alex grows older he will need all the strength we can provide him now, all the decency we can give him now."

"All right," I said. "All right, for God's sake, Ethel, let it alone." There was a senseless anger in my throat, because I felt she was right.

She came over and stood for a silent moment beside my chair. I leaned my head against her breast and smelled the flour on her apron.

"Eat," she said gently, and her small soft fingers rubbed my neck in a soothing caress. "Eat your food before it gets cold."

I ate a little more and left the table. I called Alex and got him ready for a walk. He rolled on the floor while I tried to pull on his leggings. I crouched above him and he pressed his tiny hands against my chest, begging me to crush him. My chest dipped against his body and he squealed with fear and delight. I got up and slipped on my jacket and tied a muffler around his throat.

In the yard the ground felt cold and hard beneath my feet. The dark gabled roofs of the mill loomed at the end of the block, throwing a shadow across the houses built closely side by side. The shrill whistle of a crane rang through the clear cold air.

We walked into the garage and Pa and Orchowski were bent over their checkerboard on a small table. Even though the small oil stove in the corner glowed with a steady flame, Pa wore his coat and had a wool scarf wrapped around his throat. Orchowski was dressed in a sweater and jacket and a pilot's cap with the flaps pulled down over his big shapeless ears.

Alex broke from my hand and made a dash for Pa, tumbling into his lap. Orchowski grabbed the board and held it aloft while Pa wrestled with the kid.

"If it ain't the steel man." Orchowski smirked between his pitted cheeks. He was a bull of an old man, a roller and turn foreman in the old days, and a terror on Saturday nights. "Tell me, steel man," he said. "You still picking up hot slabs with bare hands and swinging on the crane like Tarzan?"

"Leave the boy alone, you bastard," Pa said. "Today they make steel with their heads, not their backs like we used to do."

"I know," Orchowski sneered. "Sure, sure." He scratched his nose. "Play checkers. You're losing and you're trying to turn over the goddam board."

The kid listened to them intently and I remembered what Ethel had said. I stood there a moment and shivered in the chill of the garage.

"Why don't you guys play inside?" I burst out. "This place is an icebox."

Orchowski and Pa looked at me. Even Alex stopped wiggling between

Pa's legs and stared up at me as if he understood I had said something foolish. Orchowski looked at me with that smirk cracking his lips. Then he turned back to the board and waved impatiently for Pa to move.

Pa kept watching me with concern. "This is fine, Mike." He shook his head at me, slowly at first, then faster and beginning to grin. "Teddy and me like it fine out here."

For a moment Orchowski did not look up. Then he seemed to feel the waiting in the silence and raised his head. Something in Pa's cheeks must have stung him.

"To hell with playing inside," he growled. "Out here we can breathe." Then he slapped his leg with his fist. "You gonna play checkers!" he yelled at Pa. "If you don't make a move I'm gonna go get a goddam beer!"

"Shut up, you bastard!" Pa cried. "You're a poor loser and a scab!"

I took Alex by the hand and we left the garage. We stood outside in the yard and the shifts had changed and the millmen walked past our fence. Some called greetings to us and some walked tired and silent with their heads bent against the cold. After a while Alex told me he was getting cold and I took him into the house.

After supper that night, while Ethel decorated the cake, I took Alex upstairs and put him into the tub. While I soaped and rinsed him with the spray, Pa sat on the laundry hamper and laughed as he watched him splash. When I lifted him dripping out of the tub, Pa caught him in a big towel and began to rub him gently dry. Then he carried him into the bedroom and they tussled on the bed while Alex screamed.

"I got to dress him, Pa," I said.

"OK," Pa said, and he gave Alex a soft final swat across the fanny. "I'll go down and give Ethel a hand."

I finished dressing Alex and combed his hair. He was a handsome boy with Ethel's fine features. I looked at him with pride and love, thinking of him as a part of my flesh.

Ethel came upstairs and she smelled from the warm and fragrant kitchen. She gave Alex a kiss and waited until he left the room. When she turned to me there were bright spots in her cheeks and a weariness around her mouth.

"Mike," she said, "Pa wants to decorate the dining room and he's making a mess of it. I told him Blanche was bringing a few Japanese lanterns to put over the lights, but he's found some old faded crepe paper in the basement." She paused a moment, with her cheeks pale, and moved her fingers to tug helplessly at her apron. "I hate myself," she said, and she spoke softly, almost in a whisper. "I hate myself every time I complain. He's got no one but us and I want him to know this is his house, too. But I can't help myself." Her eyes became red and I could see her trying hard not to cry.

"I'll tell him," I said. "I'll tell him I want to fix it a certain way."

She shook her head, sorry suddenly that she had come upstairs, sorry that she had spoken. "Let him alone," she said. "Don't tell him anything. Don't make me feel more ashamed than I am already."

"If he would take a walk," I said, "up to the corner or over to Orchowski's for a half hour, we could finish decorating the way you want." I paused. "Orchowski is coming to the party, isn't he? You told Pa to ask him, didn't you?"

I could see the misery working behind her cheeks. Then it was my turn to feel ashamed, because I was glad she had not invited Orchowski, not for any reason but that he made Pa seem worse than he was.

We did not speak again. There didn't seem to be anything either of us could say. I started down the stairs and Pa waited for me at the bottom. I muttered something about turning the thermostat higher to warm the house.

"Is Ethel all right?" he asked. I looked away, because he seemed to sense quick when something was wrong.

"She's got a little headache," I said.

He turned away and I looked down on his gray-haired and strong head and the slight slump that rounded his big shoulders.

"If you think Ethel won't be needing me for anything special," he said, "I might take a little walk. Maybe there's something she wants from the store." He had to pass me to reach into the closet for his coat. I looked at him closely, but he only smiled.

"That's OK, Pa," I said. "I'll see if she needs anything." I called up to Ethel and knew that she was standing silently on the landing at the top of the stairs. For a long moment she did not answer, as if she were trying to compose her voice.

"No," she said, "but tell Pa to hurry back. He's sitting next to Alex at the head of the table."

Pa tugged on his coat and walked to the door and closed it behind him.

In about an hour the dozen or so guests for the party had arrived. Ethel's sister, Blanche, had come from the North Side with her husband, who was an insurance executive. He kept walking around sniffing the house. There were a couple of the turn foremen with their wives. Pa had not come back.

We waited a while longer and Ethel passed around some more cheese and crackers and I opened some more beer. Everybody was getting restless. Alex, becoming impatient, began to whine. I went next door finally, to Max's place, and asked to use their phone. I called the Burley

Club, but the bartender hadn't seen Pa. I called Orchowski's brother-in-law's house, but no one answered. On the way back I peered into the garage, but it was dark.

In the house I told Ethel to cut the cake. Alex was crabby and didn't want to blow out the candles. The insurance executive and Blanche had bought him a $22 dump truck and he didn't want to even open the other presents. I was angry and suddenly sick with worry about Pa, thinking something might have happened to him. I went into the kitchen to get another pint of ice cream and when I got back to the dining room everything was strangely quiet.

Pa stood in the front hallway. His hair was mussed, his collar unbuttoned, and his eyes were bright and glistening. Orchowski, an idiot's grin on his pitted cheeks, stood behind him. The stink of whiskey covered them both like a cloud and fell across them into the room.

I looked once at Ethel and her cheeks were the color of chalk. Pa took a step forward and stumbled and then braced himself against the doorway of the room.

He swept his arm up recklessly in a swing that included everybody in the room. He kept staring at all of us and then he fumbled behind him, catching Orchowski by the coat and tugging him forward.

"I brought my goddam friend home for the party," Pa said, and the words came slurred and thick from his tongue. "My goddam friend who worked with me at the plate mill for thirty-six years."

"Thirty-seven years," Orchowski said, swaying and grinning beside him.

Alex yelped for his grandpa and one of the foremen laughed and walked forward to greet them. Ethel moved and smiled across the pale band of her cheeks. I helped Pa off with his coat and Ethel took Orchowski's jacket, and for a moment in the closet I felt her hand, cold and trembling against my own.

A short while later I got Pa upstairs and helped him undress. He was sobering, his eyes suddenly blurred and melting, and he kept mumbling under his breath. When he was under the covers, I sat down on the edge of the bed near his head. I heard the last of the guests saying good night and the door closed for the last time. Ethel brought the kid upstairs and put him to bed. All the while, the old man lay there with his eyes wide open, staring up at the ceiling.

Ethel came into the room. She stood for just a moment inside the door and then she walked to the bed and leaned down and put her cheek against Pa's cheek.

"It's all right, Pa," she said, and she was crying, the tears running silently down her cheeks. "It's all right and I'm glad you brought Mr. Orchowski."

Pa touched her cheek with his fingers and moved his lips without making any sound. He touched her cheek that was wet with tears, in a kind of caress, and tried to smile to reassure her, and then turned his head helplessly to the wall. I motioned to Ethel to leave the room.

I sat for a while longer beside him. He twisted and thrashed beneath the blankets.

"I was drunk," he said. "Honest to God, boy, if I hadn't been loaded I wouldn't have come in like a goddam fool. I wouldn't have hurt Ethel like that."

"Let it alone, Pa," I said. "What are you making such a big thing of it for? Ethel said it was all right. We were wrong."

But he would not be comforted. He would lie still for a few moments with his eyes closed and I thought he had fallen asleep. Then he seemed to startle awake and his fingers moved in restless tremblings along the spread.

I got scared and left the room and called the doctor. He came and gave Pa a shot. After a while Pa fell asleep, his rough breathing eased and quieted.

It was not very long after that night, only a couple of months later at the beginning of summer, that the old man died. In May we sowed a bed of columbines and Pa talked of seeing them flower and just a few days after that he was dead.

When he died he had been in the hospital two days with a hard and heavy pain in his chest. The second night a blood clot formed and he died in his sleep. We had seen him early in the afternoon of that day, and when they called us back to the hospital, all I remember noticing was how really thin his wrists had become, how slim and pale his strong fingers were.

We buried him three days later. The old rollers and turn foremen who were still alive came, and a bunch of the men from my turn. It rained a little on our way to the cemetery, the drops glistened on the bankings of flowers around the grave. Ethel cried a lot and she was near enough her time for giving birth that I was scared for her and for the baby.

On the way out of the cemetery I saw Orchowski. He was dressed in a baggy gray suit, a stiff collar around his broad throat. I wanted to talk to him a few moments, there beside the old man's grave, but someone took my arm and I lost him.

We stopped on the way home to pick up Alex from Mrs. Feldman, who had looked after him. The rest of the way, Alex between us in the car, Ethel and I didn't speak. I parked the car and carried the kid into the house because of the puddles that still gleamed in the gutters and made small pools along the side of the walks.

The house was damp and quiet. I turned on some lights and put up the heat. Ethel came in behind me and we stood like that for moments, listening as if there were sounds and noises we expected to hear.

"I'm tired," Ethel said. "I've got a headache. I'll get Alex ready for bed and go to bed myself."

"I'll bring him up in a minute," I said. "Let him play for a while."

She stood in the hall and slipped off her coat and the jacket of her suit. The light fell across her body and I could see the great swell of her belly, the slow labored movement of her arms. She saw me watching her and came over and kissed me on the cheek. I held her close in the circle of my arm.

"We tried," she said, and there was a thin tight edge to her voice, and she looked at me out of her weary and swollen eyes. "We did what we could for him, didn't we, Mike? Didn't we?"

I remembered the night of Alex's birthday and the way she cried against the old man's cheek.

"Sure," I said. "Sure, baby, you did."

I sat for a while in the back room watching Alex play with his toy cars on the floor. Outside, the cars passed in the twilight and from the mill I heard the whistling of the slab-mill crane.

I listened to the kid humming a foolish song as he played. I thought suddenly of Ethel dead, someday, like my ma, and me having to live with the kid and his wife.

I got up and went into the kitchen. Through the window, night had fallen over the back yard. A few fireflies flickered over the garden. The outline of the garage loomed silent and dark against the lighter sky. I moved to the sink, feeling a tightness breaking in my throat.

When I began to cry, the water running so the kid would not hear, I didn't know for a few crazy moments who I was really crying for—the lost old man or myself.

I have written few stories with young college students as principal characters. This story was published by a campus literary magazine, but I seem to remember one or more of my sons observing I had not really understood the young people in the story.

Perhaps they are right. Any man and woman who have raised children are eminently qualified by that experience only to disqualify themselves as far as understanding them goes. I think this truth applies equally to the ignoramus and the sage. Parenthood may well be the last true democracy, all of us leveled by our bewilderment into one great, classless society.

THE SWEET LIFE

Mark and Jerry had gone to see the film "La Dolce Vita" a few days before they were to return to Michigan State for the fall semester. They first noticed the two girls in the lobby of the theatre during the intermission. Both girls were dark-haired, one tall and large-breasted with long strong legs and the other girl slender and smaller. She had a fragile high-cheeked face and great dark eyes and her black hair was brushed back into a simple coiled bun that gave her a smoldering Castilian beauty.

They were both smoking up a fog and talking loudly about the picture in a way that demanded to be noticed. Jerry worked his way over to them and Mark followed him. Jerry asked them with his swinging charm if they weren't a couple of Italian starlets touring with the picture for publicity purposes. They started laughing and the big girl, Norma, had a hoarse and throaty laugh and Senta laughed with a soft quivering of her lips around her small even white teeth. By the time the intermission was over they had made arrangements to meet after the movie. On the way back to their seats Mark and Jerry counted their money and agreed that Jerry had Norma while Mark would take Senta.

When the lights went on at the end of the film, the boys hurried through the press of people up the aisle. The girls were waiting for them in the lobby and they walked over to Rush Street and entered a tavern and sat down in a shadowed booth. Norma ordered a Bloody Mary and Senta ordered a Daiquiri. The waiter asked to see her I.D. card. Jerry and Norma teased her as she dug irritably into her purse and showed the card to the waiter. Mark learned she was nineteen and a junior at Ohio State. Mark and Jerry ordered beer.

"I liked the ending of the picture," Senta said. "The marvelous expression on the little girl's face as she called to Marcello."

"She resented missing the party," Jerry said. "She wanted Marcello so they could have a party of their own."

Norma laughed loudly in appreciation and Jerry joined her, pleased with his wit. Senta made an effort to laugh politely but it didn't quite come off and Mark felt drawn to her because of her reaction.

"That perfectly horrible fish," Norma shuddered in disgust. "That round dead eye staring up at them. It made my skin crawl. What kind of fish was that?"

"A schooner fish," Jerry said.

"The fish was a symbol," Mark said. "A bloated monster reflecting the uselessness of their own lives."

Jerry grinned and motioned at Mark. "When he graduates next June he wants to become a writer like Marcello," he said. "I think his real reason is that he wants to go to parties like that blast in the film."

"I think he looks a little like Marcello," Senta said.

"The hell he does," Jerry snickered.

"More like the fish," Mark said.

"I mean it," Senta said seriously. "You have the same sensitive eyes."

"Don't let that sensitive look fool you," Jerry said. "He uses that look to draw a girl into his web and then . . ."

"Cut it out," Mark said.

The waiter brought their drinks. They cheerfully toasted each other. Jerry took a long swill of beer and shifted closer to Norma who made no effort to slide away.

"The best scene in the picture was that party," Jerry said. "That crazy doll who did the strip and those fairies prancing around and Marcello trying to paste the chicken feathers all over the blonde."

"Remember the way she flapped her arms," Norma said. She flapped her own firm bare arms and crowed, "Oo-oo-ahroo!"

"Take it easy," Mark said. "They'll throw us out of here."

"It was sure a great party," Jerry said. "Maybe I can get the guys in the frat house to throw one like it."

"Be sure to invite me," Norma said.

"I'll invite you right now," Jerry slipped his arm around her shoulders, "and let you know the date later on." They both exploded into laughter and Mark looked wryly at Senta.

"I've been to some pretty good parties myself," Norma said.

"The hell you say," Jerry said. "Tell us about them."

"You college rah-rahs ever hear of musical chairs?" Norma laughed. "Well, I have played the same game with beds."

Jerry chortled with delight. He let his hand slip over Norma's shoulder, his fingers hanging very near her breast.

"She's just showing off," Senta said sharply to Jerry. "She has a good job in an advertising office and helps support her mom and dad."

"Mama doesn't think a girl needs any fun after a day's work in a lousy office," Norma gave Senta a quick bitter look. "After we graduated from high school, Senta was able to go on to college but I had to go to work. That doesn't mean I have to sit home and feel my arteries hardening."

"Not if I can help it, doll," Jerry said soothingly. He signaled the waiter to bring another round of drinks.

"Let's talk about the movie," Senta said with a silent plea to Mark. The dim lights of the tavern threw restless shadows across her pale cheeks and dark eyes. "I thought Fellini did a marvelous job, a kind of parable of the emptiness of our materialistic culture."

"It was all right," Norma said, "but I still think it was a pretty dirty picture."

"It wasn't dirty at all," Mark said. "It was a very moral portrayal of immorality."

"Don't tell me he had to go into that much loving detail to make a moral point," Norma snickered. "All those nymphomaniacs and homosexuals and fairies."

"Fairies and homosexuals are the same thing," Jerry said.

"I know that," Norma gave him a slight playful shove. "Don't you think I know that?"

"Mark is right," Senta said. "There were many haunting and beautiful scenes that I will never forget."

"I liked the scenes with Steiner," Mark said.

"Why did Steiner kill himself?" Norma asked.

"I'm not sure why," Senta said.

"I'm not sure either," Mark said. "He seems to have had everything a man could want. A beautiful family, literary success and artistic friends. But he was terrified of something no one else could see."

"I liked the part where Marcello's old man visits him," Jerry said. "He lectures Marcello about sin and then wants to go to a nightclub where the old rip begins to fondle one of the dolls in the chorus. He sure reminded me of my old man. I know for a fact he's had at least a half-dozen girlfriends in the last ten years. I wouldn't be surprised if my old lady knew it too even though all she cares about is playing cards five nights a week."

"There's been a change in the structure of society," Senta said.

"Marital loyalty for fifty years to the same person is sheer hypocrisy."

"Now who is showing off?" Norma asked loudly.

"I mean it!" Senta said and her eyes flashed. "In Hollywood movies, sex is a daydream for people who are scared they will never find the real thing. In French and Italian movies the people don't moon around wondering what sex is really like. If they want sex, they have it, and when they are done they forget about it until next time. It's more honest that way."

"I think you gals are both a little too fast for us," Jerry said and winked at Mark. He tried to catch the waiter's attention.

"I don't think we'd better have any more to drink," Mark said. He figured their combined funds would about cover the drinks they already had.

"If you're short I know how it is," Senta said. "Norma and I will be glad to share the bill."

"Speak for yourself, honey," Norma said. "That might be the way you little college girls do it, but I work hard for my money."

"We wouldn't consider it anyway," Jerry said and grinned. "I've got a better idea. My folks are in Washington. My old lady goes along on the old man's business trips to keep an eye on him. Our house is empty and the bar is loaded."

Senta gave Norma a long warning look. "I'm staying with Norma at her house," she said. "Her mom and dad asked us not to be late."

"By this time mama and papa will be sound asleep," Norma said, "their fannies snuggled and both snoring like bears." She smiled coyly at Jerry. "My papa is faithful to my mama," she said, "but he does have a cabinet full of nude girlie photos in the basement."

"What does your mama do for kicks?" Jerry asked with a snicker.

"She adores Cary Grant," Norma said. "She sees all his pictures at least a half-dozen times and dreams about him almost every night."

"They'll never miss you then," Jerry said. "C'mon let's go."

Norma looked hesitantly at Senta and then shrugged and rose. "I don't feel sleepy yet anyway," she said. "Tomorrow's Saturday and we don't have to get up till late."

They paid the check and left the tavern. Jerry walked with his arm around Norma's waist, his fingers spread slightly on her thigh. Senta and Mark walked slowly behind them.

"They sure hit it off well together," Mark said. They walked in silence for a few moments. The summer night was marked with a trace of early burning leaves.

"Norma is a fine girl," Senta said. "She was my best friend in high school. We used to talk all night. She was terribly disappointed when she couldn't go to college."

"You are both very different," Mark said.

Senta was silent and when she finally spoke, her voice was pensive. "Two years can be a long time," she said. "I can even see the change at home. My mother and father think I have grown callous and hard. My father is a pharmacist and thinks all life can be reduced to the exact measure for a prescription."

"I know what you mean," Mark said. "After my second year in college I couldn't stand the whole summer at home. I took jobs in other cities. It seemed I couldn't say or do anything anymore without hurting my parents in some way."

They turned off Rush Street and left the bright noisy cafes. A wind came off the lake and blew the scent of burning leaves more strongly about their heads. Mark studied Senta's face in the light of a passing streetlamp.

"You're lovely," he said suddenly. "You're a very lovely girl." He couldn't tell whether she was pleased. "I bet you've heard that from many fellows before me."

"I don't object when someone tells me that I'm pretty," Senta said quietly, "but looks can be a handicap too. Men can be distracted by surface allure and forget a girl is also a human being."

"I understand that," Mark said quickly. "In addition to beauty you have a sharp and sensitive mind."

He could tell that pleased her and after a moment he took her hand. They walked a short way in silence.

"I enjoy reading a great deal," Senta said.

"What writers do you like?"

"Tolstoy and Dostoevski in the novel and Sartre in the drama," Senta said. "A lot of poetry but mostly the work of Pablo Neruda."

"I don't know him," Mark said. "I guess I should, but I don't."

"He's a great Chilean poet," Senta said. "And I love foreign films and my favorite actress is Sophia Loren . . . she's a woman in every sense of the word."

They reached the lot where Jerry had parked the car and could not see him or Norma. They walked to the car and saw the figures in the shadowed front seat curled in a tight embrace. Mark looked at Senta with a faint embarrassed smile and knocked on the windshield. Jerry and Norma disengaged themselves slowly and Jerry motioned for them to get in the back. Mark held the door open for Senta and climbed in after her.

"I'm sorry we disturbed you," Mark said with sarcasm.

"Never mind," Jerry laughed. "We can always pick up where we left off."

They pulled into the driveway of Jerry's house, a large spacious ranch building on a lot landscaped with evergreens and myriad trees. Norma gave a low whistle of appreciation.

"It's all right," Jerry shrugged. "The old man takes the suckers for plenty in his law practice."

He drove straight for the garage and the door opened. He parked the sport coupe beside a long gleaming Cadillac. On the dark steps before entering the kitchen Jerry walked behind Norma and suddenly she squealed. "You naughty boy!" she cried.

They passed through a long kitchen with a massive twin-doored refrigerator and a stainless steel stove into a living-room paneled in walnut with an imposing array of lamps and sculpture.

"Lovely," Norma said with awe. "Just lovely."

"Wait till you see this," Jerry said. He walked to a corner and pushed a button. The wall panel slid back to reveal a compact bar with a glittering assortment of glasses and bottles.

"Better than any Rush Street tavern," Norma marveled. "If it's for real, make me another Bloody Mary."

Jerry moved briskly behind the bar and began mixing the drink. Senta sat down stiffly on the couch.

"What will you have?" Mark asked her.

"I don't think I want another drink," she said.

"Come on, honey," Jerry said. "Give me a chance to show how good a bartender I am."

"I just don't want another drink," Senta said.

"I'll take scotch on the rocks," Mark said.

When Jerry had finished mixing their drinks he picked up a glass and a nearly full bottle of Bourbon and came out from behind the bar. He stood looking at Norma with his broad shoulders hunched slightly and a reckless glint in his eyes. "I'm taking my bottle upstairs," he said slowly. "Anybody want to see the bedrooms?"

Mark looked uneasily at Senta. "For cri' sakes slow down," he said to Jerry.

Jerry loosed a short brusque snicker. "What the hell for? We sat in the bar an hour and a half. We all know why we came here. Let's not waste the whole damn night sparring around." He motioned with the bottle to Norma. "Coming, doll?"

Norma glanced hesitantly at Senta.

"Or was all that talk about musical beds just showing off," Jerry said. "The little working girl trying to impress the college crowd."

Norma turned back to Jerry with a defiant glitter in her eyes.

"You could at least put on some damn music," Mark said to Jerry.

"You play all the mood music you want," Jerry said in a flat hard voice. "Read some poetry too. Spend the whole damn night talking. I'm going upstairs now."

Senta gave him a scathing contemptuous look but he ignored her. Norma rose slowly from her chair and stood a moment staring at Senta.

"Enjoy yourself, honey," Norma said in a tight and brittle voice. "La Dolce Vita."

She turned then and started up the stairs, carrying her drink, her firm thighs pressing against the skirt of her dress. Conscious of them watching her she affected a certain casual disdain. Jerry started after her with a cool smile of triumph. "The first floor is all yours," he said to Mark. He followed Norma upstairs.

Mark watched him out of sight and glanced uneasily at Senta. She sat a little stiffly in silence and after a moment laughed shortly.

"He must be the prize bull of sorority row," she said.

"He does pretty well."

"And how about you?" Senta said. "Do you do pretty well too?"

"Not nearly as well as Jerry," Mark said. He took a long swallow of scotch.

"You're the sensitive kind," Senta said.

"Sure," Mark said sharply. "That's why I brought you here."

"You didn't bring me," Senta said. "Your fast friend brought me. You came along."

"All right," Mark said. "Don't bite my head off. I'm not going to attack you. You can just relax and read a good book until your friend comes down."

Senta rose and walked to the fireplace. She stood for an instant with her back to him and then whirled around. Her dark eyes glistened angrily.

"I'll do what I want to do!" she said. "The whole business isn't that important. If only people would stop hacking at it like woodchoppers and show a little grace."

"Okay, okay," Mark said. "Your friend is over twenty-one but I'm sorry we came here. I didn't mean to hurt your feelings."

The tight angry circles loosened slightly in her face. She returned to the couch and sat down.

"Do you believe in fate?" Senta asked quietly.

"In what way?"

"Do you believe that whatever happens to us is predestined to happen long before we are born?"

"I don't think I buy that," Mark said.

"I feel that way about love," Senta said. "That I will find it someday as it was planned long before my life began." She looked so lovely, the shadows sweeping her face and her lips gleaming. Mark leaned over suddenly and kissed her, feeling her lips surprisingly soft under his mouth.

He pulled back sharply expecting her to protest. She sat looking at him quietly without a trace of warmth in the firm carved lines around her mouth.

He kissed her again pressing his lips harder over her mouth. She twisted in his arms and he thought he felt her kissing him back. A wild urgency caught at his body and he pulled her against him in a hard embrace that robbed them both of breath. He felt the agitation of her heart. His hand rose to touch the trembling swell of her small firm breast and she began to struggle. For an instant he thought it was because she was excited until he realized she was fighting him. He paused in surprise still holding her arms.

"What's the matter?" he asked.

She looked at him with her dark eyes open so wide they resembled cups. "I won't!" she said.

"What?"

"I won't!" she cried. "I won't!"

He had heard those words as a prelude before and he ignored them and bent to kiss her again. She began to struggle violently and he was startled at the strength in her slim body. He fought to hold her and suddenly she went limp in his arms. After a moment he relaxed his grip. Almost at once she cried out and with a hard vengeful sweep of her arm raked his cheek with her nails, tearing his flesh. He cried out in shock and pain and slipped to his knees beside the couch holding his torn cheek.

"Oh my God, I'm sorry," she said. "I'm so sorry." She sat there pale and scared, her blouse pulled askew showing the flesh of her shoulder.

Mark rose slowly to his feet. "That's all right," he said and his voice sounded strange in his ears. He turned and started from the room.

"Where are you going?" she asked quickly.

"To get some iodine," he said. "Do you mind?" He walked to the bathroom. He snapped on the lights and the faces that stared back at him from the multiple mirrors did not seem his own. The scratch ran an ugly red scar down his cheek. He washed it, grimacing with pain, and then found a bottle of iodine in the cabinet.

"Let me do that, please." She had come to stand quietly in the doorway. She didn't wait for him to answer but took the bottle from his hand. She began to apply the dauber to the long scratch.

"Take it easy," he said wincing.

"I'm sorry," she said.

"That's about the tenth time you've said you're sorry," he said with sarcasm. "Change the broken record."

When she finished applying the iodine, he looked at himself in the mirror.

"I look like a goddam Indian," he said dejectedly. "I don't know how I'm going to explain this to Jerry."

"Can't you tell him you cut yourself shaving?"

"Cut myself like this?" he asked. "Are you nuts? What do you think I shave with, a saber?"

They stared at each other and her lips quivered in a faint smile.

"Go ahead and laugh," he said angrily. "If you had scratched Jerry like this, he would probably have beaten hell out of you."

"You're not Jerry," she said. "That's why I like you."

"God, I'm lucky," he said and loosed a short harsh laugh. "You like me so Jerry gets laid and I get a torn face to carry around like a badge of honor for days."

She stood watching him and he noticed the sadness of her eyes. She raised her hand and touched his cheek, her fingers fluttering softly as a bird's wing beneath the raw red line of the scratch. He had a strange feeling that she was touching the bone beneath the flesh of his face.

Something in her fingertips made him reach uncertainly for her again. She raised her small somber face to him, and he kissed her again, warily at first, and then with a growing jubilation as he felt her responding. He started to tug her into the livingroom and their feet tangled and she nearly fell. He held her in the circle of his arm while he snapped off the main light switch to darken the livingroom except for a small lamp in the corner.

"Tell me you love me," she whispered, and there was a dark anguish in her voice.

"I love you, Senta," he said, and the words tumbled from his lips. "I love you very much."

They were on the couch and he felt the frantic trembling of her body. For a moment a sharp remorse and shame possessed him. Then it was lost in a furious fumbling and twisting of their bodies.

A little before dawn it began to rain. A thin drizzle fell across the evergreens and walks and cast a shimmering mist around the post light near the gate. The first faint trace of daylight cut the rim of the dark night sky. Mark snapped off the post light and walked into the kitchen where Senta had made coffee.

Her cheeks were scrubbed clean of any remaining powder and without a stain of lipstick her lips appeared to be drained of blood. She had brushed back her hair and tied it with a strip of ribbon. He sat down across from her and poured himself a cup of coffee.

"Do you want sugar and cream?" she asked.

"Just a little sugar," he said.

They lapsed into silence and drank their coffee slowly. He gave a short and rueful laugh.

"Do you ever see those corny commercials on television?" he asked. "The ones that show the adoring newlyweds saying, 'Good morning, Mr. Jones,' and 'good morning, Mrs. Jones,' and a lot of jazz like that."

"I may have seen them," she said quietly.

"They should have a commercial for us," he said. "Some aspirin company should show us sitting like this, not talking, drinking our coffee with a kind of quiet desperation."

He fell silent again staring into his cup.

"Are you sorry?" he asked.

"I don't know," she said. "I don't really know what I feel."

He twisted restlessly in his chair.

"It's my fault," he said. "I'll assume the full blame if you feel like blaming somebody." He shook his head. "It was kind of a mess anyway," he said. "I guess the excitement and the booze didn't help much. I mean . . ."

"I don't blame you," she said.

"You're not mad?" he asked.

She shook her head slowly. "I'm just confused," she said. "I talked about people in the foreign films doing it when they wanted to do it and afterwards not worrying. But we can't be like that. I don't know why. We go at it like Jerry trying to prove something, or like me, mooning and brooding about whether to or not. We grow up into women like Norma's mother, dreaming of Cary Grant, and men like Jerry's father searching for something we cannot find." She paused and looked at him with a shaken sadness. "And in the end," she said, "a day may even come when we'll no longer remember that it once belonged to love."

Norma entered the kitchen, her face gray and weary in the neon light. Her legs were bare and she pulled at her dress which was wrinkled and showed the lace hem of her slip.

"God, I could use some coffee," she said. "Pour me a cup of black and then let's go. My old lady will kill me."

Senta poured her a cup of steaming coffee from the pot. Norma took the cup and did not sit down but stood blowing across the coffee to cool it. She looked over the rim of the cup at Senta and then at Mark. For the first time she noticed the stained scratch on his cheek. "Some night," she said grimly. "Some night we all had."

She handed the car keys to Mark. "I took them from his pants pocket," she said. "He's out like a dead man. I tried to wake him thinking he might want to drive his little sweetie home," she laughed without mirth. "He opened one eye and looked at me like I was nuts." She took a sip of coffee and grimaced as the steam curled from the corners of her mouth. "You know he resembled the fish in the picture," she said. "That goddam fish with the ugly dead eye."

They drove home to Norma's place silently except for Norma's directions to Mark. The three of them sat in the front seat watching the cold day sweep aside the final shadows of night.

Mark parked the car before Norma's small frame bungalow. Norma slipped out of the car, nervously watching the house, and motioned for

Senta to hurry. Mark started to get out of the car to take Senta to the door but she caught his arm and shook her head. They stared at each other for a moment and then he looked away. "If I don't get a chance to see you before you leave for school," he said awkwardly, "Good luck to you."

"The same to you," she said. She twisted then to slide her legs from the car. She turned back to him and with a sudden impulsive gesture raised her hands to his cheeks. She held his face for an instant and then kissed him softly on the lips, a sad and fleeting kiss of farewell. Afterwards she left the car and walked quickly toward the house. Norma waited for her on the porch with the door open and they walked inside and the door closed. The gray still silence swept back across the house.

Mark sat there in the car for a long time. A curious weariness possessed him. His head felt heavy and his arms were burdens.

He turned the key, pressed down on the gas, and the car began to move slowly and then more quickly as he gathered speed. He opened the window and let the rush of cool damp morning air strike his face.

This is the most recent story I've written. I worked on it for almost a month, beginning with one intention that altered, during the writing, into a startlingly different story. No matter how many times a writer experiences the redirection that occurs when a story assumes a life of its own, it is a humbling emotion. He understands how much he is the servant of a muse and not its master.

When the story was finished, I reread it several times over a few days, wondering if I could detect a villain or a villainess. I couldn't really find anyone to blame. The characters, like most of us, are sometimes unwise, not loving enough or loving too much, stumbling through unrehearsed deceptions. They are, in other words, human.

Finally, I ended the story the way I thought life might have ended it. That is simply my ending. Blossom, Ted, and Angie might have other endings I wasn't wise enough to understand.

SONG OF SONGS

In August of that year Ted Varnas and his wife, Angie, celebrated their 26th wedding anniversary. He'd been twenty-four when they married and she'd been twenty-one. For those same twenty-six years he'd operated the Spartan Food and Liquor Mart on Harrison Street in a neighborhood of restaurants and small shops. Angie's father had owned the store and Ted had been working for him when he died. Since Angie was an only child, her father left them the business on condition they provide a regular monthly income to his widow which they did until her death ten years later.

Ted had worked hard, improving what had already been a successful business. He and Angie hadn't become wealthy but they had a substantial sum in treasury bonds and in savings accounts. They owned, clear of any mortgage, a seven room brick bungalow in Oak Park and a Buick Le Sabre he traded in on a new model every other year. From the time their daughters, Colleen and Nancy, were children, until both girls married, the family took at least two vacations a year. In the summer they stayed in a cabin on a lake in Wisconsin and fished (he and his daughters fished while Angie read) and in the winter they went to Disneyland. Although Ted had lost count, they'd probably been to Disneyland more than a dozen times. His daughters met their future husbands on these vacations when they were teenagers and now one daughter, Colleen (expecting her first baby in a few months), lived in Milwaukee and Nancy lived in San Diego. He wondered, sometimes, if they'd taken their vacations in Canada and Mexico whether the girls might have married natives of those places.

Ted was a sturdily-built man (he'd played football in high school) of medium height with a thatch of dark hair beginning to grey. He'd never considered himself a handsome man but he'd been told he had a strong, friendly face. Except for being fifteen pounds overweight and having problems with his blood pressure, he felt in fairly good health. On his fiftieth birthday a few months earlier, he'd mentioned to Vasili Pappas, his friend who owned a dry cleaners a half block from his store, that he was starting middle age. Vasili, an acerbic man some years older than Ted, with gaunt cheeks and a crooked smile, laughed.

"Hey, Teddy, how many people you know live to be a hundred? Middle age started when you were thirty-five so you're fifteen years over the hill now."

He didn't feel over the hill but the truth was he no longer felt young. Each year seemed to increase his apathy and resignation. He didn't know whether that was part of the aging process or because of the monotony of his days. Twenty-six years in the unchanging routine of the store hardly made for a dramatic life. Yet he wasn't sure what else he wanted or if a nagging, recurring feeling that he'd missed something in his life was valid. He knew countless other men would have gladly changed places with him in his business and in his home.

His wife, Angie, was a pretty woman with large brown eyes, full lips and small, well-formed ears. She'd been a little thin when they married but with stunning legs and a shapely behind. Those were the first things he'd noticed about her on the Sunday after church when she ascended the streetcar before him. They'd dated for about a year and then become engaged. Since both of them were Greek, their parents had no objections. The passage of years and bearing the two children had added some weight to her frame and her legs were faintly blemished by tracings of varicose veins. But her figure was still attractively slender and her skin remained sleek and smooth. When they stood together in church or attended a social gathering, he felt warmed with gratitude and affection because she was his wife.

She was a sensible, practical woman, as well. Though she didn't spend an excessive amount of money on her clothing, she always looked trim and well-dressed. "My dress store is my closet," she often said. "I've plenty of nice things there. If someone remembers I've worn this dress a few times before, that's just too bad. I'd rather save money for other things."

Angie also had a placid, even temperament. When they argued about something, her voice remained low. Even if he lost his temper and shouted, she'd withdraw behind a quiet reproval that thwarted his anger. There were times he wished her more emotional and responsive but he realized that wasn't her nature. He had to be thankful he didn't have a shrew like Vasili's wife, Aspasia, who had an explosive temper.

"Her jaw could kill a man," Vasili told him grimly. "She belongs in the Bible where it writes about Samson slaying a multitude with the jawbone of an ass. He must have used a jawbone like Aspasia's."

Earlier that autumn, the Armenian woman who ran a small watch repair shop across the street and half a block up from his store, closed her business. The store remained vacant for almost two months and if it hadn't been across the street, Ted would have leased it for storage. By the middle of October he thought it would remain unrented for the winter. Then, on his way to work one morning, he saw a painter's truck outside the store and a carpenter building a new trellis for the window. Later that morning when he and Vasili were having coffee, Ted asked him about the business going in across the street.

"I walked over and asked one of the painters," Vasili winked slyly, "and he told me it was going to be called 'Intimate Garments.' "

"What's that mean?"

"It means what it says," Vasili said. "You know, the intimate, personal apparel women wear next to their naked skin."

"That's underwear."

"Underwear doesn't sound intimate or exotic," Vasili said. "Underwear is what my wife wears. Intimate garments are what I'd give an expensive mistress if I could afford one."

"Bullshit!" Ted said. "Intimate garments is just a fancy name for underwear that costs more. We don't need that kind of gyp joint in this neighborhood."

For the following week Ted observed the progress of the store. Walking across the street from it one morning he noticed the exterior had been painted and a row of lights hung in the window. That afternoon, while he was arranging tiers of pears and peaches in his window, a truck pulled up in front of the new shop. For the next hour several men with pulleys and ladders raised and suspended a gaudy, rose-colored sign above the front door. After the workmen left Ted walked outside his store to see the lettering on the sign. It read INTIMATE GARMENTS which is what Vasili told him they would be selling. He shook his head in disgust, thinking whoever had the idea of such a business prospering on their street was a loser.

He spent the following morning at South Water Market negotiating for half a truckload of produce and didn't get to his store until noon. After he parked his car in the alley, noticing the window of the new shop contained merchandise, he hesitated an instant and then crossed the street.

He had seen female underwear before, Angie's slips and brassieres and the panties and brassieres his daughters had worn. Some of them were ridiculously skimpy and frilly but nothing he'd seen prepared him for the underwear (if that's what it was) displayed in the window. There was a headless mannequin wearing a black, pinch-waisted and lacy corset from which two black garters with tiny scarlet bows held the hems of sheer black silk stockings. The wire of the corset's brassiere cupped the mannequin's breasts in such a way that they were thrust out rather than contained. The other items in the window were equally indecent. There were pink and red nylon panties with detachable flaps at the crotches. There were black and crimson panty-hose with the buttocks cut out and black G-strings and flowered orange and yellow hosiery with tiny slave bracelets around the ankles.

His first reaction was indignation. He couldn't understand the purpose of such a shop in their neighborhood of respectable Greek and Italian families. If his daughters had still been children at home, he'd have been ashamed to have them see these things in the window.

That evening as Angie put their dinner on the table, he told her about the new shop.

"I think you'll feel the same way I do when you see it," Ted said. "That stuff may be all right for South Wabash or one of those sleazy streets of porno shops up north, but it cheapens our neighborhood."

"Just about anything goes these days," Angie said. "Look at the bikinis the girls are wearing now on the beaches. It may not be as indecent as you think."

"The beach is one thing," Ted said. "You expect people to be almost naked there. But this just doesn't belong in our neighborhood, right across the street from our store. Besides, those corsets and G-strings don't look like anything a woman can really wear. They're just on display to sucker people inside. They must have more practical merchandise on sale in the store."

"Maybe I'll take the train in one afternoon next week and have a look," Angie said. "We might have dinner at the Athens and drive home together. It may not be as bad as you say."

"If you come in to take a look, don't go inside and buy anything," he said. He laughed and Angie smiled because the only underwear she'd bought for years were beige cotton briefs. Seeing them stacked with the other wash, there'd been times he wondered why she couldn't at least choose another color. If he'd asked her, he knew she'd reply that beige was the most practical shade.

Later that evening he sat reading a newspaper while Angie ironed and watched Mary Tyler Moore on TV. She stood with her back to him and he found himself staring at her. She was wearing a thin, flowered housedress, her legs bare and her feet in sandals. The frock was an old, worn one that had shrunk through many washings and stretched tightly across her thighs. When she extended her arm to iron one of the sleeves of his shirt, the frock hiked up her legs, her buttocks pressing against the fabric.

For a few restless moments he fantasized what Angie's attractive figure would look like in one of those scanty, lacy corsets. He found the image difficult to sustain because he hadn't seen her in anything sheerer than a silk slip in years. She'd had a few frilly nightgowns when they married, transparent enough so her nipples and pubic hair were visible through the material. He enjoyed seeing her wear them but as they wore out she never replaced them, saying they weren't really comfortable. For as long as he could remember she'd bought light cotton nightgowns for summer and flannel ones for winter, usually solid colors or muted prints, that covered her body from her throat to her ankles.

When they'd undressed and gotten into bed that night, he read Newsweek for a few moments and then dropped it and turned to Angie who was reading a book. His fingers brushed the bosom of her gown, feeling the softness of her breast, letting her know he wished to make love. She resisted him slightly as she usually did when he first touched her. She didn't really reject him but, a little playfully, sought to discourage him. When he persisted, she accepted his caresses, twisting her body into his arms. As he kissed her, fondling her breasts, and then slipping his hand under her nightgown, he envisioned her wearing the bottomless panty-hose he'd seen in the shop window and it spurred his desire. She closed her eyes, beginning to breathe more rapidly, rubbing herself between the legs. He heaved himself into place above her and gripped her thighs to draw them apart. When he entered her, for a few fevered seconds they rocked back and forth, Angie releasing a series of short, soft moans. After his orgasm, he hugged her tightly while he gasped for breath.

A few moments later she went to the bathroom. When she returned to bed she kissed him gently and then turned on her side. He switched off the lamp and nestled against her warm body, swept by tenderness and love for her, marveling how well-suited they were to each other.

But he couldn't sleep. Their lovemaking, swift as it had always been, left him tense and unfulfilled. Hearing Angie breathing softly in her sleep, he lay awake recalling the years they'd been married. Nagging discontents and thwarted longings sustained his sleeplessness.

He remembered Angie as a bride, slim-bodied, long-legged, lovely in her shimmering white gown and veil. She'd been a virgin on their wedding night and although he'd had intercourse with a few girls, he was clumsy and nervous and hurt her. After a while they tried again and when she bled, they were both delighted and toasted one another with champagne.

For the first year after they married, they lived with Angie's parents and found it almost impossible to make love in their bedroom that adjoined her father and mother's room. Angie worried about the bedsprings creaking and while he argued vehemently that there was nothing wrong with married people making love, he also found the stern-visaged old man with whom he worked in the store an austere and forbidding figure.

While he worked in the grocery, Angie worked as a salesgirl in a downtown department store. They saved enough money so by their first anniversary they were able to leave her parent's home and rent a third floor studio apartment. The kitchen was cramped and the bed had to be lowered from the closet at night, but they savored their privacy. Their sex became more frequent but he discerned a pattern in Angie's lovemaking. She appeared to enjoy intercourse but hastened him through the initial caresses. Ted suspected part of her anxiety was her feeling that her breasts were too small. When he kissed her nipples, she invariably tugged him away and up to her lips. No matter how hard he tried to reassure her that he loved her breasts as they were, she seemed convinced all men loved women with voluptuous breasts.

Another difficulty was their using condoms for birth control because they felt they couldn't yet afford to have a baby. The awkwardness of pausing in their lovemaking while he slipped on the rubber sheath, stifled their passion. On those occasions when they made love without that protection, at the final instant before he ejaculated, Angie made him withdraw.

Before Ted married, his closest friend who had graduated with him from high school, was Lucca Genovise. He was a dark-haired, extremely handsome and bold-eyed Italian youth who had successfully pursued at least a half dozen of the prettiest girls in school including a lovely cheer-leader that Ted and half the football team was after.

After their graduation and before he married, Ted spent several evenings a week with Lucca. They'd drink in bars or go to dances where Lucca's charm and good looks helped them pick up girls. Ted had his first intercourse with a girl he'd picked up on a date with Lucca.

Angie had met Lucca before their marriage and sternly disapproved of him. She felt he was a harmful influence on Ted and refused to have him up for dinner despite Ted pleading that he couldn't simply forsake his best friend. Finally, Angie relented and agreed to allow Lucca to come to dinner one time. He arrived with a huge bouquet of roses for Angie and carrying two bottles of wine. The evening passed swiftly and buoyantly and Ted was delighted at the way Angie laughed and glowed.

Less than a week later she suggested they invite Lucca for dinner once more. That evening passed as full of mirth and good humor as their first dinner. After that Lucca came for dinner two or three evenings a week. Angie would cook some special dish and their parties became friendlier and unrestrained. After drinking several bottles of wine they'd sprawl on the livingroom floor, joking and laughing. Angie who didn't hold her liquor well became giddy and merry. Ted wrestled playfully with her, knowing that Lucca would see her sleek, flashing legs. Both he and Lucca would tease Angie by smacking her bottom. She'd pretend indignation and flounce out of the room. But she always returned, kicking off her shoes so she'd be barefooted as well as barelegged and their prankish, bantering games would resume. After Lucca left, Ted and Angie made love, both more excited than usual but still using the precaution of a condom.

On a few occasions Lucca would bring one of his girlfriends up for dinner. Ted remembered a smoldering-eyed Jewish girl, a girl part Cherokee Indian, and a particularly lovely Swedish girl with long, golden hair. The night Lucca brought her to dinner, they all drank more recklessly than usual. Afterwards Lucca and the Swedish girl began making love on the livingroom floor. They advanced swiftly from hot kissing to caressing one another, the girl's blouse open so her flowered brassiere and buxom breasts were visible to Angie and Ted who sat on the couch. Angie went into the kitchen while Ted continued to watch Lucca boldy fondling the girl's breasts and slipping his hand beneath her panties to stroke her thighs. For an animated instant Ted thought they were going to have sex in front of him and then, laughing and lusty, Lucca and the girl left. Ted imagined the two of them so hot they screwed in Lucca's car.

That evening was one of the rare times Ted saw Angie truly angry. She told him she'd been sickened at the shameless way Lucca had carried on with the brazen girl in front of them. She resolved to tell Lucca she wouldn't tolerate that manner of behavior from him again in her house.

But Angie never told him. The next time Lucca came up for dinner he was alone and no one mentioned the Swedish girl. After dinner and a couple of bottles of wine, they resumed their laughing, crazy banter with Angie the focus of attention again.

Ted recalled with a wistful nostalgia Angie's erotic beauty that night.

She resembled a barefooted and lovely nymph, possessed by an intemperate, sensual vivacity. She danced first with Ted and then with Lucca until both of them collapsed. Then, breathless and laughing, she continued dancing alone, whirling with such animation that her dress whipped high about her legs so he and Lucca could see she was naked beneath it. When Lucca went to the kitchen for another glass of wine, Ted pulled Angie to the carpet. They began making ardent love, continuing to kiss and caress one another after Lucca returned and sat grinning on the couch as he watched them.

Ted was astonished at the ardor and passion in Angie that night, her tongue darting in and out of his mouth, her eyes taunting him to be reckless. He grew bolder, expecting her to stop him, but she encouraged him instead, all the hesitations and repressions about her banished. She wriggled on the floor, thrashing her legs so her naked thighs gleamed in the lamplight.

Ted yearned suddenly for Lucca to join them, to have his best friend kiss and caress Angie, as well. When he looked toward the couch and saw Lucca had risen and put down his glass of wine, for a frenzied moment he thought it was going to happen. But Lucca walked by them slowly, for the first time appearing nervous and shy himself, and then he left.

Afterwards Angie became a fiery tigress in his arms and he impaled her with a size and hardness he didn't know he possessed. Neither of them gave any thought to a condom until they'd finished. Lying side by side, both of them trembling and exhausted, he marveled at the force unleashed in that ancient urge to couple the male and female bodies.

About a month later Angie began getting nauseated in the mornings. When they found out from the doctor that she was pregnant, both of them understood they'd conceived the night of their passion.

He rose from the bed to go to the bathroom, tossing the covers toward Angie, hoping she might wake. He wanted to hold her in his arms and perhaps they'd whisper in the dark as they used to do on nights early in their marriage. When he returned to bed she was still asleep and he resigned himself to the silence and loneliness. He sighed and turned the luminated dial of the clock on the sidetable away from him so he wouldn't notice how slowly the hours were trailing his thoughts.

In the twenty-five years that had passed since the night they'd conceived their first daughter, he couldn't ever remember Angie revealing such passion again. As if she were frightened or ashamed of what she'd revealed about herself then, a part of her withdrew from their embraces. She gave him her body, gripping him tightly and uttering her quick, soft moans of pleasure. But that urgency to finish the union prevailed, their interludes of intimacy and love never lingering.

That night was also the last time Lucca came to their apartment. Angie stopped asking Ted to invite him to dinner and, after a while, they lost track of him except for a Christmas card when Lucca was living or visiting in California. Some years later a friend who'd known them both in high school told Ted he'd heard Lucca had been married and was living in Denver.

Not that Ted had time to mourn lost passion or a lost friend. When their second daughter was born, two years after the birth of their first child, raising the babies and running the business occupied almost all of his and Angie's time. They were also responsible for Angie's mother and, from time to time, had to take the children to see his mother who lived with his sister in Astoria, New York.

As the years went by, he accepted the infrequency and swiftness of their lovemaking as an inevitable consequence of maturing and growing responsibilities. If he endured moments of sexual frustration, he relieved himself, sometimes, in the privacy of his bathroom or, after closing the store when he was alone in his office where he kept magazines of nude women locked in a drawer of his desk.

On two occasions during those years he'd been unfaithful to Angie. Both transgressions were brief, unsatisfying encounters. One of the women had been a divorcee who was a regular customer in his store and, one evening, invited him to her apartment to have a drink. The years of swift, infrequent lovemaking had left him a clumsy, insecure lover and he suffered rather than enjoyed their sex. He saw the woman several times after that first night, torn between desire and fearful someone would see him going into her apartment or that Angie might sense he'd been with another woman.

The other affair was with a clerk he'd hired in the store, a much younger girl who was restless and blatantly the aggressor, making brazen suggestions to him whenever the two of them were alone. Not really desiring her, but incited by her boldness and coarse proposals, he made love to her after closing the store, the girl sprawled awkwardly over a blanket spread across his desk. When he went home afterwards and saw his lovely, angelic little daughters asleep, he cried in poignant remorse for his debauchery and betrayal. The following day he told the young clerk she'd have to leave and, to assuage his conscience or to buy her silence, he gave her a month's extra pay.

For the last few years he'd begun to find numerous reasons to justify his conviction that most married men were in the same predicament as he was. One couldn't live together as long as he and Angie had been and expect to maintain desire and excitement. Sexual intemperance and carnal pleasure belonged in the movies and in the pages of cheap, lurid novels. The true meaning of life, he told himself, rested in the companionship and devotion of a loyal, loving spouse.

When he noticed the grey light of dawn at the window of their bedroom, he was astonished how much of his life had been compressed into the sleepless hours of a solitary night. He rose before the alarm clock rang, switching it off so Angie might sleep a while longer.

Walking from his car to the store that morning, he gave the apparel shop no more than a cursory glance. He snapped at several of his clerks and apologized to them later. He considered going home early and, meanwhile, stopped in to have a cup of coffee with Vasili. While he was there a woman customer brought in several dresses to be cleaned. As Vasili wrote up her ticket, the woman explained she was the new owner of the Intimate Garments shop across the street. Vasili shook hands with her and, after introducing Ted as the owner of the food and liquor store, invited her to join them for coffee.

Her name was Blossom Denby Fairheart and, at first glance, Ted saw she was a plumpish, matronly woman of indeterminate age with her hair dyed a glinting chestnut-brown shade. She wore excessive powder and rouge that highlighted her cheekbones, heavy brows and deep-set hazel eyes. He didn't find her at all attractive.

But as she sipped a cup of coffee with them, he found himself curiously fascinated by her. He wasn't certain just why. She had a lilting voice that ranged from a husky whisper to an ebullient burst of laughter. She had unusually tiny fingers and hands and an exceptionally tiny mouth, one of the smallest he'd ever seen. When she spoke or laughed, her mouth opened to reveal teeth that radiated a sparkling whiteness.

There was something flirtatious and teasing in her manner and speech, as well, a blend of innocence and carnality. She gave an impression of timidity and refinement and then she told them a bawdy story in which she used the words 'Fuck' and 'Shit.'

"Perhaps now you'll think poorly of your new neighbor," she said plaintively. "You've just met me and you'll think all I do is utter crude words and tell naughty stories." She smiled that stunning flash of white teeth. "You'll go home and tell your wives you met the most brazen woman who's just opened a business in the neighborhood."

"I don't tell my wife anything," Vasili shrugged. "She doesn't stop hollering long enough for me to get in a word."

"She's an unhappy woman," Blossom said gently. "A woman is unhappy because a man isn't taking proper care of her."

"How can I make her happy?" Vasili protested. "That woman was born unhappy, spitting at the doctor who delivered her." He looked at

Ted for confirmation as another customer entered the store. Vasili left the back room to wait on her, leaving Blossom and Ted alone.

"What about your wife, Mr. Varnas?" she asked softly. "Is she unhappy too?"

"My wife's fine," he said a little stiffly.

"Then she's a fortunate woman," Blossom said and bobbed her head in vivacious affirmation of her words. "I've been married and widowed twice, but while my blessed husbands were alive, we made each other happy. Have you been married more than once, Mr. Varnas?"

"You don't have to call me Mr. Varnas," he said. "Everyone in the neighborhood calls me Ted." He shook his head. "I've only been married one time."

"Once can be enough," she said. "I wouldn't have remarried if my first husband hadn't passed away. Then I lost my dear second one too. That doesn't seem fair except that the joy we brought each other meant more than the years." Once more he felt the unreined force of her eyes. "Ted must be a shortened name?"

"I was christened Theodore," he said, "but nobody's used that name for years."

"I'd like to call you Theodore," she said. "It's a strong, masculine name with three syllables. Three syllable male names join a confluence of three benevolent stars."

He was flustered and grateful when Vasili joined them.

"I must get back to my shop," Blossom said. "I'm delighted to have met both you gentlemen. Please come visit me soon. I'll serve you some mint herbal tea that's blended for me in Mexico and that I think you'll enjoy."

"I'll come for tea but don't look for me to buy anything," Vasili grinned. "My wife wouldn't look good in any of those things you sell. Besides, she thinks nakedness is a worse sin than murder."

Blossom laughed buoyantly in response and Ted joined her. Although he'd heard Vasili's remark a number of times and no longer thought it humorous, there was something contagious in the woman's laughter, an exhilaration and delight that ignited his own laughter. Almost at once he felt better.

After she'd left the store, Vasili emitted a low, hoarse whistle.

"Isn't she something?" he said. "Have you ever seen anything like her? There's a woman who's consoled an army of men by snuggling them against her big boobs."

"She's not very good-looking," Ted said. "She's too plump and the color she's dyed her hair looks unnatural."

"You're right about that," Vasili said, "but there's a scent of sex around her that stabbed me right down to my atrophied balls. Her eyes got devils in them!" He winked at Ted. "She really went for you."

"Bullshit!" Ted said. "She didn't show any more interest in me than she did in you."

"I was watching her closer than you were," Vasili said. "Believe me, Teddy, she was looking you over the way a spider sights a fly."

Ted made a gesture of derision and impatience and returned to his store.

For the balance of the day he thought about the woman. In recollection he compared her to Angie who came out ahead in every respect. Angie was much prettier with an attractive face and a shapelier figure. In addition, Angie would never use the coarse expressions or tell the bawdy stories the woman had told.

He also remembered what she had said about men being the cause of unhappy women. He didn't believe Angie was unhappy but perhaps he'd missed being as considerate of her as he might have been. He couldn't recall when he'd last bought her flowers and he vowed to buy her a bouquet of roses, her favorite flowers, on his way home.

Later that afternoon, the sky darkened and it began to rain, a downpour that lashed the sidewalks and streets. When the rain passed, the sky above the roofs of the buildings formed a strange, splendid swirl of crimsons, golds, and purples. He saw the colors tint the window of the apparel shop so it sparkled like a rainbow. The thought came to him that instead of flowers he might find something in the woman's merchandise as a special gift for Angie. Nothing too immodest that she'd find offensive, perhaps simply some of the flowered hosiery.

He left his store at six, cautioning his clerks as he always did about locking up properly. He leaped across the puddles of water in the gutters and, before the apparel shop, he peered between the diaphanous garments in the window to see if there were customers inside. That portion of the interior visible to him appeared empty and, glancing nervously up and down the street, he opened the door. A small bell tinkled melodiously as he entered.

He gasped, thinking he'd intruded on a nearly-naked woman he hadn't seen from the street. Then he realized it was an incredibly lifelike mannequin in one of the shop corners, a full figured model of a woman clad in a lace bodysuit with a flap dangling open at her crotch. In another corner a second mannequin wore a white corset which flared above the scantiest of white bikini panties. From its hem two white silk garters and a sequined ribbon curled together and disappeared between her legs.

In the center of the shop were a half dozen racks from which dangled scores of diminutive brassieres, panties and garter belts, a bounty of erotic garments that quickened his pulse and constricted his breath.

He was startled when Blossom appeared from the back of the shop.

She watched him for an instant with a gently tolerant smile as if understanding the effect the apparel had upon him.

"I thought I'd buy a small gift for my wife," he made an effort to smile against the tension he felt in his cheeks. "Nothing too extreme," he added quickly. "I don't think she'd like it."

"A woman must be introduced to intimate apparel slowly," she said. "Often it opens new vistas of sensation for her and for her husband." She paused. "Do you have a few moments to drink a cup of tea, Theodore? We can chat a little and I'll get some idea what your wife might like."

"I'd like some tea, thank you," he said. "I can only stay a few minutes."

She led him past several fitting rooms, small, secluded cubicles where he imagined lovely women trying on the daring garments and through a draped doorway at the rear of the shop. Expecting an office he was surprised to have entered a fully-furnished, single room apartment. There was a compact kitchen, a livingroom area with sofa and armchairs and, in a recessed alcove, a canopied bed with a fringed, peach-colored spread.

"It's much less expensive than renting an apartment elsewhere," she said. "This way I'm here if one of my special customers prefers to shop at night." She gestured toward the sofa. "Please sit down, Theodore, and I'll bring our tea."

When he sat down and stared at the wall facing the sofa, he saw a large, ornately-framed painting, the naked figures in it as startlingly real as if it were a photograph. One was a voluptuously beautiful woman, every dimple, hillock, hollow and flow of thigh and arm radiant and bountiful. The other figure was a handsome, curly-haired youth. His adoration for the woman was evident in his face and in the way his arm and hand extended toward her breast in veneration and longing, his fingers falling just short of touching the glowing bounty.

"They portray Cupid and Venus," Blossom came to stand beside him. "A painting in the style of Rubens done for me by a young art student." She sighed. "He was passionately in love with me and labored on this painting for more than a year. Of course, you understand, that was a long time ago."

"It's just as wonderful as the paintings that hang in the Art Institute," he said, wondering if she'd posed for the young artist who adored her. He was conscious, suddenly, of a scent in the air, a fragrance that he remembered trailing the woman when she entered Vasili's shop.

She brought the pot of tea and poured him a cup.

"Lemon or sugar?"

"Just some lemon, thank you."

She sat in an armchair across from him. As she raised her cup to her lips, he observed, once again, the delicate smallness of her fingers.

"Now, Theodore, please tell me something about your wife."

He sipped his tea to allow himself a moment's reprieve.

"She's an attractive woman," he said. "She looks younger than her age. Not that she's old." He paused, wondering why he'd entered the shop in the first place. "She's just a very good-looking woman with a good personality."

"I'm sure she is," Blossom said gravely. "And you said before that she was happy?"

"I think she's happy," Ted said. "She doesn't complain about things and we don't fight or argue. She's never told me she wasn't happy."

"Does she hum or sing around the house?"

He recognized the question as an important one.

"I don't really remember," he said. "She's a quiet woman. Maybe she hums and sings when I can't hear her."

"That's very important," Blossom said. "A happy woman can't restrain her joy in love and life. It will burst from her like a bird's song. A silent woman is an unhappy woman." She shook her head pensively. "So many unhappy women are like unopened rosebuds and never bloom all their lives."

He listened intently to her words while noticing with fascination how they emerged from her tiny mouth, popping like puffs of air between her white, glistening teeth. So earnestly was he watching her that he was startled when he heard her say.

"You're a devilishly handsome man."

He stared at her, wondering if she were teasing him.

"I don't think I'm handsome," he said flatly.

"Of course you are!"

"I'm overweight," he said. He was going to mention his other impediments to male handsomeness but her glowing face restrained him.

"A man's attractiveness isn't in his weight or in other visible things," she said. "It springs from his sensuality, his ability to be sensitive to a woman's moods and needs, his inner strength. It comes, also, from his penis."

He felt his cheeks flush at the word emerging from her tiny, pristine mouth.

"You'll think me indelicate," she said, "but it's true. Penis. Pennniiisss..." Her tongue caressed the syllables. "That prong, bar, rod, bone that men carry between their legs." She laughed softly. "The world turns on that shaft. All hunger, power, love, hate, begin and end there."

She raised her hand and waved a tiny finger at him in reproach. He felt her reprimand had the force to leap the distance between them.

"A man who doesn't understand the power he carries, or how to use that power to awaken a woman's body and her soul is a eunuch," she said. "A true man must release a woman's divine qualities, that goddess and priestess that exists in every woman. He must nourish her longing to bring life, to sustain and enrich life, and, eventually, to take life away."

He weighed her words and their meanings, making an earnest effort to understand.

"But you'll think I've gone too far," she said. "You've only met me today and you'll think I'm brazen and shameless."

"I don't think that at all," he said quickly.

"Do you mean it?"

"Yes, I mean it." He wasn't sure just what he meant.

"It would be wonderful if you understood so quickly," she said. "I'm speaking about love, about the Prince of the Mountains, and the Lady of the Flowers, and how together they weave the fabric of life."

She leaned forward in her chair, staring at a vision beyond him, a serenity and loveliness in her face.

"My beloved spake and said unto me," she said softly, "Rise up my love, my fair one, and come away . . . come away with me."

He found her sweet voice soothing.

"As the apple tree among the trees of the wood," she went on, "so is my beloved among the sons. I sat down under his shadow with great delight, and his fruit was sweet to my taste."

He waited to make sure she had finished.

"That is one of the most beautiful love poems ever written," she said. "That is the Song of Solomon from the Bible."

"It's very beautiful," he said gravely.

"Will you have another cup of tea?" she asked.

"Thank you," he said. He settled back against the cushions, warmed by the feeling that the poetry she'd shared with him fashioned an intimacy between them.

When she returned with hot tea, she sat on the sofa beside him. The fragrance he had sensed about her earlier became overpowering, a scent that roused his blood. They talked more, or rather, she spoke and he listened to a stream of poetry, aphorisms, observations about men and women he had never considered before but which appeared to him to have the fidelity of truth. She told him of peasants in Europe who would copulate in fields they had just sown to induce fertility in their crops, of birds as the symbol of love, of Lorelei, combing her golden hair on the bank of the Rhine, enrapturing passing boatmen, of the bare-breasted goddess of Knossos, of something she called the 'Yang' and the 'Yin.' Interspersed between lines of lovely poetry, she recited several bawdy limericks and used, without a measure of self-consciousness, the words, 'cock' and 'cunt.'

He wasn't sure how long he sat there or how many cups of the exotic tea he drank, but he was loath to leave. He felt as if he'd been drinking wine or whiskey instead of tea, his body tingling and his spirit mellow. He was charmed by her vitality, by her knowledge and wisdom, and by the peals of laughter from her he was compelled to join.

Then, uncertain which of them moved closer, their arms and thighs touched. He saw her tiny alluring mouth and, with her lips so close, he kissed her. The kiss was gentle but with a ripple passing from her body to him that conveyed a storm.

He was afraid suddenly he'd acted recklessly. But there wasn't any anger or reproach in her face, only the sensitive satisfaction of a woman who'd given nourishment to a thirsty man.

"Now you'll be convinced I'm a wicked woman," she whispered.

"I don't think that," he said. "Not at all, Blossom." Her name lingered on his lips like the echo of a poem.

She rose from the couch and he rose to his feet beside her. He felt unsteady, bewildered at what had transpired so swiftly between them.

Holding his arm, she walked him to the door of the shop. She kissed him again, quickly on the cheek, whispering a word into his ear he couldn't understand but which he felt was an endearment. Leaving the shop, he heard the little bell tinkle once more. When he crossed the street, he turned and saw Blossom's shadow in the doorway. He waved to her although he doubted she could see him.

He walked on with a new vigor through the night freshened by the rain, a glimmering of the earlier colors lingering on the horizon. He inhaled deeply, relishing each breath, trembling with a curious anticipation, as if he'd embarked on a dangerous but thrilling journey.

Less than a week after the first night he visited the apparel shop, he and Blossom became lovers. It came about as naturally and easily as their kiss that first evening. They'd kissed on successive evenings when he'd visited her and then, one night, the kiss became a prelude for more intimate caresses. Staring at the painting of Venus and Cupid, sharing the young man's longing to touch the goddess, his fingers grazed Blossom's breast. She sighed as if that sign of his desire were anticipated and welcome. Leading him to her canopied bed, she slowly helped him undress, guiding his awkwardness, reassuring his anxiety. Engulfed in that nest of satin sheets and assorted fragrances, she awakened his body to feelings of maleness and strength he'd never experienced before. In her arms, caressing and caressed, he felt totally embraced and loved for the first time in his life.

From morning until the night when he could visit her again, Blossom pervaded his thoughts. A score of times during the day, appearing to sort rows of fruit in his window, he glanced longingly at the shop across the street. When one of his clerks asked him a question or a customer spoke to him, he answered while thinking how endlessly the time was dragging before he could return to her arms.

He tried to comprehend the explosion of emotion that had taken place in him. He was a man of fifty and, he would have sworn, long beyond any romantic revelation. He had an attractive, devoted wife and two loving daughters, one of them pregnant with his first grandchild. He had resigned himself to living out his years temperately and quietly. Then, in the span of a few hours, he had fallen deeply, irrevocably in love. All those emotions he had previously thought to be love, the flarings of desire and release he'd known with Angie and a few other women were sputtering bonfires beside the conflagration he experienced with Blossom. In her arms he understood that the bodies of a man and woman joined in love had the primal force of volcanos and tides. Imbued with an astonishing virility and power, he felt each of their unions so omnipotent he thought only the instant of death could be more supreme.

Feeling he must share his peerless secret with someone, after swearing him to silence, he told Vasili. His friend stared at him as if he'd confessed to being demented.

"You're too old for that!"

"Too old for what?"

"For falling in love just like that," Vasili said. "Banging a woman is one thing you shouldn't get mixed up with love."

"Bullshit!" Ted said. "Love is what makes Blossom and me different and special." He considered reciting one of Blossom's lines of poetry to Vasili but he felt his friend wouldn't understand.

"You really mean it?" Vasili asked somberly.

"I mean it."

Vasili shook his head in dismay.

"I can't believe you know what you're saying," he said. "She's a woman you just met, she's not even young or very pretty, and she's buried two husbands. I think you've gone crazy."

"I can't explain how it happened," Ted said. "But I know it's love, Vasili. I feel it's a miracle to give me another chance at life."

They sat in silence for a long time, Vasili's customarily sardonic tongue strangely muted. Finally, he spoke.

"What're you going to do about Angie?"

Confronted with the stark question, Ted couldn't answer. He didn't wish to hurt Angie. Thinking of leaving her filled him with remorse. The only punishment he'd find worse would be losing Blossom.

He had told Angie that one of his clerks was ill and he'd have to work several hours later each night for a while. She hadn't any reason to believe he wasn't telling her the truth. When he arrived home, late in the evening, he was wary and quiet, complaining that he was tired. He undressed and slipped quickly into bed. When Angie came to bed she asked him a few questions about the store or told him of an event of her own day. He'd mumble an answer, pretending he was nearly asleep, fearful she'd hear the rapid beating of his heart.

By that end of that first week he knew he should go home one or two evenings to ease Angie's concern. But he was reluctant to give up even a single night's love with Blossom. He'd wait anxiously all day until he could leave his store at the usual time. Through the twilight he'd walk half a block beyond the apparel shop and then return through the alley to her back door that Blossom left unlocked for him.

Sometimes she'd have a customer and he waited impatiently, listening as she bantered to put her shoppers at ease. He admired the way she exercised her magic on others. She sold her intimate garments convinced they would add spice and luster to the relationships between men and women, allowing them to conjure their fantasies into reality. She was like a bountiful mother, Ted thought with awe, whose compassionate heart healed the anxious and the insecure.

One evening after he'd entered by the back door, he heard Blossom in animated conversation with someone in the shop. After listening for a few moments he realized she was talking to an apparel salesman. Peering through the slit in the drape that mantled the doorway, Ted saw the salesman was an exceedingly handsome young man with a thatch of bright red hair. He was displaying silk chemises and teddies from two large, flowered sample bags that were the gaudiest and most garish Ted had ever seen. Blossom was teasing the young man whose cheeks were almost as red as his hair.

"How long did you say you'd been selling intimates?"

"About six months now."

"Are you doing well?"

The young salesman hesitated. "Not real well yet," he said.

"But you'll do wonderfully well!" Blossom said in her lilting voice. "When you gain confidence you'll outsell all the salesmen I see here! The women won't be able to resist so enchanting a commercial traveler! You're as handsome as a young God or an Ajax Red Knight with his everready lance!"

She laughed buoyantly and the salesman joined her with a shy, embarrassed laugh. Although Ted understood Blossom was playing a tantalizing game she often indulged with customers, the youth and attractiveness of the salesman produced a stab of jealousy in him more rancorous than anything he'd ever felt with Angie.

"How about giving me an order today?" the salesman tried to match Blossom's jauntiness.

"Do you have anything I haven't seen?"

Blossom and the salesman laughed again and Ted glared through the drape, by his resentment and outrage willing the salesman to get out.

"I shouldn't reward you with an order," Blossom said, "because you're a wicked, seductive young man who pretends to be innocent and shy. Oh, I'm on to you. But you can send me three of those pink chemises anyway. You'll have something for your visit and will want to hurry back."

Ted suffered while the salesman wrote up the order. The man finally carted his crude, flashy sample bags out the door. Blossom remained at the window for a few moments and then, as if sensing Ted was watching her, she snapped the lock on the door and flipped the sign to CLOSED. She flicked off the store lights, leaving only the window illuminated behind her. With that soft light reflecting a radiance across her hair, she walked slowly and enticingly toward him, pausing to fondle the breasts and thighs of each of the mannequins, as if to rouse their own desires. They watched her longingly until she reached the doorway where he waited, choked with anticipation and delight.

They made ardent love that night as they had been doing each evening for a week, unleashing a tireless potency in him he never believed he could sustain. But Blossom immersed him in a whirlwind of sensation, providing him an emotional as well as physical release. He felt all his secret desires and thwarted longings were being unfettered for the first time. Her tiny, perfect fingers caressed his flesh with tenderness and skill, inflaming his body from his head to his toes. While he kissed the silky down on her honey-tinted flesh, he inhaled the fragrance that belonged distinctly to her. When she beckoned him to fondle one of her diminutive, bare feet, he thought it the most beautiful foot in the world, ankle curved and shapely, and every delicate, shell-sheened toe flawless, as well.

"My beloved is mine and I am his," she whispered to him. "My beloved spake and said unto me, rise up, my love, rise up my fair one and let me nestle among the lilies . . ."

"I love you too, Blossom," he whispered. He heard his fervent words echo and reecho in his ears as if they were a strange, uncommon tongue he had never uttered before.

But he couldn't pretend any longer to be working late to Angie. In the beginning she waited to eat with him, but when his delays continued, his excuses incoherent and defensive, she ate her dinner before he arrived. When he got home she heated his dinner for him and left him to eat alone, returning to her reading or to watching TV. After a while they'd go to bed, having exchanged no more than a dozen words. In the darkness of their bed, knowing she was awake beside him, he struggled for words to explain to her what had happened. He was tempted to embrace her, believing if he made love to her, she might feel reassured. But he was exhausted from his lovemaking with Blossom and disabled by the knowledge that he didn't desire Angie anymore.

Finally, on a night two weeks after he'd first visited Blossom, he went directly home after work. He and Angie passed the evening in a tense, baneful silence. Several times he caught her watching him and he was tempted to speak but she turned her face away. When they went to bed, he couldn't sleep, his mind wracked with ways to resolve his dilemma.

On the following evening, the prospect of another grim, wordless night with Angie strengthened his resolve. He determined he'd tell her the truth. If she became angry and screamed at him, he'd leave and perhaps spend the night with Blossom.

When he got home, the kitchen was dark. Angie was reading in the livingroom, sitting at one end of the couch under the glow of the lamp. She wore her bathrobe and cotton nightgown with a small, faded ribbon at the bodice. She looked up from her book when he entered the room and he had the feeling she'd been waiting for him.

Quickly then, fearful he'd lose his courage, he told her he'd met another woman that he loved very much. He said it was impossible to explain how this might have happened to him after so many years but he couldn't help himself. He felt it only fair to tell her the truth.

She listened to him with little change of expression except for a paleness in her cheeks. She closed her book and he waited for her to say something. When she didn't speak, he nervously continued.

"You've been a real good wife and mother, Angie," he said. "I'd be the first one to admit that. But I know now there's always been something missing between us. I just never understood before what real love could be like."

Once again he waited vainly for her reponse. He knew her passive temperament but he was surprised that the shock of his disclosure wouldn't cause her to vent emotion.

"We haven't been unhappy," he said. "But I just can't go on like this anymore. I don't know how we'll work out a divorce but there's no reason to hurt one another. I'll be fair and square with you."

She stared at him and he couldn't fathom what she was thinking. A surge of frustration at her silence swept over him.

"Don't you have anything to say?" he asked.

She spoke then for the first time.

"What do you expect me to say?" she asked quietly.

"I wouldn't blame you if you were hurt and angry with me."

"You've found someone you love and I'm glad for you," she said.

Her patience and understanding sharpened his guilt and remorse.

"How can you be glad for me when I tell you I love another woman?" his voice rose. "That's not normal, Angie!"

For the first time a taut, cold smile hovered about her lips.

"You're in love with another woman," she said. "You don't want us to be married anymore. That happens all the time."

"I know it does," he said, "but I didn't think you'd take it so quietly. God's truth, Angie, I didn't plan this to happen. I thought we were going to grow old together." He paused, feeling a moistness in his eyes. "I know the girls will be hurt. I'll write them and tell them it's my fault. Don't worry about that."

"The girls will be fine," she said. "They're not children living at home anymore. They have their own lives now."

He nodded, trying to adjust to her calmness.

"I guess we're handling this in a civilized way," he said. "I always respected you as a sensible person, Angie, and you're proving that now."

"Did you think all these years that I was frigid?" the suddenness of the question startled him.

"I didn't think you were frigid," he said warily. "I thought maybe sex just wasn't that important to you. You've been a good wife and a good mother. I guess I needed more." Something Blossom had told him returned to him then. "We need that one person who's just right for us, someone we can love in a way that makes us full of joy to be alive."

"I feel love like that," she said.

"I'm sorry you feel it for me and I don't feel it in the same way for you, Angie," he said earnestly. "Life isn't always fair. I'm sorry for . . ."

A quick motion of her hand cut him off. He felt the air between them suddenly altered, become hostile and bitter.

"I never loved you like that," she said.

He stared at her numbly. She didn't wait for him to ask the question.

"I love Lucca Genovise," she said.

"We haven't seen Lucca in twenty-five years!" he cried.

"You haven't seen Lucca," she said. For the first time her eyes glittered with a cruelty he'd never seen in them before. "I've been sleeping with Lucca for years."

He struggled to comprehend her words, hearing them echo like thunder in his head. He was almost persuaded she was contriving a lie to get even with him.

"I don't believe you!"

"It began after he'd come to our apartment for those dinners," she said. "We'd meet while you were working. We stopped for a while and then started again after Colleen was born. Sometimes we'd only see each other once or twice a month. But I lived and waited for those hours with him."

She rose from the couch, moving slowly toward him, the glitter in her eyes become a blaze.

"I'm glad for you, Ted," she said, "but you're way behind. It took you twenty-five years longer than me to understand what love is about."

He felt a tightness in his throat, a constricting of his breath. He remembered the games with Lucca in their apartment, the way Angie had danced, her passion sparked by Lucca the night their first daughter was conceived. All became clear to him then and, with that awareness, he felt wounded and betrayed.

"Why didn't you leave me?" he cried. "If you loved him so goddam much, why didn't you leave me? Didn't he want you?"

"You were his best friend," she said. "He'd make love to me because we wanted each other but he wouldn't break up our marriage, especially after Colleen was born. Then he got married too."

"Was it over then?" he said with his voice trembling. "Did you stop seeing him then?"

"I kept seeing him a few times a year," she said. "Just for an afternoon or an evening. But each reunion made me able to come back and wait until the next time I could see him."

She circled him slowly, stalking him, as if seeking another vulnerable place to strike him again.

"It's wonderful, isn't it, Ted?" her smile was heartless and cold. "That feeling that comes over your body when it's touched by someone you really love. Every part of you tingling with joy. I'm glad you finally felt that too even if it took you twenty-five more years."

He had to get away from her and he moved to leave the house. At the door he turned back, unable to resist asking one final question.

"When did you last see him?"

"About three weeks ago," she said.

"After twenty-five years!" he cried in disbelief. "You're still seeing him after all these years!"

"That's love, Ted," she said. "You understand what love is now, don't you?"

He hurried from the house towards his car, his heart pounding, waves of nausea rising in his belly. He needed to talk to Blossom and hold her in his arms. He started his car and drove it down the streets of misted streetlamps to the expressway. All the way downtown he kept his window open despite the cold rushing air that chilled him to his bone.

He parked his car in the alley behind the apparel shop, walked to Blossom's back door and found it locked. He knocked once and, when there wasn't any answer, he knocked again. He walked quickly from the alley to the street and up to the CLOSED sign on the glass door. He knocked on the glass several times, softly and then loudly, an urgency and desperation in his blows.

He peered through the glass, the light from the illuminated window revealing a portion of the shadowed interior of the shop. He decided Blossom was out and he resigned himself to wait for her. As he turned from the door, something familiar caught his glance. On the floor near the draped doorway that led into Blossom's apartment, he saw the garish, flowered sample bags of the young, red-haired salesman.

He kept staring at the bags. Then he looked up at the corsets and garter-belts, the diaphanous pink and scarlet bikinis, one more delicate and alluring than another, a world of delight he'd held within his grasp.

A hoarse shriek of bewilderment and pain whirled from his throat, and he fled into the night.